Donato Carrisi was born in 1973 and studied law and criminology. He won four Italian literature prizes for his bestselling debut *The Whisperer*. Since 1999 he has been working as a TV screenwriter, and he lives in Rome.

Also by Donato Carrisi

The Whisperer
The Lost Girls of Rome
The Vanished Ones

THE HUNTER OF THE DARK

DONATO CARRISI

TRANSLATED BY HOWARD CURTIS

ABACUS

First published in Italy in 2014 as *Il Cacciatore Del Buio* by Longanesi & C.
First published in Great Britain in 2015 by Abacus
This paperback edition published in 2016 by Abacus

ISBN 978-0-349-14117-6

Typeset in Horley by M Rules
Printed and bound in Great Britain by
Clays Ltd, St Ives plc

Papers used by Abacus are from well-managed forests
and other responsible sources.

Abacus
An imprint of
Little, Brown Book Group
Carmelite House
50 Victoria Embankment
London EC4Y 0DZ

An Hachette UK Company
www.hachette.co.uk

www.littlebrown.co.uk

For he had commanded the unclean spirit to come out of the man. For oftentimes it had caught him: and he was kept bound with chains and in fetters; and he brake the bands, and was driven of the devil into the wilderness. And Jesus asked him, saying, What is thy name? And he said, Legion: because many devils were entered into him.

The Gospel according to St Luke, 8: 29–30

As flies to wanton boys are we to th' gods,
They kill us for their sport.

Shakespeare, *King Lear*

Prologue

The Hunter of the Dark

We come into the world and we die forgetting.

The very thing that had happened to him. He had been born a second time, but first he had had to die. The price had been forgetting who he was.

I don't exist, he kept telling himself, because it was the one truth he knew.

The bullet that had penetrated his temple had taken away his past and, with it, his identity. But it hadn't eaten into his background factual memory or the language centres of his brain, and – strangely – he could speak several languages.

This rare gift for languages was the one thing he knew for certain about himself.

As he waited in a hospital bed in Prague to find out who he was, he woke one night to find a mild-looking man by his bed, a man with neatly combed black hair parted at the side, and a boyish face, who smiled at him and said just one sentence.

'I know who you are.'

Those words should have liberated him, instead of which they were merely the prelude to a new mystery, because, at that point, the black-clad man put two sealed envelopes in front of him.

In one, he told him, was a bearer cheque for twenty thousand euros and a passport with a fictitious name and only the photograph missing.

In the other was the truth.

The man granted him all the time he needed to decide. Because it was not always a good thing to know all about yourself, and he was actually being given a second chance.

'Think it over carefully,' he advised him. 'How many men would love to be in your position? How many would like to have every mistake or failing or pain of their past wiped out by amnesia and be able to start all over again, wherever they wished? If you choose that option, then listen to me: throw the other envelope away without even opening it.'

To make the decision easier, he told him that nobody out there was looking for him or waiting for him. He had no close relationships, no family.

Then the man left, taking his secrets with him.

He looked at the two envelopes for the rest of that night and all the following days. Something told him that, deep down, that man already knew which he would choose.

The problem was that he himself didn't know.

The idea that he might not like the contents of the second envelope was implicit in that strange proposal. 'I don't know who I am,' he kept saying to himself, but he soon realised that there was a part of himself he knew well: the part that couldn't spend the rest of his life with that doubt.

That was why, the evening before they discharged him from hospital, he got rid of the envelope with the cheque and the passport with the fictitious identity – so that there couldn't be any second thoughts. Then he opened the envelope that was supposed to reveal all.

It contained a train ticket for Rome, some money, and the address of a church.

San Luigi dei Francesi.

It took him a day to get to his destination. He sat down on one of the pews at the back of the central nave of that masterpiece – a perfect synthesis of Renaissance and Baroque – and stayed there for hours. The tourists who thronged the place, their attention focused on the art, did not even notice him. And he too discovered the wonder of being surrounded by so much beauty. Among all the new pieces of knowledge feeding into his virgin memory, the knowledge of the works of art he had around him was something he wouldn't forget easily, he was sure of that.

But he still didn't know what any of this had to do with him.

When, late in the evening, the parties of visitors started streaming out of the church, hastened on their way by a coming storm, he hid in one of the confessionals. He had no idea where else to go.

The doors had been bolted and the lights turned off, and only the votive candles remained to illumine the place. Outside, the rain had started falling. The rumble of thunder made the air inside the church vibrate.

It was then that a voice echoed, 'Come and see, Marcus.'

So that was what he was called. Hearing his name hadn't had the hoped-for effect on him. It was a sound like any other: it wasn't familiar to him.

Marcus emerged from his hiding place and searched for the man he had met only once before, in Prague. He spotted him beyond a pillar: standing motionless, with his back to him, facing one of the side chapels.

'Who am I?'

The man didn't reply. He kept looking straight ahead of him, at the three large paintings on the walls of the little chapel.

'Caravaggio painted these between 1599 and 1602. The Vocation, The Inspiration *and* The Martyrdom of St Matthew. *The last one is my favourite.' He pointed to the one on the right. Then he turned to Marcus. 'According to Christian tradition, St Matthew, apostle and evangelist, was murdered.'*

In the painting, the saint was lying on his back on the ground while his killer was brandishing a sword, ready to strike. Around them, those present were fleeing in horror from what was happening, making way for the evil about to be committed. Instead of trying to escape his fate, Matthew was opening his arms wide, awaiting the blade that would bring him martyrdom and, with it, eternal sainthood.

'Caravaggio was a debauchee: he frequented the most rotten and corrupt circles in Rome and often took the inspiration for his works from what he saw in the streets. In this case, violence. So try to imagine that there is nothing sacred or redemptive in this scene; try to picture it with common everyday characters . . . Now what do you see?'

Marcus thought about it for a moment. 'Just another homicide.'

The other man nodded slowly. 'Someone shot you in the head in a hotel room in Prague.'

The sound of the rain had become more intense, amplified by the echo in the church. Marcus assumed that the man had shown him the painting for a specific purpose. To force him to think about who he himself could have been in that scene. The victim or the murderer?

'Others see salvation in this painting, but all I can see is evil,' Marcus said. 'Why?'

As a flash of lightning lit up the windows, the man smiled. 'My name is Clemente. We're priests.'

The revelation shook Marcus to the core.

'Part of you, which you have forgotten, can spot the signs of evil. The anomalies.'

Marcus couldn't believe he had such a talent.

Clemente placed a hand on his shoulder. 'There is a place in which the world of light meets the world of darkness. It is there that everything happens: in the land of shadows, where everything is vague, confused, undefined. You were a guard appointed to defend that border. Because every now and again something manages to get through. Your task was to chase it back into the darkness.'

Clemente let the sound of that sentence fade in the tumult of the storm.

'A long time ago you took an oath: nobody must know of your existence. Ever. You will be able to say who you are only in the time that elapses between the lightning and the thunder.'

In the time that elapses between the lightning and the thunder . . .

'Who am I?' Marcus asked. He was making an effort to understand.

'The last representative of a holy order. A penitenziere. You have forgotten the world, but the world has also forgotten all of you. Once, though, people called you hunters of the dark.'

Vatican City is the smallest sovereign state in the world.

Less than a quarter of a square mile bang in the centre of Rome, it stretches behind the basilica of St Peter's. Its borders are protected by an imposing perimeter wall.

The whole of the Eternal City once belonged to the Pope. But in 1870, when Rome was annexed to the newly formed Kingdom of Italy, the pontiff withdrew into this small enclave where he could continue to exercise his power.

As an autonomous state, the Vatican has a territory, a population, and organs of government. Its citizens are divided between ecclesiastics, who have taken vows, and lay people, who haven't. Some live within the walls, others outside, on Italian territory, and every day the latter travel back and forth to reach their place of work in one of the many offices and departments, going in and out through one of the five gates that give access.

Within the walls there are facilities and services. A supermarket, a post office, a small hospital, a pharmacy, a court that adjudicates on the basis of canon law, and a small electricity-generating plant. There is also a heliport and even a railway station, for the exclusive use of the pontiff.

The official language is Latin.

Apart from the basilica, the papal residence and the government buildings, the area of the small state is occupied by extensive gardens and by the Vatican Museums, visited every day by thousands of tourists from all over the world, who conclude their tour by looking up in the air and gazing in awe at Michelangelo's wonderful fresco of the Last Judgement on the ceiling of the Sistine Chapel.

That was where the emergency began.

About four in the afternoon, two hours before the official closing of the museums, the guards began to move the visitors out without any explanation. At the same moment, in the rest of the small state, the lay staff were asked to go back to their own homes, outside or inside the walls. Those who lived within the walls were advised to stay indoors until further orders were issued. The same advice was given to the ecclesiastics, who were invited to go back to their private residences or to withdraw to the various internal monasteries.

The Swiss Guard, the Pope's military corps, whose members, originally mercenaries, since 1506 had been recruited exclusively from the Catholic cantons of Switzerland, were given orders to lock all the entrances to the city, beginning with the main one, the Porta Sant'Anna. All direct phone lines were cut, as was the mobile phone signal.

By six o'clock on that cold winter's day, the city was completely isolated from the rest of the world. Nobody could go in or out or communicate with the exterior.

Nobody except the two individuals walking through the San Damaso courtyard and the Loggia of Raphael, in the dark.

The electricity-generating plant had cut off the energy supply throughout the vast area of the gardens. Their footsteps echoed in the silence.

'Let's hurry, we only have thirty minutes,' Clemente said.

Marcus was aware that the isolation could not last too long, or those on the outside would start getting suspicious. According to

Clemente, a version had already been prepared for the media: the official reason for this quarantine was that a new emergency evacuation plan was being tested.

The real reason, however, had to remain absolutely confidential.

The two priests lit their torches and entered the gardens. These occupied twenty-three hectares, half the entire territory of Vatican City. They were divided into Italian, English and French gardens, and contained botanical species from all corners of the world. They were the pride of every pontiff. Many popes had strolled, meditated and prayed among these plants.

Marcus and Clemente walked along the avenues lined with box hedges, perfectly pruned by the gardeners until they looked like marble statues. They passed beneath the great palms and cedars of Lebanon, accompanied by the sound of the hundred fountains that adorned the grounds, and the rose garden commissioned by John XXIII, where the roses that bore his name bloomed in the spring.

Beyond the high walls was the chaos of Rome's traffic. But, on their side, the silence and peace were absolute.

This was not peace, though, Marcus thought. At least, not any more. It had been spoilt by what had happened that same afternoon, when the discovery had been made.

In the place where the two penitenzieri were heading, nature had not been tamed as it had elsewhere in the grounds. Within these gardens, in fact, there was an area where the trees and plants were allowed to grow freely. A wood extending over three hectares. The only maintenance to which it was subjected was the periodic removal of dry branches. Which was what the gardener had been doing when he'd raised the alarm.

Marcus and Clemente clambered up on to a little mound. From the top, they shone their torches into the depression below, in the centre of which the Gendarmerie – the Vatican police force – had marked off a small area with yellow tape. They had already carried out an investigation and examined the spot, before receiving orders to abandon the area.

To make way for us, Marcus told himself. So he approached the tape, shone his torch, and saw it.

A human torso.

It was naked. It immediately reminded him of the Belvedere Torso, the gigantic mutilated statue of Hercules kept in the Vatican Museums, from which Michelangelo had taken his inspiration. But there was nothing poetic in the remains of the poor woman subjected to such bestial treatment. Someone had severed her head, arms and legs. They lay scattered a few yards away, along with her dark, lacerated clothes.

'Do we know who she is?'

'A nun.' Clemente pointed straight ahead. 'There's a small enclosed convent over there, beyond the wood. Her identity is a secret: it's one of the rules of her order. Not that it matters much at this point.'

Marcus bent down to take a closer look. The pale complexion, the small breasts, the indecently displayed sexual organs. The very short blonde hair, once covered by a veil, now exposed on the severed head. Her blue eyes, raised to heaven as if in supplication. Who are you? he asked her with his eyes. Because there was a fate worse than death: to die without a name. Who did this to you?

'Every now and again, the nuns stroll in this wood,' Clemente went on. 'Almost nobody ever comes here, and they can pray undisturbed.'

The victim had chosen an enclosed order, Marcus thought. She had taken vows to isolate herself from humanity with her fellow nuns. Nobody would ever again see her face. Instead she had become the obscene display of somebody's wickedness.

'It's difficult to comprehend the choice these women make,'

Clemente said, as if reading his thoughts. 'Many people think they should go out and do good in the world instead of shutting themselves up within the walls of a convent. But, as my grandmother always said, we don't know how many times these sisters may have saved the world with their prayers.'

Marcus did not know whether to believe this. As far as he was concerned, and despite everything that he had learned during the past two years of training with Clemente, the world could hardly say it had been saved when faced with a death like this.

'In all the centuries, nothing like this has ever happened here,' Clemente went on. 'We aren't prepared. The Gendarmerie will carry out an internal investigation, but they don't have the means to handle a case like this. So there's no pathologist, no forensics team. No post mortem, no fingerprints, no DNA.'

Marcus turned to look at him. 'Then why not ask the Italian authorities for help?'

According to the treaties that linked the two states, the Vatican could call in the Italian police if they needed to. But they only ever did so to control the many pilgrims who flooded to the basilica or to prevent the petty crimes that took place in the square. The Italian police had no jurisdiction beyond the foot of the steps that led up to the entrance to St Peter's. Unless there was a specific request.

'It won't happen – it's already been decided,' Clemente said.

'How can I investigate inside the Vatican without anybody noticing me or, worse still, discovering who I am?'

'Quite simply, you won't. Whoever it was came from outside.'

Marcus didn't understand. 'How do you know that?'

'We know his face.'

The reply took Marcus by surprise.

'The body has been here for at least eight or nine hours,' Clemente continued. 'This morning, very early, the security cameras filmed a suspicious man wandering around the gardens.

He was dressed like a Vatican employee, but it turns out the uniform had been stolen.'

'Why him?'

'Look for yourself.'

Clemente handed him a printout of an image. It showed a man dressed as a gardener, his face partly hidden by the visor of a small cap. Caucasian, indeterminate age but definitely over fifty. He had with him a grey shoulder bag, at the bottom of which a dark stain was visible.

'The gendarmes are convinced that inside that bag there was a small hatchet or something similar. He must have used it recently: the stain you see is probably blood.'

'Why a hatchet?'

'Because it was the one kind of weapon he could have found here. There's no way he could have brought anything in from outside, with all the security checks and metal detectors.'

'But he took it away with him to cover his tracks, in case the gendarmes called in the Italian police.'

'It's easier on the way out: there are no checks. And to get away without being seen, all you have to do is mingle with the stream of pilgrims and tourists.'

'A gardening implement . . .'

'They're still checking if anything's missing.'

Marcus looked again at the remains of the young nun. Without realising it, with one hand he was squeezing the little medallion he wore around his neck, depicting the Archangel Michael – the protector of the penitenzieri – brandishing a fiery sword.

'We have to go,' Clemente said. 'Our time is up.'

Just then, there was a rustling in the wood, coming in their direction. Marcus looked up and saw a group of shadowy figures emerging from the darkness. Some were holding candles. In the dim light of those little flames, he noticed that they all had dark veils over their faces.

'Her fellow nuns,' Clemente said. 'They've come to take her.'

In life, only these women had been allowed to know what she looked like. In death, only they could take care of her remains. That was the rule.

Clemente and Marcus retreated to leave the place free. The nuns took up their places in silence around the wretched remains. Each of them knew what she had to do. Some laid out white sheets on the ground, others gathered up the body parts.

Only then did Marcus notice the sound. A concordant hum coming from beneath the cloths that covered those faces. A litany. They were praying in Latin.

Clemente took him by the arm to draw him away. Marcus made to follow him, but just then one of the nuns passed close to him. And he heard her say something quite distinctly.

'*Hic est diabolus.*'

The devil is here.

PART ONE

The Child of Salt

1

A cold nocturnal Rome lay at Clemente's feet.

Nobody would have guessed that the dark-clad man leaning on the stone balustrade of the Pincio terrace was a priest. Before him lay an expanse of palaces and domes dominated by the Basilica of St Peter. A majestic panorama, unchanged for centuries, through which tiny figures swarmed.

Clemente stood there gazing down at the city, heedless of the sound of steps approaching him from behind. 'So, what's the answer?' he asked before Marcus had even come level with him. They were alone.

'Nothing.'

Clemente nodded, not at all surprised, then turned to examine his fellow penitenziere. Marcus looked dishevelled, with several days' growth of beard.

'Today makes a year.'

Clemente was silent for a moment, looking him straight in the eye. He knew what he was referring to: it was the first anniversary of the finding of the dismembered body of the nun in the Vatican gardens. In all that time, Marcus's investigations had led nowhere.

No leads, no clues, no suspect. *Nothing*.

'Do you intend to give up?' Clemente asked.

'Why, do you think I could?' Marcus replied, stung. This case had tried him to the limit. The hunt for the man in that security-camera image – Caucasian, over fifty – had proved fruitless. 'Nobody knows him, nobody has ever seen him. The thing that makes me particularly angry is that we know his face.' He paused and looked at his friend. 'We have to take another look at the lay people who work in the Vatican. And, if nothing comes from that, we'll have to move on to the ecclesiastics.'

'None of them looks anything like the photograph, so why waste time?'

'Who's to say the murderer didn't have help from someone on the inside? Somebody who's been covering for him? The answers are within the walls: that's where I should be investigating.'

'You know we can't. There's an obligation of confidentiality.'

Marcus knew that the question of confidentiality was only an excuse. Quite simply, they were afraid that, if he stuck his nose in their affairs, he might discover something else, something unconnected with this case. 'I'm only interested in catching the killer. You have to persuade the prelature to remove the obligation.'

Clemente immediately dismissed the idea with a gesture of his hand, as if it was absurd. 'I don't even know who has the power to do so.'

Beneath them, the Piazza del Popolo was filled by parties of tourists on a night tour of the beauties of the city. They probably didn't know that there had once been a walnut tree down there, beneath which was the burial place of the Emperor Nero, the monster who, according to a rumour invented by his enemies, had ordered the burning of Rome in 64 AD. The Romans had believed the place was overrun with demons. That was why, around the year 1100, Pope Paschal II had ordered the walnut tree to be burnt, together with the Emperor's exhumed ashes.

The church of Santa Maria del Popolo had been built on the site, its high altar still decorated with bas-reliefs showing the Pope about to cut down Nero's tree.

That's Rome, Marcus thought fleetingly. A place where every revealed truth hid another secret, the whole of it wrapped up in myth. That way, nobody could really know what was hidden behind everything. Just so as not to unduly upset the minds of men – those small, insignificant creatures, unaware of the war that was constantly, surreptitiously being fought around them.

'We should start to consider the possibility that we'll never catch him,' Clemente said.

But Marcus couldn't accept that. 'Whoever it was knew how to move around inside those walls. He'd studied the place, the control procedures, he got though security.'

What he had done to the nun was brutal, animalistic. But the way he had planned it all had had a logic, a design.

'I've grasped one thing,' Marcus said, confidently. 'The choice of the place, the choice of the victim, the means of execution: they're a message.'

'To whom?'

Hic est diabolus, Marcus thought. The devil had entered the Vatican. 'Someone wants us to know that there's something terrible inside the Vatican. It's a test, don't you see? A test. He knew what would happen: he knew the investigation would lead nowhere. And that the higher echelons would prefer to let suspicion fester rather than dig deeper and risk bringing God knows what into the light. Maybe some other buried truth.'

'You know that's a very serious accusation, don't you?'

'But don't you realise that's exactly what the killer wants?' Marcus continued, unperturbed.

'How can you be so sure?'

'He would have killed again. The reason he hasn't done so is because it's enough for him to know that suspicion has already taken root and that the brutal murder of a poor nun is small beer, because there are far more terrible secrets that need safeguarding.'

Clemente tried, as ever, to be conciliatory. 'You have no proof. It's just a theory. You've been thinking too much about this whole thing.'

But Marcus would not let go. 'I beg you: you have to let me talk to them, I might be able to convince them.' He was referring to the ecclesiastical hierarchy from which his friend took his instructions and orders.

Ever since, three years earlier, he had taken him from a hospital bed in Prague, deprived of memory and full of fears, Clemente had never told him a lie. He would often wait for the right moment to reveal things to him, but he had never lied.

That was why Marcus trusted him.

It could even be said that Clemente was his family. In those three years, apart from rare exceptions, he had been his one contact with the human race.

'Nobody must know about you and what you do,' he always said to him. 'What's at stake is the survival of what we represent and the future of the task that has been entrusted to us.'

He had always told him that the hierarchy knew of his existence but didn't know his face.

Only Clemente knew that.

When Marcus had asked the reason for such secrecy, his friend had replied, 'That way you can protect them even from themselves. Don't you understand? If all other measures were to fail, if the barriers turned out to be futile, there would still be someone to keep guard. You are their last defence.'

Marcus had often wondered: if he represented the lowest rung of the ladder – the man who worked in silence, the devoted servant called upon to get his hands dirty – and Clemente was only a go-between, who occupied the top rung?

In those three years he had committed himself totally, trying to appear dutiful in the eyes of whoever – and he was sure there was someone – was watching his actions from above. He had hoped that this would eventually lead to his being admitted to a higher knowledge, to finally meeting someone who would explain to him why such a thankless task had been created. And why he had been the one chosen to carry it out. Having lost his memory, he was in no position to say if it had been his own decision, if the Marcus from before Prague had had a role in all this.

But it hadn't happened.

Clemente conveyed orders and assignments to him that seemed to answer only to the prudent and sometimes indecipherable wisdom of the Church. Behind every mission, however, the same shadow could be glimpsed, the shadow of somebody.

Whenever he tried to find out more, Clemente shut down the discussion with the same words, uttered in a patient tone and accompanied by a kindly expression of the face. He used them again now, on this terrace, looking down on the splendour that concealed a secret city, in order to put an end to Marcus's demands.

'It is not for us to ask, it is not for us to know. We must simply obey.'

2

Three years earlier, the doctors had told him he had been reborn.

It wasn't true.

He had died and that was it. And the fate of the dead was to vanish forever or to remain imprisoned in their previous lives as ghosts.

That was how he felt. *I don't exist*.

The fate of a ghost is a sad one. He observes the grey existence of the living, their suffering, as they strive to keep up with time, as they get angry over trifles. He watches them struggle with the problems that fate presents them with on a day-to-day basis. And he envies them.

A resentful ghost, he told himself. That's what I am. Because the living would always have an advantage over him. They had a way out: they could still die.

Marcus was walking through the alleys of the old quarter. People passed without noticing him. He slowed down amid the stream of pedestrians. Usually, it was enough for him to brush against them. That minimal contact was the only thing that made him feel still part of the human race.

Trastevere had always been the heart of working-class

Rome. Far from the noble majesty of the centre, it had its own peculiar charm. The succession of different periods was visible in the architecture: medieval buildings stood side by side with eighteenth-century dwellings, all brought into a harmonious whole by history. The *sampietrini* – the traditional basalt paving stones used in Rome since the days of Pope Sixtus V – were a mantle of black velvet stretched along narrow, winding streets, and gave the footsteps of those passing along them an incomparable, age-old sound. Anyone walking here had the impression of being projected into the past.

Marcus slowed down at the corner of the Via della Renella. In front of him, the river of people steaming through the quarter every night continued to flow placidly to the sound of music and chatter in the bars and restaurants that made Trastevere a magnet for young tourists from all over the world. However different they were, these people all seemed the same to Marcus.

He passed a small group of American girls in their twenties, wearing shorts that were too short and flip-flops, maybe taken in by the idea that in Rome it was always summer. Their legs were purple with cold and they hurried past, hugging themselves in their college sweatshirts, in search of a bar where they could find refuge and alcohol to warm up.

A couple of lovers in their forties came out of a *trattoria*. They lingered in the doorway. She was laughing; he had his arm around her. The woman leaned back slightly against her partner's shoulder. He grasped the invitation and kissed her. A Bengali street vendor with a tray of roses and cigarette lighters spotted them and stood by them waiting for the clinch to come to an end, in the hope that they might want to seal the moment with a flower.

Three young men were walking along with their hands in their pockets, looking around. Marcus was sure they wanted to buy drugs. They didn't yet know it, but on the other side of the street a North African was approaching who would soon grant their wish.

Thanks to his ability to go unnoticed, Marcus had a privileged view of men and their weaknesses. But so could anyone who looked closely enough. His talent – his curse – was rather different.

He saw what others didn't see. He saw evil.

He detected it in the details, in the *anomalies*. Tiny tears in the fabric of normality. A low-frequency sound hidden in the chaos.

It happened to him constantly. He might not have wanted that gift, but he had it.

First he saw the girl. She was walking close to the wall, little more than a dark patch moving against the peeling plaster. Her hands were stuffed into the pockets of her bomber jacket and her back was stooped. She was looking down. A strand of fuchsia hair hid her face. Her boots made her look taller than she really was.

Marcus noticed the man walking ahead of her only because he kept slowing down and turning to check on her. He was keeping her on a leash with his eyes. He was well over fifty. A light-coloured cashmere overcoat, shiny and expensive brown shoes.

To an inexpert eye they might have seemed like father and daughter. He might be a manager or a successful professional, she could be a rebellious teenager, and he'd gone to pick her up from a bar to take her home. But it wasn't as simple as that. Coming to a door, the man stopped and waited for the girl to go in, but then he did something clearly inconsistent with the father/daughter story: before going in after the girl, he looked around to make sure that nobody was watching them.

Anomaly.

Evil paraded before him every day, and Marcus knew there was no solution. Nobody would be able to correct all the imperfections of the world. And, even though he didn't like it, he had learned a new lesson.

To survive evil, you sometimes have to ignore it.

A voice distracted him from the door as it closed. 'Thanks for the ride,' said the blonde woman getting out of the car to the friend who had given her a lift.

Marcus withdrew into the corner to be less conspicuous, and she passed him with her eyes fixed on the screen of the mobile phone she was clutching in one hand. In the other, she was carrying a large bag.

Marcus came here often, just to look at her.

They had met no more than four times, when, almost three years ago, just two or three months after his own arrival, she had come to Rome from Milan to discover how her husband had died. Marcus could remember every word they had exchanged, every single detail of her face. It was one of the positive effects of amnesia: you had a new memory to fill.

Sandra Vega was the only woman with whom he had communicated in all that time. And the only stranger to whom he had revealed who he was.

He remembered Clemente's words. In his previous life, Marcus had taken an oath: nobody was to know of his existence. For everyone he was invisible. A penitenziere could show himself to others, revealing his true identity, *only in the time that elapses between the lightning and the thunder*. A fragile interval that could last a moment or a small eternity, nobody could tell. Everything was possible in that juncture when you were aware that the air was filled with energy and expectation. That was the moment, precarious and uncertain, when ghosts once again assumed human form. And appeared to the living.

That had happened to him, during a heavy storm, on the threshold of a sacristy. Sandra had asked him who he was and he had replied, 'A priest.' It had been a risk. He didn't know exactly why he had run it. Or maybe he did know, but only now was able to admit it to himself.

He had strange feelings for her. There was something familiar connecting him to her. And he also respected her, because she had managed to put her grief behind her. She had chosen this city to start over again, getting herself transferred to a new police department and taking a small apartment in Trastevere. She had new friends, new interests. She had started to smile again.

Marcus always felt a certain awe at the idea of change. Perhaps because for him it was impossible.

He knew Sandra's movements, her timetable, her little habits. He knew where she did her shopping, where she liked to buy her clothes, the pizzeria where she ate on Sundays after going to the cinema. Sometimes, like tonight, she came home late. But she didn't seem exhausted, just tired: the acceptable consequence of a life lived intensely, a feeling you could shake off with a hot shower and sleep. The debris of happiness.

Every now and again, while waiting for her in the evening not far from her building, he thought of how it would be to step out of the shadows and show himself to her. He didn't even know if she would recognise him.

But he had never done it.

Did she still think about him? Or had she left him behind, together with her grief? The very thought of it hurt him. Like the thought that, even if he had summoned up the courage to approach her, it would be pointless, because there could be no follow-up.

And yet he couldn't stop seeking her out.

He saw her enter her building and, through the windows on the landings, walk up a couple of flights of stairs to her apartment. She stopped outside the door and searched for her keys. But the door opened and a man appeared.

Sandra smiled at him and he leaned forward to give her a kiss.

Marcus would have liked to look away, but he couldn't. He saw them go into the apartment and close the door behind them. And, with it, the past, ghosts like him, and all the evil in the world.

Electronic sounds. The man was naked, lying flat on his back on the double bed, in the semi-darkness. As he waited, he played a videogame on his mobile phone. He paused it for a moment and lifted his head to look beyond his prominent stomach.

'Hey, hurry up,' he yelled to the young girl with the fuchsia hair, who was in the bathroom, injecting heroin into her arm. Then he went back to his game.

Suddenly, something soft fell on his face. But the pleasant sensation of the cashmere lasted barely a few moments, because then he felt as if he was choking.

Someone was pressing his own coat down on to his face.

Instinctively, he flailed about with his arms and legs in search of something to latch on to: he was drowning even though there was no water. He grabbed the forearms of the unknown person pinning him down and tried to loosen his grip, but this other man, whoever he was, was stronger. He tried to scream, but only shrill moans and gurgles emerged from his mouth. Then he heard a whisper in his ear.

'Do you believe in ghosts?'

He couldn't answer. And, even if he could, he wouldn't have known what to say.

'What kind of monster are you: a werewolf, a vampire?'

He gasped for breath. The coloured dots dancing in front of his eyes had become flashes of light.

'Should I shoot you with a silver bullet or drive an ash stake through your heart? Do you know why ash and not another wood? Because Christ's cross was made of ash.'

The strength of despair was the only resource left to him,

because the asphyxia was starting to affect his body. He remembered what he had been told by the scuba-diving instructor during his trip to the Maldives with his wife and children two years earlier. All those warnings about the symptoms of hypoxia. They were of no use to him right now, but he remembered them all the same. They'd had a great time there, going underwater to look at the coral reef: the children had loved it. It had been a wonderful holiday.

'I want to help you be reborn,' the stranger said. 'But first you have to die.'

The idea of drowning terrified him. Not now, not here, he told himself. I'm not ready yet. But he was starting to feel weak. His hands lost their grip on the attacker's forearms and he started to move them about wildly in the air.

'I know what it means to die. It'll all be over soon, you'll see.'

The man let his arms fall to his sides, his breathing as weak now as it was futile. I want to make a phone call, he thought. Just one phone call. To say goodbye.

'You're losing consciousness. When you wake up again – if you wake up again – you'll go back to your family, your friends, and whoever likes you even a little in this dirty world. And you'll be different. They'll never know, but you will. And if you're lucky you'll forget tonight, you'll forget this girl and all those like her. But you won't forget me. And I won't forget you either. So listen carefully . . . I'm saving your life.' Then he said emphatically, 'Make sure you deserve it.'

The man had stopped moving.

'Is he dead?'

The girl was looking at him from the foot of the bed. She was naked, unsteady on her feet. Her arms were covered in bruises from too many injections.

'No,' Marcus said, taking the cashmere coat off the man's head.

'Who are you?' Squinting as if trying to bring the scene into focus, she was clearly dazed by the drug.

Marcus saw a wallet lying on the bedside table. He picked it up and took out all the money. He stood up and approached the girl, who instinctively retreated, almost losing her balance. He grabbed her by one arm and put the money into her hand. 'Get out of here,' he said harshly.

Eyes wandering over Marcus's face, she took a while to grasp what he was saying. Then she bent down to pick up her clothes and put them on as she headed for the door. She opened it but, before leaving, turned as if she had forgotten something.

She pointed to her face.

Marcus instinctively raised his hand to his face and felt something sticky on his fingertips.

His nose was bleeding.

He always had a nosebleed whenever he chose not to apply the lesson that sometimes, in order to survive evil, you needed to ignore it.

'Thank you,' he said, as if she had been the one to save him and not the other way round.

'Don't mention it.'

3

It was their fifth date.

They had been going out for nearly three weeks now. They had met at the gym, where they tended to go at the same times. She suspected that he had arranged that deliberately so that he could meet her, which she'd found flattering.

'Hi, I'm Giorgio.'

'Diana.'

He was twenty-four, three years older than her. He was at university and was about to graduate in economics. Diana was crazy about his curly hair and green eyes. And that smile, those perfect teeth, apart from the left incisor, which was a little too prominent. An unruly detail that she really liked. Because too much perfection could also be tiring.

Diana knew she was pretty. She wasn't tall, but she had a good figure, light brown eyes and beautiful black hair. She had stopped studying after high school and was an assistant in a perfume shop. The salary wasn't great, but she liked advising the customers. And besides, the owner of the shop had taken a shine to her. But what she really wanted was to find a nice boy and get married. She didn't think that was asking too much of life. And Giorgio might be 'Mr Right'.

They had kissed the first time they had gone out, and there had been other things too, but not much. That holding back was nice, it made everything seem more beautiful.

That morning, though, she had received a text on her mobile phone.

Can I drop by at nine? I love you.

The message had given her an unexpected energy. She had often wondered what happiness was. Now she knew it was something secret, impossible to explain to other people. It was as if someone had created this feeling especially for her.

It was exclusivity.

Diana's happiness had shone through in all her smiles, everything she said that day, like a kind of cheerful contagion. She didn't know if the customers or her colleagues in the shop had noticed. She felt self-confident. She had savoured the wait, her heart occasionally giving her a jolt to remind her that the date was coming closer.

At nine, as she was descending the stairs of her building to join Giorgio, who was waiting below, that happiness assumed a different form. Diana was grateful for that day. If it weren't for the secret promise of the future, she would have liked it never to end.

She thought again about Giorgio's last text. She had replied only with a *yes* and a smiley face. She hadn't returned the *I love you*, because she was planning on doing it in person tonight.

Yes, he was 'Mr Right' – the one person to whom she could say those words.

They drank a sparkling white wine. The alcohol gave Diana the courage to start sending him unmistakable signals. About eleven, they got back in his car to drive back to Rome.

She felt cold in her skirt, and Giorgio put the heating on maximum. But she also leaned in towards him and put her head on his shoulder as he drove. She looked up at him. Neither of them spoke.

A Sigur Rós CD was playing on the car stereo.

Bracing herself on her heels, she slipped off her shoes. First one, then the other fell with a slight thud on the rug. Now that she was his girl, she could take the liberty of making herself more comfortable.

Keeping his eyes on the road, he reached out his hand to caress her leg. She rubbed herself against his arm, almost purring. Then she felt his palm glide up her stocking, until it reached the hem of her skirt. She let him, and, when she felt his fingers moving into the middle, she slightly parted her legs. Even through the tights and the knickers, he could feel how strong her desire was.

She half-closed her eyes and noticed that the car had slowed down and was turning off the main road on to the side streets that led into the big pine wood.

Diana had hoped this would happen.

They drove a few hundred yards at reduced speed, along an avenue lined by very tall pines. The fallen needles on the road cracked beneath the tyres. Then Giorgio veered left, entering the trees.

Even though they were going slowly, the car jolted over the ground. To avoid the jolts, Diana kept very still on the seat.

After a while, Giorgio stopped the car and switched off the engine. The music stopped too. All that could be heard was the residual ticking of the engine and, over it all, the wind blowing through the trees. They might not even have noticed it before, but now it seemed to Diana as if they had discovered a secret sound.

He moved the seat back a little, then put his arms around her and kissed her. Diana felt the caress of his tongue between her lips. She returned the kiss. Then he undid the buttons of her twinset. He lifted her T-shirt and sought out her bra. He stopped for a moment, feeling the fabric. He slid his fingers inside, freed one breast and cupped it with his hand.

What a unique feeling it is, being discovered by someone for the first time, Diana thought. Giving yourself to him, and simultaneously imagining what he's feeling. Feeling his excitement, his surprise.

She reached out her hands to remove his belt and unbutton his trousers, while he tried to slip off her skirt together with the nylons. All this without their mouths ever stopping searching each other, as if, without those kisses, they might choke.

For a moment Diana looked at the time on the dashboard, hoping that it wasn't too late, briefly afraid that her mother might ring her on her mobile at any moment and break the spell.

Their gestures became more impatient, the caresses deeper. Soon they were naked, gazing at each other in those few moments when they opened their eyes between kisses. But they didn't need to look at each other, they were getting to know each other with their other senses.

Then he placed one hand on her cheek and she realised that the moment had come. She moved away from him, sure that Giorgio would wonder why, maybe imagining that she'd had second thoughts. In fact she was about to say the *I love you* that she had held back all day. But instead of taking notice of her, Giorgio slowly turned towards the windscreen. Her pride was punctured: did she suddenly not warrant his total attention? She wanted to ask him for an explanation, but she stopped herself. There was a look of surprise in Giorgio's eyes. So Diana also turned.

Someone was standing in front of the bonnet. Staring at them.

4

A phone call had dragged her out of bed.

Her orders were to get to the pine wood in Ostia as soon as possible. That was all.

As she hurriedly put on her uniform, as quietly as possible in order not to wake Max, Sandra tried to clear her head. Calls like this happened rarely. But when they came it was like receiving a punch in the stomach, a shot of adrenaline and fear.

That was why it was best to be prepared for the worst.

How many crime scenes had she visited with her camera? How many corpses had she found waiting for her? Mutilated, humiliated, or simply frozen in an absurd posture. It was Sandra Vega's thankless task to capture a final image of them.

Whose death was going to need a photographic record this time?

It wasn't easy to find the exact spot. There was as yet no police cordon keeping at a distance those who had no right to be there. No flashing lights. No deployment of men and resources. When she arrived, most of the troops had still to get there. It was all for show anyway. For the benefit of the media and the authorities, so that people felt safe.

Right now, there was a single patrol car at the start of the road that led into the wood and, a bit further on, a van and a couple of cars. Still no parade for the newly dead. The time for an elaborate display of strength was still to come.

But the army would arrive on the battlefield already defeated.

That was why all the people who were really needed for the investigation were already there, gathered in that meagre group. Before she joined them, Sandra took the bag with her equipment from the boot of her car and put on white overalls with a hood in order to not contaminate the scene. She didn't yet know what to expect.

Superintendent Crespi came up to her. He summed up the situation in a terse sentence: 'You won't like it.'

Together, they entered the trees.

Before Forensics started searching for evidence. Before her police colleagues started trying to figure out what had happened and why. Before the ritual of the investigation officially started, it was all up to her.

And they were all there, waiting. Sandra felt like a latecomer at a party. They were talking among themselves in low voices, sneaking surreptitious glances at her as she passed them, hoping only that she would do her work quickly enough to let them get on with it. Two officers were questioning the runner who, during his morning training run, had discovered the horror that had brought them there. He was squatting on a dry trunk with his head in his hands.

Sandra walked behind Crespi. The unreal peace of the pine wood was marred by the sound of their steps on the pine needles but, above all, by the muffled ringing of a mobile phone. She barely paid any attention to it, concentrating instead on the scene she was starting to get a glimpse of.

Her colleagues had simply marked off the area with red and white tape. In the middle stood a car with all its doors open. In accordance with procedure, the only person to have crossed that border so far was the pathologist.

'Astolfi has just certified the deaths,' Superintendent Crespi announced.

Sandra saw him: a thin little man who looked like a bureaucrat. Having finished his task, he had come back across the tape and was now mechanically smoking a cigarette and collecting the ashes in the palm of his hand. But he was still looking at the car, as if hypnotised by some thought or other.

When Sandra and Crespi came level with him, he spoke without taking his eyes off the scene. 'I need at least a couple of shots of each wound for my report.'

It was only now that Sandra realised what it was that had captured the pathologist's attention.

The ringing of the mobile phone in the background.

And she also realised why nobody had the power to make the sound stop. It was coming from the car.

'It's the girl's,' Crespi said, without her asking him. 'It's in her handbag on the back seat.'

Obviously, someone was alarmed because she hadn't come home last night and was trying to contact her.

How long had it been ringing? They couldn't do anything about it. The show had to proceed in a specified order, it was still too early for the final number. And she would have to take her photographs with that heartrending accompaniment.

'Eyes open or closed?' she asked.

It was a question that meant something only to those who frequented crime scenes. Sometimes killers, even the most brutal ones, closed their victims' eyes. It wasn't a gesture of pity, but of shame.

'Eyes open,' Astolfi replied.

This killer had wanted to be seen.

*

The mobile phone continued ringing, loud and indifferent.

Sandra's task was to freeze the scene before time and the search for answers altered it. She used her camera as a screen between herself and the horror, between herself and the pain. But, because of the ringing, those emotions risked overflowing beyond that screen and hurting her.

She took refuge in the routine of her profession, in the rules she had learned years earlier, during her training. If she followed procedure, everything would soon be over and she might be able to go back home and slip back into bed beside Max, seeking the warmth of his body and pretending that this freezing cold winter's day hadn't yet started.

From the general to the particular. She raised her camera and started shooting.

The flashes broke like waves on the face of the girl before fading into the cold, pale light of dawn. Sandra had taken up position in front of the bonnet but, after taking a dozen photographs of the car, she lowered her camera.

The girl was staring at her through the windscreen.

There was an unwritten rule she had been taught. Like her colleagues, she applied it scrupulously.

If the corpse has its eyes open, make sure they are never looking straight at the camera.

It was to avoid the pathos of an effect – 'photocall with dead model'. The girl last, she told herself. She decided to begin with the second body.

It lay on the ground, naked, a few yards from the car, face covered by pine needles, arms thrust forward.

'Man, between twenty and twenty-five approximately,' Sandra said into the microphone connected to the recorder in the pocket of her overalls. 'Firearm wound on back of neck.'

The hair around the entry wound showed evident traces of burning, a sign that the killer had fired at close range.

Sandra looked with her camera for footprints. She spotted a few in the damp earth. The heel part was as deep as the tip. He wasn't escaping, he was walking.

He didn't run away, Sandra thought. 'The killer made him get out of the car and took up position behind him. Then he opened fire.'

It had been an execution.

She saw more prints, shoeprints this time. 'Signs of trampling, covering a circular area.'

They belonged to the killer. She followed the steps with the camera in front of her, diligently continuing to collect images that would be stored in the digital memory. As she approached one of the trees she saw a little patch at the base that had been cleared of pine needles. She dictated the location into the recorder.

'Ten feet southeast: the earth has been moved on the surface, as if someone has been clearing it.'

It was here that everything began, she thought. It was here that he lay in wait. She lifted the lens, trying to replicate the killer's point of view. From here, through the trees, it was easy to see without being seen.

You enjoyed the spectacle, didn't you? Or did it make you angry? How long did you stay here watching them?

From there she began moving backwards, shooting as she did so, along a diagonal towards the car, reproducing the trajectory the killer must have taken. Back at the bonnet, Sandra again felt the girl's eyes on her: they actually seemed to be looking for her.

She ignored them a second time, concentrating instead on the car.

She moved round towards the back seat. There, scattered, lay the victims' clothes. She felt a pang in her heart. An image came into her mind of the two lovers getting ready to go out together, standing by their wardrobes, thinking of what to put on in order to appear more attractive to the other person, an entirely altruistic pleasure.

Were they already naked when the killer surprised them, or did he force them to undress? Had he watched them while they were making love or had he interrupted them? Sandra dismissed these thoughts: it wasn't up to her to supply the answers. She made an effort to recover her concentration.

In the middle of the clothes was the black handbag in which the phone had been ringing. Luckily it had stopped for a while, but it would start up again soon. Sandra stepped up the pace. That phone was a source of pain, and she didn't want to be too close to it.

The wide-open door on the passenger side revealed the girl's body. Sandra crouched beside her.

'Woman, approximate age twenty. The corpse is naked.'

Her arms were down by her sides, and she was pinned to her seat – which was reclining at an angle of about a hundred and twenty degrees – by a climbing rope that was wound several times around her, the part around the headrest strangling her.

In the middle of that tangle was a big hunting knife, the handle sticking out of her sternum. It had been driven in with such force that it couldn't be pulled out, Sandra concluded: the killer had been forced to leave it there.

Sandra photographed the trail of dried blood that ran down the victim's belly, soaking the seat and collecting in a little pool on the rug, between her bare feet and a pair of high-heeled shoes. Elegant high-heeled shoes, she corrected herself mentally. It had clearly been meant as a romantic evening.

Finally, she summoned up the courage to photograph the face in close-up.

The head was slightly tilted to the left, the black hair dishevelled: Sandra had the impulse to rearrange it, like a sister. She noted that the girl was very pretty, with the delicate features only youth could sculpt. And, where the tears hadn't blurred it, a touch of make-up could still be detected. It seemed applied with care, as if the girl was used to doing it. Perhaps she worked in the beauty industry, Sandra thought.

Her mouth, though, was turned down in an unnatural manner, and she wore glossy lipstick.

It made a strange impression on Sandra. There was something wrong, although for the moment she couldn't figure out what it was.

She leaned into the car to get a better view of the face. In accordance with the forensic photographers' unwritten rule, she looked for angles that allowed her to avoid that direct gaze into the camera. She found it hard looking into those eyes anyway, and she certainly didn't want them staring back at her.

The mobile phone started ringing again.

Violating what she had been taught, she instinctively closed her eyes, letting the camera take the last shots by itself. She was forced to think of those who were present at that scene, even without being there physically. The girl's mother and father, waiting for a reply that would free them from their anxiety. The young man's parents, who maybe still hadn't realised that their son hadn't come home that night. The architect of so much pain, who was probably miles away by now, enjoying the secret pleasure of killers – a sadistic itch in the heart – and basking in his own invisibility.

Sandra Vega let the camera finish its task, then pulled herself out of that cramped space that smelt of urine and young blood.

'Who?'

That was the recurring question in the heads of those present. Who could have done something like this? Who could have planned it?

When you can't give a monster a face, anyone could be him. People look at each other suspiciously, wondering what is hidden behind appearances, conscious of being observed by others with the same question in their eyes.

When a man commits a terrible crime, suspicion extends to the whole human race.

That was why even the cops, that morning, avoided looking at each other too much. Only when the killer was captured would the curse of suspicion be lifted.

Failing that, there remained the identities of the victims.

The girl didn't yet have a name. And that was a good thing from Sandra's point of view. She didn't want to know it. The young man's name, on the other hand, they had managed to discover through the car's registration number.

'His name was Giorgio Montefiori,' Crespi said to the pathologist.

Astolfi made a note of this on one of the forms he carried in a small folder. To write, he leaned on the mortuary van, which had just arrived on the scene to collect the bodies.

'I want to do the post mortem as soon as possible,' he said.

Sandra assumed that his haste was due to his wish to contribute to the investigation, but had to think again when he went on, without a shred of pity in his voice, 'I already have a road accident to deal with today, not to mention an expert opinion I have to write for a trial.'

Bureaucrat, Sandra thought. She couldn't bear these two dead young people getting less compassion than they were entitled to.

In the meantime, the forensics team had taken possession of the scene and were starting to search the area and collect evidence. And now that the girl's mobile phone could finally be picked up, it had stopped ringing.

Sandra turned away from the conversation between Astolfi and Crespi and watched as one of the technicians, having recovered the phone from the bag in the car, now walked towards the red and white tape and handed it over to a policewoman. It would be up to her to answer as soon as someone called. Sandra didn't envy her.

'Can you do it this morning?'

Sandra was distracted and didn't catch Crespi's last words. 'What?'

'I was asking if you can hand over the material this morning,' Crespi repeated, indicating the camera, which she had put back in the boot of the car.

'Oh, yes, of course,' she hastened to assure him.

'Can you do it now?'

She would have liked to get away and continue once she was back at Headquarters. But, faced with her superior's insistence, she couldn't refuse. 'All right.'

She started connecting the camera to her laptop so that she could transfer all the images on to it. Then she would email them, and at last she would be free of this nightmare. She was among the first to arrive at crime scenes, but was also the first to leave. Her work finished there. Unlike her colleagues, she could forget.

As she did this, another officer brought Crespi the dead girl's handbag. The superintendent opened it to check if there were papers in it. Sandra saw the girl's face on the identity card.

'Diana Delgaudio,' Crespi read, in a thin voice. 'Only twenty, dammit.'

A brief silence followed this statement.

Still looking at the card, he made the sign of the cross. He was a religious man. Sandra didn't know him well; he wasn't the show-off type. At Headquarters he was respected more for his length of service than for his actual merits. But maybe he was the right man for a crime like this. A person capable of handling a horrible case without trying to make capital out of it with the media to advance his career.

For the two dead people, a merciful cop was a good thing.

Crespi turned again to the officer who had brought him the handbag and handed it back. He took a deep breath. 'OK, let's go and inform the parents.'

They walked away, leaving Sandra to her work. In the meantime, the photographs she had taken started to appear on the computer screen as they loaded from the memory card. Observing them, she quickly went over that morning's work. There were almost four hundred photographs. One after the other, like stills from a silent film.

She was distracted by the ringing of the mobile phone, which everyone had been waiting for. She turned towards the policewoman, who was checking the name on the display. She passed a hand over her forehead, and finally answered it. 'Good morning, Signora Delgaudio, this is the police.'

Sandra had no idea what the mother was saying at the other end, but it was easy to imagine what she had felt, hearing a strange voice and the word 'police'. What until then had been only a nasty premonition was now taking on the semblance of a massive grief.

'A police car will be coming to your house to explain the situation,' the officer continued.

Sandra could not bear to listen. She focused her attention back on the images as they succeeded one another on the computer, hoping the program would hurry up downloading them. She had decided she would never have children, because her greatest fear was that they might end up in photographs like these. Diana's face. The absent expression. The dishevelled black hair. The make-up blurred by tears. The mouth twisted into a kind of sad smile. The eyes contemplating nothingness.

The download had almost finished when a close-up appeared fleetingly that was different from the others.

Instinctively, Sandra pressed a button to stop the process. Her heart pounding, she clicked back to that particular image. Around her, everything disappeared as if sucked into a black hole. There was only that image on the screen. How had she not noticed it?

In the photograph, the girl's face was still motionless.

Sandra turned rapidly in the direction of the crime scene beyond the red and white tape. Then she started running.

Diana Delgaudio had moved her eyes towards the camera.

5

'How could this have happened?'

The Commissioner's shouting bounced off the frescoed ceiling of the conference room and echoed around the second floor of the old palace on Via San Vitale which served as Rome's Police Headquarters.

The brunt of his fury was borne by those who had been at the crime scene that morning.

Diana Delgaudio had survived. But, because she had not been given aid in time, she was now fighting for her life in an operating theatre.

The main target of the commissioner's invective was the pathologist, Dr Astolfi. He sat hunched on his chair, with everyone looking at him. He had been the first to intervene and had certified the two deaths: it was up to him to answer for such negligence.

According to his account, the girl had had no pulse. The night-time temperature to which her naked body had been exposed, as well as the seriousness of the wounds, was 'incompatible with survival'. 'In such a situation,' Astolfi said in his defence, 'an objective analysis was sufficient to conclude that nothing could be done.'

'But, all the same, she survived,' the Commissioner retorted, increasingly furious.

It had been a 'lucky combination of events'. The crux of it all was the knife in the sternum. It had got caught between the ribs and the killer hadn't even tried to pull it out, he had been forced to leave it there. But it had also prevented the victim from losing too much blood. In addition, the blade had become embedded without harming any of the arteries. But what had really saved the girl's life was the fact that she had been unable to move because her body had been immobilised by the climbing rope. This had helped to stem the internal haemorrhaging, preventing it from becoming fatal.

'So the hypothermia turned into an advantage,' Astolfi concluded. 'It allowed the vital functions to continue.'

Sandra couldn't see any 'luck' in that sequence. The clinical outlook for Diana Delgaudio was still extremely grim. Even if the emergency operation she was undergoing at that very moment succeeded, nobody was certain what kind of life awaited her.

'We'd only just informed the mother and father that their daughter was dead!' the Commissioner said, to make sure that all those present realised the damage a mistake like that could do to the police's image.

Sandra looked around. Maybe some of her colleagues thought that those parents had at least been given the gift of hope. She knew that Superintendent Crespi was thinking precisely that. But in his case the practising Catholic in him had prevailed over the policeman. To someone with faith, God moved in mysterious ways, and there was always a message, a test or a lesson in everything that happened, however painful. But she didn't believe that. On the contrary, she was convinced that, very soon, fate would knock at those parents' door again, like a postman who had forgotten to deliver a package and went back with it.

Part of Sandra was secretly relieved at the fact that everybody considered Astolfi the person responsible for that morning's disaster.

But she too was guilty.

If, at the end of the procedure, she hadn't closed her eyes and let the camera take the last shots, she would have noticed the movement in Diana's eyes – that silent, desperate call for help – earlier.

It had been the girl's mobile phone that had distracted her, but that was no excuse. The thought of how things might have gone if she had only realised it hours later, maybe when she was at home or in the police laboratory, tormented her.

She too would have been an accomplice to that night's homicide. Did I save her? she asked herself. Was it really me? The truth was that Diana had saved herself. And Sandra would get the credit for it unfairly. And she would have to keep quiet to help the police save face. That was why she couldn't bring herself to totally condemn Astolfi.

In the meantime, the Commissioner had finished his diatribe. 'All right, get out of here, all of you.'

They all rose from their seats, but it was Astolfi who left the room first.

'Not you, Officer Vega.'

Sandra turned to look at the Commissioner, wondering why he wanted to detain her. But he immediately said to Crespi, 'You stay too, Superintendent.'

Sandra realised that another group was standing just outside the door through which her colleagues were streaming, ready to take their places in the room. They were members of the Central Operations Team, a special squad dealing with organised crime, undercover operations, serial killings, the hunt for escaped prisoners and other major crimes.

As they sat down again, Sandra recognised Deputy Commissioner Moro.

He was relatively young but already had the reputation of a consummate veteran. He had gained it by capturing a Mafia boss who had been on the run for thirty years. He had kept after him with such tenacity, putting his life on hold and ruining his own marriage, that even the fugitive himself had congratulated him when Moro finally put the handcuffs on him.

He was highly respected. Everyone wanted to be in Moro's team. An elite within the elite of the State Police. But Moro almost always worked with the same people, some fifteen of them. Men he trusted because they'd shared his efforts and his sacrifices. Men accustomed to leaving home in the morning without knowing when – or if – they would see their loved ones again. Moro chose them unmarried: he said he didn't like having to console widows and orphans. They were a family in themselves. Even outside work, they were always together. Unity was their strength.

In Sandra's eyes, they were like Zen monks. Linked by a vow that went beyond the uniform they wore.

'He'll do it again.'

Moro announced this with his back to the audience as he walked to the light switch and turned off the lights in the room. The words swept over those present as they were plunged into darkness. The silence that followed made Sandra shudder. For a moment, she felt lost in the dark. But then the iridescent beam of the video projector made the world around her suddenly reappear.

On the screen, one of the photographs she herself had taken that morning appeared.

The car with its doors open, the girl with the knife planted in her sternum.

None of those present turned their eyes away in horror. These were men who were prepared for anything, but it was also true that, as the hours had passed, pity and revulsion had given way to a different feeling. What Sandra called 'the illusion of distance'. It wasn't indifference, it was acclimatisation.

'This is just the beginning,' Moro went on. 'It may take a day, a month, ten years, but he'll strike again, you can be sure of it. That's why we have to stop him first. We have no choice.' He moved towards the centre of the screen, so that the image was now projected on to him too, making it hard to make out his face, as if it the horror on the screen had become a perfect camouflage. 'We're looking very closely into the lives of these two young people to see if anybody might have harboured any hatred or resentment towards them or their families: disappointed ex-fiancés or lovers, relatives with reasons to hold a grudge, angry creditors or debtors, connections with organised crime, the wrong thing said to the wrong person ... But, even though we don't know anything yet, I'm convinced that all those things can be ruled out as of now.' He raised his arm to the screen. 'Right now, though, I'm not going to talk to you about lines of inquiry, evidence, clues. Let's leave aside for a moment all our police methods, forget procedure. Instead, I want you to concentrate on these images. Look at them carefully.' He fell silent, clicking from image to image with the remote. 'There's method in all this, don't you think? This isn't someone who improvises: he's planned all this in advance. Strange as it may seem, there's no hatred in his actions. He's diligent, scrupulous. Get it into your heads that this is his job, and he does it extremely well.'

Sandra was struck by Moro's approach. He had set aside the traditional methods of investigation because he wanted an emotional reaction from his men.

'I ask you to memorise these photographs because if we look for a rational explanation we'll never catch him. Instead, we have to feel what he feels. We may not like it at first, but it's the only way, believe me.'

The first images of the dead man appeared. The wound in the back of the neck, the blood, his pale, ostentatious nakedness: it all seemed like an act. Police officers sometimes smiled when faced with a scene like that. Sandra had seen that happen more than once, but it wasn't cynicism or a lack of respect. It was a kind of self-defence. Their minds rejected the reality of it in the same way we reject something absurd, by ridiculing it. Moro was trying to avoid that. He needed their anger.

He continued moving from one photograph to the next. 'Don't let yourselves be deceived by the messiness of the slaughter: that's just appearance. He leaves nothing to chance. He's thought it through, he's planned it and carried it out. He isn't mad. On the contrary, it's likely that he's socially well adjusted.'

To a lay person, these words might have seemed jarring, as if he were expressing genuine admiration. But Moro was simply trying to avoid the mistake that many police officers made: underestimating the adversary.

He moved out of the beam of light from the projector and peered around at those present. 'There's a sexual element to these murders, because he chose a young couple making love, but he doesn't abuse the victims. The doctors have assured us that the girl was not assaulted and the preliminary post mortem results suggest the man wasn't either. So when our man kills he isn't driven by instinctual urges or by a desire to achieve orgasm. He won't masturbate over the bodies and leave DNA if that's what you're hoping. He strikes, disappears and, above all, watches: from now on he will be watching us, the police. Now he's come out into the open, he knows that he can't allow himself to make any mistakes. But he's not the only one being put to the test – we are too. In the end it won't be the best man who wins, but whoever's taken most advantage of the other man's mistakes. And he already has one advantage over us . . . ' He turned his wrist and showed the audience his watch. 'Time. We're in a race with this bastard and we have to win it. But that doesn't mean haste: haste is a very bad ally. Instead, we have to be as unpredictable as he is. That's the only way we'll be able to stop him. Because – and you can be certain of this – he's already planning something else.' He stopped the succession of images on the very last one.

The close-up of Diana Delgaudio.

Sandra could imagine the girl's desperation as, paralysed and half-conscious, she tried to indicate that she was still alive. Looking at her rigid face, though, she also remembered the impression she had had as she took that photograph. The make-up blurred by tears but still quite tidy. The eyeshadow, the blusher, the lipstick.

Yes, there really was something wrong.

'Take a good look,' Moro resumed, interrupting her thoughts. 'This is what he does, because this is what he likes doing. If by some miracle Diana Delgaudio survives, we'll have a witness who can identify him.'

Nobody reacted to that statement, not even with a nod. It was a secret hope, nothing more.

Unexpectedly, Moro turned to Sandra. 'Officer Vega.'

'Yes, sir.'

'You did a very good job this morning.'

This compliment made Sandra feel flustered.

'We'd like you with us, Vega.'

She had been dreading that invitation. Any other police-woman would have felt flattered to be offered a place in Moro's team. Not her. 'I don't know if I'm up to it, sir.'

In the semi-darkness, Moro tried to bring her into focus. 'Now's not the time for modesty.'

'It isn't modesty. It's just that I've never dealt with this kind of crime before.'

Sandra noticed that Superintendent Crespi was shaking his head as if to reprimand her.

Moro pointed at the door. 'Then let's put it this way: *we* don't need you, it's two young people out there who need you, two young people who don't know that very soon it's going to be their turn. Because that will happen. I know it and you know it, Officer Vega. Even just talking about it, we've already wasted too much of the time those two young people have left.'

He was clearly determined. Sandra did not have the strength to retaliate and, besides, Moro had already turned away and was changing the subject.

'Our people are still finishing their examination of the pine wood at Ostia, so we'll soon be able to analyse what they find, reconstruct what happened, and learn more about the killer's *modus operandi*. In the meantime, I want you to focus on what you feel in your guts, in your bones, in the most hidden and shameful part of yourselves. Go home, sleep on it. Tomorrow, we start sifting through the evidence. And tomorrow I don't want to see any trace of emotion. You have to stay clear-headed and rational. The meeting is over.'

Moro was the first to walk out. The others also rose to leave the room. Sandra, though, stayed seated, still staring at the photograph of Diana on the screen. As they all filed past her, she didn't take her eyes off that image. She would have liked someone to turn off the projector: that final exhibition seemed somehow pointless and disrespectful.

Moro had put them through a kind of emotional training, but the next day he wanted them 'clear-headed and rational'. But Diana Delgaudio had already stopped being a girl of twenty with dreams, ambitions, plans. She had lost her identity. She had become material for an investigation, the generic individual who, having suffered a crime, could now take on the fleeting title of victim. And the transfiguration had happened right there, in front of everyone, during the meeting.

Acclimatisation, Sandra remembered. The antibody that

allowed police officers to survive evil. So, while everyone ignored the photograph of Diana, Sandra felt it her duty to pay attention to it, at least as long as she was alone in the room. And the more she looked at that close-up, the more she had a sense that something jarred.

A detail that was out of place.

In the smudged make-up on the girl's face, there was something that really wasn't right. Sandra at last identified it.

It was the lipstick.

6

'Learn to photograph emptiness.'

That was what the forensic photography instructor at the academy had said. At the time, Sandra was just over twenty and, to her and her companions, those words had sounded absurd. Just another of those set phrases, the kind of life lesson veteran officers were always coming out with, like 'learn from your enemy' or 'never abandon your colleagues'. For her – so sure of herself, so cocky – such expressions were part of the brainwashing recruits were subjected to so that they wouldn't have to face the truth. Which was that the human race was disgusting and, in doing that job, they would very soon feel revulsion at being part of it.

'Indifference is your greatest ally,' the instructor had added, 'because it isn't what you have in front of your camera that matters, but what isn't there.' Then he had repeated, 'Learn to photograph emptiness.'

And then, one at a time, he had admitted them to a room for a drill. It was a kind of set: the furnished living room of a perfectly ordinary apartment. But first he had announced that a crime had taken place in it. Their task was to figure out what kind of crime.

No blood, no bodies, no weapons. Just ordinary furnishings.

To achieve their aim, they had to learn to ignore the stains of baby food on the sofa, which would indicate that a child lived in that house, and the smell of air-freshener, clearly chosen by a house-proud woman. The crossword abandoned on an armchair, half-finished – would anyone ever finish it? The travel magazines scattered on the coffee table, put there by someone imagining a happy future, unaware that something nasty was about to happen.

Details of an abruptly interrupted existence. The lesson was an obvious one: empathy confuses. And in order to photograph emptiness, you first have to create it within yourself.

And Sandra had succeeded, surprising even herself. She had identified with the potential victim, not with what she herself felt. She had used the victim's point of view, not her own. Imagining that the victim had been lying on the floor, on her back, she too had lain down. And that was how she had seen a message under a chair.

FAB

The scene was the reproduction of an actual apartment in which a dying woman had found the strength to write, in her own blood, the first three letters of her killer's name.

Fabrizio.

She had pointed the finger at her own husband.

Sandra subsequently discovered that for twenty-five years this particular woman had been on the list of missing persons, while her husband mourned her in public and on TV appeals. And that the truth hidden beneath the chair had emerged only when he had decided to sell the house furnished. The discovery had been made by the new owner.

The idea that posthumous justice was possible had reassured

Sandra. A killer could never feel safe. But, even though the mystery had been solved, the woman's body had never been found.

'Learn to photograph emptiness,' Sandra repeated now to herself in the silence of her own car. Basically it was what Deputy Commissioner Moro had asked: indulge in your own emotions but then, once you have come out of them, restore the necessary coldness.

Sandra, though, hadn't returned home to reflect on what she felt in preparation for tomorrow's meeting, when the hunt for the killer would officially be launched. Ahead of her, beyond the windscreen, was the pine wood at Ostia, lit up by floodlights. The noise of the diesel generators and the intense brightness of the lights reminded her of country dance festivals. But it wasn't summer and no music would start up. Instead, there was grim winter weather and the only thing echoing through the wood were the voices of the police officers in their white overalls moving around the crime scene as if in a dance of ghosts.

The search had gone on all day. Sandra had returned to the scene at the end of her shift, and was parked some distance away, watching her colleagues at work. Nobody had asked her why she was there, waiting for everybody to go away. But there was a reason.

Her intuition about Diana's lipstick.

The girl worked in a perfume shop. Sandra hadn't been wrong when, after noticing the make-up on her face, she had hypothesised that she really knew her stuff. Having guessed that aspect of her life, though, had further reduced the distance between them. And that wasn't a good thing. She must never become too involved. It was dangerous.

She had learned that to her own cost nearly three years earlier, when her husband had died and she had been forced to investigate, all by herself, something that had been hastily written off as an accident. It had taken a great deal of clear-headedness not to let her ideas be clouded by anger or regret. It had been a risky enterprise. But at the time she had been alone, and she could afford to do it.

Now there was Max.

He was perfect for the life she had chosen. The transfer to Rome, the apartment in Trastevere, new faces, new colleagues. The right time and place to lay down new memories. Max was the ideal companion to share them.

A history teacher in high school, he lived for his books. He would spend hours reading in his study. Sandra was sure that if she weren't there he would even forget to feed himself or go to the toilet. He was as far from anything to do with police work as it was possible to get. The only horror he was likely to witness was one of his pupils doing a particularly poor oral exam.

Anyone who devoted himself to words could not be touched by the ugliness of the world.

Max was delighted whenever Sandra asked him to talk to her about his subject. Then he would launch into a passionate exposition, waving his arms about, eyes shining. He was born in Nottingham, but had lived in Italy for twenty years. 'There's only one place in the world for a history teacher,' he would say, 'and that's Rome.'

Sandra hadn't disillusioned him by telling him how much evil was concentrated in this city. That was why she never talked about her work. But this time she was actually going to lie. She dialled the phone number and sat waiting for his voice.

'Vega, you should have been home by now,' he said good-humouredly. He called her by her surname, like her colleagues.

'There's a big case on and they've asked us to do overtime,' she said – that was the excuse she had chosen.

'All right, then we'll have dinner a little later.'

'I don't think I can make it for dinner. I may be out for a while.'

'Oh,' was Max's only reaction to the news. He wasn't angry, only surprised. She'd never had to do such long overtime before.

Sandra half-closed her eyes. She felt really bad. She knew she had to fill that brief silence before it undermined the credibility of her story. 'You have no idea what a pain it is. There seems to be some kind of flu bug going around the photographic team.'

'Are you dressed warmly enough? I saw the forecast: it's going to be cold tonight.'

The fact that he was worried about her made her feel even worse. 'Of course.'

'Would you like me to wait up for you?'

'There's no need,' she said quickly. 'Seriously, go to bed. I may get through it all quite fast.'

'OK, but wake me up when you get home.'

Sandra hung up. The sense of guilt didn't make her change her mind. She had got it into her head that she had done a bad job because, like Astolfi, she had been in a hurry to get away from the crime scene. The final discovery that had elevated her in the estimation of her colleagues and Deputy Commissioner Moro was merely the result of a coincidence. If she had followed the photographic protocol to the letter she would have protected the evidence, not herself. Instead of using the camera to probe the crime scene, she had made use of it as a shelter.

She had to make amends. The only way was to repeat the procedure, to make sure she hadn't neglected anything else.

In the pine wood, the police officers and the forensics team were starting to disband. Very soon she would be alone. She had a mission to carry out.

To photograph emptiness.

The young couple's car had been removed, and the police cars that had guarded the area had also gone. They had forgotten to take away the red and white tape. The wind made it sway along with the branches of the pines, but now it enclosed an empty space.

Sandra checked the time: just after midnight. She had parked three hundred yards away, but she wondered if that was far enough. She didn't want anyone to notice her car.

The moonlight was obscured by a thin layer of clouds. She couldn't use a torch: there was a risk someone might see it, and, besides, it would alter her perception of the place. She would use the infrared sight on her camera to orientate herself, but in the meantime she let her eyes grow accustomed to the pale glimmer of the moon.

She got out of her car and headed for the centre of the crime scene. As she walked through the pine wood, the thought sprang into her mind that maybe what she was doing was stupid. She was exposing herself to danger. Nobody knew she was there and it was impossible for her to know the killer's intentions. What if he came back to check on things? Or to relive the sensations he had felt the night before? Some killers did that.

Sandra knew that this pessimistic vision was actually part of a kind of propitiatory ritual. You prepared for the worst with the sole purpose of being proved wrong. But at that moment a ray of light broke free of the clouds and came to rest on the ground.

It was then that she noticed a dark figure between the trees a hundred yards away.

On the alert, she slowed down, although she couldn't stop immediately. Fear had taken control of her body and she took another crunching step on the pine needles. In the meantime, the shadowy figure was moving across what had been the crime scene and looking around. Sandra was petrified. Then she saw the man do something unexpected.

He made the sign of the cross.

For a moment she felt relieved: this was a man of faith. But a second later her mind caught up with what she had seen, replaying it in slow motion.

The sign had been inverted – *from right to left, from bottom to top*.

'Get down!'

The words emerged like a whisper from the darkness, a few yards behind her. For Sandra it was like waking up with a start, but from one nightmare into another. She was about to cry out, but the man who had spoken stepped forward: he had a scar on his temple and he motioned to her to squat down with him behind a tree. Sandra knew him, but it took her a few seconds to realise who he was.

Marcus. The priest she had met almost three years earlier.

He again motioned to her to squat, then came and took her hand, slowly pulling her down. She obeyed, then stared at him, still incredulous. But he was looking straight in front of him.

Ahead of them, the unknown man had knelt and was feeling the ground with the palm of his hand, as if searching for something.

'What's he doing?' Sandra asked in a low voice, her heart still pounding.

Marcus did not reply.

'We have to go in,' she said. It was halfway between a statement and a question, because she wasn't sure of anything at that moment.

'Do you have a weapon on you?'

'No,' she admitted.

Marcus shook his head, as if to say that they couldn't afford to take any risks.

'Do you want to let him go?' She was incredulous.

In the meantime, the unknown man had got back on his feet. He stood there for a few more seconds, motionless. Then he walked off into the darkness, in the opposite direction from them.

Sandra leapt forward.

'Wait,' Marcus said, trying to stop her.

'The number plate,' she said, referring to the car he had probably used to get there.

The unknown man seemed to be walking faster now, even though he couldn't have known he was being followed. Sandra tried to keep up with him, but her footsteps on those damned pine needles risked revealing her presence, so she was forced to slow down.

It was because of that that she noticed something familiar about the unknown man. Maybe it was the way he walked, or maybe his posture. The sensation was a fleeting one, lasting barely a second.

The man climbed over a hillock and disappeared from her field of vision. As she was wondering where he had got to, she heard the noise of a car door closing, then an engine starting up.

Sandra started running as fast as she could. She stumbled over a branch but managed to keep her balance. Her calf hurting, she forced the pace because she didn't want to lose him. Images of the two dead young people flashed before her eyes. If this really was their killer, she couldn't let him get away like this. No, she wouldn't allow it.

As she reached the edges of the wood, though, she saw the car driving away with its lights off. In the pale moonlight, the rear number plate was unreadable.

'Shit,' she cursed. Then she turned. Marcus was standing a few paces behind her. 'Who was it?' she asked.

'I don't know.'

She had hoped to get a different answer. She was struck by how controlled his reaction was. It was as if he didn't care that he had missed the opportunity to give the killer a face and a name. Or maybe he was just more pragmatic than she was. 'You were here for him, weren't you? You're also hunting for him.'

'Yes.' He didn't want to tell her that he was there because of her, that he often stood outside her building, or waited for her to finish work so that he could accompany her home without her knowing. That he liked watching her from a distance. And that, when she hadn't headed in the direction of home at the end of her shift tonight, he had decided to follow her from Police Headquarters.

But Sandra was too shaken by what had just happened to realise that he had lied to her. 'We were so close to him.'

He looked at her impassively, then turned abruptly. 'Let's go,' he said.

'Where?'

'When he knelt, he may have buried something.'

7

Using the light from Sandra's smartphone, they went in search of the spot where the unknown man had been digging.

'Here we are,' Marcus announced.

Both of them bent over a small heap of earth that had recently been moved.

Marcus took a latex glove from his jacket pocket and put it on. Then he started shifting the earth, slowly and carefully. Sandra watched impatiently, still shining the light from her phone on it. After a while, Marcus stopped.

'Why don't you carry on?' she asked.

'There's nothing here.'

'But you said—'

'I know,' he interrupted her calmly. 'I don't understand: the earth has been moved, you saw it too.'

They got back on their feet and stood for a while in silence. Marcus was afraid that Sandra would ask him again what he was doing there. In order not to arouse her suspicions, he was obliged to put off for the moment any further discussion of what had happened. 'What do you know about this business?' he asked her.

She seemed to think it over for a moment, uncertain what to do.

'You aren't obliged to tell me. But maybe I can give you a hand.'

'How?' she asked, suspiciously.

'Exchange of information.'

Sandra weighed up the offer. She had seen him in action almost three years earlier: she knew he was good and that he saw things differently from the way a police officer did. He couldn't 'photograph emptiness', as she could with her camera, but he was able to detect the invisible traces left by evil. So she decided to trust him and started telling him about the two young people and that morning's incredible final development: Diana Delgaudio surviving both a deep wound and the cold of a winter's night.

'Can I see the photographs?' Marcus asked.

Once again, Sandra stiffened.

'If you want to understand what happened tonight and what that man was doing here, you have to show me the images of the crime scene.'

After a while, Sandra returned from her car with a couple of torches and a tablet. Marcus reached out his hand. But before giving it to him she wanted to make things clear. 'I'm contravening regulations, and I'm also breaking the law.' Then she passed him the tablet, together with one of the torches.

He looked at the first photographs. They showed the tree where the murderer had taken up position.

'That's where he stood to spy on them,' she said.

'Show me the place.'

She led him there. The patch from which the pine needles had been cleared was still visible on the ground. Sandra had no idea what was going to happen. It was a method quite different from that of police profilers.

Marcus looked down, then raised his eyes and started observing what he had in front of him. 'All right, let's begin.'

First of all, he made the sign of the cross, but not an inverted one like the unknown man earlier. Sandra noticed how Marcus's face changed, undergoing a series of imperceptible transformations. The lines around his eyes relaxed, his breath became deeper. He wasn't simply concentrating; something was emerging from inside him.

'How long did I stay here?' he asked himself, starting to identify with the killer. 'Ten, fifteen minutes? I study them carefully, savouring the moment before going into action.'

I know what you felt, Marcus told himself. The rush of adrenaline, that tense feeling in the stomach. A mixture of excitement and anxiety. Like when you played hide and seek as a child. That little itch at the back of the neck, the electric quiver that makes the hair on your arms stand up.

Sandra was starting to understand what was happening: nobody could enter the mind of a murderer, but Marcus was able to evoke the evil he carried inside him. She decided to humour this simulation and address him as if he were really the killer. 'Did you follow them here?' she asked. 'Maybe you knew the girl, you liked her and you followed her.'

'No. I waited for them. I don't know them. I didn't choose the victims, only the hunting ground. I examine it and then I prepare.'

The pine wood at Ostia was becoming a refuge for lovers, especially in summer. In winter, on the other hand, not many ventured there. The killer must have spent many days roaming the wood, waiting for an opportunity. In the end, he had been rewarded.

'Why did you clear the ground?'

Marcus looked down. 'I have a bag with me, maybe a rucksack: I don't want to dirty it on the pine needles. I'm very fond of it, because it's where I keep my tricks, my conjuring tricks. Because I'm like a magician.'

He chooses the right moment and slowly approaches the victim, he reflected. He counts on the effect of surprise: that's part of the conjuring act.

Marcus moved away from the tree and started advancing towards the centre of the scene. Sandra followed him at a short distance, surprised by how the reconstruction was coming along.

'I get to the car without being seen.'

Marcus looked through the next set of images. The naked victims.

'Were they already undressed or did you force them to strip?' Sandra asked. 'Had they already made love or were they just starting?'

'I choose couples because I can't relate to other people. I can't have an emotional or sexual relationship. There's something in me that keeps people away. I act out of envy. Yes, I envy them . . . That's why I like watching. And then I kill them, to punish their happiness.'

He said this with a lack of emotion that froze Sandra's blood. All at once, she grew afraid of his expressionless eyes. There was no anger in him, just a lucid detachment. Marcus wasn't simply identifying with the killer.

He had become the killer.

She felt a sense of confusion.

'I'm sexually immature,' Marcus continued. 'I'm between twenty-five and forty-five.' It was usually in those years that the accumulated frustration of an unsatisfied sex life exploded into violence. 'I don't abuse my victims.'

Sure enough, Sandra remembered, there had been no sexual assault.

Marcus looked at the photograph of the car and placed himself level with the bonnet. 'I appear out of nowhere and aim the gun to stop them restarting the car and getting away. What objects do I have with me?'

'A gun, a hunting knife and a climbing rope,' Sandra said.

'I give the rope to the boy and *persuade* him to tie his partner to the seat.'

'You force him, you mean.'

'It isn't a threat. I never raise my voice, I say things gently: I'm a seducer.' He hadn't even needed to fire a warning shot, just to demonstrate that he meant business. All he had had to do was make the boy believe that he had a chance to save himself: that, if he obeyed, if he behaved himself, in the end he would be rewarded. 'Obviously, the boy did as he was told. I watched to make sure he tied her properly.'

Marcus was right, Sandra thought. People often ignored the power of persuasion of a firearm. For some reason, they all thought they could handle a situation like that.

Looking through the photographs, Marcus arrived at the one showing the girl with the knife in her sternum.

'You stabbed her but she was lucky,' Sandra said, and immediately regretted using that word. 'The internal bleeding only stopped because you left the knife where it was. If you'd pulled it out, she probably wouldn't have been saved.'

Marcus shook his head. 'I wasn't the one who killed the girl. That's why I left the knife. For all of you, to let you know.'

Sandra was incredulous.

'I offered him a swap: his life in exchange for hers.'

She seemed horrified. 'How do you know that?'

'You'll see, you'll find the boy's fingerprints on the knife handle, not mine.' He wanted to degrade what they felt for each other, he thought. 'It's a test of love.'

'But, if he obeyed you, why then did you kill him too? After all, you made him get out of the car and shot him in the back of the neck at close range. It was an execution.'

'Because my promises are lies, just like the love that couples say they feel for each other. And, if I demonstrate that another human being is capable of killing out of pure selfishness, then my own actions will also be absolved of all guilt.'

The wind rose, shaking the trees. A single great shudder that went through the wood and then faded away in the darkness. But to Sandra it seemed as if that lifeless wind came from Marcus.

He realised how upset she was and, from whatever place he was in at that moment, he was suddenly brought back to reality. Aware of the fear in her eyes, he felt ashamed. He didn't want her to look at him like that. He saw her instinctively take a small step back, as if wanting to place a safe distance between them.

Sandra looked away, embarrassed. But, after what she had seen, she couldn't hide her unease. To get out of the impasse, she took the tablet from his hands. 'I want to show you something.'

She skimmed through the photographs until she got to a close-up of Diana Delgaudio.

'The girl works in a perfume shop,' she said. 'The make-up she has on her face, where it hasn't been smudged by tears, has been put on with care. Including the lipstick.'

Marcus looked at the image blankly. He was still shaken, and maybe that was why he didn't immediately grasp the significance of that detail.

Sandra tried to make it clearer. 'When I took the photograph, it struck me as strange. There was something wrong, but it wasn't until later that I realised what it was. Just now you said we're dealing with a killer with voyeuristic tendencies: he waits for the sexual act to take place before he shows himself. But, if Diana and her boyfriend had been in the throes of passion, why does she still have lipstick on?'

Marcus understood. 'He put it on her, afterwards.'

Sandra nodded. 'I think he photographed her. In fact, I'm sure of it.'

Marcus registered the information with great interest. He still didn't know how to incorporate it into the killer's pattern, but he was convinced that it had a specific place in the ritual. 'Evil is the anomaly in front of everybody's eyes but which nobody can see,' he said as if to himself.

'What do you mean?'

Marcus looked at her again. 'The answers are all here, and it's here that you have to look for them.' It was like in the painting of *The Martyrdom of St Matthew* in San Luigi dei Francesi: you just had to know how to look. 'The killer is still here, even though we can't see him. We have to search for him in this place, not anywhere else.'

Sandra understood. 'You're talking about the man we saw earlier. You don't think he was the killer.'

'What would be the point of coming back here hours later? A killer assuages his burden of morbid and destructive desires with the death and humiliation of his victims. His urges are satisfied. He's a seducer, remember? He's already looking for his next conquest.'

Sandra was convinced that wasn't all, that Marcus was hiding the real reason from her. His was a rational argument, but she could tell from his disturbed state that there was something else. 'That's why he crossed himself, isn't it?'

That inverted sign of the cross had clearly made a big impression on Marcus too.

'So who was it, in your opinion?' Sandra insisted.

'Look for the anomaly, Officer Vega, don't be content with details. What did he come here to do?'

Sandra thought over what she had seen. 'He knelt on the ground, and dug a hole. But there was nothing inside . . .'

'Precisely,' Marcus said. 'He didn't bury anything. He dug something up.'

'This is the second lesson of your training,' Clemente had announced.

He had found Marcus accommodation in an attic room in the Via dei Serpenti. It wasn't very large. There was nothing in it but a lamp and a camp bed against the wall. But from the small window he had a unique view of the roofs of Rome.

Marcus had raised his hand to the plaster that still covered the wound on his temple. It had become a kind of nervous tic. He did it almost unconsciously. Since his loss of memory, it had sometimes seemed to him that everything was the result of a dream or his imagination. So it was as if that gesture was necessary in order to prove to himself that he was real. 'All right, I'm ready.'

'I'll be your only point of reference. You won't have any other contacts: you won't know where your orders and your missions come from. In addition, you will have to reduce your relations with other people to a minimum. Years ago, you took a vow of solitude. You are not enclosed within the walls of a monastery, but in the world that surrounds you.'

Marcus wondered if it was possible to survive in such conditions. Part of him, though, told him that he didn't need other people, that he was already accustomed to being alone.

'There exist some categories of crimes that attract the attention of the Church,' Clemente continued. 'What makes them different is

that they contain an anomaly. Over the centuries such anomalies have received various definitions: absolute evil, mortal sin, the devil. But these are nothing but imperfect attempts to give a name to something inexplicable: the secret wickedness of human nature. From the start, the Church has looked for crimes that had this characteristic, analysed them, classified them. To do so, it uses a special category of priests: the penitenzieri, the hunters of the dark.'

'Is that what I did before?'

'Your task is to find evil on behalf of the Church. Your training won't be any different from that of a criminologist or a police profiler, but in addition you will be able to distinguish details that others do not grasp.' Then he added, 'There are things that men do not want to admit or to see.'

But Marcus still did not fully understand the sense of his mission. 'Why me?'

'Evil is the rule, Marcus. Good is the exception.'

Even though Clemente had not answered his question, those words struck him more than any others. The sense was clear. He was an instrument. Unlike other people, he possessed the awareness that evil was a constant of existence. In the life of a penitenziere there was no place for things like friends, family, love for a woman. Joy was a distraction, and he had to agree to do without it.

'How will I know when I'm ready?'

'You will know. But, to be aware of evil, you first have to learn to work on behalf of good.' At that point, Clemente gave him an address, then handed him an object.

A key.

Marcus proceeded to the place without knowing what to expect.

It was a small two-storey villa in an area on the outskirts of the city. On his arrival, he saw a group of people standing outside. A cross of purple velvet had been placed on the front door: the unmistakable sign that there was a dead person inside.

He went in and passed among friends and relations of the family without anybody paying him any attention. They were speaking among themselves in low voices: nobody was crying but the atmosphere was heavy with genuine grief.

The misfortune that had befallen the house was the death of a young girl. Marcus immediately recognised the parents: while everyone else was standing, they were the only people sitting in the room. Their faces told a story not so much of grief as of confusion.

For a moment, his eyes and those of the father met. A robust man in his fifties, the kind who could have bent a steel bar with his bare hands. Now, though, he looked defeated, the picture of powerless strength.

The coffin was open and those present were filing past it. Marcus joined the line, and when he saw the girl he immediately understood that death had started to act on her while she was still alive. Overhearing what other people were saying, he discovered that her disease had been herself.

The drugs had rapidly eaten away at her existence.

Marcus, though, did not understand how he could do good in this situation. Everything seemed lost, irredeemable. Then he took from his pocket the key that Clemente had entrusted to him, and looked at it in the palm of his hand.

What did it open?

Diligently, he did the one thing he could do: try it in every door. He started moving around the house, taking care not to attract attention, searching for the right one. But without any luck.

He was about to give up when he noticed a door at the back. It was the only one without a lock. He opened it by simply pushing it with his hand. Beyond it was a staircase. He descended into the semi-darkness of a cellar.

There was old furniture, and a counter with DIY tools. But then he turned and noticed a wooden cabin. A sauna.

He went to the porthole in the door and tried to look inside, but the glass was thick and it was too dark. So he decided to test the key. To his great surprise, the lock started to turn.

He opened the door and was immediately overcome by the stench. Vomit, sweat, excrement. Instinctively, he retreated. Then he moved forward again.

There was someone on the floor of that narrow space. His clothes were torn, his hair dishevelled, and he had a long beard. It was clear from his heavily swollen eye, from the dried blood that covered his nose and the corners of his mouth and from his numerous bruises that he had been soundly beaten many times. On the skin of his arms, blackened by dirt, parts of a tattoo could be seen: a skull and crossbones. On his neck, another tattoo: a swastika.

From the state he was in, Marcus immediately worked out that he had been locked in here for some time.

Turning towards him, the man shielded his one good eye with one hand, because even that dim light bothered him. There was genuine fear in his eyes. After a few seconds, he realised that Marcus was a new character in this nightmare. Maybe that was why he summoned up the courage to speak to him.

'It wasn't my fault . . . These kids come to me, ready to do anything to score . . . She asked me if she could prostitute herself, she needed money . . . I simply did as she asked me, it was nothing to do with me . . .'

The enthusiasm with which he had begun these words gradually faded, and with it his hope. He lay down again, resigned. Like a rabid dog that had been chained up, that barked but then lay down again because it knew it would never be free.

'The girl is dead.'

At these words, the man bowed his head.

Marcus stood there looking at him, wondering why Clemente had subjected him to such a test. The real question, though, was a different one.

What was the right thing to do?

He had before him a wicked man. The symbols he had tattooed on him clearly stated what side he was on. He deserved punishment, but this wasn't the way. If he freed him, he would probably continue to make other people suffer. Then the blame would also be his. Just as he would make himself an accomplice to cruelty if he decided to leave him there.

Where was good and where was evil in this situation? What should he do? Free the prisoner or close the door and go?

'Evil is the rule. Good is the exception.' But, at that moment, he couldn't tell the difference.

8

They used voicemail to communicate.

Whenever one of the two had something to report to the other, he would call a particular number and leave a message. The number changed periodically, but there was no fixed period. They might use it for a few months, or Clemente might change it after just a few days. Marcus knew there were security reasons for this, but he had never asked what the decision depended on. Even that banal question, though, was indicative of the existence of a whole world about which his friend kept him in the dark. And Marcus was finding it hard to be left out. Even though Clemente was doing it for a good reason or to safeguard their secret, he felt used. That was why relations between them had been so tense lately.

After the night spent with Sandra in the pine wood at Ostia, Marcus had called the voicemail to ask for a meeting. But, to his great surprise, his friend had got in first with a message.

The appointment was for eight o'clock at the minor basilica of Sant'Apollinare.

Marcus crossed the Piazza Navona, which at that hour was starting to fill with the stalls of artists displaying pictures of the most beautiful places in Rome. The bars were putting out their tables, which in winter were arranged around big gas stoves.

Sant'Apollinare was in the nearby square of the same name. The church wasn't opulent or particularly beautiful, but its simple architecture blended in well with the buildings surrounding it. It was part of a complex that had once been the headquarters of the Collegium Germanicum et Hungaricum. For some years now, it had housed the Pontifical University of the Holy Cross.

The peculiarity of the little basilica, though, lay in two stories, one older and one more recent. Both had to do with a secret presence.

The first, dating back to the fifteenth century, involved an image of the Madonna. When in 1494 the soldiers of Charles V of France had camped in front of the church, the faithful had covered the sacred effigy with plaster to spare the Virgin the sight of the soldiers' nefarious deeds. But, because of that, the image had been forgotten for a century and a half, until an earthquake in 1647 had brought down the screen concealing it.

The second story, which was much more recent, concerned the curious fact that Enrico De Pedis was buried in the church. De Pedis, known as Renatino, had been a member of the bloodthirsty Magliana gang, a criminal organisation rampant in Rome from the middle of the seventies and implicated in some of the city's more obscure episodes, some even involving the Vatican. Although the gang had been almost wiped out by trials and killings, some people said it still operated in the shadows.

Marcus had always wondered why the most ferocious of its members had been granted an honour reserved in the past only for saints and great benefactors of the Church, as well as two popes, cardinals and bishops. He recalled the scandal that had arisen when someone had revealed that dubious presence to the world, and the ecclesiastical authorities had been forced to evict the body – but only after a long campaign, which had been firmly and inexplicably opposed by the Curia.

Some maintained that buried alongside De Pedis was a young girl who had disappeared years ago not far from Sant'Apollinare and who had never been seen again. Emanuela Orlandi was the daughter of an employee of Vatican City, and there was a theory that she had been kidnapped to blackmail the Pope. But the exhumation of De Pedis's body had revealed that this was only the latest in a series of false trails in the story.

Thinking back on all this, Marcus wondered why Clemente had chosen this particular place for their meeting. He hadn't liked the way they had quarrelled the last time, or the way in which his friend had dismissed his request to meet his superiors over the case of the nun who had been dismembered a year before in the Vatican gardens.

'It is not for us to ask, it is not for us to know. We must simply obey.'

He hoped that Clemente's summons was a way of begging forgiveness, or that he had had second thoughts. That was why Marcus walked a little faster when he reached the square in front of Sant'Apollinare.

When he went in, the church was deserted. His steps echoed on the marble of the central nave, along which were carved the names of cardinals and bishops.

Clemente was already sitting in one of the front pews. On his knees was a black leather bag. He turned to look at Marcus and calmly motioned to him to sit down next to him. 'I imagine you're still angry with me.'

'Did you send for me to tell me that the higher-ups have decided to co-operate?'

'No,' Clemente replied bluntly.

Marcus was disappointed, but didn't want to let it show. 'So what's going on?'

'Last night something terrible happened in the pine wood at Ostia. A young man is dead, and a young woman may not survive.'

'I read about it in the newspapers,' Marcus lied. In reality, he already knew everything thanks to Sandra. But he certainly couldn't tell Clemente that he had been following a woman in secret because he might have feelings for her. Feelings he himself didn't understand.

Clemente looked at Marcus as if he had guessed he was lying. 'You are to handle the case.'

The request caught him off guard. The police were already putting their best men and resources into it: Deputy Commissioner Moro's team was well placed to track down the killer. 'Why?'

Clemente was never explicit about the reasons that lay behind any of their investigations. He often referred to reasons of expediency or the Church's general interest in a particular crime being solved. That was why Marcus never knew the real motive for his assignments. But this time his friend granted him an explanation.

'There is a serious threat hanging over Rome. What happened the other night is having a profound effect on people.' Clemente's tone was unexpectedly alarmist. 'It isn't the crime in itself but what it represents: the killings are heavy with symbolic elements.'

Marcus thought again of the way the killer had staged it all: the young man forced to murder his girlfriend to save his own life, then executed with a shot to the back of the neck, in cold blood. The killer knew that when the police arrived on the scene they would be faced with questions they wouldn't be able to answer. The spectacle was for their eyes only.

And then there was the sex. Even though the monster hadn't abused the victims, the sexual aspect of what he had done was evident. Crimes of that nature were more worrying because they generated a morbid interest on the part of the public. Even though many denied it, they felt a dangerous attraction, which they concealed with a show of disgust. But there was something else.

Sex was a dangerous vehicle.

Whenever, for example, a statistic concerning rape was issued, in the days that followed, instances of the crime increased exponentially. Instead of creating indignation, the figure – especially if it was high – generated emulation. It was as if even latent rapists, who until then had managed to control their own impulses, suddenly felt authorised to go into action by seeing themselves as part of a large, anonymous group.

The crime is less serious if the guilt is shared, Marcus remembered. That was why most police forces in the world no longer put out figures about sexual crimes. But he was convinced that there was something else. 'Why on earth this sudden interest in what happened in the pine wood at Ostia?'

'You see that confessional?' Clemente was pointing to the second chapel on the left. 'No priest ever goes in there. But every now and again someone does use it to confess.'

Marcus was curious to know what was behind this statement.

'In the past, criminals used it to pass messages to the police. There's a tape recorder in the confessional. It's set off every time somebody kneels. We dreamed up the idea so that whoever needed to could talk to the police without running the risk of being arrested. Sometimes those messages contained valuable information, and in return the police turned a blind eye to certain things. It may surprise you, but the two sides communicated with each other through us. Of course nobody ever knew. Our mediation saved many lives.'

This pact was the reason the body of a criminal like De Pedis had been preserved there until a short time ago. That much was clear now, even to Marcus: Sant'Apollinare was a safe haven, a neutral area.

'You're speaking in the past tense, meaning it doesn't happen any more.'

'There are more effective means of communication now,' Clemente said. 'The intercession of the Church is no longer necessary, and is even viewed with suspicion.'

Marcus was starting to understand. 'But the tape recorder is still there . . . '

'We thought we'd at least keep that going, assuming it might prove useful again one day. And we weren't wrong.' Clemente opened the black leather bag that he had brought with him and took out an old cassette player. Then he put a cassette in the appropriate compartment. 'Five days ago – in other words, before the two young people were attacked in the pine wood at Ostia – somebody knelt in that confessional and uttered these words . . .'

He pressed play. A rustling sound filled the nave then faded away in the echo. The quality of the recording was very poor. But after a while, a voice emerged from that invisible grey river.

'. . . a time . . . It happened at night . . . And everyone came running to where his knife had been planted . . . '

It was like a distant whisper, neither male nor female. It was if it came from another world, another dimension. It was the voice of a dead man trying to imitate the living, maybe because he had forgotten he was dead. Every now and again it vanished into the background static, taking fragments of sentences with it.

'. . . his time had come . . . the children died . . . the false bearers of false love . . . and he was pitiless with them . . . of the child of salt . . . if he isn't stopped, he won't stop.'

That was the last thing the voice said. Clemente stopped the tape.

To Marcus, it was immediately clear that this recording was no coincidence. 'He talks about himself in the third person, but it's him.' It was the killer's voice that was recorded on that tape. His words were unequivocal, at least as unequivocal as the resentment that underlay them.

'*. . . And everyone came running to where his knife had been planted . . .*'

As Clemente observed him in silence, Marcus started to analyse the message.

'*A time,*' Marcus repeated. 'The first part of the sentence is missing: what does he mean? And why does he talk in the past about what was going to happen in the future?'

Apart from the proclamations and the threats, which were part of the usual repertory of exhibitionist killers, there were some other passages that had attracted his attention.

'*The children died,*' he repeated in a low voice. The choice of the word 'children' was deliberate. It meant that the target was partly the parents of the two young people in Ostia. The killer had struck at their own blood and, inevitably, had also killed them. His hatred had reverberated like the shock of an earthquake. The epicentre was the two young people, but from them an evil seismic wave had spread that would harm anyone who was around them – family members, friends, acquaintances – until it reached all those mothers and fathers who had no links with the two young people but who were now sharing in the general anguish and grief at what had happened in the pine wood, thinking it might happen to their own children.

'*The false bearers of false love,*' Marcus said, and thought again of the test to which the killer had subjected Giorgio Montefiori, tricking him into thinking that he could choose between his own death and Diana's. Giorgio had preferred to live and had agreed to stab the girl who trusted him and believed that he loved her.

'We should hand this tape over to the investigating team,' Marcus said, with great conviction. 'It's obvious that the killer wants to be stopped, otherwise he wouldn't have announced what he was about to do. And if in the past the confessional was used to communicate with the police, then the message is addressed to them.'

'No,' Clemente said immediately. 'You'll have to work alone.'

'Why?'

'It's been decided.'

Once again, a mysterious upper level was fixing the rules on the basis of some apparently incomprehensible motive.

'What's the child of salt?'

'The only clue you have.'

9

When she had got home that night, she had woken Max with a kiss and then they had made love.

It had been strange. The act should have helped to free her, to remove the unease lurking deep inside her. The effort of sex had indeed washed clean her soul, but had done nothing to get rid of the image of Marcus.

Because, while making love with Max, she had thought of him.

Marcus represented all the pain she had left behind her. Seeing him again was likely to bring old traumas to the surface, like a marsh which in the course of time regurgitated everything it had swallowed. And indeed, in Sandra's life, it was as if old chests full of memories had reappeared, houses in which she had lived, clothes she had discarded. And a strange nostalgia. But, much to her astonishment, it wasn't for her dead husband.

Marcus was to blame.

When Sandra woke, about seven, she stayed in bed, thinking about these things. Max was already up, and she waited for him to leave for school before getting up herself. She didn't want to have to answer his questions: she was afraid he had noticed something and might ask for an explanation.

Before she stepped into the shower, she switched on the radio to hear the news.

The jet of warm water ran over the back of her neck. She closed her eyes and let herself be caressed. The newsreader was providing an account of the day in politics.

Sandra did not listen. She tried to bring what had happened last night into focus. Seeing Marcus at work had been a kind of shock. The way he had penetrated the mind of the killer had made her feel as if she had the real killer in front of her.

Part of her was full of admiration, the other horrified.

'*Look for the anomaly, Officer Vega, don't be content with details.*' That was what he had said. '*Evil is the anomaly in front of everybody's eyes but which nobody can see.*'

And what had she seen that night? A man moving around the pine wood like a shadow in the moonlight. And bending to dig a hole.

'*He didn't bury anything. He dug something up,*' Marcus had said.

Dug up what?

The unknown man had made the sign of the cross. But an inverted one – *from right to left, from down to up*.

What did it mean?

At that moment, the newsreader on the radio went on to the crime news. Sandra turned off the water to hear it and stood there in the shower stall, dripping, with one hand resting on the tiled wall.

The main news was the attack on the two young people. The tone was worried. Couples were recommended to avoid going to isolated places. The police would be increasing their presence to guarantee the safety of the citizens. To discourage the killer, the authorities had announced night patrols in areas on the outskirts of the city and in the countryside. But Sandra knew it was just propaganda: it was a vast territory, and it would be impossible to cover all of it.

When he had finished detailing how the police forces were reacting to the emergency, the newsreader went on to supply a bulletin on the condition of the surviving victim. Diana Delgaudio had survived the difficult operation she had undergone. Now she was in a state of induced coma, but the doctors were not issuing any prognosis. In practical terms, they were unable to say when and, above all, if she would regain consciousness.

Sandra looked down, as if the words coming out of the radio were flowing together with the rivulets of water into the shower drain. The thought of the girl had become an illness. If Diana remained like that, what kind of life awaited her? The weird thing was that she might not even be able to provide any useful information that would help capture the person who had reduced her to that state. Which meant that the killer had achieved his aim after all, because you could kill a person while still leaving them alive.

It wasn't Diana, but the killer who had been lucky.

If Sandra thought about the events of the two previous nights, there were too many things that didn't make sense. The attack on the two young people and then the actions of the unknown man in the moonlight. Had the killer deliberately left something at the scene of the crime? Had he buried it so that someone else could go and dig it up? It was hard to see why he would have done something like that, but the first of the two questions was a pertinent one.

Whatever the object was, the killer wasn't the one who had buried it, she told herself. It had been someone else, who had intervened later. That person had hidden the object so that he could subsequently recover it at his leisure. It was someone who didn't want anybody else to discover what he had found at the scene.

Who?

As she had been following the man through the pine wood, she had felt a momentary sense of familiarity. She hadn't been able to pin it down, but it had been more than a mere feeling.

It was only now that Sandra noticed that she was cold, just like the evening before when she had been with Marcus. But it wasn't because for more than five minutes she had been standing in the shower stall with the water off. No, this cold came from inside her. It was caused by a hunch. A dangerous hunch that might have truly serious consequences.

'*Evil is the anomaly in front of everybody's eyes but which nobody can see*,' she repeated in a low voice.

Diana still being alive was the anomaly.

The Central Operations Team briefing was fixed for eleven. She had time. For the moment she had no intention of informing anyone of her initiative, partly because she had no idea how to justify it.

The Department of Forensic Medicine was situated in a small four-storey building from the fifties. The façade was anonymous, a row of high windows next to a ramp that allowed vehicles to park in front of the entrance. The mortuary vans used a more discreet entrance at the back. From there you could get straight to the basement where the cold cells and the autopsy rooms were located.

Sandra chose the main entrance and headed for the old lift. She had only been here a couple of times, but she knew that the doctors occupied the top floor.

There was a smell of disinfectant and formaldehyde in the corridors. Contrary to what might have been imagined, there was a constant coming and going of people and the atmosphere was that of a normal place of work. Even though the material they dealt with was death, nobody seemed too bothered about it. In her years spent in the police, Sandra had known many pathologists. They all had a marked sense of humour and a positive cynicism. Except one.

Dr Astolfi's office was the last room on the right.

As she approached it, she saw that the door was open. She stopped in the doorway. The doctor was sitting at his desk in a white coat, busy writing something. Next to him was the inevitable packet of cigarettes, with a lighter resting on it.

She knocked on the door frame and waited. Astolfi let a few seconds pass before looking up from his papers. He saw her and there was an immediate question in his eyes: why was there a uniformed officer in his doorway? 'Come in.'

'Good morning, Doctor. I'm Officer Vega, remember?'

'Yes, I remember.' He was as standoffish as usual. 'What is it?'

Sandra walked into the room. From a rapid glance, she guessed that he had been here for at least thirty years. There were shelves of books with yellowed covers and a leather sofa that had seen better days. The walls needed whitewashing, and there were faded certificates and diplomas. A smell of stale nicotine hung in the air. 'Do you have a few minutes? I need to speak to you.'

Without putting down his pen, Astolfi motioned to her to sit down. 'Provided it doesn't take too long. I'm in a bit of a hurry.'

Sandra took a seat in front of the desk. 'I wanted to tell you that I'm sorry that all the blame fell on you yesterday.'

Astolfi gave her a sidelong glance. 'What do you mean? What's it got to do with you?'

'Well, I could have noticed earlier that Diana Delgaudio was alive. If only I hadn't avoided looking her in the eyes . . .'

'You didn't notice, but nor did your colleagues from Forensics who came along just after you. The blame is all mine.'

'Actually, I came here because I'd like to offer you a chance to redeem yourself.'

An incredulous grimace appeared on Astolfi's face. 'They took me off the case, it's nothing to do with me any more.'

'I think something serious happened,' she went on.

'Why don't you talk to your superiors?'

'Because I'm not sure yet.'

Astolfi seemed annoyed. 'So am I supposed to provide you with certainty?'

'Maybe.'

'All right, what's it about?'

Sandra was pleased that he hadn't yet shown her the door. 'As I was taking another look at the photographs I took in the pine wood, I noticed something I'd overlooked before.'

'That can happen,' Astolfi said, but only to get her to hurry up with her story.

'It was the fact that on the ground, not far from the car, there was a spot where the earth had been moved.'

This time Astolfi said nothing, but put his ballpoint pen down on the table.

'My hypothesis is that the killer may have buried something.'

'That's a bit random, don't you think?'

Good, she told herself: he hadn't asked her why on earth she was telling this to him, of all people. 'Yes, but then I went back to check.'

'And?'

Sandra looked at him. 'There was nothing there.'

Astolfi did not immediately look away, nor did he ask her when she had gone to check. 'Officer Vega, I don't have time for idle chatter.'

'But what if it was one of our people?' Sandra blurted out the words in one go, knowing she had reached the point of no return. It was a major accusation, and if she was wrong there might be serious consequences. 'One of our people steals evidence from the crime scene. As he can't risk taking it away with him, he hides it in the ground and goes back later to get it.'

Astolfi seemed horrified. 'You're talking about an accomplice, Officer Vega. Have I understood correctly?'

'Yes, Doctor.' She tried to sound as confident in her convictions as she could.

'Someone from Forensics? A police officer? Or maybe even me.' He was beside himself. 'You do know what a serious accusation that is?'

'I'm sorry, but you haven't grasped what this means. I was present at the scene too, so I could be just as involved as any of the others. In fact, what I missed puts me at the top of the list of suspects.'

'I advise you to drop this. I'm telling you for your own good. You have no proof.'

'And you have an impeccable service record,' Sandra retorted. 'I've checked. How many years have you been doing this work?' She didn't let him answer. 'Did you really not realise that the girl was still alive? How can anyone make such a mistake?'

'You're mad, Officer Vega.'

'If the crime scene really was altered, then even the fact that nobody noticed Diana Delgaudio was still alive has to be seen in a new light. Not a mere oversight, but a deliberate attempt to aid the killer.'

Astolfi rose to his feet, pointing a finger at her. 'This is just speculation. If you had any proof you wouldn't be here talking to me, you would have gone straight to Deputy Commissioner Moro.'

Sandra did not say a word. Instead, slowly, she made an inverted sign of the cross – *from right to left, from down to up*.

From Astolfi's expression, Sandra knew that the man in the wood the night before really had been him. And that he had worked out that she had seen him.

Sandra deliberately moved her hand towards her belt, to which the holster with the pistol was attached. 'It was you who killed those two young people. Then you went back to the pine wood in your capacity as a pathologist, you discovered that Diana was still alive, and you decided to let her die. In the meantime, you cleared the scene of a piece of evidence that might have pointed to you. You hid it and then went back to recover it when everyone had gone.'

'No,' he retorted, calmly but resolutely. 'I was called out to do my work, there's a duty rota: it wasn't premeditated.'

'A stroke of luck,' Sandra replied, even though she didn't believe in coincidences. 'Or else it's true: it wasn't you who attacked them, but you know who it was, and you're covering for him.'

Astolfi collapsed on his chair. 'It's my word against yours. But if you go around telling this story you'll ruin me.'

Sandra said nothing.

'I need a smoke.' Without waiting for her consent, he took the packet of cigarettes and lit one.

They sat there in silence, looking at each other like two strangers in a waiting room. Astolfi was right: Sandra had no proof to back up her accusations. She didn't have the power to arrest him, or to force him to follow her to the nearest police station. All the same, he hadn't sent her away.

It was obvious that he was looking for a way out, and not only because he risked seeing his own career in ruins. Sandra was convinced that, if they investigated him a little more, something compromising would come out. Maybe the very thing he had taken from the crime scene, even though she was sure he had already got rid of it. Or maybe he hadn't?

Astolfi stubbed out his cigarette in an ashtray and got to his feet, keeping his eyes fixed on Sandra. He walked to a closed door that probably led to his own personal toilet. His eyes were defiant.

Sandra had no power to stop him.

He closed the door behind him and turned the key. Shit, she said to herself, standing up and going to see if she could hear what he was doing.

On the other side there was a long silence, interrupted by the sudden sound of a toilet flushing.

I've been an idiot, I should have known this would happen, she thought, getting angry with herself. But, while she waited for Astolfi to come out of the toilet, she thought she heard screams. She wondered if she had only imagined them.

They weren't in the building, they came from outside.

She rushed to the window and saw people running towards the building. She opened the window and leaned out.

Four floors below her, on the asphalt, lay Astolfi's body.

For a moment Sandra stood there in dismay, then turned again towards the toilet door. She had to do something.

She tried to force the door with her shoulder. Once, twice. At last it yielded, and she found herself projected inside. She was knocked back by the blast of air coming in through the wide-open window through which Astolfi had thrown himself. Ignoring it, she threw herself on all fours at the toilet bowl. Without hesitation, she put her arm into the transparent water, hoping that whatever Astolfi had thrown in hadn't gone all the way down. She pushed her hand as far in as she could and her fingers brushed against something, grabbed it, then lost it again. She got hold of it again and tried to drag it towards her and pull it out, but, before she could, the object escaped her.

'Shit,' she cursed.

But then she realised that her fingertips bore the fleeting memory of a shape: something round and rough, with things attached to it. The image that immediately came to mind was that of a foetus. But then she thought again.

It was a kind of doll.

10

The name of the club was SX.

There were no signs, just a black plate with the two gold letters next to the door. To get in, you had to use the entryphone. Marcus pressed the button and waited. It wasn't instinct that had brought him here but a simple observation: if the killer had chosen the confessional of Sant'Apollinare to communicate, then he knew the criminal underworld quite well. If that really was the case, then Marcus was in the right place.

After a couple of minutes, a female voice answered with a laconic, 'Yes?' Behind her, heavy metal music could be heard pounding away at very high volume.

'Cosmo Barditi,' he said.

'Do you have an appointment?'

'No.'

The voice disappeared, as if swallowed by the din. A few seconds passed, then the door clicked open.

Marcus went in and found himself in a passage with concrete walls. The only light came from a fluorescent strip that was flickering as if about to blow at any moment.

At the end of the passage was a red door.

Marcus walked towards it. The throbbing of the bass in the

music could be heard, muffled. As he got nearer, the music grew in volume. The door opened before he reached it, liberating those ghastly sounds, which rushed out to greet him like demons escaping from hell.

A woman appeared, presumably the woman who had spoken to him earlier through the entryphone. She was wearing vertiginously high heels, a very short leather skirt and a silver top with a plunging neckline. There was a moth tattooed on her left breast. She had platinum-blonde hair and was heavily made up. As she waited for him to come closer, she chewed gum and leaned one arm on the doorframe. She looked him up and down without a word, then turned her back on him and walked away, clearly intending him to follow her.

Marcus entered the club. SX stood for sex, but without the E. There was no mistaking the kind of place it was. The whole atmosphere was decidedly S&M.

A large room with a low ceiling. The walls were black. In the middle there was a circular platform with three lap-dancing poles on it. All around were small red leather sofas and tables of the same colour. The lights were dim, and pornographic images of torture and corporal punishment flashed on screens.

On the stage, a girl, topless, was performing a listless dance number with a chainsaw in time to the heavy metal music. The singer was repeating over and over: *'Heaven is for those who kill gently.'*

As he walked behind the blonde, Marcus counted at least six customers scattered through the room. All men. They weren't displaying skulls or studs, nor did they seem fierce, as might have been expected. They were just anonymous men of different ages, dressed normally and looking vaguely bored. In a dark corner, a seventh customer was masturbating.

'Hey, put that thing away!' the blonde yelled at him.

The man ignored her. She shook her head angrily, but did

nothing. After crossing the entire room, they entered a narrow corridor with private rooms on either side. There was a men's toilet and, beyond it, a door with the words NO ENTRY.

The woman stopped and looked at Marcus. 'Nobody here calls Cosmo by his real name. That's why he decided to see you.'

She knocked and motioned to him to go in. Marcus watched her walk away, then opened the door.

There were posters of hardcore films from the seventies, a bar counter, shelves with a stereo and various knick-knacks. The room was lit only by a table lamp, which created a kind of bubble of light around a very tidy black desk.

Behind the desk sat Cosmo Barditi.

Marcus closed the door behind him, blotting out the music, but stood there for a moment outside the circle of light to get a better look at him.

He was wearing reading glasses on the tip of his nose, which rather clashed with his crewcut hair and his denim shirt with the rolled-up sleeves. Marcus immediately spotted the skull and crossbones on his forearms, as well as the swastika on his neck.

'Well, who the fuck are you?' the man said.

Marcus took a step forward into the light, so that his face could be seen.

Cosmo sat there stunned for a while, trying to focus his memory on the face. 'It's you,' he said at last.

The prisoner in the sauna had recognised him.

Marcus still remembered the test to which Clemente had subjected him, sending him to the house of two parents overcome with grief at the death of their daughter with only a key in his hand.

Evil is the rule. Good is the exception.

'I thought that after I freed you, you would change your life.'

The man smiled. 'I don't know if you're aware of this, but it isn't easy to get a regular job with a past like mine.'

Marcus pointed around him. 'Then why all this?'

'It's a job, isn't it? My girls are all clean, no drugs, and they don't have sex with the customers: here, people only watch.' Then he turned serious. 'I have a woman now who loves me. And also a two-year-old daughter.' He was trying to show that he had deserved his release.

'Good for you, Cosmo,' Marcus said. 'Good for you.'

'Have you come to present me with an invoice?'

'No, to ask you a favour.'

'I don't even know who you are or what you were doing there that day.'

'It doesn't matter.'

Cosmo Barditi scratched the back of his neck. 'What do I have to do?'

Marcus took another step towards the desk. 'I'm looking for a man.'

'Do I know him, or should I know him?'

'I don't know. I don't think so. But you might be able to help me to find him.'

'Why me?'

How many times had Marcus asked that question of himself, or Clemente? The answer was always the same: fate, or, for those who believed in it, providence. 'Because the man I'm looking for has special tastes when it comes to sex, and I think that in the past he may have experimented with his fantasies in places like this.'

Marcus knew that there was always an incubation period before violence. The killer did not yet know that he wanted to kill. He would feed the beast that he carried inside him with experiences of extreme sex, and in doing so gradually get nearer to the most deeply hidden part of himself.

Barditi seemed interested. 'Tell me about him.'

'He likes knives and guns, and it's likely that he has problems of a sexual nature: using weapons is the only way he can get satisfaction. He likes watching other people having sex – young couples – but he may also have frequented swingers' clubs. He likes to take photographs. I think he keeps images of all the encounters he's had over the years.'

Cosmo was taking notes like a diligent schoolboy. Then he raised his eyes from the sheet of paper on which he was writing. 'Anything else?'

'Yes, the most important thing: he feels inferior to other people and that makes him angry. To demonstrate that he's better than them, he puts them to the test.'

'How?'

Marcus thought again of the young man who had had to stab to death the woman he loved, after being tricked into believing he would save his own life.

The false bearers of false love.

That was what the killer had called them in his message at Sant'Apollinare. 'He plays a kind of game with them, a game with no rewards, which is intended only to humiliate them.'

Cosmo thought about this for a moment. 'Does this by any chance have anything to do with what happened in Ostia?'

Marcus did not reply.

Cosmo laughed briefly. 'The violence here is just a show, my friend. The people you saw out there come to my club because they think they're being transgressive, but in the real world they're insignificant people who wouldn't hurt a fly. What you're talking about is serious stuff, certainly not the work of any of those losers.'

'So where should I look?'

Cosmo turned away for a moment to think this over, doubtless wondering whether it was in his interest to trust him. 'I have nothing to do with those kinds of people any more, but I have heard about something . . . There's a group of people who get together to celebrate whenever there's a violent crime in Rome. They say that, every time an innocent life is sacrificed, negative energies are released. They hold these parties in which they evoke what happened, but it's just an excuse to take drugs and have sex.'

'Who goes to these things?'

'People with serious mental problems, if you ask me. But also people with money. You have no idea how many people believe that bullshit. It's all anonymous, you can only get in on very specific conditions – privacy means a lot to them. Tonight there's going to be a party to celebrate what happened in Ostia.'

'Can you get me in?'

'They choose different places to meet. It won't be easy to find out where tonight's party will be.' Cosmo's indecision was obvious: he didn't want to get mixed up in that kind of thing. Maybe he was thinking of the safety of the woman and daughter who were waiting for him at home. 'I'll have to get back in touch with my old contacts,' he said reluctantly.

'I'm sure that won't be a problem.'

'I'll make a few phone calls,' Cosmo promised. 'You can't get into places like that if you're not invited. You'll have to be very careful, though, because these are dangerous people.'

'I'll be as careful as possible.'

'And what if I can't help you?'

'How many deaths do you want on your conscience?'

'OK, I get it. I'll do what I can.'

Marcus went to the table, took the pen and the sheet of paper on which Cosmo had been taking notes and wrote something on it. 'As soon as you find out how to get me into the party, call me on this voicemail number.'

He handed back the piece of paper, and Cosmo saw that

something else was written on it apart from the number. 'What's the child of salt?'

'If you feel like mentioning that when you make your phone calls, I'd be very grateful to you.'

Cosmo nodded, pensively. Marcus had finished, he could go. But, just as he was about to walk out through the door, Cosmo asked him a question.

'Why did you free me that day?'

'I don't know,' Marcus said without turning around.

11

At the age of sixty, Batista Erriaga considered himself a cautious man.

But he had not always been like that. When he was just a boy, in the Philippines, he didn't know what caution was. On the contrary, he had many times challenged fate – and death – because of his bad character. When you looked at it closely, the one advantage he drew from being a bully had to do with pride.

Not money, not power, let alone respect.

It was pride that would be the cause of a great misfortune, an event that would mark the rest of his life, although he didn't know it yet.

At the time he was only sixteen and he back-combed his hair to make himself look taller. He loved his raven-black head of hair, it was his pride and joy. He washed it every evening and then rubbed palm oil into it. He had an ivory comb that he had stolen from a stall. He carried it in the back pocket of his trousers and every now and again would pull it out and touch up his thick quiff.

He would strut down the streets of his village in the tight-fitting jeans his mother had sewn for him using the canvas from a tent, leather boots bought from a shoemaker for very little money because they were actually made of pressed cardboard blackened with shoe polish, and a green shirt with a pointed collar, ironed to perfection and always immaculate.

Everyone in the village knew him as 'Batista the sharp dresser'. He was proud of that nickname, until he realised that they were actually making fun of him and among themselves called him 'the son of the trained monkey', because his father, an alcoholic, was ready to do anything for a drink and often performed ridiculous and humiliating little shows for the amusement of customers in the tavern, hoping they would stand him a drink.

Batista hated his father. He hated the way he had always lived, doing back-breaking work on plantations and then begging in order to sustain his own vices. The only times he was ever tough were when he was with his wife, when he came back drunk in the evening and took out on her the oppression he had been subjected to by others. Batista's mother could have defended herself and overpowered him easily, given that he could not even stand up straight. Instead, she passively submitted to the blows just so as not to add humiliation to humiliation. He was still her man, and this was his way of loving and protecting her. That was why Batista hated her too.

In the village, the Erriagas belonged to a kind of inferior caste because of their Spanish surname. It had been Batista's great-grandfather who had chosen to call himself that, long ago in 1849 under Governor-General Narciso Clavería. The Filipinos didn't use surnames and Clavería forced them to choose one. Many borrowed those of the colonisers to ensure their goodwill, unaware that by doing this they would brand themselves and future generations: despised by the Spaniards who couldn't stand being lumped in with them, and hated by the other Filipinos for betraying their own origins.

And Batista also had the burden of that first name, chosen by his mother to indicate their Catholic faith.

Only one person didn't seem to care about any of that. His name was Min and he was Batista Erriaga's best friend. He was a tall fellow, a real giant. He instilled fear in those who saw him for the first time, but actually he would never have hurt anyone. Not that he was stupid, but he was very innocent. A hard worker who dreamed of becoming a priest.

Batista and Min spent a lot of time together. There was a big age gap between them – his friend was more than thirty – but they didn't care about that. It was as if Min had taken his father's place in Batista's life. He protected him and gave him invaluable advice. That was why Batista hadn't told him about his plans.

The fact was, the week of the event that would change his life, young Batista had gained entry to a gang: Los Soldados del Diablo. He had been wooing them for months. They were more or less his age – the eldest, who was also the leader, was nineteen. To join, Batista had had to perform a whole series of tests: shooting a pig, running across a bonfire of tyres, robbing a house. He had passed them all with flying colours and had been given a leather wristband, which was the symbol of the gang. Thanks to that sign of recognition, the members were entitled to all kinds of privileges, like drinking for free in the bars, going with prostitutes without paying, and demanding the right of way from anyone they met on the street. Actually, nobody had granted them these rights, they just bullied them out of people.

Batista had been part of the group for a few days and felt comfortable with them. He had finally redeemed his own name from his father's cowardice. Nobody would ever again dare to show him a lack of respect, nobody would ever again call him 'the son of the trained monkey'.

Until, one evening, he had met Min while he was with his new companions.

Seeing him swaggering with the gang, wearing that ridiculous leather wristband, his friend started making fun of him. He even called him a 'trained monkey', like his father.

Min's intentions were good, Batista had known that, deep down. He was only trying to tell him that he was making a mistake. But Min's attitude and the way in which he treated him had left Batista no choice. He started to shove him and hit him, because he was sure that Min wouldn't retaliate. But that just made Min laugh all the louder.

Batista would never be able to explain what happened: where he found the stick, when he struck the first blow. He didn't remember any of those things. Afterwards it was like waking up from a kind of sleep: he was sweating and covered in blood, his companions had vanished into thin air, leaving him alone, and his best friend lay there with his skull smashed in and a fixed grin on his face.

Batista Erriaga had spent the next fifteen years in prison. His mother had fallen seriously ill and in the village where he was born and had grown up he was no longer even worthy of a mocking nickname.

But in spite of everything the death of Min, the giant who had wanted to become a priest, had proved a positive thing. Many years afterwards, on the plane taking him from Manila to Rome, Batista Erriaga had thought again of that event.

After learning what had happened in the pine wood in Ostia, he had got on the first available flight. He had travelled tourist class, wearing anonymous clothes and a cloth cap with a peak in order to mingle with his compatriots going to Italy to work as domestic servants. He hadn't talked to anyone during the journey for fear that someone might recognise him. But he had had time to think.

Arriving in the city, he had taken a room in a modest tourist hotel in the centre.

Now he was sitting on a worn bedspread, watching the TV news in order to get the latest on the man everybody had now dubbed 'the Monster of Rome'.

It had really happened, he told himself. That thought was torturing him. But maybe there was still a way to put things right.

Erriaga turned down the volume on the TV and walked over to the little table on which he had placed his tablet. Pressing a button on the screen, he started the recording.

'. . . *a time . . . It happened at night . . . And everyone came running to where his knife had been planted . . . his time had come . . . the children died . . . the false bearers of false love . . . and he was pitiless with them . . . of the child of salt . . . if he isn't stopped, he won't stop.*'

A few phrases from an obscure message left in a confessional in Sant'Apollinare, once used by criminals to communicate with the police.

Erriaga turned back to the silent TV screen. The Monster of Rome, he repeated to himself. What fools! They had no idea of the real danger hanging over them.

He switched off the TV with the remote. He had work to do, but he had to be careful.

Nobody must know that Batista Erriaga was in Rome.

12

'A doll?'

'Yes, sir.'

Deputy Commissioner Moro wanted to be sure that he had heard correctly. Sandra was quite convinced, but with the passing of time she had started to question her own perceptions.

When he had learned of Astolfi's suicide, especially the fact that he had performed that desperate act because he had been discovered stealing evidence from the crime scene, Moro had activated all the confidentiality procedures and assumed complete control of the investigation.

From now on, nothing that was connected to the case could be touched or thrown away, even if it was just a note made casually on a piece of paper. An operations room had been set up with computers linked between themselves and dependent on a server different from that of Headquarters. To prevent leaks, all phone calls going in or out would be recorded. Even though it was not possible to monitor all mobile or private phones, those working on the investigation would have to sign a document committing themselves not to divulge information, on pain of dismissal or being charged with aiding and abetting.

Moro's main fear, though, was that other evidence might be destroyed.

As far as Sandra knew, while they were conferring in the new operations room, specialised technicians, in collaboration with Forensics, were inspecting the drainpipes at the Department of Forensic Medicine. She didn't dare imagine the conditions these men must be operating in, but the system in the building was an old one and there was real hope that the doll she thought she had recognised by touch in Astolfi's toilet might still be there.

'So last night,' Moro said, leaning towards her, 'you went back to the pine wood to check that you had performed the photographic procedure correctly.'

'That's right,' Sandra replied, trying to conceal her unease.

'And you saw a man digging something up. You thought it was Dr Astolfi, so this morning you went to talk to him.' He was repeating the version of events she had just given him, but he seemed to be doing so only to point out to her how absurd it was.

'I thought that, before you were informed, he should be given a chance to explain himself,' Sandra said, hoping that would seem more credible. 'Did I do the wrong thing?'

Moro thought this over for a moment. 'No. I'd have done the same.'

'I obviously couldn't imagine that when he had his back to the wall he'd decide to kill himself.'

Moro was drumming with a pencil on the desk, never taking his eyes off her. Sandra felt under pressure. Obviously, she had neglected to mention Marcus.

'In your opinion, Officer Vega, did Astolfi know the killer?'

Apart from the pipes in the Department of Forensic Medicine, the men were taking a look at the pathologist's life. His office and home were being subjected to a meticulous search. His phones, his computers, his emails were all being checked. His bank accounts and expenditure were being analysed. They would leave nothing out: relatives, work colleagues, even casual acquaintances. Moro was convinced that something would come out, some small clue as to why Astolfi should have been driven to take a piece of evidence from the crime scene and do his best to make sure that Diana Delgaudio did not survive. In both cases, the doctor had almost failed. Or maybe it was more correct to say that he had almost succeeded. But, in spite of the resources and technology he had put in place, Moro still needed a more personal opinion. That was why he had asked Sandra that question.

'Astolfi endangered his reputation, his career, his freedom,' she said. 'A person doesn't risk everything like that without a powerful motive. So yes, I think he did know who it was. The proof of that is that he preferred to die rather than reveal the killer's identity.'

'Someone close: a child, a relative, a friend.' Moro paused. 'But the doctor had nobody. No wife, no children. He was a loner.'

Sandra suspected that the thorough check Astolfi's life was being put through wasn't bringing the results that Moro had hoped. 'How did Astolfi come to be at the crime scene? Was it chance, or was there something behind it? Honestly, sir, I find it incredible that the doctor should have known the killer and should also have found himself dealing with the case out of pure coincidence.'

'The pathologists' rota changes from week to week. Astolfi wasn't clairvoyant, he couldn't have known he'd be on that shift. In fact, he wasn't due to be on duty the other morning, he was only called in because he was the best expert in Rome on this kind of violent crime.'

'In other words, he was predestined.'

'Precisely my point. Given his specific area of expertise, it was natural that he would be the one to be called in. And he knew that perfectly well.' Moro stood up from his chair and walked to the other side of the room. 'It's clear he was involved in the murder. He was covering for someone. Maybe he recognised the killer's *modus operandi* because he'd already seen him at work in the past, so we're checking through all his old cases.'

Sandra followed him. 'Sir, have you thought about my hypothesis that the killer put make-up on Diana Delgaudio? I'm more and more convinced that he also photographed her. Otherwise, why take the trouble?'

Moro stopped by one of the workplaces. He bent down towards the computer screen to check something and replied without looking at her, 'The lipstick thing . . . Yes, I have thought about it, and I think you're right. I've had it added to the list.' He indicated the wall behind them.

There was an enormous board to which the main elements of the case, as revealed by the forensics reports and those of the pathologists, were listed:

Objects: rucksack, climbing rope, hunting knife, Ruger SP101 revolver.

Prints of the young man on the climbing rope and on the knife left in the sternum of the young woman: he ordered him to tie the girl up and stab her if he wanted to save his life.

Kills the young man by shooting him in back of neck.

Puts lipstick on the girl (to photograph her?).

Ballistics had identified the killer's firearm, a Ruger. But what surprised Sandra was that Moro had realised that the killer had had Diana killed by Giorgio. The same conclusion Marcus had reached. But, whereas Moro had obtained that result with the help of science and technology, Marcus had intuited it all by observing the photographs of the crime scene and the crime scene itself.

'Come with me,' Moro said, interrupting her thoughts. 'There's something I want to show you.'

He led her to an adjoining room. It was narrow and windowless. The only light came from a table with a luminous top in the middle of the room. Sandra's attention focused on the walls that surrounded it, entirely covered with photographs of the crimes. Overall views and details. The photographic work she had begun had been continued by colleagues in Forensics, who had done searches, measurements, tests of every kind.

'I like to come here to think,' Moro said.

Sandra remembered what Marcus had told her about how the culprit had to be looked for at the scene of the crime. 'The killer is still here, even though we can't see him,' he had said. 'We have to search for him in this place, not anywhere else.'

'This is where we'll catch him, Officer Vega. In this room.'

Sandra turned away from the photographs on the walls and looked at him. Only then did she notice the two bundles on the table, wrapped in transparent cellophane, like the ones used by laundries. Inside them, clothes were folded. She recognised them. They belonged to Diana Delgaudio and Giorgio Montefiori. They were the clothes they had chosen for their date, which had lain scattered on the back seat of the car in which they had been attacked.

Sandra felt a sense of anguish and unease as she looked at them. It was as if the two young people were there on that table, side by side.

As elegant as two phantom spouses.

There had been no need to wash the clothes, there were no bloodstains on them. And they did not constitute evidence.

'We'll give them back to the families,' Moro said. 'Giorgio Montefiori's mother keeps coming here to ask for her son's personal effects. I don't know why. It seems so pointless. But everyone has their own way of reacting to grief. Especially parents. Sometimes it seems to drive them mad and their requests become absurd.'

'I've heard that Diana Delgaudio is making progress. Maybe she'll be able to help us.'

Moro shook his head and smiled bitterly. 'If you're referring to what they're saying in the papers, it would be better if she hadn't survived the operation.'

Sandra hadn't been expecting that answer. 'What do you mean?'

'That she'll be a vegetable for the rest of her life.' Moro came close to her. 'When all this is over and we look the killer in the face, we'll all feel like idiots, Officer Vega. We'll look at him and realise that he isn't at all the way we imagine him. Most of all, we'll realise that he isn't a monster but a normal person, someone just like us, in fact. We'll dig into his little, ordinary life and find nothing but boredom, mediocrity and resentment. We'll discover that he likes to kill people but maybe hates those who mistreat animals, and that he loves dogs. That he has children, a family, maybe even someone he genuinely loves. We'll stop being afraid of him and instead we'll be surprised at ourselves for having been deceived by such a banal human being.'

Sandra was struck by the way he was speaking. She was still wondering why he had brought her here.

'You've done an excellent job so far, Officer Vega.'

'Thank you, sir.'

'But don't even think of keeping me in the dark again, the way you did with this Astolfi business. I have to be informed of everything my people do, even what they're thinking.'

Faced with Moro's calm steadfastness, Sandra felt deeply embarrassed and lowered her gaze. 'All right, sir.'

Moro was silent for a while, and when he spoke again, his tone changed. 'You're an attractive woman.'

Sandra hadn't been expecting a compliment like that, and she felt herself blush with embarrassment. It struck her as inappropriate for her superior to address her that way.

'How long is it since you last handled a gun?'

Sandra was taken aback by the question, which seemed to have nothing to do with what he had just said. She tried to answer as best she could. 'I practise every month at the range, as per regulations, but I've never been assigned to active service.'

'I have a plan,' Moro said. 'To flush out the killer, I've decided to use bait: unmarked cars with men and women on board who are actually plain-clothes officers. From tonight, they'll be covering the outskirts of the city, stopping every hour in a different place. I've called it Operation Shield.'

'Fake couples.'

'Precisely. But we're short of women officers. That's why I asked you if you're still capable of using a gun.'

'Sir, I'm not sure.'

'I'll exempt you from tonight's shift, but I'd like you to be part of the operation as of tomorrow. We need all our resources to—' He was interrupted by the ringing of his mobile phone. He replied, completely ignoring Sandra, who stood there, not knowing where to look.

Moro limited himself to replying with curt monosyllables, as if he was simply registering the information. The call didn't last long and, when it finished, he turned back to her. 'They've just finished inspecting the pipes and the drains at the Department of Forensic Medicine. I'm sorry, Officer Vega, but they haven't found any doll, or anything that looks like one.'

Sandra's unease increased noticeably. She had been hoping that a piece of good news might help her regain a little respect. 'How is that possible? I assure you, sir, I touched something with my fingertips, I didn't imagine it.'

Moro was silent for a few moments. 'I suppose this may seem

trivial to you . . . but when you told me that before Astolfi killed himself he'd got rid of an object by throwing it in the toilet, I asked Forensics to analyse his hands. You never know, we might have had a stroke of luck.'

Sandra didn't believe in luck, but now she was hoping for it.

'On one, they found traces of sodium chloride.' He paused again. 'That's why we didn't find the object you touched, Officer Vega: it dissolved in the water. Whatever it was, it was made of salt.'

13

Rome had been founded with a murder.

According to legend, Romulus had murdered his brother Remus, conferring his own name on the city and becoming its first king.

But that had been only the first in a whole series of bloody episodes. The long history of the Eternal City was studded with murders, and it was often impossible to distinguish what was myth from what had actually happened. But it could honestly be stated that the greatness of Rome had been fed with blood. And, over the centuries, even the papacy had contributed to that.

So it was hardly surprising if even today, in secret, the city celebrated violent death.

Cosmo Barditi had been as good as his word: he had found Marcus a way to get into the private party being held that night, which had as a macabre theme what had happened at Ostia. Marcus did not yet know what to expect, but from a phone booth in the bus station at Tiburtina he listened carefully to the message Cosmo had left on his voicemail.

'Each guest has their own alphanumeric code. You have to learn it by heart. Whatever you do, don't write it down.'

That was no problem: in order to avoid leaving traces of their own existence, the penitenzieri never took notes.

'689A473CS43.'

Marcus repeated it in his mind.

'The appointment is for midnight.'

Then Cosmo gave him an address on the Appia Antica. He memorised that too.

'One more thing: I may have a promising lead . . . I still have to check my sources, so I don't want to say anything yet.'

Marcus wondered what it might be. But Cosmo's tone of voice sounded hopeful and even vaguely smug.

The message concluded with a warning: *'If you decide to go to the villa, you won't be able to have second thoughts. Once you're inside, there's no turning back.'*

The area of Appia Antica took its name from the road built by the Roman censor and consul Appius Claudius Caecus in 312 AD.

The Romans had called it *regina viarum* because, unlike other roads, it was a real engineering masterpiece, quite forward-looking for its time. Its flagstone paving meant it could be used by all kinds of vehicles and in all weather conditions. In case of rain, there was a drainage system to avoid wheels getting stuck. The road was originally more than four yards wide, allowing vehicles to go down it in two directions, and it was also lined with pavements to allow pedestrian traffic.

The Appian Way was so much in advance of its time that large stretches of it still remained, perfectly preserved. Around the remains, magnificent villas had sprung up which today were the residences of rich, privileged people.

The one that interested Marcus was the most isolated.

It had an art nouveau façade, half-covered with climbing ivy, which, stripped of its leaves, looked like the skeleton of a gigantic prehistoric snake. A tower, topped by an observatory, dominated the west side. The windows were large and dark. Every now and again a passing car, sweeping its headlights across the windows, revealed the colourful designs in the glass: great orchids, magnolias, peacocks and butterflies.

A huge wrought-iron gate resembling a tangle of branches and flowers led to a drive lined with Roman pines, more than fifty feet high, with slender, slightly inclined trunks, the foliage pruned into globes, so that they resembled old ladies with their Sunday hats on.

The house looked as if it had been uninhabited for decades. What revealed the presence of someone, though, was a security camera at the top of a pole, which every now and again moved to check the road in front of it. The road itself was lit by a single lamp that gave out an orange light.

Marcus reached the place a long time before the hour arranged. He took up position some ninety feet from the entrance, in a niche in the perimeter wall. From there he could keep a careful watch on the villa while waiting for midnight.

The countryside was in the grip of an intense cold. It was as if everything had hibernated, even the sounds. The air was motionless and everything hung suspended. Marcus felt a sense of solitude, like someone having to contemplate what lurked beyond his own death. A few yards from him was the passageway to a secret world, a world hidden from the eyes of common people.

There had been other times when he had felt as if he were one step away from the entrance to a kind of hell. It had happened once on board the charter plane that left Ciampino Airport every Tuesday at two in the morning, with only men as passengers. The lights on the plane had been dimmed so that they could avoid looking at each other, even though everybody was there for the same purpose. Passing along the aisle, Marcus had peered at the faces of those normal men, imagining them in their everyday lives – respectable workers, heads of families, football fans. Outwardly they were on a flight to a tropical destination; in reality they were going to some third-world country to buy young lives in order to satisfy a vice their mothers, wives, girlfriends, acquaintances and work colleagues had, and would always have, no inkling of.

The same anguish had come over Marcus as he looked into the weary, resigned eyes of Nigerian prostitutes, lured to the West with the promise of work and ending up in a dark basement to be sold at prices that varied according to what was included, even torture.

Marcus would never forget the sense of dismay and horror he had felt after accessing extreme pornography on the internet. A parallel dimension, a web within the web. A place where children were no longer children and violence became an instrument of pleasure. A place where anyone, from the safety of his own home, maybe sitting comfortably in pyjamas and slippers, could find material to give vent to his own most shameful and hidden urges.

And now, what would he find in the villa he was about to enter?

As he was thinking these things, midnight had come. The guests started arriving for the party.

They got out of taxis or chauffeured cars that then drove on. Some arrived on foot from God knew where. Some were in pairs, some alone. Beneath their coats and furs they wore evening clothes. And they had hats or scarves covering their faces. Or else they had their collars turned up to avoid being recognised.

They all went through the same routine. At the gate, they would ring the bell and wait for a sound from the loudspeaker: a brief musical note. Then they would recite their alphanumeric code. The lock would click and they would go in.

Marcus waited until one in the morning and counted at least a hundred people. Then he emerged from the shadows and walked to the gate.

'689A473CS43,' he said into the entryphone after the musical note had sounded.

The lock clicked open, and he went in.

A massive individual, clearly a security guard, came to greet him and without saying a word led him along a corridor. They were alone; there was no trace of the people Marcus had seen arriving earlier. What struck him most, though, was that there was no sound in the house.

The man led him into a room, came in after him and placed himself at his back. Marcus found himself in front of a mahogany table behind which sat a young woman in a purple evening dress with one shoulder bare. She had tapering fingers and green eyes like a cat's, and her hair was gathered into an elegant bun. Next to her was a silver tray with a water jug and some glasses.

'Welcome,' she said with a complicit smile. 'Is this your first time?'

Marcus nodded.

'There's only one rule here, and it's a simple one: everything is permitted as long as the other person consents. But if the other person says no, it's no.'

'Understood.'

'Do you have a mobile phone with you?'

'No.'

'Any weapons or objects that could be harmful?'

'No.'

'We have to search you all the same. Do you mind?'

Marcus knew he had no choice. He opened his arms wide and waited for the man behind him to do his duty. When he had finished, he went back to his place.

At this point, the woman filled one of the glasses she had next to her. Then she opened a drawer, closed it again and showed him a shiny black pill.

Marcus hesitated.

'This is the key,' she said reassuringly, holding out her hand with the pill in the palm. 'You have to take it, or you won't be able to go in.'

Marcus reached out his hand, took the pill in his fingers, lifted it to his mouth and swallowed it down with all of the water.

He had barely had time to put down the empty glass when a sudden hot wave rose from deep inside him, swept up through his body, and exploded in his eyes. The outlines of everything around him started to sway. He was afraid he was going to lose his balance. Then he felt himself being supported by two powerful arms.

He clearly heard a laugh, which then shattered like crystal. 'You'll get used to it in a few seconds,' the woman said, amused. 'In the meantime, let it take effect, don't resist it. It'll last about three hours.'

Marcus tried to follow the advice . . . Some time later, without knowing how, he found himself leaning against the wall of a room filled with voices that sounded like the singing of birds trapped in an aviary. Everything was wrapped in a semi-darkness that slowly cleared. He realised that his eyes were simply becoming accustomed to the change of lighting.

When he felt sure enough of his own balance, he took his first steps into the room. Elegant music pervaded the air – maybe Bach. The lights were dim and seemed like distant halos. A smell of wax and candles, but also the all-pervasive smell of sex.

There were other people with him. He couldn't see them clearly, but he was aware of them.

The pill he had taken must have been some kind of drug that amplified sensations while at the same time preventing him from memorising what was around him. He would look at a face and immediately forget it. That was the secondary purpose of the drug: nobody would recognise anyone.

Human figures passed close to him, glanced briefly at him or else smiled. A woman caressed him then walked away. Some of the people were naked.

On a sofa there was a tangle of faceless bodies. Nothing but breasts, arms, legs. Mouths searching for other mouths, hungry for pleasure. Everything was passing in front of Marcus like a speeded-up film.

If he couldn't make out these people, then there was no point in his having come here. He had to think of a way. He realised that, although the overall picture was evanescent, the details weren't. He had to concentrate on those. If he lowered his eyes, his vision became more distinct. Something didn't vanish.

The shoes.

Marcus tried to memorise them. Some with heels, some with laces. Black, shiny, red. He walked among them and let himself be led. Until, suddenly, they started to move together. Like a stream, they were converging towards the middle of the room, attracted by something. Marcus made his way in that direction. Peering over the barricade of people's backs, he saw a naked body, lying face-down, blood apparently oozing from the back of the neck.

Giorgio Montefiori, Marcus thought immediately. Two women were kneeling by him, caressing him.

. . . his time had come . . . the children died . . . That was what the killer had said in his message in Sant'Apollinare.

Some distance away, a car seat to which a naked girl had been tied, her breasts imprisoned by a climbing rope. She was wearing a paper mask: the smiling face of Diana Delgaudio, taken from the photograph in a newspaper or on the internet.

. . . the false bearers of false love . . .

A large, powerful-looking man in a black leather hood, his sculptural physique smeared in oil, was sitting astride the girl. In one hand he brandished a knife with a silvery blade.

. . . and he was pitiless with them . . . of the child of salt . . .

The scene of the two young people attacked in the pine wood at Ostia was the malign crux of this whole evening. From time to time, some of the spectators would break away from the others and walk away together to have sex.

. . . if he isn't stopped, he won't stop.

Marcus felt a sudden retching. He turned and, forcing his way through the throng with his arms, managed to get to a corner of the room. He rested one hand on the wall and took a deep breath. He wished he could vomit. That way he might get rid of some of the drug and be able to leave here. But he also knew that he wasn't likely to emerge quickly from the kind of trance he was in. And, besides, he didn't want to turn back now. He had to see this through to the end, there was no other way.

It was at that moment that he looked up and saw a shadowy figure standing to one side, observing the spectacle. The figure was clad in overalls, or maybe it was a raincoat, or a jacket that was too big. But what struck him was a strange black object that stuck out from beneath a flap. The figure was trying to hide it. It looked like a gun.

Marcus wondered how he had managed to bring it into the party. Hadn't he been searched on the way in? But then he realised that it wasn't a gun at all.

It was a camera.

He remembered Sandra's words about the lipstick that the killer had placed on Diana Delgaudio's lips.

'I think he photographed her. In fact, I'm sure of it.'

He's come here to get a souvenir, Marcus told himself. So he detached himself from the wall and walked towards him. As he advanced, he made an effort to focus on the features of the man's face. But it was like looking at a mirage: the closer he got, the more it vanished.

The man must have noticed him, because he turned to look at him.

Marcus felt the power of those two black eyes on him, immobilising him, pinning him down as though he were a moth in a display case. He forced himself to keep walking, but the figure retreated. Marcus tried to walk faster, but it was impossible. He felt as if he were moving through an ocean of water and sand.

The figure began walking away from him, turning from time to time as if to check that he was still there.

Marcus tried to keep up, but it was hard. He even reached out one arm, in the mistaken belief that he could stop him. But he was already panting, as if walking up a very steep slope. Then an idea occurred to him. He stopped and waited for the figure to turn and look at him.

When he did so, Marcus made an inverted sign of the cross.

The figure slowed down, as if trying to figure out the meaning of that gesture. But then he carried on walking.

Marcus set off again. He saw the man go out through a French window. Maybe that was the way he had come in, thus avoiding the security checks. Now Marcus, too, stepped out, and for a moment the rush of the cold night air seemed to reawaken his drug-dazed senses.

The figure had headed for the wood. He was already some distance away. Marcus had no intention of letting him go.

. . . if he isn't stopped, he won't stop.

But, just as he was recovering some of his faculties, something heavy came down on the back of his head. There was a flash of pain. Someone had struck him. As he fell, he lost consciousness. And as he lost consciousness, he saw, an inch or two from his face, the shoes his attacker was wearing.

They were blue.

PART TWO

The Man with the Wolf's Head

1

The wind kept coming in sudden gusts then dropping.

According to the weather forecast, it was going to be an unsettled night. Between the trees a milky, rain-laden sky could be glimpsed. It had already turned bitterly cold, like an omen.

And she was wearing this damned miniskirt.

'Do you think we should kiss?'

'Fuck off, Stefano,' she replied.

Of all the colleagues she could have ended up with for this duty, it had to be that idiot Carboni.

They were out in the country, in a white Fiat 500. They had to look like a courting couple who had found a secluded spot for a bit of privacy, but Officer Pia Romani couldn't keep calm. She didn't like the idea of Operation Shield, she considered it a pointless waste of manpower and resources. It was an impossible task to cover the outskirts of Rome with barely forty cars as bait.

Trying to capture the Monster this way was a little like trying to win the lottery at your first attempt.

Plus, there was something sexist about the way she had been selected.

Like the other female officers, she had been chosen for her looks. A different yardstick had clearly been used for their partners. The proof of that was sitting beside her: Stefano Carboni, the creepiest, least attractive man in Headquarters.

The next day she would have to talk about it with her other female colleagues who were working tonight. They would have to consult their union.

But there was another truth that Pia Rimonti wasn't telling herself. Which was that she was scared. And it wasn't only because of her miniskirt that she felt a shudder climbing up her legs.

Every now and again, she moved her hand to the pocket in the door, in search of her pistol. She knew it was there, but touching it gave her a sense of security.

Carboni, though, seemed to be enjoying himself. He clearly couldn't believe he was alone in a car with the woman he'd been trying to chat up for more than two and a half years. Did he really think this situation would change things? What an idiot! Sure enough, he continued provoking her with jokes and *double entendres*.

'Can you imagine?' he laughed. 'I'll be able to say we spent the night together.'

'Why don't you shut up and concentrate on your work?'

'What work?' Carboni said, pointing to the surrounding scene. 'We're in the middle of nowhere and nobody will come. That strutting peacock Moro doesn't understand a damn thing, take my word for it. But I'm glad I'm here.' He leaned towards her with a half-smile. 'Might as well take advantage.'

Pia put a hand on his chest and pushed him away. 'Maybe you won't mind my telling Ivan.'

Ivan, her boyfriend, was very jealous. Though most likely, like all jealous men, he would be angrier with her than with

Carboni. He would blame her for not informing her superiors and making sure she was assigned a different colleague. He would accuse her of secretly liking the idea, like all women, of being wooed. In other words, in the end the blame would be entirely hers. It was pointless telling him that, apart from all the other difficulties of the profession, a policewoman had to constantly demonstrate that she was equal to her male colleagues. That was why she couldn't go and whine to her superiors every time someone didn't treat her like a princess. No, best to leave Ivan out of this.

Stefano Carboni was an arsehole, and would boast to his colleagues tomorrow even if he didn't manage to do anything tonight. Might as well let him talk. She would just have to keep him at a distance until the end of the shift.

But the real problem now was that she needed a pee.

She had been holding it back for more than an hour, and now she felt as if she might explode at any moment. It was partly the cold, and partly the tension. But she had found a way to resist by crossing her legs and leaning her weight on her left side.

'What the hell are you doing?'

'Putting on a bit of music, do you mind?'

Carboni had switched on the radio, but Pia switched it off almost immediately. 'I want to hear if anybody's coming close to the car.'

Carboni snorted. 'Rimonti, don't worry, relax. You're just like my girlfriend.'

'You have a girlfriend?'

'Of course,' he retorted, indignantly.

Pia couldn't believe it.

'Wait, I'll show you.' Carboni took out his mobile phone and showed her the photograph he used as a screensaver. There he was, by the sea, his arm around a girl.

She was pretty, Pia noted. And then she thought: poor thing.

'Would she mind if she knew you were trying it on with me?' she teased him.

'A man has to do what a man has to do,' he said. 'If I didn't try it on in a situation like this, I wouldn't deserve to be called a man. I don't think my girlfriend would like to know that she was with only half a man.'

Pia shook her head. His logic didn't make sense. But, instead of amusing her, it reminded her of Diana Delgaudio. The man she had gone out with on the evening of the attack in the pine wood at Ostia hadn't defended her. On the contrary, in order to save himself, he had agreed to stick a knife in her chest. How much of a man was a man like that? And how would Ivan have acted in her place?

Or Stefano Carboni?

That was the question she had avoided asking herself all night. If they really were attacked by the Monster of Rome, would her colleague be capable of protecting her? Or else would the man who had been hitting on her for more than two hours simply do as the killer said?

As she was thinking these things, a voice emerged from the car radio: '*Rimonti, Carboni: everything OK where you are?*'

It was the central switchboard. Every hour they checked in with the cars scattered around the countryside to find out how things were going. Pia grabbed the transmitter. 'Affirmative, nothing happening here.'

'*Keep your eyes open, guys: the night is still young.*'

As Pia hung up, she glanced at the digital clock on the dashboard. It was only just one o'clock. Yes, the night is young all right, she thought. At that moment, Carboni placed a hand on her leg. Pia first glared at him, then punched him in the forearm.

'Ouch!' he yelled.

It wasn't so much the gesture that made her angry as the fact that he had forced her to change her position on the seat. That made the urge to urinate unbearable. She grabbed Carboni by the lapel. 'Listen, I'm getting out to look for a tree.'

'To do what?'

Pia couldn't believe that he could really be so stupid. Ignoring his question, she said, 'You stand by the car and don't move until I finish. Got that?'

Carboni nodded.

Pia got out of the car with her pistol in her hand, and Carboni did the same.

'Don't worry, partner. I'm here.'

Pia shook her head and started to walk away. Behind her, Carboni started whistling, and then she heard the sound of a jet of liquid hitting the ground. He too had decided to urinate.

'The advantage of being a man is that we can do it whenever and wherever we like,' he boasted in a loud voice, then started whistling again.

Pia, though, was finding it hard to walk over the uneven ground. Her bladder hurt and that bloody miniskirt was hampering her movements. Not to mention the damned wind tugging at her like an invisible, spiteful hand.

She had her pistol and her mobile phone with her. She tried to see where she was going by using the light from the phone. At last, she chose a tree and increased her pace. As she approached the tree, she looked carefully around. She placed the pistol and phone on the ground. Then, a little apprehensively, she pulled down her tights and knickers, lifted her skirt up to her pelvis and squatted.

Her backside was cold, and she felt uncomfortable. But, despite the pressing need, she couldn't get it out. It was as if she was blocked. 'Pleasepleaseplease,' she said.

It was the fear.

She picked up the pistol and held it tight against her belly. Carboni's whistling echoed through the wood from the distance, making her feel calmer. With every gust of wind, though, it faded. All at once, it stopped altogether.

'Please, could you start whistling again?' she said, and immediately regretted her imploring tone.

'Of course!' he cried, and started again.

At last, her bladder let go. Pia half-closed her eyes with the pleasure of liberating herself. The hot liquid came out of her in a headlong rush.

Carboni stopped whistling again.

'What an arsehole,' she said to herself, even though the whistling once again started up.

She had almost finished when a stronger gust than the others made her sway. It was then that she heard a bang.

Pia stiffened. What had it been? Was it real or had she just imagined it? It had happened too quickly and the wind had muffled it. Now she wished Carboni would stop whistling, because that was all she could hear.

She was overcome by an irrational fear. She got to her feet and pulled up her tights as best she could. She grabbed her phone and pistol, then set off at a run, her miniskirt riding all the way up to her belly button. In her panic, she couldn't have been a pretty sight.

She thrust herself forward, constantly on the point of falling, with Carboni's whistling as her only guide.

Please don't stop.

She had the impression that somebody was following her. It might be her imagination, but she didn't care. Her only thought was to get back to the car.

When she finally came out into the little clearing where they were parked, she saw that her colleague was sitting in the car with the door open. She jumped into the passenger seat.

'Stefano, stop whistling, there's someone there!' she said in alarm.

But he didn't stop. Pia would have liked to slap him for being so stupid, but then she froze at the sight of his wide-open eyes and gaping mouth. There was a hole in his chest, from which black, sticky blood gushed. The explosion had been a gunshot.

And someone was still whistling, somewhere near her.

2

At dawn, the birds woke him.

Marcus opened his eyes and recognised the singing. But then he felt a spasm that pierced his skull. He tried to figure out where the pain was coming from, but it hurt everywhere.

And he felt cold.

He was lying on the ground in an awkward position, the left side of his face pressed into the hard earth, his arms down by his sides, one leg stretched out, the other bent awkwardly at the knee.

He must have fallen on his stomach, without trying to cushion his fall with his hands.

He tried first to raise his arm. Then, using his elbows, he started to sit up. Everything was spinning. He had to resist the temptation to close his eyes again. The threat of fainting was stronger than any dizziness.

He was finally able to sit up and look down. On the ground was the dark outline of his body, surrounded by a carpet of night frost all round it. He felt the dampness on himself, on his back, his legs and arms, his head.

The back of his head, he thought. That was the main source of the pain.

He touched it with one hand to see if there was a wound. In the spot where he had been hit, though, there was no blood. Only a huge lump and maybe a slight abrasion.

He was scared of losing his memory again. So he tried to quickly go through what he could remember.

For some reason, the first thing that came into his mind was the image of the dismembered nun in the Vatican gardens a year ago. But he immediately replaced it with the thought of Sandra, the kiss he had seen her exchange with the man she was in love with, their encounter in the pine wood at Ostia. Then came all the rest . . . The tape recorder in the church of Sant'Apollinare, Clemente's words: 'There is a serious threat hanging over Rome. What happened the other night is having a profound effect on people.' The child of salt . . . And finally the party – the orgy, rather – that he had witnessed last night, the shadowy figure with the camera, his trailing of that figure under the effect of the drug, the blow on the head. The last image he remembered, though, was the feet of his attacker as he walked away. He had been wearing a pair of blue shoes.

Someone had been protecting that shadowy figure. *Why?*

At last Marcus managed to get back on his feet. He felt the effects of the beginnings of hypothermia. At some moment in his past life, before the amnesia had blotted so much out, his body had learned to resist cold.

The pale light of dawn gave the grounds of the villa a ghostly appearance. He went back to the French window he had come out of, but it was closed. He tried to push it open, but he wasn't strong enough. So he picked up a stone and threw it at the glass. Then he stuck his arm in and opened it.

Inside, there was no trace of the party. The house looked as if it had been uninhabited for decades. The furniture was covered with white sheets, and there was a musty smell in the air.

Could he really have imagined everything? Was the drug he had taken so powerful? But then he noticed a detail – an anomaly – that told him it had all been real.

There was no dust.

Everything was too clean: the patina of neglect hadn't yet settled on things.

He removed a sheet from one of the sofas and put it around his shoulders to warm himself. Then he tried to switch on an electric light, but there was no current. So he groped his way up the stairs that led to the first floor, in search of a bathroom.

He found an en-suite one inside one of the bedrooms.

The weak light of day filtered through the slats of the Persian blinds. Marcus rinsed his face several times in the washbasin. Then he looked at himself in the mirror. His eyes were circled in black from the blow he had received. He hoped he hadn't suffered any cranial trauma.

He remembered Cosmo Barditi's voicemail message. *'One more thing: I may have a promising lead . . . I still have to check my sources, so I don't want to say anything yet.'*

'Cosmo,' Marcus repeated in a low voice. It was Cosmo who had told him about the party, then had found a way to get him into the villa. Could he also have betrayed him?

Something, however, told him that Cosmo had nothing to do with it. It had happened because he had started following the shadowy figure. Maybe that was not what had earned him that blow to the head, maybe he had provoked it by making the inverted sign of the cross. But the shadowy figure hadn't understood that gesture. Even though he couldn't remember his face because of the drug, Marcus still remembered being aware of the uncertain way he had stood looking at him.

But someone else had understood. *Blue shoes.*

He ought to inform Clemente, and then find out if Cosmo

really did have something for him. For the moment, though, all he wanted was to leave the villa.

A short while later, he walked into the cafeteria of a service station. The woman behind the counter looked at him as if she were seeing a corpse.

Marcus was still unsteady on his feet, and it hadn't been easy for him to drive here. He must look awful. He searched in his pockets for coins, then placed a couple of euros on the counter.

'A weak coffee, please.'

As he waited for the drink to be served, he looked up at a TV in a corner of the room.

A news reporter was standing in an isolated spot, in the middle of the countryside. Behind him, police officers were coming and going. Marcus recognised Sandra.

'*. . . the two officers killed last night were Stefano Carboni and Pia Rimonti,*' the reporter was saying. '*The monster followed almost the same ritual as in the first attack: he shot the man in the chest and then the woman in the stomach, perhaps because he noticed that she was armed. But he didn't kill her immediately: after wounding her, he tied her to a tree and attacked her with a knife. From what we have learned, according to the pathologist the torture would have been prolonged. In later bulletins we hope to supply more details . . .*'

Marcus noticed a public phone in a corner. He forgot about his coffee and rushed to the booth. He dialled the voicemail number and was about to leave a message when an electronic voice informed him that there was already one there, which he hadn't yet listened to.

He dialled his own code and stood waiting. Sure that he would hear Clemente's voice, he actually heard Cosmo Barditi's. He had left him a second message after that of the previous evening. Unlike the first, the tone was not at all calm: this time it betrayed a deep anxiety, a genuine terror.

'*. . . We have to meet right away . . .* ' the voice panted. '*It's much worse than I could ever have imagined . . .* ' He was so agitated, it sounded as if he was crying. '*We're in danger, serious danger,*' he continued. '*I can't tell you now, so come to my club as soon as you hear this message. I'll wait for you until eight, then get my daughter and partner and take them out of Rome.*'

The message ended. Marcus looked at the time: 7.10. He could still make it, but he had to hurry.

Right now, what interested him was not so much what Cosmo had discovered as the reason he was so scared.

3

Sandra had known Pia Rimonti.

They had spoken often. The last time, they had exchanged opinions about a sportswear shop. She had also frequented a gym and had been planning to start a Pilates course.

She wasn't married, but it was clear from what she said that she would like to start a family with her boyfriend, whose name, if Sandra remembered correctly, was Ivan. She had told her that he was jealous and possessive and that was why she had asked for a transfer from active duty to office work, so that at least he would always know where she was. She would gladly have accepted the change. Sandra would never forget her limpid smile, or how at the Headquarters cafeteria she liked her coffee with a little cube of ice.

After photographing Pia's naked, lacerated body that morning, Sandra found it hard to think clearly. She had carried out her work in a mechanical manner, as if part of her was anaesthetised to the horror. She didn't like feeling that way, but without that protective shell she wouldn't have been able to stand it for more than a few minutes.

Last night, when the Monster had realised that he was dealing with two police officers, he had launched a savage attack on Pia.

After shooting her in the stomach to render her harmless, he had stripped her, then kept going at her for at least half an hour. They had found her body wrapped around a tree trunk, handcuffed. The Monster had cut her skin with a hunting knife. Stefano Carboni had got off more lightly. According to the pathologist, the killer had shot him in the chest, hitting an artery. He had died instantaneously.

When the central switchboard had tried to contact the two officers by radio, as happened on average every sixty minutes, there had been no reply. At that point a patrol car had been sent out to check, and the macabre discovery had been made.

The media already knew about it, in spite of all the precautions taken by Headquarters to avoid leaks.

The double homicide had happened near the Via Appia Antica. An unusual amount of traffic had been recorded there the previous night: for now, that was the only strange element they could cling to.

Deputy Commissioner Moro was beside himself with rage. Operation Shield had proved a disaster. And the deaths of two officers was a major failure for the police.

In addition, the Monster had violated the corpse of Pia Rimonti, making it up with blusher and lipstick. Maybe in this case, too, he had taken photographs as souvenirs of his work. Whatever the purpose of the ritual, Sandra found it repulsive.

And this time too, there was no DNA of the killer, and no fingerprints.

Together with the men of the Central Operations Team, with Moro at their head, Sandra went in through the entrance of Headquarters on returning from the crime scene. There was a crowd of reporters and photographers waiting specifically for Moro, who forced his way through to the lift and refused to make a statement.

Among those present in the lobby, Sandra noted Giorgio Montefiori's mother. The woman, who had been so insistent that the police give her back her son's clothes, was holding in her hands a plastic bag with which she was trying to attract Moro's attention.

Moro turned to one of his men and said in a low voice, 'Get rid of her for me. Be gentle but firm.'

Overhearing this, Sandra felt sorry for her, but she could understand Moro's impatience. Two of their own people had been killed; they didn't have time to humour a mother's madness, however justified by grief.

'This investigation starts again from scratch,' he announced soon afterwards to the audience gathered in the operations room. Then he started to update the board showing the salient elements, adding those found at the latest crime scene.

Homicide in pine wood at Ostia:

Objects: rucksack, climbing rope, hunting knife, Ruger SP101 revolver.

Prints of the young man on the climbing rope and on the knife left in the sternum of the young woman: he ordered him to tie the girl up and stab her if he wanted to save his life.

Kills the young man by shooting him in back of neck.

Puts lipstick on the girl (to photograph her?).

Leaves a figure of salt next to the victims (a doll?).

Homicide of Officers Rimonti and Carboni:

Objects: hunting knife, Ruger SP101 revolver.

Kills Officer Stefano Carboni with a gunshot to the chest.

Shoots Officer Pia Rimonti, wounding her in the stomach. Then strips her, cuffs her to a tree, tortures her, and finishes her off with a hunting knife. Puts make-up on her (to photograph her?).

As Moro wrote, Sandra immediately noticed the difference between the elements gathered at the first and second crime scenes. In the latter, there were fewer of them and they appeared even less revealing.

And this time the killer had left nothing for them. No fetish, no signature.

When he had finished, Morrow addressed the audience. 'I want you to go out and dig up every pervert or maniac with a record for sexual crimes in this city. Grill them, make them spit out everything they know. We have to go over their profiles, word by word . . . check all their movements in the last few months, even the last few years, if necessary. I want to know the contents of their computers, which internet sites they've visited and what filthy material they've masturbated over. Get hold of their phone records and call those numbers, one by one, until something comes up. They have to feel they're in a corner, with us breathing down their necks. Our man can't have come out of nowhere, he must have a past. So read over the results we have so far, look at every tiny detail we may have neglected. And bring me something on this son of a bitch.' Moro concluded his harangue by punching the table. The meeting was over.

To Sandra, it merely confirmed that they had nothing to go on. That thought aroused a sudden sense of insecurity in her. She was convinced she wasn't the only one to feel that way. Confusion was obvious in her colleagues' expressions.

As they all left the room, her eyes met Superintendent Crespi's. He seemed weary, as if the events of the last few days had tried him to the limit. 'So, how did it go at Astolfi's place?' she asked him.

Crespi had handled the search of the pathologist's apartment. 'No link with the murder.'

Sandra was surprised. 'So how do you explain what he did?'

'I don't. The team has turned his life upside down, without finding anything.'

It wasn't possible, she didn't believe it. 'He could have helped us save Diana Delgaudio, but he wanted her to die. And then he hid and destroyed a piece of evidence. Nobody becomes the accomplice to a crime if he doesn't have a personal interest.'

Crespi noticed she was talking a bit too loudly, so he took her by one arm and drew her away from the others. 'Look, I don't know what got into Astolfi, but think about it: why should he have destroyed a doll made of salt? The truth is, he was a loner. Let's be honest, nobody liked him. Maybe he had his reasons for being bitter towards the police, or the human race, who knows? It happens to some sociopathic individuals: they do terrible, incomprehensible things.'

'Are you telling me that Astolfi was insane?'

'Insane, no, but maybe he lost his head.' He paused. 'I once arrested a paediatrician who, every hundred and eleven prescriptions, wrote down the wrong medicine. Children got ill because of it and nobody knew the reason.'

'Why a hundred and eleven?'

'Nobody knows. But that was the detail that gave him away. In every other respect he was a good doctor, in fact more scrupulous than most. Maybe he just needed to release his dark side every now and again.'

Sandra, though, wasn't convinced by this explanation.

Crespi put a hand on her arm. 'I know it's annoying, because you were the one who discovered what he'd done. But serial killers don't have accomplices, you know that: they act alone. And besides, the likelihood that Astolfi knew the killer and just happened to be called to the scene of the crime is pretty remote.'

Reluctantly, she had to admit that what the superintendent was saying made sense. But that made her feel even more fragile and powerless in the face of the evil that had been committed.

She wondered where Marcus was right now. She would have liked to talk to him. Maybe he could have reassured her.

Marcus reached the SX with just a few minutes to spare before eight o'clock. The street where the club was located was deserted at that hour of the morning. He walked to the entrance, pressed the entryphone, and waited for a reply. None came.

He wondered if Cosmo, tired of waiting for him, had decided to bring forward his escape with his family. The man was scared. And you couldn't predict how the mind of someone who felt threatened would function.

But Marcus couldn't afford to neglect any lead, however flimsy. So, having made sure that there really was nobody around, he reached into his pocket for the small retractable screwdriver he always carried with him and used it to open the lock.

He walked down the long concrete corridor leading to the red door. The fluorescent strip that usually lit it was off. He repeated the operation he had performed just now with the front door and entered the club.

There was only one light on, and it came from the central stage.

Marcus crossed the room, taking care not to bump into sofas and tables. He went out the back, where Cosmo's office was. When he got to the door, he stopped.

There was something strange about all this silence.

Without even touching the handle, he had a premonition that a corpse was waiting for him on the other side of the door.

When he finally walked through the door, he saw through the gloom the body of Cosmo Barditi lying on its back on the desk. He went closer and lit the lamp. Cosmo was clutching a gun in one hand and there was a bullet hole in his temple. His eyes were wide open and his left cheek lay in a pool of blood that had reached the edge of the desk and was dripping on the floor. It was supposed to look like a suicide, but Marcus knew it wasn't. Even though there was no sign of a struggle, Cosmo would never have taken his own life. He had a daughter now, he had talked of her with pride. He would never have abandoned her.

He had been killed because he had discovered something important. In the last message left on the voicemail he had said some disturbing things.

'*It's much worse than I could ever have imagined. We're in danger, serious danger.*'

What was Barditi referring to? What had scared him?

Hoping he had found a way to leave some clue before dying, Marcus started searching around the corpse. He put on latex gloves, opened the desk drawers, searched the dead man's pockets, moved furniture and fittings, upturned the wastepaper basket.

He had the impression though, that someone had done this before him.

This was confirmed when he realised that Cosmo's mobile phone was missing. Had whoever killed him taken it? Maybe there was a record on it of the calls Cosmo had made to gather information. Maybe, thanks to those very calls, he had discovered something so important that it had led to his death.

Maybe.

Marcus realised that this was all speculation. As far as he knew, Cosmo might never even have owned a mobile phone.

In the office, though, there was a landline. Marcus picked up the receiver and pressed the button that recalled the last number dialled. It rang a few times, then a woman's voice replied. 'Cosmo, is that you? Where are you?'

The tone was apprehensive. Marcus put the phone down. Probably it was his partner, who must be in an anxious state after he had failed to come home.

He took a last look around the room, but there was nothing of interest. As he was about to leave, he looked one last time at the swastika tattoo on Cosmo's neck.

Some years earlier, he had saved his life, or rather, he had given him the opportunity to change it. That symbol of hate no longer represented Cosmo Barditi, but whoever found his corpse would think that it did, and maybe wouldn't feel for him the pity he deserved.

Marcus raised his hand and gave him a blessing. Sometimes he remembered that he was also a priest.

4

The secret consisted of three levels. The first was 'the child of salt'.

Even though someone had managed to uncover that part of the puzzle, there were still the other two to be deciphered.

Nobody had managed that so far.

All the same, Batista Erriaga was nervous. He had dreamed about Min, that good friend he had killed as a young man in the Philippines. He had often thought of him in the last few days, maybe that was why. But, every time that happened, Batista was overcome with anxiety. That was never a good sign. It was as if Min was trying to warn him about something. Danger was gathering like a storm cloud around him. But the terrible secret of his youth was a small thing compared with the one he was trying to protect now.

Events were happening too quickly. A risky mechanism had been set in motion, and he didn't know how to slow it down.

There had been a new attack the previous night, leading to a double homicide.

Death didn't make him indignant, and the deaths of innocent people aroused no compassion in him. It was simply the way things were. He was no hypocrite. The truth was that, faced with the deaths of other people, we cry for ourselves. It isn't a noble sentiment, it's just fear that one day the same fate will befall us.

The only thing that mattered to him was that this time two police officers had died. That would complicate things.

He had to admit, though, that they had had a stroke of luck. The pathologist's suicide had put a brake on things. That idiot Astolfi had got found out, but had been sufficiently far-sighted to take his own life before the police could figure out his involvement.

But Erriaga simply had to find out if someone was following the trail of the child of salt, even though he knew that after a while they would come up against a brick wall.

And then their secret would be safe.

Many years earlier, a mistake had been made: a serious danger had been underestimated. The time had come to remedy that. But things were going too fast. That was why he needed to know exactly how far the police investigation had got.

There was only one way to find out: he had to give up his original idea of remaining incognito while he was in Rome.

At least one person would have to know he was here.

The Hotel de Russie was at the end of the Via del Babuino, an elegant street joining the Piazza del Popolo with the Piazza di Spagna, which took its name from the statue of Silenus lying on a little fountain dating back to 1571. The face of the sculpture was so ugly that the Romans had immediately compared it to a baboon.

Batista Erriaga walked into the hotel with the peak of his cap down over his eyes in order not to be noticed, and headed straight for the Stravinskij Bar, an exclusive spot where you could find excellent cocktails and sophisticated cuisine, and where you could drink and dine alfresco in the adjoining gardens from spring onwards.

A business lunch was in progress. A man in his seventies, elegant and authoritative in appearance, was entertaining his business partners from China.

His name was Tommaso Oghi. A Roman for many generations, descended from a very poor family, he had made his fortune in construction at a time when the city was being plundered by unscrupulous entrepreneurs whose only purpose was to get rich. Oghi was a friend of powerful people, including political figures of dubious morality, many of them Freemasons. His specialities were speculation and corruption, and in both he was a master. Several times he had been investigated, accused of having interests in common with organised crime. But he had always emerged scot-free, with not a single stain on his reputation.

Strangely, people like him who came through any kind of adversity unscathed rose in other people's estimation and acquired ever more power. Sure enough, Tommaso Oghi was considered one of the godfathers of Rome.

Erriaga was ten years younger than him, and yet he envied his demeanour, his worldliness. That fine head of neatly combed-back silvery hair. The discreet tan that gave him a healthy, glowing look. He recognised him immediately in his elegant Caraceni suit and made-to-measure English shoes. Batista asked a waiter to bring him a paper and a pen, then wrote a message and indicated the man to whom it was to be handed.

When Tommaso Oghi received the note, his expression changed abruptly. The tan vanished along with the smile, giving way to an anxious pallor. He excused himself to his guests and headed for the toilets, just as he had been ordered.

When he opened the door and saw Erriaga, he recognised him immediately. 'So it really is you.'

'Nobody must know I'm in Rome, apart from you,' Erriaga said immediately, taking off his cap and locking the door.

'Nobody will,' Oghi assured him. 'But I have people in there. I can't keep them waiting.'

Erriaga came and stood in front of him and looked him straight in the eyes. 'This won't take long. I just have a small request.'

Oghi, who was a shrewd man, seemed to grasp immediately that Erriaga's 'small request' probably wasn't so small, or he wouldn't have lowered himself to talking to him in a toilet. That wasn't like him. 'What's it about?'

'The Monster of Rome. I want you to get me copies of the police reports.'

'Isn't what you read in the papers enough for you?'

'I want to know the details that aren't divulged to the press.'

Oghi laughed. 'The case is being handled by Deputy Commissioner Moro, a bulldog from the Central Operations Team. Nobody can get close to him.'

'That's why I came to you,' Erriaga sneered.

'Even I can't do anything this time. I'm sorry.'

Erriaga shook his head and clicked his tongue irritably several times. 'You disappoint me, my friend: I thought you were more powerful.'

'Well, you're wrong. There are people I can't get to.'

'In spite of your contacts and your deals?' Erriaga asked – he enjoyed reminding other people how mean and underhand they were.

'In spite of my contacts and my deals,' Oghi said, with a show of self-confidence.

Erriaga turned to the large mirror that hung over the washbasins and looked at Oghi's reflection. 'How many grandchildren do you have? Eleven, twelve?'

'Twelve,' Oghi said, uneasy now.

'A nice big family, congratulations. And tell me: how old are they?'

'The oldest has just turned sixteen. Why do you ask?'

'What would he say if he found out his grandad liked having fun with young girls the same age as he is?'

Oghi was furious, but forced himself to keep calm. He was at a disadvantage. 'That old story . . . How many more times are you going to use it, Erriaga?'

'I would have stopped ages ago. But you seem to want exactly the opposite, my friend.' He turned back to him. 'I saw the photographs of your last holiday in Bangladesh: you did well, holding hands with that minor. And I know the address of the woman in the suburbs here who lets you amuse yourself with her daughter every Thursday afternoon: are you helping her with her homework, by any chance?'

Oghi grabbed him by the lapel. 'I'm not going to let you blackmail me again.'

'You're wrong, I'm not blackmailing anyone any more. I just take what belongs to me by right.' Calmly, he pulled Oghi's hand away. 'And remember: I know you better than you know yourself. You may be angry, but you'll do exactly what I ask. Because you know that I won't expose you now. You know that I'll leave you be and wait until the next time you touch a minor, and only then will I tell the press everything. Tell me, my friend: would you be able to resist the temptation?'

Oghi said nothing.

'It isn't the fear of losing face that bothers you, it's the thought that you won't be able to do what you like any more . . . am I right?' Battista Erriaga bent and picked up his cap, which had fallen a little earlier without his noticing. He put it back on his head. 'When you die, your soul will go to hell, you know that. But as long as you're here it belongs to me.'

5

Operation Shield had been blown wide open by the media.

In the hours following the second double homicide, the press had been harsh in their criticism of the Central Operations Team, and Deputy Commissioner Moro in particular. The words that had recurred most often were 'inadequacy' and 'inefficiency'. Among the public, feelings of commiseration for the deaths of the two police officers had been replaced by a mounting anger.

Fear was having an effect on people. The Monster was winning the game.

Moro had been forced to call off Operation Shield to avoid more controversy. He had then barricaded himself in Headquarters with his most trusted men, looking for a new angle for the investigation.

'What's going on?' There was a touch of anxiety in Max's question. 'You're not in any danger, are you?'

'Don't take any notice of what you hear on TV,' Sandra replied. 'They don't know what they're talking about, they just have to sell the news to the public, so they use scare tactics.' She knew that this statement wasn't completely truthful, but she didn't know a better way to reassure him.

'When will you be home?'

'As soon as we've finished here.' This too was a lie. In reality, they didn't have much to work on, they were simply going over the elements of the case and looking for individuals with previous convictions for sexual offences to question. Apart from that, they were groping in the dark.

'Are you all right?'

'I'm fine.'

'That isn't true, Vega. I can tell from your voice.'

'You're right,' she admitted. 'It's this case. I've become unused to so much violence.'

'You've been evasive for the last couple of days.'

'I'm sorry, but I can't talk about it right now.' She had taken refuge in the lobby to make this call. She couldn't stand being with the others any more and had taken advantage of the fact that Headquarters was less crowded after nightfall to look for a little privacy. But now she regretted having thought of calling Max. She was afraid he had realised the main reason why she was like this. 'I can't always be a hundred per cent. You understand that, don't you?'

'Then why not quit?'

They had already talked about that. His solution to everything was for Sandra to change her job. He really couldn't understand how a person could choose to be surrounded by dead people.

'You have school, your history lessons, your pupils . . . ' she replied, trying to be patient. 'I have this.'

'I respect what you do, I'm just saying that maybe you could consider leading a different kind of life. That's all.'

He was partly right: Sandra was too involved. She felt a weight deep down in her stomach, as if a big parasite had taken up residence there and was draining her strength, replacing it with anxiety. 'When my husband died, everybody told me that I should change profession. My family, my friends. I was so stubborn, I told them I could manage. The fact is, I've tried to avoid the most violent cases these past three years. When I couldn't, I hid behind my camera. The result is that I've tried to get away from the blood as quickly as possible and haven't done my job as well as I should have done: that's why I didn't realise immediately that Diana Delgaudio was still alive. It was my fault, Max. I was at the scene, but it was as if I wasn't there.'

Max sighed at the other end of the line. 'I love you, Vega, and I know it may seem selfish on my part, but I have to tell you that you're still hiding. I don't know from what, but you are.'

Sandra knew he was saying this for her own good, because he was sincerely worried about their future. 'Maybe you're right, I'm the one who exaggerates. But I promise you that when this whole thing is over we'll talk about it again.'

These words succeeded in reassuring him. 'Come home soon, I'm waiting.'

Sandra hung up, but then stood looking at the mobile phone in the palm of her hand. Was she really all right? This time it was she and not Max who formulated the question. But she had been unable to answer him, and she was unable to answer herself either.

It had been a very long day and it was late. But none of Moro's team would leave the building without giving their all for the investigation, especially now that it involved the deaths of two colleagues.

Sandra was about to take the lift back up to the operations room when she noticed that Giorgio Montefiori's mother was still sitting on one of the plastic chairs in the lobby reserved for visitors. She looked composed and patient. And on her knees she was holding the plastic bag she had tried to hand over to Moro a few hours earlier.

Sandra turned her back on her, for fear that she had seen her with Moro and might want to talk to her. She pressed the button for the lift. But when the doors opened, she couldn't go in. They closed again and she turned and walked over to the woman. 'Good evening, Signora Montefiori, my name is Sandra Vega, I'm working with the Central Operations Team. Can I be of any help?'

The woman shook the hand Sandra held out to her, although without much conviction, perhaps because she couldn't believe someone was actually paying attention to her. 'I spoke with some of your colleagues, they told me to wait, but I can't.'

She sounded dazed. Sandra was afraid she might faint at any moment. 'The cafeteria's closed, but there are machines: why don't you eat something?'

The woman heaved a deep sigh. 'Losing a son is heartbreaking.'

Sandra didn't understand the connection, but the woman continued speaking.

'Nobody, though, tells you the real truth, which is that it's such a bother.' There was bitterness in her eyes, but also a kind of lucidity. 'It's a bother having to get out of bed in the morning, it's a bother to walk, even to go to the bathroom or simply look at the wall. As I look at you, I find it hard to open and close my eyes, can you believe that?'

'Yes, I can,' Sandra said.

'Then don't ask me if I need to eat something and listen to what I have to tell you instead.'

Sandra understood: this mother didn't need compassion, but attention. 'All right, I'm here, go ahead.'

The woman showed her the plastic bag. 'There's been a mistake.'

'What mistake? I don't understand . . .'

'I asked for Giorgio's personal effects.'

'Yes, I know.' Sandra remembered the bundles of transparent

cellophane, containing the clothes of Diana and her boyfriend. Moro had shown them to her and told her that Giorgio's mother was insisting on having her son's effects handed over to her. He had described this as one of the many absurdities produced by grief.

'I checked,' she said, opening the bag to display the contents: a white shirt. 'This isn't my son's. They gave me someone else's.'

Sandra looked at it. It was the very one she had seen, scattered together with the other clothes, on the back seat of the car while she was taking photographs.

But the woman insisted, 'Maybe it belonged to another boy who died. And now his mother's wondering what happened to her son's shirt.'

She would have liked to tell her that there was no other dead boy, and no other desperate mother. What grief was doing to this woman was terrible, so she tried to be as patient as she could. 'I'm sure there hasn't been any mistake, *signora*.'

But Signora Montefiore now took the shirt out of the bag. 'Look here: this shirt is medium. Giorgio always wore large.' Then she showed her the sleeve. 'And it doesn't have his initials on the cuffs. All his shirts have his initials, I sewed them on myself.'

She was perfectly serious. At any other moment, Sandra would have thought of getting rid of her, gently but firmly. Instead she was struck by a sudden presentiment, and a shiver trickled down her spine. What if it wasn't a mistake?

There was only one explanation.

She ran into the operations room and went straight to the board showing the salient elements of the case. She took the felt-tip pen and wrote:

After killing he changes clothes.

Moro, who had been sitting with his feet up on the desk, now sat up and looked at her with a questioning air. Nobody present understood what was going on.

'How do you know?' Moro asked.

Sandra showed him the plastic bag with the shirt. 'Giorgio Montefiori's mother brought this in, she says it doesn't belong to her son. She thinks there was a mistake, and she's right, only we weren't the ones who made it.' She was galvanised by the discovery. 'We gave her the one that was found in the car in the pine wood at Ostia, but the shirts were swapped earlier: in the dark, the killer took Giorgio's shirt thinking it was his. And that can be explained only one way . . .'

'He takes off his clothes at the scene,' Moro said. A new awareness was growing inside him, dispelling the depression that had afflicted him all day. 'Maybe in case they get bloodstains on them, or so as not to look conspicuous later.'

'Precisely,' Sandra stated, radiant. But this precautionary measure, common to other killers, might have a further and unexpected consequence in this case. 'That's why, if this is the killer's shirt in the bag . . .'

Moro got in ahead of her. '. . . then it has his DNA on it.'

6

He had waited in the street, not far from the entrance to the SX, for someone to find Cosmo Barditi's body.

In the end, it had fallen to one of the girls who worked in the club to make that macabre discovery. Marcus had heard the screams and walked away.

He had to get back on the scent of the lead Cosmo had been following, or saving his life years earlier, and his death now, would both have been pointless.

But what had Cosmo discovered that was so serious as to put his life in danger?

In the afternoon, Marcus had returned to the attic where he lived, in the Via dei Serpenti. He'd needed to get his thoughts in some kind of order. A fierce migraine was attacking his temples. He had stretched out on the camp bed. The spot on the back of his head where he had been hit was aching, and his stomach was still upset because of the drug he had taken before the party. A vague sense of nausea came to the surface from time to time.

The walls of the room were as bare as those of a cell, except for a photograph nailed to the wall: the image from the security footage showing the presumed killer of the nun in the Vatican gardens. The man with the grey shoulder bag whom Marcus had spent a year looking for, without success.

Hic est diabolus.

Marcus had hung it there in order not to forget it. But at that moment he had closed his eyes. And he had thought of Sandra.

He would have liked to talk to her again. Had he ever been with a woman? He couldn't remember. Clemente had revealed to him that his vows went back many years, to when he was still a young man in Argentina. What did it feel like to be loved and desired by someone?

He had fallen asleep with these thoughts. Then a dream had made him toss and turn in bed. It was a repetitive dream: just when it seemed to have finished, it started all over again. It was the shadowy figure of the unknown man with the camera walking away through the grounds of the villa on the Appia Antica. Every time Marcus was about to catch up with him and look him in the face, he was hit on the back of his head. That night, death had given him a warning. That night, death had worn blue shoes.

When he opened his eyes again, it was already dark.

He sat up and looked at the time. After eleven. There was a positive aspect to having slept so long: his headache had subsided.

He took a quick shower in the little bathroom. He knew he ought to eat something, but he wasn't hungry. He put on clean clothes – dark as usual, like the rest of the things he kept in an open suitcase on the floor.

He had to go somewhere.

Under a brick in the ceiling, he hid the money that Clemente passed on to him. He used it for his missions, spending little on himself. He didn't need much.

He counted out ten thousand euros, then left.

Half an hour later, he was outside Cosmo Barditi's front door. He rang the bell and waited. He saw something moving behind the spy hole. Nobody asked him who he was. Marcus, though, knew that Cosmo's partner was on the other side of the door, and that she was understandably worried by a visit at that hour.

'I'm a friend of Cosmo's.' It was a lie – they had never been friends. 'I saved his life around three years ago.'

It might be the key to overcoming the woman's resistance, he thought, because it was something only he and Cosmo knew about. He hoped that the man had shared that secret with his partner.

After a few moments' hesitation, he heard the lock open, and a young woman appeared in the doorway. She had shoulder-length hair and bright eyes reddened by tears.

'He told me about you,' she said immediately. She had a rolled-up handkerchief in the palm of one hand. 'Cosmo's dead.'

'I know,' Marcus said. 'That's why I'm here.'

The apartment was dark. Asking him to be quiet in order not to wake the child, she led him to the kitchen. They sat down at the table on which the little family ate its meals, overhung by a low lamp that emitted a warm and welcoming light.

The woman offered to make him a coffee. Marcus declined.

'I'm going to make it anyway,' she insisted. 'You don't have to drink it if you don't want to, but I really can't keep still.'

'Cosmo didn't kill himself,' Marcus said when she had her back to him. He saw her stiffen. 'He was murdered because he was helping me.'

The woman said nothing for a while. 'Who was it?' she said at last. 'Why? He never did anything wrong, I'm sure of it.'

She looked as if she was about to start crying. Marcus hoped she wouldn't. 'That's all I can tell you. It's for your safety, and that of your child. You have to trust me: it's best if you know as little as possible about this business.'

For a moment he wished she would react, start lashing out at him, throw him out. But she didn't.

'He was worried,' she said in a thin voice. 'When he came home yesterday, he asked me to start packing. When I asked him why, he changed the subject.' As the coffee maker simmered on the stove, she turned to Marcus. 'You shouldn't feel guilty over his death. Cosmo had three more years to live thanks to you. Three years to change, to fall in love with me and bring a little girl into the world. I think that, in his place, anyone would have chosen the same fate.'

It wasn't much consolation for Marcus. 'He may have died pointlessly, that's why I'm here . . . Didn't he leave you anything for me? A message, a number, something . . . '

The woman shook her head. 'He came back very late last night. He told me I should pack, but didn't say where we were going. We were supposed to leave this morning. I think he wanted to go abroad, at least that's the idea I got. He was only at home for an hour. He put the child to bed, he'd brought her a book of fairytales. I think that in his heart he knew he might never see her again, that's why he had a gift for her.'

Marcus felt a strange sense of powerlessness and anger. He had to change the subject. 'Did Cosmo have a mobile phone?'

'Yes, but the police didn't find it in his office. And it wasn't in his car either.'

He registered the information. The disappearance of the phone supported the homicide theory.

Cosmo must have called someone who had given him a piece of information. Who?

'You saved Cosmo, Cosmo saved me,' the woman said. 'I think sometimes, if a person does something good, then that good action is repeated.'

Marcus would have liked to say that it was so, but what he really thought was that only evil had such a talent. It reverberated like an echo. In fact, Cosmo Barditi, however innocent, had paid for the bad things he had done in the past.

'You have to leave anyway,' Marcus said. 'It isn't safe here.'

'But I don't know where to go and I don't have any money! Cosmo invested everything in the club and things weren't going well.'

Marcus put the ten thousand euros he had brought with him down on the table. 'This should be enough for a while.'

The woman looked at the pile of banknotes. Then she started crying again softly. Marcus would have liked to get up and go and embrace her, but he didn't know how to perform certain gestures. He constantly saw people expressing affection and compassion, but he wasn't capable of doing so himself.

The coffee-maker on the stove started puffing steam, and the liquid was boiling over. The woman, though, did not lift it from the flame. Marcus stood up and did it for her. 'It's best I go now,' he said.

The woman nodded between her sobs. Marcus headed alone for the exit. As he walked back along the corridor, he noticed a door that was slightly ajar, with dim moonlight filtering through it. He went closer.

A star-shaped lamp softly illumined the semi-darkness. A little girl with blonde hair was sleeping serenely in her cot. She lay on her side, with a dummy in her mouth and her hands together. She had thrown off the blankets. Marcus approached and, with a gesture that surprised even himself, pulled them up.

He stood there looking at her, wondering if this was the reward for having saved Cosmo Barditi years before. If, when it came down to it, this new life had also come into being thanks to him.

Evil is the rule, good the exception, he reminded himself.

So no, he had nothing to do with it. He decided to leave this apartment immediately, because he felt out of place.

But, as he was about to take a step towards the door, his eye fell on the cover of a book lying on a table-top in the little room. It was the fairytale that Cosmo had given his daughter the previous night. The title struck him like a fist.

The Amazing Story of the Child of Glass.

Clemente's third lesson had come on a sultry summer afternoon.

They had arranged to meet in the Piazza Barberini and from there had walked along the street of the same name, before plunging into the side streets that led to the Trevi Fountain. They cut through the mass of tourists thronged around the monument, intent on taking photos and throwing coins in the water – the old ritual according to which anybody who did so would come back to Rome at some point during his lifetime.

As the visitors gazed at the Eternal City, awed by its beauty, Marcus watched them, conscious of his own distance from the rest of the human race. He was like one of those shadows crossing the walls as if to escape the light of the sun.

Clemente seemed particularly calm that day. He had great confidence in the training and was sure that, very soon, Marcus would be ready to undertake his mission.

Their walk ended in front of the baroque church of San Marcello al Corso. Its concave façade seemed to be trying to embrace the faithful.

'This church contains a great lesson,' Clemente announced.

They went in and were greeted by a sudden coolness. It was as if the marble was breathing. The church wasn't very large and had a single central nave with five chapels on each side.

Clemente walked straight to the central altar, over which hung a splendid crucifix of dark wood, from the fourteenth-century Sienese school.

'Look at that Christ,' he said. 'Beautiful, isn't it?'

Marcus nodded. But he wasn't sure if Clemente was referring to the work of art or, as a priest, to the spiritual nature of the symbol.

'According to the inhabitants of Rome, that crucifix is miraculous. This church, as we see it today, was rebuilt after a fire destroyed it on the night of May 23, 1519. The only thing that was saved from the flames was that Christ you see on the altar today.'

Struck by the story, Marcus started looking at the work with different eyes.

'And that's not all,' Clemente continued. 'In 1522 the plague struck Rome, killing hundreds of people. The population remembered the miraculous crucifix and it was decided to carry it in procession through the streets of the city, in spite of the opposition of the authorities, who feared that all those people following the cortège might help the epidemic to spread.' At this point, Clemente paused. 'The procession lasted sixteen days and the plague disappeared from Rome.'

Faced with that unexpected revelation, Marcus was unable to utter a word, spellbound by the mystical power of that piece of wood.

'But wait,' Clemente admonished him. 'There's another story connected with this work . . . Take a good look at the face of Christ suffering on the cross.'

The signs of pain on that face were vivid. You could almost hear a moan escaping the wood. Those eyes, the lips, the lines faithfully portrayed the emotion of death.

Clemente turned solemn. 'The artist who carved that sculpture was anonymous. But it is said that he was filled with such faith that he wanted to give Christians a work capable of moving them and, at the same time, impressing them with its realism. And so he became a murderer. He chose a poor charcoal-burner as a model, then killed him very slowly, to capture his expressions and his suffering as he died.'

'Why have you told me both stories?' Marcus asked, although he already suspected why.

'Because for centuries people have enjoyed telling both. Atheists, obviously, prefer the more macabre of the two. Believers like the first . . . But they don't turn their noses up at the second story either, because human nature is attracted by the mystery of wickedness. The point, though, is: which do you believe?'

Marcus thought about this for a while. 'No, the real question is: can something good come out of something evil?'

Clemente seemed pleased with this answer. 'Good and evil are never well-defined categories. Often it is necessary to decide which is one and which the other. The judgement depends on us.'

'Depends on us,' Marcus repeated, as if assimilating the words.

'When you examine a crime scene, maybe one in which innocent blood has been shed, you can't focus only on the who and the why. Instead, you have to imagine the perpetrator of that crime in the past that led him there, without neglecting those who love him or have loved him. You have to imagine him as he laughs and cries, when he's happy or sad. As a child, in his mother's arms. And as an adult, doing the shopping or catching the bus, sleeping and eating. And loving. Because there is no man, even the most terrible, who cannot feel love.'

Marcus understood the lesson.

'The way to capture a bad person is to understand how he loves.'

7

Deputy Commissioner Moro was driving along the eastern ring road in an unmarked car, the kind the police used to carry out surveillance and stakeouts without being recognised. They were often vehicles that had been confiscated after being used in crimes and subsequently made available to Headquarters.

The car driven by Moro had belonged to a drug-trafficker. It looked like an ordinary saloon car, but in fact it had an upgraded engine and a double body shell: in the gap between the two, the customs officers had found fifty kilos of the purest cocaine.

Moro had remembered that false floor and it had struck him as the ideal place to transport something without being conspicuous.

He had used a side exit from Headquarters in order to put reporters off the scent. They were all after him right now, trying to obtain a statement and simultaneously to attack him over the deaths of the two police officers. Officially, he never got involved in controversy. Over the course of his brilliant career he had often run up against the press and had his actions called into question. It was one of the prices to pay for fame, although they were certainly small wounds to his pride. But this time it was different. If the journalists had discovered what he was trying to hide with all these precautions, the price would have been very high indeed.

A pale and iridescent sun illuminated the Roman morning but did not warm it. The traffic was going at a snail's pace. There are things it's dangerous to talk about, Moro thought as he looked at the faces of the occupants of the other cars in the queue. There are things it's best not to know. These people wouldn't understand. Might as well let them live in peace, no point disturbing them with things even he couldn't explain.

Moro took nearly an hour to reach his destination: a concrete apartment block surrounded by others that were identical, built at a time when certain areas of the city had been fertile ground for developers.

He parked in a side street. One of his men was waiting for him in plain clothes at the entrance to the building. He came towards him and Moro handed him the keys of the car.

'They're all up there,' the officer said.

'Good,' Moro said, heading for the main door.

He stepped into the narrow lift and pressed the button for the eleventh floor. Reaching the landing, he identified the door that interested him and rang the bell. A technician in a white coat came and let him in.

'How far have you got?' Moro asked.

'We've almost finished.'

The area was foul with the smell of the chemical reagents used by Forensics, but beneath it – like a persistent layer – there was the unmistakable smell of stale nicotine and mustiness.

The apartment was dark and not very large. There was a narrow corridor with four rooms leading off it. At the entrance, there was a dresser with a large mirror, and in a corner a coat-stand with overcoats hanging on it.

Moro walked along the corridor, stopping at the door of each room. The first was a study. There was a bookcase with volumes on anatomy and medicine, but also a desk covered with sheets of newspaper on which stood an unfinished model of a three-masted ship, and next to it glue, brushes and a telescopic lamp.

There were models of aeroplanes, ships and trains, arranged on the shelves or else scattered just anywhere, even on the floor. Moro recognised an RAF De Havilland DH95 Flamingo from the Second World War, a Phoenician bireme, and one of the first electric locomotives.

All the models were covered with a thick layer of dust, making the room look like a scrapyard. And probably that was what it was: once he had finished each model, their creator would lose interest. He had nobody to show his work to, Moro thought, looking at the ashtrays filled with cigarette ends. Time and solitude had joined hands, the cigarettes bore witness to that.

The Forensics team were bustling around the abandoned relics with ultraviolet lamps and photographic equipment. It was like being present at the scene of a disaster in miniature.

In the kitchen, two technicians were emptying and cataloguing the contents of a refrigerator, a model that was certainly more than thirty years old. Here, too, there was an untidiness that seemed to have settled year after year.

The third room was a bathroom. White tiles, a tub with yellowed ceramics, a toilet with a pile of magazines and a number of rolls of toilet paper next to it. On the sink, a shelf with nothing on it but a can of shaving foam and a plastic razor.

Since the failure of his first marriage, Moro too had been single. But he wondered how anybody could let themselves go like this.

'Astolfi was a loner, and the apartment is a mess.'

It was Superintendent Crespi who had spoken. He was in charge of the search.

Moro turned. 'Have you kept Vega out of this?'

'Yes, sir. When she asked me, I told her we hadn't found anything important. I convinced her that Astolfi had lost his head and that his taking a piece of evidence from the crime scene was simply a meaningless act of madness.'

'Good,' Moro said, even though he wasn't completely sure that Sandra Vega would accept that without asking questions. She was clever, she wouldn't be content. But maybe that version of events would keep her quiet for a while. 'What do the neighbours say about Astolfi?'

'Some of them didn't even know he was dead.'

The funeral had taken place that very morning, but nobody had attended. It was a sad thing, Moro thought. Nobody cared about the pathologist's death. The man had created a void around him. A deliberate distance, stoked over the years with neglect. The only human beings he had any relations with were the corpses that he sliced up on his table. But, judging from the place where he lived, Astolfi had already become part of that silent throng a long time before killing himself.

'Had he made a will? Who will his things go to?'

'He left no instructions and had no relatives,' Crespi said. 'Can you imagine solitude like that?'

No, Moro really couldn't. But he knew that such men existed. He had come across apartments like this one more than once, and people who possessed the gift of invisibility. Nobody noticed them until they were dead, when the stink of their corpses reached their neighbours. Once that was gone, though, nothing remained of them and they could go back to being anonymous, as if they had never existed.

Astolfi, though, had left something. Something for which he would never be forgotten.

'Do you want to see the rest?' Crespi asked.

There are things it's dangerous to talk about, Moro remembered. There are things it's best not to know. But he was one of those people who couldn't keep away. 'OK, let's see it.'

The bedroom was the last room at the end. It was there that they had made the discovery.

There was the single bed on which Astolfi slept. Next to it, a bedside table with a marble top. On it were an old alarm clock that needed winding, a reading lamp, a glass of water and the inevitable ashtray. There was a heavy-looking wardrobe of dark wood. A worn leather armchair and a coat stand. An overhead light with three branches and a window with the blinds down.

A perfectly ordinary bedroom.

'I came here in an unmarked car with a false bottom,' Moro said. 'I want the finds taken to Headquarters without anybody seeing. Now tell me everything . . .'

'We checked the contents of every cupboard and drawer,' Crespi said. 'That madman never threw anything away. It was like going through his whole useless existence. He accumulated stuff but had no souvenirs. The thing that struck me most is that we didn't find any photographs of him as a child, or of his parents. Not a single letter from a friend, not even a postcard.'

He accumulated stuff but had no souvenirs, Moro repeated to himself as he looked around. Could you really live like this, without any purpose? But maybe that was what Astolfi had wanted them to believe.

A world of dark secrets was hidden within people.

'We'd just finished turning the apartment upside down and were about to leave when . . .'

'What happened exactly?'

Crespi turned towards the wall next to the door. 'There are three light switches,' he said. 'The first turns on the overhead light, the second is connected to the lamp on the bedside table.

But what about the third?' He paused. 'A lot of apartments have light switches that aren't used any more. They stay there for years and in the end you can't even remember what they used to be for.'

This wasn't the case here, however. Moro reached out his hand and pressed the buttons that switched off the overhead light and the lamp on the bedside table. The room was plunged into darkness. But now Moro activated the third light switch.

A dim light insinuated itself into the room. It was filtering through the skirting board of one of the walls. A long, very thin line of light that went from one corner to the other.

'The wall is made of plasterboard,' Crespi said. 'On the other side there must be an air space. The room was originally larger.'

Moro sighed deeply, wondering what to expect.

'The way in is on the right.' Crespi indicated a point low down on the wall, where there was a kind of door about a foot and a half wide and just over a foot high. He went to it and pressed it with the palm of his hand. The lock snapped open, revealing an entrance.

Moro crouched on the ground to look inside.

'Wait,' Crespi said. 'You have to realise what we're dealing with . . . '

At this point, he pressed the light switch again, turning off the light on the other side of the wall. Then he passed him a torch.

'When you're ready, let me know,' Crespi said.

Moro turned towards the dark entrance. He lay down on his stomach and, propping himself on his arms, slid into the opening.

As soon as he was on the other side, he felt as if he was cut off from the rest of the world.

'Are you all right?' Crespi's voice sounded muffled and distant, even though they were separated only by a wall an inch or two thick.

'Yes,' Moro said, getting to his feet. Then he switched on the torch.

He shone it first right, then left. And it was on the left, at the end, on the opposite side of this narrow space, that he saw something.

A small wooden table. On it was some kind of stylised structure. It seemed as light as a spider's web. It was about a foot high and was made up of superimposed and intertwined branches.

Moro approached cautiously, trying to figure out the meaning of the composition. The shape revealed nothing, it was as if the pieces of wood had been placed there at random. A perfect piece of model work, he said to himself, thinking again of the glue and brushes he had seen in the study. When he had it there in front of him, he realised he was wrong.

They weren't branches, but bones. Small, blackened bones. Not human, but animal.

Moro wondered how something like this was possible. What mind could have conceived this?

He noticed the light bulb hanging by a thread from the ceiling and ending just behind this macabre sculpture.

'I'm ready,' he said out loud.

He switched off the torch and from outside Crespi again pressed the switch. The bulb came to life, diffusing its yellowish light.

Moro didn't understand. What was so strange?

'Now turn,' the inspector said.

He did so. When he saw it, he gave a start. A start he would remember for as long as he lived.

On the opposite wall, his own shadow was superimposed on that cast by the bone structure.

The bones had not been put together at random. The proof of that was the image that had formed on the wall.

A tall anthropomorphic figure. A human body with a wolf's head.

A wolf with holes for eyes. But the most disturbing thing was that it was holding its arms out wide. That was the image that had made Moro jump.

The creature's shadow was embracing his.

8

Sandra saw him on the bench at the Piazza della Repubblica metro station. He was trying to mingle with the other passengers, but it was obvious that he was waiting for her.

She got off the train and saw Marcus walk away, clearly wanting her to follow him. She did so. She climbed the stairs leading to the exit and saw him turn left. She kept at a distance, while he proceeded unhurriedly. Then she saw him stop by a metal door with a sign saying *Staff Only*. He went in all the same. Soon afterwards, so did she.

They were in the well of a service staircase.

'I was right: someone took a piece of evidence from the crime scene, didn't they?' Marcus began. His voice echoed in the stairwell.

'I can't talk to you about the investigation,' Sandra said, immediately on the defensive.

'I don't want you to feel forced,' he replied seraphically.

She was angry with him. 'So you knew ... You knew someone had taken something away and you suspected one of us.'

'Yes, but I wanted you to get there by yourself.' He paused. 'I read about the pathologist's suicide. Maybe he couldn't stand the sense of guilt for having almost let Diana Delgaudio die . . . '

No sense of guilt, Sandra would have liked to tell him. But she was sure that Marcus had grasped that part of the story too. 'Stop playing with me,' she said.

'It was something made of salt, wasn't it?'

Sandra was astonished. 'How on earth do you . . . ' But then she immediately went on, 'Astolfi managed to destroy it before we could get to it. I touched it briefly for a moment, and it felt like a little doll.'

'It was probably a kind of statuette.' Then Marcus took from his jacket the fairytale book he had found in Cosmo Barditi's daughter's room.

'*The Amazing Story of the Child of Glass*,' Sandra read, then looked at him. 'What does it mean?'

Marcus did not reply.

Sandra started leafing through the book. It was only a few pages long, mostly filled with drawings. It was the story of a boy who was different from the others because he was made of glass. He was very fragile, but every time part of him broke he risked hurting children of flesh and blood.

'He'll become like the others,' Marcus said, anticipating what happened at the end.

'What?'

'It's a kind of educational parable: there are two blank pages before the end. I think the child who reads the book is asked to provide the solution.'

Sandra leafed through. Sure enough, on the last two pages the drawings were replaced by lines, like those of an exercise book. Whatever had been written there had been crossed out, although you could still see pencil marks. Sandra closed the book and checked the cover. 'There's no author's name, or even who published it.'

Marcus had already noticed that.

'Why should this fairytale have anything to do with the doll made of salt?'

'Because a man died to give me this.' Marcus did not mention the recording in Sant'Apollinare, the message left in the confessional by the killer five days before attacking the two young people in the pine wood at Ostia. Instead, he said, 'I saw him.'

'How . . . ' Sandra was incredulous.

'I saw the killer. He had a camera with him. When he noticed me he ran away.'

'Did you see his face?'

'No.'

'Where did this happen?'

'In a villa on the Appia Antica. There was a kind of party or orgy. People celebrating violent death. And he was there.'

Appia Antica, the very area where the two officers taking part in Operation Shield had been murdered. 'Why didn't you stop him?'

'Because somebody stopped me, with a blow to the back of my head.' The man with the blue shoes, he remembered.

Sandra still didn't understand.

'The pathologist stealing evidence, the murder of my informer, the attack on me . . . Sandra, the Monster has protection.'

Sandra felt a certain unease: Superintendent Crespi had assured her that Astolfi had nothing to do with the case, that what he had done must have been an act of madness, because nothing had emerged from a close examination of his life. Could he have lied to her? 'We have his DNA,' she found herself saying, without even knowing why. Or rather, she did know: Marcus was the only person she trusted.

'That won't help you catch him, believe me. We aren't dealing only with him. There are other forces at work in the shadows. Powerful forces.'

Sandra guessed that Marcus wanted something from her, otherwise he wouldn't have asked to see her.

'A friend once told me that to catch an evil person you have to understand how he loves.'

'Do you really think someone like that is capable of love?'

'Maybe not any more, but in the past, yes. This is a story about children, Sandra. If I can find the child of salt, I'll discover who or what he's become as an adult.'

'And what do you want me to do?'

'Cosmo Barditi, my informant who was killed . . . they tried to make it look like suicide. Which is credible because according to his partner he was heavily in debt. But I know that's not what happened.' Marcus felt himself seething, thinking that he was partly to blame. 'Someone took Barditi's mobile phone after killing him. Maybe because of the calls he made to get hold of this book. Clearly he met someone.'

Sandra wanted to know where he was going with all this. 'To get the phone records you need authorisation by a judge.'

Marcus looked at her. 'If you really want to help me, there's no other way.'

Sandra leaned on the banisters of the iron staircase. She felt as if she was trapped between two barriers slowly closing in on her like a vice. On one side there was what she was supposed to do, on the other what it was right to do. And she didn't know which to choose.

Marcus placed himself in front of her. 'I can stop him.'

Sandra was familiar with the inspector who had been assigned the investigation into the death of Barditi. She was sure that, being classed as a suicide, the case would soon be shelved.

She couldn't ask a favour of a colleague, even on a pretext. She was a photographer, she didn't have a valid excuse, and anyway he wouldn't believe her.

Even though it wasn't an important case, she couldn't get access to the file. The documentation was in the Headquarters database, and only the officers in charge of the case, plus the Prosecutor's Department that was handling the file, had the password.

In the course of the morning, Sandra left the operations room several times and went down to the floor below, where her colleague's office was situated. There, she would linger and chat with the other officers, just so that she could keep an eye on him.

The door of the room was always open, and she noticed that the inspector was in the habit of making notes on Post-its that he left scattered about his desk. She had an idea. She waited for him to go to lunch, then went and got her camera. She didn't have much time, someone might see her. When there was nobody in the corridors, she went into his office and took a series of photographs of the desk.

Back upstairs, she looked at them on her computer, trying to find something interesting. Her hope was that the inspector had noted down the password of the Barditi file in order not to forget it.

Sandra found a code on one of the Post-its. She typed it into the only terminal in the operations room that was linked to the Headquarters database, and out came the file.

She had to hurry. There was a risk that someone among those present might be suspicious. Fortunately, Moro and Crespi had been out for hours.

As she had predicted, the documentation on Cosmo Barditi was somewhat meagre. There were his previous convictions for drug-trafficking and living off immoral earnings, as well as his mugshots. Sandra felt a sense of unease at the sight of the swastika tattoo on Barditi's neck. She wondered how Marcus could have trusted him, because he seemed genuinely saddened by his death. Maybe it was only prejudice on her part, she was aware of that. Maybe Barditi had been better than he appeared, in spite of that symbol of hate he'd had stamped on himself.

Sandra preferred not to let her thoughts run away with her. She went back to the file and noticed that there was no request to the examining magistrate to obtain the dead man's phone records. She filled out the form, indicating high priority, and sent it. The inspector probably wouldn't even notice.

The Prosecutor's Department ratified the request and, around the middle of the afternoon, the telephone company finally sent her what she had requested.

Going through the long list of calls made by Barditi during the last day of his life, Sandra immediately noticed that the man had been very busy gathering information. The people the numbers were registered to all had criminal records. She didn't know how Marcus would find the person he was looking for, given that they were all suspicious. But then she noticed that one of the numbers recurred at least five times. She highlighted it, together with the corresponding name.

Half an hour later, as per instructions, the printout of the phone records and the criminal record of the man most often called by Cosmo Barditi were deposited in a collection box in the church of the Santi Apostoli.

9

Sandra Vega had kept her word. In fact, she had done much more. She had given him a name.

Nicola Gavi, though, was untraceable.

His mobile phone was switched off, and when Marcus paid a visit to his apartment he got the impression the man had been away from home for at least a few days.

Nicola Gavi was thirty-two years old, but according to his criminal record had spent much of that time, first in reform school, then in prison. He had a long series of offences to his name: drug-dealing, theft, armed robbery, grievous bodily harm.

Lately, to maintain his dependence on crack, he had prostituted himself.

Marcus enquired about the places where he solicited clients – clubs for men only, spots where male prostitutes hung out. Then he set about finding him, offering money in return for information. The last time that anyone had seen him around had been forty-eight hours earlier.

Marcus came to the conclusion that Gavi was either dead, or so afraid that he had gone into hiding.

He decided to go with the second hypothesis, partly because there was a way to verify it. If it really had been two days since the man had last been seen in the places he usually frequented, that meant he'd be running out of the drug and would soon need to come out in search of a fix.

Crack was the answer. Abstinence would flush him out, force him to run risks.

Marcus didn't think Nicola had any money to fall back on – he knew drug addicts, he knew that they spent their last penny shooting up. Not having worked for days, he would have to find a client to pay for a fix. Marcus could go back to the male prostitutes' haunts. In the end, though, there was only one place he would definitely go.

The Pigneto district was the kingdom of crack dealers. When darkness fell, Marcus started to scour the area in the hope of seeing him.

Around seven-thirty, when the evening air had turned colder, he had taken up a position not far from a street corner where a dealer was distributing his merchandise. Everything happened by sleight of hand. The junkies knew they shouldn't queue up in order not to be too conspicuous, so they orbited at a distance. It was easy to recognise them: they moved nervously, their eyes fixed on a single objective. Then, in turn, one of them would break away and approach the dealer, grab his fix and walk away.

Marcus noticed the arrival of a massively built man in a black sweatshirt. His head was covered with a hood and he had his hands in his pockets. In those temperatures, the light clothing made Marcus suspicious. He was dressed like someone who had been forced to leave home in a great hurry.

The man did the swap with the dealer and walked quickly away. As he looked around, Marcus saw the face beneath the hood.

It was Nicola Gavi.

He followed him, sure he wouldn't go far. Sure enough, Gavi slipped into a public toilet to consume the crack.

Marcus went in after him. No sooner had he crossed the threshold than he was overcome with the stench. The place was filthy, but Nicola had to make up for his abstinence. Sure enough, he had locked himself in one of the cubicles. Marcus waited. After a while, a puff of grey smoke appeared over the top of the cubicle. A few minutes passed, then the man came out. He walked to the one washbasin and started washing his hands.

Marcus was behind him, in a corner, watching, knowing that Gavi hadn't seen him. He hadn't been mistaken: the man had the muscles of a bodybuilder and, without his hood, his shaven head and sturdy neck were quite fearsome.

'Nicola.'

The man turned abruptly, and his eyes opened wide.

'I just want to talk to you,' Marcus said, raising his hands.

Finding himself confronted with an unknown face, Gavi leapt forward suddenly. With his bulk, he knocked Marcus aside, as if in a rugby tackle. Marcus felt the breath suddenly go out of him and he fell, hitting his back on the filthy floor, but also managed to reach out an arm and grab his assailant's calf, making him stumble.

Gavi collapsed to the ground with a dull thud, but, despite his size, he was very agile. He got back on his feet and landed a kick in Marcus's ribs. Marcus felt the full impact of it and his eyes clouded over. He would have liked to say something to stop him, but Gavi planted the sole of a large shoe on his head, then raised himself up, trying to crush him with all of his weight. Marcus found the strength to grab him by the calf with both hands and again make him lose his balance. This time, Gavi was sent crashing into one of the cubicle doors, which caved in.

Marcus tried to get up. He knew he didn't have much time. He heard Gavi's groans, but was conscious that he would recover soon and be on him again. Marcus pressed down with his hands on the dirty floor and pushed himself up. The bathroom seemed to sway around him. He somehow got back up on his feet, but his legs wouldn't support him. When at last he was more certain of his balance, he saw that Gavi had ended up on one of the toilet bowls. He had hit his huge head, and his forehead was covered in blood.

It was pure luck that Marcus had managed to neutralise him like this. Otherwise Gavi would have killed him, he was sure of it. Marcus approached the dazed giant and returned the kick to the ribs.

Gavi screamed like a little boy.

Marcus squatted beside him. 'When someone tells you they just want to talk to you, you should listen to them first, then hit them if you have to. Understand?'

Gavi nodded.

Marcus searched in his pocket and threw him a couple of fifty-euro banknotes. 'You can have more if you help me.'

Gavi nodded again, his eyes filling with tears.

'Cosmo Barditi,' Marcus said. 'He came to see you, didn't he?'

'That arsehole landed me in the shit.'

The statement confirmed Marcus's suspicions: Gavi was afraid someone would hurt him, that was why he had vanished. 'He's dead,' Marcus said, and saw the dismay and fear on Gavi's face.

Gavi was back by the washbasin, trying to dab the wound on his forehead with toilet paper. 'I heard that there was someone asking for information about a pervert who loved knives and photography. I immediately realised he was talking about this killer of couples. So I looked for the guy who was asking the questions, to get a bit of money out of him.'

Cosmo Barditi hadn't been cautious. He had gone around asking questions, but someone else apart from Gavi had had his ears pricked. Someone dangerous. 'You didn't know anything, did you?'

'No, but I could have made up a story about running into a client who resembled this sicko. I get a lot of weird people, trust me.'

'But Barditi didn't fall for it.'

'The bastard hit me.'

Marcus found that hard to believe, given Gavi's size and the treatment he had just meted out to him. 'And did it end there?'

'No.' Obviously, Nicholas's fear related to that. 'After a while, he mentioned the child of salt. That was when I remembered the old book I had at home. I told him about it and we started negotiating.'

That explained the telephone calls that Cosmo had made to him before he was killed.

'He paid me and I gave him the goods. Everybody satisfied.'

At this point, Gavi turned unexpectedly and pulled up his sweater to show his back: there was a large plaster near his right kidney. 'After we'd done the swap, someone tried to stab me. I got away only because I was bigger than him and I deflected his hand and ran away.'

Once again, someone had tried to cover up this business. At all costs.

But now Marcus had to ask the most important question. 'Why did Cosmo buy the book? What led him to think that it wasn't just a coincidence? That there was a connection with the child of salt?'

Gavi smiled. 'Because I convinced him.' On his face a pained expression appeared, but it was an old pain that had nothing to do with the wound on his forehead. 'There's nothing you can do: wherever you try to escape, your childhood follows you.'

Marcus realised he was talking about himself.

'Have you ever killed somebody you love?' Gavi said, smiling and shaking his head. 'I loved that bastard, but he knew right away that I wasn't like the other kids. And he'd hit me, trying to change something in me I hadn't yet understood completely myself.' He sniffed. 'So, one day I discovered where he hid his gun and I shot him while he was asleep. Goodnight, Daddy.'

Marcus felt profoundly sorry for him. 'But there's nothing about that in your record.'

Gavi let out a brief laugh. 'At the age of nine they don't put you in prison, they don't even put you on trial. They hand you over to the social services and slam you in one of those places where adults try to figure out why you did it and whether or not you'll do it again. Nobody really cares about saving you. They brainwash you, they pump you full of drugs and justify it by saying it's for your own good.'

'What's the name of the place?' Marcus asked, sensing the relevance to what he was looking for.

'The Kropp Institute,' Gavi said immediately, his face darkening. 'After I shot my father, someone called the police. They shut me up in a room with a psychologist, but we hardly said anything to each other. Then they came and took me away. It was night-time. When I asked where we were going, the officers said they couldn't tell me. What they did say was that I'd never get out of there, and I saw the smiles on their faces as they said it. But I wouldn't have tried to run away anyway, because I didn't know where else to go.'

Marcus saw a shadow pass over his face, as if the memory had materialised out of his words. He waited for him to continue.

'In the years I spent there, in the Institute, I never knew exactly where I was. As far as I was concerned, it could have been on the moon.' He paused. 'Ever since I left it, I've often wondered if it was all true or if I had only imagined it.'

That remark aroused Marcus's curiosity.

'You won't believe me,' Gavi said, laughing bitterly, before turning serious again. 'It was like living in a fairytale ... but without being able to get out.'

'Tell me about it.'

'There was this doctor, Professor Kropp, a psychiatrist, who had invented something he called "therapeutic fiction". Each patient was assigned a character and a story, according to their particular mental condition. I was the child of glass, because I was fragile but dangerous. Then there was a child of dust, one of straw, one of wind—'

'And the child of salt?' Marcus asked.

'In the story, he was more intelligent than other children but, for that very reason, everyone avoided him. He made food inedible, he made plants and flowers dry up. It was as if he destroyed everything he touched.'

A troublesome intelligence, Marcus thought. 'What was wrong with him?'

'Everything,' Gavi said. 'Sexual disorders, latent aggression, well-developed skills of deception. All combined with a very high IQ.'

A description that fitted the Monster well, Marcus thought. Was it really possible that Gavi had known him when they were younger? Given that someone had tried to shut him up with a knife, that might indeed be the case. 'Who *was* the child of salt?'

'I remember him well,' Gavi said, raising his hopes. 'He was Kropp's favourite. Brown eyes and hair, rather ordinary-looking. He was about eleven, but he'd already been there for a while when I got there. Shy, withdrawn, always absorbed in his own thoughts. He was puny, you'd think the others would have bullied him, and yet they let him be. They were scared of him. We were all scared of him. I can't explain why, we just were.'

'What was his name?'

Gavi shook his head. 'I'm sorry, friend: none of us knew each other's real names, it was part of the therapy. Before they put you with the others, you spent quite a bit of time alone, while Kropp and his colleagues persuaded you to forget who you were before and to wipe the crime you had committed from your memory. I think they did that because their aim was to rebuild the person inside the child, starting from scratch. I didn't remember my name or what I'd done to my father until I was sixteen and I heard a judge read out my real name in front of everyone, the day he ruled that I could go back to the real world.'

It seemed to Marcus that he had enough information now. But there was one last thing he needed to clarify. 'Who are you running away from, Nicola?'

Gavi turned on the tap to wash his hands. 'As I said, the child of salt scared everyone – and I mean, there were dangerous people in there, kids who'd committed horrible crimes without thinking twice. I wouldn't be surprised if that child who seemed so fragile and helpless was out there now, hurting people.' He looked at Marcus in the mirror. 'Maybe you should be afraid of him too. But he wasn't the one who stabbed me.'

'So you saw his face?'

'He came up behind me. But he had hands like an old man, I can be sure of that. The other thing I noticed is that he was wearing these horrible blue shoes.'

10

Astolfi's apartment had been dubbed Site 23.

The reason was that it was the latest in a series. That was what Moro was explaining to the secret meeting held late that evening in the Commissioner's office.

The participants were a select few. Apart from the Com missioner, those sitting around the table were an official from the Ministry of the Interior, the Director of the State Police, a representative of the Prosecutor's Department, and Superintendent Crespi.

'Twenty-three cases,' Moro said. 'The first dates from 1987. A boy of three thrown from the fifth-floor balcony of a tower block. Believed to be a tragic accident. A few months later, the same thing happened to a slightly younger girl, from a building in the same area. Both times, there was something strange: the bodies were missing their right shoe. What had happened to it? They hadn't lost it during the fall and, according to the parents, it was nowhere to be found in the apartment. Was it just coincidence? A girl who worked as a babysitter for both families was arrested. The two shoes turned up among her things, along with a diary that contained this.'

Moro showed those present the photocopy of a page from an

exercise book. The anthropomorphic figure from the shadow in Astolfi's apartment. The man with the wolf's head.

'The girl confesses she threw the two children from their balconies, but she can't explain the origin of this drawing. She says she wasn't the one who drew it. But given that she's confessed, the investigation stops there. Nobody looks any further into the question of the drawing, partly because the investigators are afraid it may be a pretext for the defence to claim insanity.'

The small audience were following the story attentively. Nobody had the courage to interrupt.

'After that,' Moro continued, 'the figure appears, directly or indirectly, twenty-two more times. In 1994, it is found in an apartment where a man has just killed his wife and children before killing himself. The police don't spot it immediately, it's Forensics who discover it in the course of a supplementary investigation requested by the magistrate to establish whether the man acted alone or with an accomplice. The chemical reagents show it up on the bathroom mirror where it had been drawn in the condensation, nobody's sure when.' Moro took from his papers the photograph that had been taken at that time. But he hadn't finished yet. 'We also found it in spray paint on the grave of a paedophile murdered in prison by another inmate in 2005. The curious thing is that the gravestone, by order of the authorities, who feared acts of vandalism or revenge, had no name on it. Nobody knew the identity of the dead man. Is that also coincidence?'

None of those present had an answer to that.

'I could keep you here for another hour, but the truth is, the story of this recurring image has been kept secret to avoid copycats. Someone might have been inspired to commit a crime and sign it with the same figure.'

'One of our own people involved, a pathologist: what a mess,' the Commissioner said, reminding them all of the gravity of the discovery made in Astolfi's apartment.

'Do you think there's a connection between this figure and the killer of young couples?' asked the official from the Ministry, the highest-ranking person in the room.

'There has to be a link, even though we don't yet know what it is.'

'What do you think this sign is?'

Moro knew that answering was risky, but he felt he had no choice. The truth had been avoided for too long. 'Some kind of occult symbol.'

At this point the Director of the State Police spoke up. 'Gentlemen, please. I wouldn't like to be misunderstood, but I think we should be very cautious. This "Monster of Rome" business is already causing a lot of controversy. Public opinion is volatile right now, nobody feels safe, and the media are making things worse and constantly trying to show us in a bad light.'

'It takes time to get results in a case like this,' Superintendent Crespi said.

'I'm aware of that, but this is a delicate matter. People are simple and practical. They don't want to pay too much tax and they want to be sure that what they do pay is being properly used to capture criminals. They want immediate answers, and they don't care how an investigation is carried out.'

The official from the Ministry agreed. 'If we concentrate too much on this occult stuff and it gets out, the media will say we have nothing to go on and that's why we're going after evil spirits and rubbish like that. We'll be a laughing stock.'

Moro listened to the debate in silence, because he knew this was precisely the reason why in the past nobody had wanted to delve deeper into the matter. Their fear wasn't just that they might seem ridiculous: there were other factors. No policeman who wanted to make a name for himself would ever follow a lead connected with the occult: the risk was that it would lead nowhere, the investigation would get bogged down, and his own career would be compromised. In addition, no high-ranking official would authorise such an investigation: in their case, the risk was that they would lose credibility and authority. But there was a more human factor, a natural reluctance to confront certain subjects. Maybe the inadmissible, irrational fear that there might be some truth in it. That was why they had always dropped it. And that had been a mistake.

Right now, though, Moro didn't feel up to rocking the boat, so he agreed with his superiors. 'I share your worries, gentlemen. I assure you we'll take them on board.'

The Commissioner stood up from the table and went to the window. Outside a storm was gathering. Lightning flashes lit up the night horizon, warning the city of the imminent arrival of rain. 'We have the killer's DNA, don't we? Let's concentrate on that. We'll catch him and forget all this other business.'

Crespi felt himself implicated. 'We've summoned all the criminals with records for sexual crimes and attacks. We're taking saliva samples from all of them and matching the genetic profiles, hoping that one corresponds. But it won't be a short operation.'

The Commissioner struck the wall with his hand. 'It has to be, dammit! Or else this investigation is going to cost us millions of euros: we're talking about more than twenty thousand cases in Rome alone, and that's just in the past year!'

Sexual crimes were the most common crimes of all, even though the number was kept secret to avoid some pervert thinking he could go unpunished.

'If I'm not mistaken,' the official from the Ministry said, summing up what had happened, 'the DNA found on the shirt left in the car at the first crime scene has confirmed only that we are dealing with a male. No genetic anomaly that could point to a particular kind of person, is that correct?'

'Yes, it is,' Crespi admitted. But all those present knew perfectly well that the Italian police kept only the genetic data of those who had committed crimes in which it had been necessary to carry out a DNA test to track down the culprit. Most criminals, when they were arrested, were only fingerprinted. 'So far the search hasn't yielded any results.'

While the others had gone back to discussing the more manageable aspects of the investigation, Moro was continuing to think of the shadow he had seen on the wall inside that secret space in Astolfi's apartment. The man with the wolf's head was an idea nobody in this room wanted to deal with. He thought again of the sculpture of animal bones constructed by the pathologist. The patience it must have taken to put it all together! That was why, if it had been merely a question of a killer of young couples, Moro might have felt more at ease. But there was something else, something truly terrible behind the case of the Monster of Rome.

Something that nobody wanted to hear about.

Batista Erriaga stood at the window of his modest hotel room, holding a photograph. For a moment, the lightning from the coming storm lit up the image of the bone sculpture found in Astolfi's apartment.

On the bed, the entire case file of the investigation into the Monster of Rome lay scattered. His 'friend' Tommaso Oghi had got it for him, as requested. It even included confidential documents.

Erriaga was worried.

The first level of the secret was the child of salt. The second, the man with the wolf's head. The investigators would need to understand the meaning of the first two to get to the third.

Erriaga tried to find reassurance in that. It'll never happen, he told himself. But in his head he could hear the voice of Min, his giant friend, telling him that in fact the police were getting dangerously close to the truth. For years, the wise Min had taken the place of that part of his conscience that considered the worst-case scenarios. The same part of himself that, when he was young, he had chosen systematically to ignore. But the days of the Philippines were over, and he was another person now. So he was duty-bound to take notice of his own fears.

According to the papers contained in the file, the investigators had very little to go on. There was the matter of the killer's DNA, but that didn't bother Erriaga. They would never capture the Monster with science alone. The police didn't know how to look at things.

That was why the only thing that disturbed him was the symbol that had appeared once again in the context of a violent crime. They'll stop the way they did all the other times, he told himself. Because, even if they were to discover the truth, they wouldn't be prepared to admit it.

The real problem, though, was Deputy Commissioner Moro. He was as stubborn as a mule, he wouldn't stop until he got to the bottom of the whole business.

The man with the wolf's head.

Erriaga couldn't allow that symbol to be deciphered. But as the rain began falling outside, he was struck by a premonition.

If it was, what would happen?

11

Officially, the Kropp Institute did not exist.

It had to be a secret, this place where children who had killed were taken. Nobody would ever call them murderers, but that was what they were, Marcus thought.

'*It was like living in a fairytale . . . but without being able to get out.*' That was how Nicola Gavi had described it.

There was no trace of a psychiatric institute for minors anywhere. No address, not even a fleeting mention on the internet, where even the most confidential information almost always left some kind of trace.

Nor was there much about Joseph Kropp, the Austrian-born doctor who had set up that place to deal with young people who had committed terrible crimes, crimes of whose gravity they themselves were often unaware.

Kropp was mentioned as the author of some publications on the development of guilt at an early age and the ability of pre-adolescents to commit crimes. But there was nothing else: no biography, not even his professional CV.

The only clue that Marcus had managed to dig up was in an article in praise of the educational value of fairytales.

Marcus was convinced that the reason for so much secrecy

was the desire to protect the privacy of the Institute's young inmates. The public's morbid curiosity could well jeopardise their chances of recovery. But the place couldn't be completely unknown. There must have been suppliers who'd provided it with what it needed; there must have been tax documents that proved these activities, authorisations. And staff must have worked there, hired in the normal way, paid regular salaries. So maybe the one plausible explanation was that it had had a different name, a cover name, that let it go unnoticed.

That was how Marcus had come across the Hamelin Institute for Child Assistance.

Hamelin: the name of the town in the fairytale, in which the Pied Piper had appeared one day. According to the tale, he had first used his pipe to liberate the inhabitants from a plague of rats, and then lured away all the town's children as revenge for not being paid.

It was a strange choice, Marcus thought. There was nothing pleasant about that fairytale.

The Hamelin Institute was located in a small early twentieth-century building in the southwest of the city, surrounded by grounds, which, briefly visible in the lightning flashes, showed signs of neglect. The grey stone building was not very large and consisted of just two floors. The windows at the front had been covered with panels of dark wood. Everything was in an obvious state of abandonment.

In the rain, Marcus looked at the house from outside the rusty iron gate. He thought again of Nicola Gavi's rough description of the child of salt. Brown hair and eyes, ordinary-looking. Puny and introverted, but nevertheless capable of instilling a strange fear. Why had he been there? What had he done that was so serious? The answers might well be in that building. At that hour of the night, the place repelled the inquisitive with its grim but also melancholy appearance. Like a child's secret.

Marcus couldn't wait.

He climbed over the gate, landing on a carpet of both wet and dry leaves. The wind was shifting from one side to the other of the grounds, like the spirits of children playing catch. In the rain, their laughter could be heard as part of the rustling.

Marcus walked to the front door.

The lower part of the façade was covered with spray-painted graffiti, a further sign of the neglect of the place. The front door was barred with planks of wood. So Marcus went around the building, looking for a way in. The panel of one of the windows on the ground floor had an opening. He climbed on to a cornice made slippery by the constant rain, gripped the windowsill to hoist himself up, taking care not to slip, and slid in through the narrow opening.

He found himself on the inside, dripping water on the floor. First of all, he searched in his pocket for his torch and turned it on. In front of him was a kind of refectory. Some thirty-four Formica chairs, all identical, around low circular tables. The very tidy arrangement clashed with the abandoned appearance of the place. It was as if the chairs and tables were still waiting for someone.

Marcus climbed down from the windowsill and shone his torch on the floor. The bricks were a mosaic of faded colours. He set off to explore the other rooms.

They were all alike. Maybe because, apart from the carcasses of a few items of furniture, they were empty. There were no doors and the walls were white, where the plaster hadn't come away because of the damp. There was a persistent odour of mould and the dripping of the rain coming in echoed through the building. The Institute was like the wreck of an ocean liner at the mercy of a storm.

Marcus's footsteps added a new sound to this setting – sad, solitary steps like those of a guest who had arrived too late. He wondered what had happened to this place, what curse had struck it that it should end up in such an undignified state.

At the same time, he could feel a strange vibration. Once again, he was very close to the truth. He was here, he said to himself, thinking of the shadowy figure he had spotted at the party on the Appia Antica. His path passed through this place many years before crossing mine that night.

He began to climb the stairs that led to the upper floor. The steps looked precarious, as if the slightest pressure would be enough to make them collapse. He stopped on the landing. A short corridor stretched on either side. He started to explore the rooms.

Rusty bunk beds, a few broken chairs. There was also a large bathroom, with matching showers and a changing room. Marcus's attention, however, was drawn to a room that was at the far end. He crossed the threshold and found himself in a room that was different from the others. The walls were covered with a kind of wallpaper.

All around him were scenes from famous fairytales.

He recognised Hansel and Gretel in front of the gingerbread house. Snow White. Cinderella at the ball. Red Riding Hood with her basket of food. The Little Match Girl. These characters seemed to have come out of a faded old book. But there was something strange about them. Running the beam of his torch over them, Marcus realised what it was.

There was no joy on their faces.

Nobody was smiling as they might have been expected to do in a fairytale. The feeling you got from looking at them was one of unease and turmoil.

A peal of thunder louder than the others. Marcus needed to leave the room. But, as he did so, he stepped on something, felt it through the sole of his shoe. He lowered the torch and saw drops of wax on the floor. They were in a neat line and led outside. Marcus picked up the trail in the corridor. It led downstairs. He decided to follow it.

It led him to a narrow space under the stairs, where the wax trail ended in front of a small wooden door. Whoever had ventured as far as this with a candle in his hand had gone beyond. Marcus tried the handle. It was open.

He aimed the torch. In front of him there was a maze of little rooms and corridors. He calculated that they occupied a much larger space than the two floors above, as if the building were actually submerged in the ground and the visible section was only a small part of it.

He carried on. The drops of wax were the only way to orientate yourself down here. Without them, he would certainly have got lost. On the ground, instead of bricks, there was rubble. And he could smell a strong odour of kerosene which, most likely, came from the old boilers.

Down here was where the furniture of the former Institute was piled up. There were mattresses rotting in the darkness and items of furniture silently worn away by damp. The basement was like an enormous stomach slowly digesting them until every trace disappeared.

But there were also lots of toys. Dolls with springs corroded by rust, little cars, a rocking horse, wooden buildings, a teddy bear with its fur rubbed away but with two bright eyes. Hamelin had been halfway between a prison and a psychiatric hospital, but these objects reminded Marcus that it was also a place for children.

After a while, the wax trail led to one of the rooms. Marcus shone the torch inside. He couldn't believe it.

It was an archive.

The room was cluttered with filing cabinets and piles of files.

They were heaped up along the walls and filled the centre of the room, all the way up to the ceiling, in a state of total chaos.

Marcus moved his torch closer to read the labels on the drawers. Each one bore a date. Thanks to these, he was able to deduce that the Hamelin Institute had been in operation for fifteen years. Then, for some obscure reason, it had closed down.

Marcus started examining the documents, taking them out at random, convinced that he would only need a brief look to know if they were of any interest. But after reading a few lines taken at random from a couple of files he realised that what he had in front of him, in this disordered form, wasn't a mere archive of medical records and bureaucratic papers.

It was the diary of Professor Joseph Kropp.

Here were the answers to all his questions. But it was precisely the vastness of this storehouse of information that was the major obstacle to the search for the truth. Without any logical yardstick, Marcus had to trust to the chaos. He started looking through Kropp's notebooks.

Just like adults, minors possess a natural propensity to kill, the psychiatrist had written, *which usually manifests itself in puberty. Adolescents, for example, are responsible for many cold-blooded school massacres using firearms. There are also young people who join gangs and commit murders, secure in the knowledge that they belong to a group.*

But Kropp went further, analysing the phenomenon of homicides occurring at an age of innocence and purity of soul.

Childhood.

12

In its fifteen years of life, some thirty children had passed through the Hamelin Institute.

The crime was always the same. Murder. Although not all had actually committed murder. Some, in fact, had merely manifested 'marked homicidal tendencies' or had been stopped before they could achieve their aim, or hadn't succeeded.

Considering the age of the criminals, thirty was a large number. The account of what they had done was not accompanied by photographs, and there were no first names.

Each child's identity was concealed by a fairytale.

Children are crueller than adults when they kill: innocence is their mask, Joseph Kropp wrote. *When they arrive here, they seem completely unaware of the gravity of what they have done or were about to do. But the innocence of their behaviour can be deceptive. Think, for example, of a child who tortures a little insect. The adult will admonish him but will think of it as a game, because minors are not considered capable of fully understanding the difference between right and wrong. Part of the child, though, knows that what he is doing is wrong, and feels an obscure sadistic pleasure.*

Marcus started reading at random.

The child of straw was twelve years old and didn't have

feelings. His mother – a single parent – had entrusted him to an uncle and aunt because she couldn't take care of him. One day, in an amusement park, he had met a five-year-old boy and, taking advantage of the little boy's babysitter being distracted, had persuaded him to follow him to an abandoned building site. There, he had led him to the edge of a cistern several yards deep and pushed him in. The younger child had broken both legs, but had not died immediately. Over the next two days, while everyone was busy searching, certain that he had been abducted by an adult, the true culprit had gone back several times to the building site and had sat down on the edge of the cistern to listen to the crying and calls for help coming from below – like a fly trapped in a jar. On the third day, the moans had ceased.

The child of dust was seven. For a long time he had been an only child, and that was why he hadn't accepted the arrival of a little brother – a hostile stranger who interrupted the chain of family affections. One day, taking advantage of his mother being busy, he had taken the baby from the crib, carried it to the bathroom, and immersed it in a tub full of water. The mother had found him impassively watching his little brother drowning and had managed to save the baby at the last moment. Even faced with the evidence, the child of dust had always stated that it hadn't been him.

According to Kropp, these crimes were sometimes carried out in a dissociative mental state. *During the act a genuine flight from reality occurs, in which the victim is perceived, not as a human being but as an object. This explains the amnesia that often follows the crime, with the young culprit unable to remember what he has done or to feel any pity or remorse.*

Marcus understood why the authorities kept quiet about these cases. It was a taboo. To divulge these stories would have been too disturbing. That was why special courts had been set up, why the documents were confidential and everything was wrapped in secrecy.

There were three children of wind, all ten years old. Their victim was a man of fifty, a sales representative with a wife and two children, who had been driving home along the highway on a normal winter's evening. The windscreen of his car had been hit by a stone thrown from a flyover and had punctured his cranium, leaving a deep hole where his face had been. The three young culprits had been identified in the footage from a security camera placed above the bridge. Apparently, they had been playing their deadly game for several weeks. They had damaged a number of vehicles, without anyone spotting them.

The child of fire was eight years old. When he had burnt his arm with a firecracker, his parents had assumed it was an accident, whereas the truth was that he had been experimenting with the mysterious power of the flame – there was something sweet deep inside that pain. For some time, he had had his eyes on a homeless man who spent his nights in an abandoned car in a car park. He had set fire to the vehicle with a jerry can of petrol stolen from his father's garage. The homeless man had been left with serious burns on seventy per cent of his body.

In commenting on these crimes, Joseph Kropp was not indulgent, but tried to bring out the deeper motives. *Many wonder how a child, a human being considered pure in himself, can perform an act as inhuman as murder and yet, unlike homicides carried out by adults in which two protagonists can be distinguished, the murderer and the victim, in those that involve children the murderer himself is a victim. Usually of a father who is either absent or punitive or not very affectionate. Or else of a dominant or unemotional mother, or one who makes sexual advances to her son. A child who suffers abuse or violence in the family, who is despised by his parents, basically feels guilty for this, and thinks he deserves mistreatment. That is why he chooses someone the same age as him, someone vulnerable and defenceless, and kills him, because he has learned that the weakest must always succumb. In reality, in this way the young murderer is punishing himself and his own inability to react to humiliation.*

That was the case in the story of the child of pewter, mistreated from an early age by both his parents, who took out their own frustrations on him. The two of them were too well respected among their acquaintances to arouse suspicion. In the eyes of strangers, their only son was awkward or simply unfortunate because he was constantly having 'little accidents' that resulted in bruises and fractures. Until that solitary child found a close friend. That relationship had been a positive thing in his life and he had started to be happy and to feel like everyone else. And yet one day he had lured his little friend into the basement of his grandmother's house, tied him up and broken the bones of his legs and arms with a heavy hammer. Then he had taken a blade and slashed him in several places. Finally he had perforated his stomach with a sharpened piece of iron – 'I had to do it because he wouldn't die.'

Marcus, who because of his amnesia knew nothing of his previous life, including his childhood, was forced to wonder when exactly, as a child, he had understood the meaning of right and wrong, and if he too had been capable of such ruthless detachment when he was small. But he had no way of answering the question. So he started again to search for the story that interested him the most.

But among the papers there was still no mention of the child of salt or of the crime he had committed. Marcus looked again at the cabinets and the heaps of documents he had around him. The search would take a long time. He shone his torch around the room, hoping that something would leap out at him. He stopped in front of the half-open drawer of a wooden desk. Looking closer, he saw it was full of old videocassettes. He pulled them out – even though something inside resisted – placed them on the floor and bent down to check the contents.

Each cassette had a label on the spine – 'Aggressive psychosis', 'Antisocial personality disorder', 'Mental backwardness aggravated by violence'. There were at least thirty of them.

Marcus started to check if among the various conditions there was one that might correspond to Nicola Gavi's description of the child of salt: sexual disorders, latent aggression, well-developed skills of deception, very high IQ. He was concentrating so much on this that the torch fell from his hands and on to the floor. When he leaned forward to pick it up, he noticed that the beam of light was pointing to something in a corner.

There on the ground was a mattress, a heap of rags and a chair pushed up against the wall on which stood some candles and a camping stove. He immediately thought of a tramp's makeshift bed, but then he noticed something else at the foot of the chair.

A pair of blue shoes.

He didn't have time to react because he felt something creeping behind him. He moved the torch to shine on it. It was an old man.

He had hair as white as moonlight and very deep blue eyes. The lines on his face made it look like a wax mask. He was looking at Marcus with a strange smile on his lips.

Marcus stood up slowly. But the old man wasn't moving. He was hiding one hand behind his back.

It was the same man who had killed Cosmo Barditi, stabbed Nicola Gavi and hit him on the back of his head in the villa on the Appia Antica. And Marcus was unarmed.

The old man finally revealed what he was hiding.

A small blue plastic cigarette lighter.

With this he made an inverted sign of the cross and ran off into the darkness.

Marcus tried to find him with the torch and saw only a figure quickly leaving the room. After a moment's hesitation, he went after him, but as soon as he got out into the corridor he noticed that the smell of kerosene from the old boilers had suddenly become stronger. A little flame rose from somewhere in that labyrinth. The glow of it was clearly visible.

Marcus vacillated. He had to get away immediately, or he would be trapped here and burnt alive. But part of him knew that, if he left without an answer, there would be no other way to stop the evil that was plaguing Rome. So, conscious of the risk he was running, he retraced his steps to the archive.

He threw himself at the pile of videocassettes he had been examining, picked them up one by one, and quickly discarded those that didn't interest him. Until one attracted his attention.

The label said: 'Psychopathic savant'. Marcus slipped it under his jacket and ran out to the exit.

The basement corridors all looked the same, and were rapidly filling with dense, acrid smoke. Marcus had covered his mouth and nose with his collar and was trying to remember the way that he had come, but it was really hard. The beam of light from the torch was now coming up against a black wall of soot.

He went down on all fours in order to breathe more easily. He felt the heat increasing around him, the flames following him, besieging him. He looked up and noticed that the smoke was going in one direction, as if it had found a way out. So he got back on his feet and followed it.

He was groping his way, forced every now and again to stop and lean against the wall to cough. But, after what seemed an interminable length of time, at last he found the stairs leading to the ground floor. He started climbing, the fire almost enveloping him.

Reaching the ground floor, he realised that the smoke would

soon overrun this too. So he couldn't go out the way he had come in: he might die of suffocation just a few steps from salvation, which struck him as absurd. If he wanted to get out of here alive, he realised, he had to go upstairs and deceive the smoke by preceding it.

He found himself again on the first floor and, with the little breath he had, managed to get to the room where the walls were covered with scenes from fairytales. The heat, though, had got there before him and it was unbearable: the wallpaper with the drawings was starting to peel away from the walls.

Marcus sensed that he didn't have much time, so he started to kick at the wooden panel across the window. One, two, three kicks, while the glow of the flames could already be seen in the corridor. At last, the panel yielded, falling out into the grounds. Marcus grabbed hold of the windowsill and was about to follow it into the darkness of the storm when, behind the peeling wallpaper, a figure appeared. An imposing figure, rising like a menacing shadow.

A man who wasn't human. He had empty eyes and the head of a wolf.

13

The rain that had been beating down on Rome all night was a vague memory the morning after.

A pale sun flooded the basilica of San Paolo fuori le Mura, second in size only to St Peter's.

It housed the tomb of the apostle Paul who, according to tradition, had suffered martyrdom by beheading just a short distance from there. It was situated on the left bank of the Tiber, beyond the Aurelian Walls, hence its name, 'outside the walls'. It was often used for solemn ceremonies, such as state funerals. Right now it was where the funerals of Pia Rimonti and Stefano Carboni, the officers brutally murdered by the Monster of Rome two nights earlier, were taking place.

The church was packed, and it was impossible to get in. Among the mourners were high-ranking police officers and representatives of various authorities. But many ordinary citizens had also come to pay tribute to the victims of a terrible crime.

Beneath the portico of the basilica were all the crews covering the event for national television. Outside the entrance, the police guard of honour in dress uniform stood ready to pay a last tribute to the coffins.

Sandra had stayed outside together with many of her colleagues and was watching everything with a feeling of resignation, and the certainty that the killer must be enjoying the spectacle being staged thanks to him.

She was in plain clothes and had a small digital camera with her, with which she was photographing those present. Other police photographers mingling with the crowd inside and outside the basilica were doing the same. They were on the lookout for anyone behaving suspiciously. The hope was that the killer had decided to be present at the service to savour the intoxication of still being free and unpunished.

He isn't that stupid, Sandra told herself. He isn't here.

The last time she had attended a funeral was when her husband had died. But her thoughts of that long-ago day had nothing to do with the pain of the loss. As she had followed David's funeral, she hadn't been able to get it out of her mind that she was officially a widow. A word that didn't suit her, especially at her young age. It was the word that bothered her. Nobody had yet used it in her presence, but she couldn't avoid seeing herself that way.

Until she had solved the mystery of the death of the man she had loved, she hadn't got rid of that title. Nor of his disquieting presence. Nobody ever admits it, she thought, but the deaths of the people we love sometimes pursue us like debts that are impossible to pay. That was why she still remembered the sense of liberation she had felt when she had let her David go.

But she had needed more time to accept that another man could enter her life. A different love, and a totally different way of loving. Another toothbrush in the bathroom, a new smell on the pillow next to hers.

Yet now she was no longer sure of Max, and she didn't know how to tell him. And the more she tried to convince herself that he was the right man, and to remind herself how perfect he was, the more the need to put an end to everything grew in her.

These thoughts were all the stronger now, on the day of her colleague Pia Rimonti's funeral. What would have happened if she had been the one in that car used as a bait to capture the monster? What images, what regrets would have occupied her mind in the last moments of her life?

Sandra was afraid of answering her own question. But maybe it was thanks to these troublesome thoughts that, as she looked through the camera to photograph a small group of people, she realised that included in the frame was Pia's boyfriend Ivan, who for some strange reason was hurrying away from the basilica before the end of the funeral.

Sandra followed him with her eyes and saw him walk all the way along the portico, turn into a side street and walk to a parked car. Even at that distance, he seemed upset. Maybe he had been unable to bear the grief and had run away. But before reaching the car, he made a gesture that struck Sandra.

He angrily took his mobile phone from his jacket pocket and threw it into a litter bin.

Sandra recalled Marcus's words about anomalies. And this was certainly anomalous behaviour. She hesitated for a moment, then decided to go and talk to the man.

Before these tragic events, she had only seen him once, waiting for Pia at the end of her shift. But in the last two days he had come often to Headquarters. He seemed unable to rest because of what had happened: he felt somehow responsible for not having protected his woman.

'Hi,' Sandra said. 'You're Ivan, aren't you?'

He turned to look at her. 'Yes, I am.'

'My name is Sandra Vega, I'm a colleague of Pia's.' She felt obliged to tell him why she had approached him. 'It isn't easy, I know. I went through it a couple of years ago when my husband died.'

'I'm sorry,' were his only words, maybe because he didn't know what else to say.

'I saw you run out of the church.' Sandra noticed that, as she said this, Ivan instinctively looked at the litter bin into which he had just thrown his mobile phone.

'Yes . . . I really couldn't stand it.'

Sandra had been wrong, there was no pain or anger in his voice. He was simply in a hurry. 'We'll get him,' she said. 'He won't go unpunished. We always catch them in the end.'

'I know you will,' Ivan said, but without conviction, as if he didn't really care.

His tone and attitude clashed with the idea of him she had had up until that moment: the boyfriend who wanted justice at all costs. Now, Sandra had the impression he was trying to hide something. Partly because he carried on throwing fleeting glances at the litter bin.

'Can I ask you why you left the funeral?'

'I already told you.'

'The real reason,' she insisted.

'It's none of your business,' he replied angrily.

Sandra stood looking at him in silence for a few seconds which to him, she was sure, must have seemed interminable. 'All right, I'm sorry,' she said before walking away. 'I'm sorry for what you're going through.'

'Wait . . . '

Sandra stopped in her tracks and turned.

'Did you know Pia well?' he asked, his tone quite different now, sadder.

'Not as well as I would have liked.'

'There's a bar near here.' He looked down at his shoes, then added, 'Do you mind if we talk a little?'

At first, Sandra did not know what to say.

'I'm not hitting on you,' he said, raising his hands as if in apology. 'But I need to tell someone . . .'

Sandra looked at him closely: whatever burden he was carrying inside him, he deserved to have someone help him get free of it. Maybe it was easier with a stranger. 'I have to finish my shift. You go ahead, I'll join you later.'

Another hour passed before Sandra managed to get away. All the time, she had kept wondering what his burden was and whether it was heavier than hers: the things she didn't have the courage to tell Max. Then, as promised, she joined him in the bar.

She found him sitting at a table, he had ordered a strong drink. As soon as he saw her he seemed to come awake again, a strange expectation in his eyes.

Sandra sat down facing him. 'So, what's going on?'

Ivan rolled his eyes as if searching for words. 'I'm a bastard. A real bastard. But I did love her.'

She wondered why on earth he had begun in that way, but she let him talk without intervening.

'Pia was a lovely person, she would never have hurt me. She said our relationship was more important to her than anything else. She was waiting for me to ask her to marry me. But I ruined everything . . .'

Sandra noticed that Ivan couldn't look her in the eyes. She reached out a hand and placed it on his. 'If you didn't love her any more, that's not your fault.'

'I *did* love her,' he said emphatically. 'But the night she died I was cheating on her.'

Sandra was startled by that revelation. Slowly, she withdrew her hand.

'I was having an affair with another woman. It had been going on for a while. And it wasn't even the first.'

'I don't think I should be hearing this.'

'Oh, I think you should.' He seemed to be begging her. 'The other night, when I found out that Pia was on duty and couldn't call me, I took the chance to see that other woman.'

'Seriously, that's enough.' She had no wish to hear the rest.

'You're a policewoman, aren't you? Then you should stay and listen to me.'

Sandra was confused by his attitude, but let him continue.

'I didn't say it before because I was afraid they would think I'm a rat. What would our friends have said about me, or her parents? And all the others? This case has been on television. All the people who don't know me would have felt entitled to judge me. I've been a coward.'

'What haven't you said?'

Ivan stared at her, his eyes full of fear, and Sandra was afraid he might start crying.

'That I received a call from Pia's phone the night she died.'

Sandra felt a shiver run up her legs to her spine. It wasn't true that the Monster hadn't left anything for them at the second crime scene. There was something. 'What are you saying?'

He searched in his pocket, took out a mobile phone and placed it on the table. In all probability, it was the one she had seen him throw away a little earlier. He pushed it slowly towards her. 'It was off,' he said. 'But then I found a message on the voicemail.'

14

He had taken refuge in a safe house, one of the many Vatican properties scattered throughout Rome. They were usually empty apartments in perfectly ordinary buildings. In case of necessity, you could find food there, medicines, a bed to rest in, a computer linked to the internet and, above all, a telephone with a secure connection.

The previous night, Marcus had used it to call Clemente, telling him that he needed to talk to him.

Clemente appeared about eleven in the morning. When Marcus opened the door it was like seeing his own reflection in a mirror, because it was clear from Clemente's face what impression his own appearance made.

'Who did that to you?'

Marcus had suffered a cranial trauma the night of the party in the villa in the Via Appia Antica, then he'd been attacked by Nicola Gavi, and, last but not least, he'd escaped a fire by the skin of his teeth by throwing himself out of a window. There were grazes on his face from the fall, and he was still having difficulty breathing because of all the soot he'd inhaled.

'It's nothing,' he said as he greeted Clemente, who had brought a black trolley suitcase with him. They went to the one furnished room in the apartment, and sat down on the edge of the unmade bed on which Marcus had been trying to sleep – unsuccessfully – for the past few hours.

'You should be seen by a doctor,' Clemente said, parking the suitcase next to him.

'I took a couple of aspirins, that should be enough.'

'Have you at least eaten something?'

Marcus didn't reply – right now, his friend's concern was getting on his nerves.

'Are you still angry with me?' Clemente was referring to the investigation into the murder in the Vatican gardens.

'I don't want to talk about it,' Marcus said immediately. But every time they met he saw again the image of the nun's dismembered body.

'You're right,' Clemente said. 'We have to deal with the Monster of Rome. That's more urgent than anything else.'

He was trying to seem resolute, and Marcus decided to indulge him.

'The murder of the two police officers followed the attack in the pine wood at Ostia by a couple of days,' Clemente said. 'Two more days have gone by. If the killer is following a specific programme he should have struck last night.'

'But last night it rained.'

'What of it?'

'The child of salt, remember? He's afraid of water.'

The idea had occurred to him the previous night, as he was running away from the Hamelin Institute in the rain. The compulsion to repeat his killings, characteristic of serial killers, was dictated by specific stages. Imagination, projection, action. All the same, after having struck, a killer usually managed to satisfy his predatory urges with memories, which could guarantee him a sense of appeasement for more or less long periods. In this case, though, the very short interval between the two attacks indicated that the killer had a very precise plan in mind. And that the deaths that had occurred were only the first stages in a journey whose ultimate destination was still obscure.

The impulse to kill, in other words, wasn't triggered by need, but by a purpose.

Whatever his objective was, the Monster of Rome was respecting the role he had assigned to himself. The message he was trying to communicate was that the child of salt from the Hamelin Institute had not in fact been cured of his condition. Rather, he had sublimated it.

'He's following a script,' Marcus stated. 'And the rain is part of it. I checked: it's going to rain tonight. If I'm right, between tomorrow and the day after tomorrow he'll strike again.'

'So how much of a head start do we have?' Clemente asked. 'Thirty-six hours? Just thirty-six hours to figure out how his mind works. In the meantime, all we can say is that he's very clever. He likes killing, he likes pulling surprises, he wants to spread panic, but we still don't know his motive. Why loving couples?'

'The story of the child of salt,' Marcus said, and told Clemente about the books used as therapy at the Hamelin Institute by Professor Joseph Kropp. 'I believe the Monster is trying to tell us his personal story. The murders are nothing but the chapters in this story. He's composing it in the present, but what he's trying to reveal to us must be an old story, filled with pain and violence.'

'A storyteller.'

Serial killers were usually divided into categories, according to their methods and the motives that drove them. 'Storytellers' were considered a subcategory of the larger category of 'visionaries', who committed murders under the control of an *alter ego* with which they communicated and from whom they received instructions, sometimes in the form of visions or 'voices'.

But storytellers needed an audience for their work. It was as if they were looking constantly for acknowledgement of what they were doing, even in the form of fear.

That was why the Monster had left a message on the tape recorder in the confessional, five days before the first attack.

'. . . a time . . . It happened at night . . . And everyone came running to where his knife had been planted . . . his time had come . . . the children died . . . the false bearers of false love . . . and he was pitiless with them . . . of the child of salt . . . if he isn't stopped, he won't stop.'

'In Sant'Apollinare he talked in the past tense, as if in a fairytale,' Marcus said. 'And the first sentence, from which the beginning is missing, is "once upon a time".'

Clemente was starting to understand.

'He won't stop until we understand the meaning of his story,' Marcus added. 'But right now the monster isn't our only problem.'

It was like fighting on two fronts. On one, a ruthless killer. On the other, a series of individuals who were doing their best to muddy the waters, murdering their pursuers or throwing them off the track, even at the cost of their own lives. So they temporarily dropped the storyteller and devoted themselves to the second aspect. Marcus brought Clemente up to date with what he had discovered.

He started with the pathologist Astolfi, who had stolen a piece of evidence, perhaps a statuette of salt, from the first crime scene. Then he told Clemente about Cosmo Barditi and how he had uncovered a lead: the book about the 'child of glass' which Nicola Gavi had sold him.

It was the questions Barditi had been asking that had drawn the attention of the person who had then killed him, making it look like a suicide. It was the same person who had tried to stab Nicola Gavi to death and who had attacked Marcus at the party in the villa on the Appia Antica: the man with the blue shoes, the old man with blue eyes who lived in the basement of the Hamelin Institute.

'Astolfi and that old man are the proof that someone is trying to hide the truth and, perhaps, to protect the Monster,' Marcus concluded.

'Protect? What makes you say that?'

'It's an impression more than anything else. The Monster needs an audience, remember? He likes to feel gratified. So I'm sure I met him that night at the villa on the Appia Antica. He was there with his camera, enjoying the celebration of his work without revealing himself. When he realised that I'd noticed him, he ran away. As I was following him, I had the idea of making an inverted sign of the cross as I'd seen Astolfi do in the pine wood at Ostia while unearthing the statuette of salt he had hidden.'

'And?'

'I'd foreseen a reaction of some kind, but the man with the camera looked at me in a puzzled way, as if that gesture meant nothing to him.'

'Whereas the old man in the blue shoes recognised the inverted sign of the cross and that was why he attacked you and left you unconscious in the grounds of the villa. Is that right?'

'I think so.'

Clemente thought this over for a while. 'The Monster's being protected but he doesn't know it . . . Why?'

'We'll get there,' Marcus promised. 'I think my visit to the Hamelin Institute put me on the right track.' He began pacing up and down the room, trying hard to make sense of what he had seen the previous night. 'In the basement, the old man made an inverted sign of the cross, then ran away and started the fire.

An apparently mad act, but I don't think madness had anything to do with it. I think it was actually a demonstration. Yes, he was trying to demonstrate to me how determined he was to keep the secret. I don't think he survived: I stood outside the villa for a while to make sure, but nobody came out. In fact, I only just managed to get out myself.'

'Like Astolfi, he preferred to take his own life rather than talk.' Clemente, though, was confused. 'What could this secret possibly be?'

'In a room in the Institute, behind the wallpaper showing characters from fairytales, was an image of an anthropomorphic figure: a man with a wolf's head. I need you to do some research for me: you have to find the meaning of that symbol. What does it represent? I'm sure there's a history behind it.'

Clemente agreed. 'Is that the one clue you found at the Institute?'

Marcus pointed to the black suitcase his friend had brought with him. 'Did you bring the video recorder with you?'

'Just as you asked me.'

'I found a videocassette. It's the only thing I managed to save from the fire, but I think it may be worth it.' Marcus took it from a chair and handed it to his friend, who read the label.

'Psychopathic savant.'

Then he explained. 'The young patients didn't use their own names and didn't know those of the others. Kropp assigned each of them a surname linked to the fairytale chosen for their therapy. His intention was to reconstruct the individual inside the child. Nicola Gavi, for example, was "fragile and dangerous", like glass, while the child of salt in the fairytale was more intelligent than the other children but, for that very reason, everyone avoided him: he destroyed everything he touched. Gavi even said that his companion had a very high IQ . . . '

Clemente was starting to see what Marcus was getting at.

'Christ described his disciples as "the salt of the earth" precisely to highlight the value of their knowledge: God's truth had been revealed to them. Since then, salt has been a synonym for knowledge. Sure enough, the child of salt is more intelligent than the others.'

'The psychopathic savant,' Marcus said. 'I think this videocassette will show us the Monster when he was just a child.'

15

The Technical Analysis Laboratory of the Rome police was among the most advanced in Europe. Its activity ranged from decoding DNA to electronic investigation.

The head of it was Leopoldo Strini, a thirty-five-year-old expert with balding hair, thick glasses and a pale complexion. 'Here we decrypt codes and reconstruct the contents of home and telephone intercepts,' he explained to Sandra. 'If, for example, a recording has gaps, we're able to fill them with the exact words, thanks to our apparatus. Just as we can extract the underlying image from a photograph taken in the dark, as if it was bright daylight.'

'How is that possible?' Sandra asked.

With a self-satisfied air, Strini went to one of the terminals in the room and gave the monitor a couple of slaps. 'Thanks to a system of very powerful state-of-the-art software, our margin of error is 0.009.'

The computers were the real secret of the place. The laboratory was equipped with technological tools that nobody else – public authorities or private companies – had at their disposal. The large room that housed them was in the basement of Police Headquarters. There were no windows, and a ventilation system maintained a constant temperature in order to keep the sophisticated instruments from damage. The servers that supported all this technology, meanwhile, were buried a good twenty feet below the foundations of the Headquarters building.

To Sandra, this place seemed like a mixture of a biology lab – the counter with microscopes and all the rest – a computer centre and an electronics workshop – with soldering irons, components and various tools.

Currently the laboratory was at work on the DNA of the Monster of Rome, found on the shirt that the killer had inadvertently left in the car of the young people he had attacked in Ostia. And it was also busy examining the finds taken from Dr Astolfi's apartment. But, in accordance with the wishes of the upper echelons at Headquarters, this second matter was secret, Leopoldo Strini remembered. So there was no way Sandra Vega, a mere forensic photographer, could have come to see him about that.

'The killer's DNA hasn't revealed anything else,' Strini said, putting his hands up. 'No matches with other cases or with any of the samples we've been getting from people with records for similar crimes.'

'I need a favour,' Sandra said, cutting short his speech. She handed him the mobile phone given to her by Pia Rimonti's boyfriend Ivan.

'What am I supposed to do with this?'

'In the voicemail, there's a message from my colleague who was killed two nights ago. First I need you to listen to it.'

Strini took the phone from Sandra's hands as if it were a relic. Then, staring at it in silence, he walked towards a terminal. He connected the mobile and dialled a series of commands on the keyboard. 'I'm extracting the message,' he announced, and pressed the button that connected directly to the voicemail. Then he raised the volume of the speakers on the table.

The call started. An electronic female voice welcomed them and announced that the voicemail contained one saved message. Then it mentioned the day and the hour when it had been left: three o'clock in the morning. At last, the recording started.

Strini was expecting to hear the voice of Pia Rimonti. Instead, there was only a prolonged silence, which lasted some thirty seconds in all. Then the line went dead.

'What does it mean?' he said, turning to Sandra. 'I don't understand.'

'That's why I haven't yet informed Moro or even Crespi,' she said. She briefly told him about her encounter with Pia's boyfriend after the funeral and how she had found out about the voice message. 'I need you to tell me if there was a mistake, in other words, if the call was started by mistake, or else if the voicemail recorded it badly, maybe because there wasn't any signal . . .'

Strini immediately understood what Vega was getting at. What she really wanted to know was whether there was something in that silence.

'I think I'll be able to tell you quite quickly,' he assured her, and got straight down to work.

A few minutes went by during which Sandra watched as Strini deconstructed the message into a series of audio traces that on the screen looked like the diagram of a seismograph. He amplified every vibration, every noise, to such an extent that the line jumped at the smallest sound.

'I've increased the background noise to maximum,' Strini said. 'I can already rule out the possibility that the voicemail recorded the message badly.' He pressed a button to play the contents again.

Now the rustle of the wind in the leaves could clearly be heard. Sandra felt as if she was there. The secret noises of a wood at night, when no one was present to hear them. She felt a strange sense of fear. Because someone had in fact been there.

'Someone deliberately started the call,' Strini confirmed. 'He kept silent for about thirty seconds then hung up. Why do something like that?'

'The timetable,' was Sandra's reply.

Strini didn't understand immediately.

'The recorded voice just told us that the message was left at three in the morning.'

'What of it?'

Sandra took out a sheet of paper she had brought with her. 'The last radio contact between the officers and the switchboard was just after one. According to the post mortem, Stefano Carboni died a few minutes later, while Pia Rimonti was tortured for at least half an hour before being killed.'

'The call was made after her death,' Strini said, astonished but also scared by the observation.

'It was made more or less at the time our people went to check and discovered the two bodies.'

There was no need to even say out loud the natural conclusion to be drawn. The killer had walked away with Pia Rimonti's phone and had made the call from somewhere else.

'Pia's phone wasn't among the objects found at the crime scene.' To back this up, Sandra showed Strini a paper with the list of objects she was talking about.

But Strini stood up, refusing to look at it. 'Why did you come to me? Why didn't you go straight to Moro or Crespi?'

'I told you before: I needed confirmation.'

'Confirmation of what?'

'I think the Monster was trying to attract our attention with that silent message. Can you trace where the call was made from?'

16

He loaded the cassette into the recorder and pressed play.

The screen filled with a greyish mist. It lasted for what seemed like a very long minute, during which Marcus and Clemente did not utter a word. At last, something appeared. The image wavered from top to bottom while the tape tried to settle down – it seemed as if it might snap at any moment. But then, all by itself, the frame stabilised, showing a scene in faded colours.

It was the room with the wallpaper covered in fairytale characters. On the floor, a number of toys, and a rocking horse in a corner. In the middle, two chairs.

On the chair on the right was a man of about forty, sitting cross-legged. Very fair hair, sideburns and glasses with dark lenses. He was wearing a doctor's white coat. Presumably, he was Professor Joseph Kropp.

On the chair on the left sat a thin young boy, his back bent, his hands between his knees. He was wearing a white shirt buttoned to the wrists and the neck, dark trousers and leather boots. His light brown hair, cut in a bob, hung down low over his eyes. He was looking down.

'Do you know where you are?' Kropp asked in a slight Germanic accent.

The boy shook his head.

The frame moved for a moment, as if someone was still arranging the camera. Sure enough, soon afterwards, a second man appeared in front of the camera. He too was wearing a white coat and carrying a folder.

'This is Dr Astolfi,' Kropp said, introducing the young man who would later become a pathologist. Astolfi took a seat and went and sat down next to him.

For Marcus, it was confirmation that he had not been mistaken: Astolfi was involved and knew the Monster.

'We want you to feel comfortable, you're among friends here.'

The child said nothing, but Kropp made a sign towards the open door. Three nurses came in, a woman with red hair and two men who went and took up position along the wall at the back.

One of the two men didn't have a left arm and wasn't wearing any prosthesis. Marcus recognised the other. 'That's the old man from the fire at the Institute, the man who attacked me at the villa on the Appia Antica.' The same blue eyes, and much sturdier-looking – at the time, he couldn't have been more than fifty. Another confirmation: those who were protecting the Monster had known him since he was a child.

'This is Giovanni,' Kropp said, introducing him. *'The lady is Signorina Olga. And that thin man with the big nose is Fernando.'* He indicated the one-armed man.

They all smiled at the joke, except for the child, who continued looking down at his own feet.

'We'll stay with you for a while, but then you'll be able to join the other children. You'll see: you may not think so now, but in the end you'll like being here.'

Marcus had already recognised two of the protagonists in the video. Now he made a mental note of the names and faces of the others. Kropp, fair-haired. Fernando, one-armed. Olga, a redhead.

'*I've made his room ready*,' the woman said with a kindly smile. She was addressing Kropp, but in reality was talking to the child. '*I've put his things in the drawers, but I think that later we'll be able to go together to the toy store-room and choose something he likes. What do you think, Professor?*'

'*I think that's a very good idea.*'

The boy didn't react in any way. Then Kropp made another sign and the three nurses left the room.

Marcus noticed that they were all very pleasant and attentive – an attitude in marked contrast to the joyless faces of the fairytale characters on the walls.

'*Now we're going to ask you some questions, all right?*' Kropp said.

The boy turned unexpectedly towards the camera.

Kropp drew his attention back. '*Do you know why you're here, Victor?*'

'His name is Victor,' Clemente said, to underline that they might now have the Monster's name. But at the moment Marcus was more interested in what was happening on the screen.

The boy looked at Kropp again, but did not answer this second question either.

Kropp persevered. '*I think you do know, but you don't want to talk about it, is that right?*'

Once again, no reaction.

'*I know you like numbers*,' Kropp said, changing the subject. '*They tell me you're very good at maths. How would you feel about showing me something?*'

At this point Astolfi rose from his chair and walked out of frame. After a short while, he came back and placed next to Victor a blackboard on which a square root had been written.

$\sqrt{78747057579457}$

Then he put down the chalk and sat down again.

'*Would you like to solve it?*' Kropp asked the boy, who had not even turned to see what Astolfi was doing.

After a few seconds' hesitation, Victor stood up, went to the blackboard and started writing the solution.

28061906,132522

Astolfi checked in his folder and indicated to Kropp that the result was correct.

'He's a little genius,' Clemente said, astonished.

'*Good, Victor,*' Kropp said enthusiastically. '*Very good.*'

Marcus knew that there were people who had exceptional gifts for mathematics or music or drawing. Some possessed incredible calculation skills, others only needed one day to learn to play an instrument perfectly, others still were capable of reproducing a view of a city after seeing it for a few seconds. Often the extraordinary gift was connected with a mental disorder like autism or Asperger's syndrome. In the past, they had been called idiot savants. But now they were referred to by the more appropriate term of savants. In spite of their extraordinary aptitudes, they were usually incapable of relating to the world around them and were significantly backward in language and in cognitive processes, as well as suffering from obsessive-compulsive disorder.

Victor must have been one of them. The psychopathic savant, he recalled.

The boy went back to his seat and assumed the same position as before, bent forward with his hands between his knees. But then he again began to stare at the camera.

'*Please, Victor, look at me,*' Kropp said gently.

His eyes were intense, and Marcus felt an unpleasant sensation. It was as if the boy could see him through the screen.

After a moment, Victor obeyed the psychiatrist, turning back to him.

'*Now we have to talk about your sister,*' Kropp said.

The words had no effect on the boy, who continued to sit there motionless.

'*What happened to your sister, Victor? Do you remember what happened to her?*' Kropp followed the question with a pause, maybe to stimulate a reaction.

A little time went by, then Victor said something. His voice, though, was too weak to be heard clearly.

'What did he say?' Clemente asked.

'*Could you repeat that, please?*' Kropp said.

The boy raised his voice, very slightly, and repeated shyly, '*It wasn't me.*'

The two doctors didn't reply, but waited for the boy to say something else. To no avail. Victor simply turned once again, for the third time, to the camera.

'*Why are you looking over there?*' Kropp asked.

The boy slowly lifted his arm and pointed to something.

'*There's nothing there. I don't understand.*'

Victor said nothing, but continued to stare.

'*Do you see an object?*'

Victor shook his head.

'*Someone, then . . . A person?*'

Victor remained motionless.

'*You're wrong, there's no one there. We're alone in the room.*'

But the boy continued looking in that direction. Marcus and Clemente both had the unpleasant impression that Victor was really looking at them.

'*We'll have to talk about your sister another time,*' Kropp said.

'It's important. But that's enough for today. You can stay here and play, if you want.'

After exchanging a brief glance, the two doctors stood up and headed for the door. They left the room, leaving the boy alone but without switching off the camera. Marcus thought that strange. Unperturbed, Victor continued looking at the camera, without moving a muscle.

Marcus tried to read his eyes, looking deeply into them. What secret was hidden in the boy's gaze? What had he done to his sister?

Almost a minute passed. Then the tape ended and the recording stopped.

'Now we know his name,' Clemente said with satisfaction.

The two fixed points were that videocassette and the recording of the Monster's voice in the confessional in Sant'Apollinare, with which his investigation had started.

'. . . a time . . . It happened at night . . . And everyone came running to where his knife had been planted . . . his time had come . . . the children died . . . the false bearers of false love . . . and he was pitiless with them . . . of the child of salt . . . if he isn't stopped, he won't stop.'

The video and the tape were the two ends of the story. The Monster when he was only a child and then as an adult. What had happened in between? And before?

'The confessional in Sant'Apollinare was used in the past by people involved in organised crime to pass information to the police,' Marcus summed up, trying to clarify his own ideas. 'The church was a safe haven, a neutral area. The Monster knew that, and that's why we took it for granted that he was a criminal.'

'It's likely that he committed other crimes after the Hamelin Institute,' Clemente said, pointing to the screen. 'Basically, we know how these things go: most children or adolescents who commit crimes continue later.'

'Their destiny is marked out,' Marcus said, but more as part of a conversation with himself. He felt that he was very close to something important. There was a sentence in the tape which, in the light of what he had seen in the video, now took on a different meaning.

The children died.

The first time he'd heard it, he had thought the Monster was referring to the parents of his young victims. That it was a sadistic warning addressed to them, because of the grief that he would make them feel.

He was wrong.

'I've realised why he chooses loving couples,' he said, emerging from his thoughts. 'The reason has nothing to do with sex or perversion. In the tape he refers to the victims as "children".'

Clemente was all ears.

'In the video, Kropp asks Victor what happened to his sister. Probably she's the reason the boy was at the Hamelin Institute: he did her harm. Sure enough, he answers, "It wasn't me".'

'Go on, I'm following you . . .'

'Our man is a storyteller. He's telling us his story through the murders.'

'Of course – the children!' Clemente got there by himself. 'In his imagination, the loving couples represent a brother and a sister.'

'In order to strike, he needs to surprise his victims when they're alone and isolated. Think about it: it's easier to find a couple of lovers than a brother and sister.'

The theory of the link between what was happening now and what had happened between Victor and his sister was also supported by the fact that the killer was more brutal towards his female victims. '"It wasn't me." He still thinks he was the victim of an injustice. And it's his sister's fault.'

'And he's making those young people pay for it.'

Now Marcus was in full flow. He got up and started pacing about the room. 'Victor does something bad to his sister and is sent to the Hamelin Institute. But, instead of changing him for the better, the place turns him into a criminal. So as he grows up, he commits other crimes.'

'If only we knew which,' Clemente regretted. 'Then we'd be able to discover his true identity.'

But it wasn't possible. The crime Victor had committed in his childhood had been wiped out forever: there was no trace of crimes committed by children in police records. Everything was concealed. The world could not accept that a pure soul could commit evil acts with such clear-headed ruthlessness.

'There is a way,' Marcus said, confidently. 'His first victim. Only the identity of the culprit was wiped out, but, if we discover what happened to Victor's sister, we'll find Victor.'

17

The silent message on the voicemail was an invitation.

It was as if the Monster was saying, 'Come and see.'

Leopoldo Strini had pinpointed the call made from Pia Rimonti's mobile that night to an area southeast of Rome, in the Alban Hills. Sandra had immediately informed Moro and Crespi. The Central Operations Team's emergency procedure had been activated. It was less than an hour to sunset, so they had to hurry.

A cortège of a dozen police cars and armoured vehicles had left Headquarters, promptly tailed by TV vans. With a couple of Augusta helicopters from the airborne division to act as guardian angels, they crossed the centre of Rome with sirens howling, attracting the attention of passers-by. Through the window of her car, Sandra Vega caught their anxious looks: they were staring at the procession, paralysed by the sound and spellbound with fear. Parents pushing pushchairs with little children, tourists who had chosen this tense time to visit the Eternal City and would never forget their holiday, women and men, old and young. All sharing the same feeling, the same uncontrollable terror.

Sandra was sitting next to Moro on the back seat of the

second lead car. He had asked her to come with him but had not yet said a word. He was lost in thought, but his nervousness was obvious. From time to time, he looked in the rear-view mirror at the satellite dishes on the TV vans. Like wild beasts, the reporters were hungry for prey.

Sandra could imagine what Moro must be thinking, his anxiety about how the police would come out of it this time. Because so far, even though nobody admitted it, they were losing the match. It was only natural, then, that one of the things he was worried about was the possibility that the case might be taken away from him. It was too juicy a case for other people not to want to get their hands on it. The Special Operations Group of the Carabinieri, for example, who also dealt with violent crime and who were champing at the bit to be involved.

As the long but compact column of vehicles drove along Provincial Highway 217, a front of icy air was falling over the city, bringing with it low, menacing clouds that scurried over their heads like an army of shadows towards the sun, which was rapidly sinking on the horizon.

The elements were against them.

The Alban Hills were actually an immense quiescent volcano that had collapsed in on itself thousands of years earlier. The various craters had become plains or else housed little freshwater lakes. All around, a belt of hills covered with dense vegetation.

The area was inhabited and there were a number of towns. Leopoldo Strini had only been able to pinpoint the location of the call to within a radius of two miles, which was a large area to check.

After about twenty minutes, they reached open country. The lead cars stopped at the edge of a wooded area, while the armoured vehicles that were transporting the men of the special teams parked in such a way as to constitute a front line.

'All right, let's begin the search,' Moro ordered by radio.

Officers emerged from the vehicles in assault uniforms, with submachine guns and bulletproof vests. They lined up along the edge of the wood. Then, at a specific signal, they moved in unison into the trees.

Moro took up position on a small hill to wait, clutching the radio in one hand. Sandra kept looking at him, wondering how a man prepared for every eventuality could live through moments like these. Hundreds of yards behind them, the TV vans, kept at bay by a police cordon, were starting to set up their cameras in order to broadcast live.

With the approach of night, tripods for the halogen lamps were starting to be set up. Linked to diesel generators, they were arranged at a distance of about thirty-five feet from each other over a very long perimeter. As the last rays of the sun were about to fade, Superintendent Crespi ordered them to be switched on. With a series of mechanical clicks that echoed through the valley, bright white light hit the barrier of vegetation.

In the meantime, the helicopters had begun sweeping the wood from above with their powerful lights, to offer the armed men on the ground a little visibility.

Almost thirty minutes passed without anything happening. Nobody had expected that anything would occur so soon, but it did. A voice came over Moro's radio.

'Sir, we've found Officer Rimonti's mobile. I think you should come and take a look.'

The lights from the helicopters filtered through the branches of the trees from above – thin beams of light that gave the wood a magical air. Sandra was walking behind Moro and Superintendent Crespi. Escorted by other officers, they advanced through the vegetation.

Each time the helicopters passed overhead, the din of the blades covered the sound of their steps, then faded in a way that reminded Sandra of the echo in a great cathedral. About a hundred yards ahead of them, someone raised and lowered a torch several times, signalling to them to head in that direction.

Reaching the place, they found a group of men from the Central Operations Team waiting for them, gathered around their senior officer.

'Where is it?' Moro asked.

'It's over here.' The man indicated a point on the ground and shone his torch on it.

Sure enough, there was a soil-covered mobile phone on the ground.

Taking a latex glove from his pocket and putting it on his right hand, Moro crouched to get a better look at the phone. 'Give me more light.' The beams of other torches converged on the spot.

It was a smartphone with a dark blue cover bearing the State Police badge. Moro recognised it because it was part of the corps' merchandising: you could buy it on the official site along with T-shirts, caps and other things. Officers were provided with these covers for free, to avoid them having objects in bright colours that didn't match the uniform. The only quirk, in this particular case, was the little heart-shaped pendant that hung from one corner.

The heart was flashing, as if it were actually beating.

'That's how we found it,' the officer said. 'We noticed the flashing. It may indicate that the battery's running low.'

'Probably,' Moro said in a low voice, as he continued to stare at the phone. Then with one finger he lifted it and tried to examine the screen. Apart from the soil, it was stained with blood.

Pia Rimonti's blood, Sandra thought.

'Call Forensics to get fingerprints off the phone, and comb through the entire area.'

When the officer had summoned Moro by radio, he had used a specific expression.

I think you should come and take a look.

That was just it. Right from the start, they had all expected to find something in this place. But, apart from the phone, there was nothing to see.

Why had the killer led them here?

From his crouching position, Moro looked first at Sandra and then at Superintendent Crespi. 'All right, let's bring the dogs here.'

Six officers from the dog-handling unit led six bloodhounds along an imaginary grid centred on the spot where the phone had been found.

The dogs zigzagged with their bodies low to the ground, moving against the wind.

Bloodhounds had recently been dubbed 'molecular dogs' by the press because they were capable of following the molecules of smell in the most adverse conditions. Unlike other breeds, they were able to identify a scent even when a long time had passed since a crime. Quite recently, they had been used to identify a maniac who had raped and killed a little girl in northern Italy: they had led the investigators to the place where he worked, and the arrest had taken place in front of photographers and TV cameras. The breed had gained an unexpected notoriety.

But among the police their name was still 'corpse dogs'.

At that moment, one of the animals stopped and immediately turned to its trainer. It was the signal that he had scented something. The trainer lifted one arm: it was a gesture intended to obtain confirmation. Sure enough, the dog barked, abandoning its crouching position and getting down on all fours to wait for a reward.

'Sir, there's something under here,' the trainer called to Moro. Then he gave the dog a pellet of dry food and moved it away from the spot indicated.

Moro approached with Crespi. Both squatted. As Crespi aimed the torch downwards, Moro brushed the earth clear of branches and dried leaves with his hand. Then he ran his palm over the bare soil.

There was a slight depression.

'Shit,' Moro said, angrily.

Sandra, who was standing fairly close by, could guess what was happening. There was a body down there. And she didn't only know that because of the bloodhounds. The ribcage of a body buried without a coffin would yield after a while beneath the weight of the earth covering it, causing a depression in the soil.

Crespi came over to her. 'Vega, maybe you should start to get ready.'

Sandra put on her white overalls with the hood and arranged the microphone of her recorder in such a way that it was close to her mouth.

The special teams had left the field to the Forensics people who now, along with the men from the morgue, started to dig. Floodlights were set up and the area was marked off with poles.

Sandra photographed the scene. As the earth was moved – delicately, with the help of small shovels – something started to appear. First fragments of denim cloth. It was immediately clear that these were trousers.

The body was buried barely one and a half feet deep, so it wasn't difficult to get to the rest. A pair of gym shoes, tennis shorts, a brown cord belt, a green canvas jacket. The body was lying on its back, the legs bent slightly towards the trunk, a sign that whoever had dug the hole hadn't quite calculated the depth correctly. Sure enough, the ribcage had collapsed and looked like a large chasm.

Sandra continued to shoot, moving around her colleagues as

they proceeded with the exhumation. They had abandoned the small shovels and were now shifting the soil with brushes.

The head was still under the ground but the hands, the only part not covered by clothes, appeared like two dark pieces of wood. Being buried like that had speeded up the process of decomposition.

Then it was time to uncover the face. This was done with great care. At last a skull emerged, the hair still attached to it – a matted mass of hair the colour of ebony.

'Male, indeterminate age,' the pathologist said after carefully examining the bones of the frontal area, the cheeks and the jaw.

'There is an entry hole at the height of the right temple,' Sandra said into her recorder, and immediately thought of the Ruger revolver used by the Monster – clearly a kind of signature. The exit hole must be at the back of the skull.

Then, zooming with her camera to get a close-up, she noticed something sticking out from the earth beneath the neck.

'There's something else under the body,' she said to the Forensics team. They looked at her for a moment in surprise, then continued digging.

Moro was a few yards away. He stood motionless with his arms folded, watching the operation. He saw the men extract the body from the hole and place it delicately on a stretcher.

That was when the second body was at last revealed beneath it.

'Woman, indeterminate age.'

She was much smaller than her companion. She was wearing flowered leggings and pink tennis shoes. From the waist up she was naked.

Sandra thought of the previous female victims. Diana Delgaudio had been naked – causing the hypothermia that had saved her life – while Pia Rimonti had been stripped before being tortured and killed with a hunting knife. The killer always gave the men a quick death. Giorgio Montefiori had been persuaded to stab Diana and then had received a bullet in the head, as in an execution. Stefano Carboni had been shot in the chest, another almost instantaneous end. And the man who was now lying next to the grave also seemed to have got off lightly, with that bullet hole in the temple.

Maybe the Monster quite simply wasn't interested in men. Then why choose couples?

In the case of the second victim, here too the ribcage had been crushed because of the weight pressing down on it. The pathologist examined her attentively. 'On the left,' he said, 'the eighth and ninth rib present small grooves with granulated profiles, a sign of possible stabbing.'

Yet again, the Monster's *modus operandi* had been confirmed.

But before the pathologist could add anything else, the corpse dogs, a few yards away, started getting excited again.

The second grave contained two rucksacks. One red, the other black. One large, the other smaller. They belonged to the victims. The most immediate and convincing explanation was that the killer, not finding room for them in the first hole, had been forced to dig a second one.

When the men from the morgue opened the woman's black rucksack and started taking out the contents, Sandra saw Moro's expression change.

His face was a picture of dismay. He picked up an object that was familiar to her.

A pregnancy test.

Silence spread like a contagion, and no one in the wood said another word. All those present felt the same horror.

'The hitchhikers,' Moro said softly.

18

'Life is just a long series of first times.'

Sandra couldn't remember who had said it, but the phrase came back to her as she left the crime scene. It had always struck her as a positive expression, filled with hope and expectation.

There was a first time for everything. For example, she remembered when her father had taught her to ride a bicycle.

'There, now you'll never forget again,' he had said. And he was right, even though she hadn't really believed him at the time.

And she recalled when she had kissed a boy for the first time. That was something else she would never forget, though she wouldn't have minded if she could, given that the boy had been a pimply teenager with breath that smelt of strawberry chewing gum, and she had thought it the least sexy thing in the world.

And there were first times that were also last times. Sandra couldn't help thinking of her marriage to David as an unrepeatable experience. That was why she would never marry Max.

In any case, first times, whether good or bad, created an indelible memory and had a strange magic. And they contained a lesson that was valuable for the future. Always. Except the one she had witnessed that night in the wood.

A killer's first time.

Bernhard Jäger and Annabel Meyer were twenty-three and nineteen respectively. He was from Berlin, she from Hamburg. He had just finished his architecture studies, while she was still at art school. They had known each other for a few months and had immediately moved in together.

Two summers ago, they had gone on a hitchhiking trip to Italy. But after a couple of weeks spent roaming around the country they had vanished into thin air. In their last phone call to their families, Bernhard and Annabel had announced the news that they would soon be having a baby.

It was with them that the Monster had learned to kill.

From a summary examination of the scene, it was clear to everybody that the pattern was the same as in the other cases, but that it had been carried out in a very approximate manner. As if by an amateur who had a vocation and knew the rudiments of the trade but didn't yet have enough experience to carry out the work to the highest standard.

In the killer's case, it was a question of details.

The bullet that had killed the man had been fired at the temple, which often did not cause instant death. The stabs inflicted on the woman had been distributed at random on the abdomen, as if the killer had acted in haste, without enjoying his own work.

And then there was the matter of the child.

The killer couldn't have known that Annabel was pregnant, it was too early for any change in her physique to be noticeable. Maybe she had told him, but when it was already too late. Or maybe he had only seen the pregnancy test afterwards. Once that *detail* had been discovered, he had realised his mistake: he had chosen a couple that did not correspond to his initial fantasy.

There were no children in the Monster's plan.

That was probably why he had decided to bury the bodies.

On his first time out, he had made a mistake and had tried to hide it from the world and, above all, from himself.

But now that he had become good enough, now that everyone, after two almost exemplary attacks, had recognised his merits, paying him the tribute of horror and dismay, he had decided to reveal his imperfect debut. As if, now, he could stop feeling ashamed about it.

Because now that 'distraction' might even turn out to be his greatest triumph.

The fact was that the disappearance of the two young people had not ended up lost among the various missing persons cases that occurred in Italy every year, which were usually dropped after a short while with just the hope that one day there might be a stroke of luck – which almost never arrived.

Annabel Meyer was the second child of a well-known German banker, a powerful man who had exerted great pressure on the government and the Italian authorities for his daughter to be found. The media had talked a lot about the case, and it had been entrusted to the most expert police officer available, Deputy Commissioner Moro.

Since the young people had been hitchhiking, hours of footage taken by security cameras on roads and motorways had been viewed, a use of manpower and resources that was unusual for an investigation of this kind. A disappearance wasn't a homicide, nor was there any evidence that this had been a kidnapping, and yet a lot of money and time had been spent.

In the end, in spite of the objective difficulty of finding anything at all, it had emerged that in July Bernhard and Annabel had been seen in the vicinity of a service station just outside Florence, on the A1, the so-called Motorway of the Sun. They were stopping motorists and asking for a lift to Rome. The security cameras in the service station had captured the moment when the two young people had got on board a runabout. A tracing of the number plate had revealed that the car had been stolen. The driver's face hadn't been captured by the cameras. But, thanks to Moro's talent, the police had managed to track down the thief.

He was a petty crook with previous convictions for theft and robbery. His speciality was offering lifts to naïve tourists and then threatening them with a gun and making them hand over their belongings. The suspect had been arrested after an extensive manhunt. In his apartment, apart from a Beretta with its licence number erased, objects belonging to the two young Germans had been found: Bernhard's wallet and a gold necklace of Annabel's.

The police's theory had been that Bernhard, who was bigger than the robber, had resisted, and the robber had been forced to shoot him. In a panic, he had killed the girl too, and then got rid of both bodies. After his arrest, the man had admitted the robbery but claimed that he had never shot anybody and that he had dropped the two hitchhikers in open country.

As it happened, the place he had indicated was about a hundred yards from where the bodies had now been found, Sandra noted.

But two years earlier nobody had looked for them because the robber had changed his story during the first stage of the trial. He had admitted the double homicide, declaring that he had got rid of the bodies by throwing them in a river.

Divers had searched the whole river, but the bodies had not been found. The court, though, had shown that it appreciated the defendant's co-operation and had sentenced him to life imprisonment but with the option of requesting a regime of day release in the not too distant future.

Now it was obvious that the confession had been part of a specific strategy on the part of his lawyers: faced with the crushing weight of the evidence, they had advised him to plead guilty, even though it wasn't true. It was one of the flaws of the legal system, but at the time the parents of the two young people, including the powerful banker, had been content with it because they at least had a culprit who had received the maximum sentence. That was probably a small consolation for the fact that they would have no actual place to mourn their children. The Italian authorities, for their part, had provided the German authorities with a demonstration of efficiency. Deputy Commissioner Moro had been smothered with congratulations and had seen his own fame increase considerably.

Everyone was happy. Until now.

As the disconcerting truth was emerging, Sandra took off her uniform and put her equipment back in the car.

A few paces from her, an embarrassed Moro was releasing a first statement for the benefit of the main newspapers, national and foreign. In the floodlights, his face looked even wearier than before. Behind him, the wood where the skeletons had been found. In front of him, a forest of microphones.

'Bernhard Jäger and Annabel Meyer.' He pronounced the names slowly, for the benefit of the cameras. 'Twenty-three and nineteen.'

'How did they die?' a reporter asked.

Moro searched for his face among the others, but he was blinded by the flashes and gave up. 'We believe they are a third couple killed by the Monster. But, given that they disappeared at least two years ago and that their remains are in an advanced state of decomposition, we can assume they were actually the first victims.'

For two years the killer had lived undisturbed and now he had become the Monster.

Marcus had said that someone was protecting him, Sandra recalled. Who could be doing something like that, and why?

Maybe it was the thought that anyone could prefer a killer over innocent young people that most angered her.

Astolfi had been part of that absurd cover-up, and she had found him out. Superintendent Crespi had assured her that he wasn't involved, that it had been an act of madness. But Marcus had disproved that thesis. That was why he was the only person Sandra now believed.

She wanted to look into the faces of the other accomplices, whoever they were. She wanted them to know that someone was aware of their plot. Given that the police had no intention of investigating Astolfi further, or the reasons for his suicide, she wanted to send a signal all the same. She was sure that Marcus would approve.

The idea came to her when she saw Superintendent Crespi making the sign of the cross as he left the wood.

Life is just a long series of first times, Sandra said to herself. And she had hidden for too long behind the protective barrier of a camera. Maybe the time had come to take risks.

So, taking advantage of the fact that she was definitely in the frame behind Moro as the TV cameras were filming him, she raised her right hand and, as she had seen Astolfi do in the pine wood at Ostia, made an inverted sign of the cross.

PART THREE

The Psychopathic Savant

The fourth lesson of Marcus's training had taken place in the largest church in the world.

St Peter's had no equal. The basilica had been rebuilt by Bramante after the demolition of the previous one. Including the portico, it was 730 feet long. The dome, up to the tip of the cross that surmounted it, was 118 feet high.

In the interior, every artefact, monument, column, frieze and niche had a story.

The first time Clemente had taken Marcus there, worshippers were mingling with tourists on a sultry Thursday in June. But it was impossible to distinguish those who were there out of devotion from those who were simply sightseeing. Unlike other places of worship, there was no sense of mystical inspiration.

In reality, what the most important symbol of Christendom celebrated above all was the temporal power of the Popes who, in the course of history, on behalf of the apostle Peter, and on the pretext of governing the things of the spirit, actually devoted themselves to material things just like any other monarchs.

The period of the Pope Kings was now over, but the mausoleums of successive pontiffs still bore witness to it. They seemed to have competed with one another to leave the most opulent sign of their own passage – with the help of great artists.

It was because of this last fact, even though it had little to do with God, that Marcus did not feel like condemning such vanity.

Many wonders were hidden in the subsoil of Rome. The remains of the Eternal City that had dominated the world with its civilisation, but also numerous graveyards, some from the Christian era: the catacombs. It was over one of these that the basilica in which they now found themselves had been built.

The catacomb in question was the one that, according to tradition, housed the grave of Christ's favourite disciple. But only in 1939 had Pius XII authorised a series of excavations to find out if Peter's remains really were in the subsoil.

It was during these excavations that, just a few yards down, a red wall was discovered, with an aedicula *that bore an inscription in ancient Greek.*

ΠΕΤΡ (ΟΣ)
ENI

'Peter is here.'

The grave beneath the aedicula*, however, was empty. Only many years after the discovery did someone remember that material found by chance near the excavation had been stored in a closet.*

It had been put into an ordinary shoebox.

Inside the box were human and animal bones, fragments of cloth, earth, small pieces of red plaster and medieval coins.

Specialists were able to establish that the bones had belonged to an individual of the male gender, rather tall and sturdy, between sixty and seventy years old. The fragments of material were from a purple cloth woven with gold. The plaster was that of the red wall that housed the aedicula*, and the earth was identical to that of the burial place. The medieval coins, on the other hand, had probably been brought there by the rats – it was their remains that had been found together with the dead man's bones.*

'It's like the plot of a great thriller,' Clemente had said after telling him the story. 'The fact is that we will never know if that man was really Peter the apostle. It might have been any Peter, maybe even a debauchee or a malefactor.' He had looked around. 'And every year thousands of people kneel at his tomb and pray. They pray to him.'

But Marcus knew that there was a practical meaning to his friend's story.

'The real point is this: what is a man? Unable to know who someone really is, we judge him by what he does. Right and wrong are our yardstick. But is that sufficient?' Then Clemente turned suddenly serious. 'The time has come for you to become acquainted with the greatest criminal records archive in history.'

Catholicism was the only religion that included the sacrament of confession: men told their sins to a priest and in return received forgiveness. Sometimes, though, the sin was so serious that the priest could not give absolution. This was the case with the so-called 'mortal sins', that is, sins regarding 'a grave matter' and committed with 'awareness and deliberate consent'.

Homicide was the major one, but also included were the betrayal of the Church and of the faith.

In such cases, the priest transcribed the text of the confession and submitted it to a higher authority: a college of high-ranking prelates called together in Rome to pass judgement on such matters.

The Tribunal of Souls.

It had been established in the twelfth century under the name Paenitentiaria Apostolica. It had come about at the time of an extraordinary influx of pilgrims into the Eternal City. Many were looking for absolution for their sins.

At the time, there were dispensations and pardons that only the highest authority of the Church, the Pope himself, could grant. But it was a huge task for him. So he had started to delegate it to some of his cardinals, and they had set up the ministry of the Paenitentiaria.

At first, once the tribunal pronounced judgement, the texts of the confessions were burnt. But after a few years the penitenzieri decided to create a secret archive . . . 'And their work has never stopped,' Clemente concluded. 'For nearly a thousand years, the worst sins committed by humanity have been kept there. Sometimes they are crimes that have never come to light. It isn't just a database, like that of the police. It's the largest and most up-to-date archive of evil in existence.'

But Marcus still didn't understand what any of this had to do with him.

'You will study the Archive of Sins. I'll provide you with the cases to examine and you will do so. In the end, you'll be a kind of profiler or criminologist. Just as you were once, before you lost your memory.'

'Why?'

'Because then you will apply your knowledge to the real world.'

This was the real crux of his training.

'Evil is in everything, but often we cannot see it,' Clemente added. 'Anomalies are the almost imperceptible sign of its presence. Unlike everybody else, you will be in a position to identify them. Remember, Marcus: evil is not an abstract idea. Evil is a dimension.'

1

The hospital room was bathed in a green half-light created by the lights from the medical equipment. In the background could be heard the piston of the automatic respirator connected to the trachea of the girl lying in the bed.

Diana Delgaudio.

Her mouth was wide open, a rivulet of dribble dropping from her chin. Her hair, combed with a side parting, made her look like a child aged before its time. Her eyes were wide open but expressionless.

The voices of two nurses approached along the corridor. They were chatting away. One of the two had problems with her boyfriend.

'I told him I don't care if before he met me he used to see his friends on Thursday evenings. Now I'm here and I have priority.'

'And how did he react?' the other one asked, apparently amused.

'He made a bit of a fuss at first, then he gave in.'

They entered the room, pushing a trolley with linen, tubes and spare cannulas. They were here to perform the usual procedure of washing the patient. One of them switched the light on.

'She's already awake,' said the other, noticing that the girl had opened her eyes.

But 'awake' wasn't the most appropriate word to describe Diana, given that she was in a state of vegetative coma. The media weren't talking about it, out of respect for her family, but also because they didn't want to upset all those people who believed that the girl's survival was a kind of miracle.

That was the only comment that the two nurses made about her. They immediately resumed talking about their own lives.

'So, as I said, I realised that's the way I always have to be with him if I want to get anything.'

As they talked, they changed Diana, washed her and put in a new cannula for the respirator, noting down everything they did on a clipboard. To replace the bedsheets, they briefly moved the girl to a wheelchair. One of the nurses placed the clipboard and the pen in her lap, because they didn't know where else to put them.

Once they had finished, the girl was again put to bed.

The nurses were getting ready to leave the room with the trolley, continuing to talk non-stop about their personal affairs.

'Wait a moment,' one of them said. 'I forgot the clipboard.'

She turned on her heel and recovered it from the wheelchair. She glanced at it distractedly, but then was forced to give it a closer look. She fell silent with amazement. She looked at Diana, who lay in bed as still and expressionless as ever. And then looked again at the clipboard she had in front of her, incredulous.

On the sheet of paper inserted in the clipboard, something had been written in an unsteady, childish hand. A single word.

THEY

2

The TV set in the café was tuned to a twenty-four-hour news channel, and this was now the third time he had seen the same bulletin.

He would gladly have done without its accompaniment while he ate, but there wasn't anything he could do about it: although he tried to look elsewhere, as soon as he got distracted his eyes automatically returned to the screen, even though there was no sound.

Leopoldo Strini reflected that it was all a result of the general dependence on technology. People could no longer be alone with themselves. And that was the most profound thought of his day.

The other customers, too, were glued to the screen – families with children, office workers taking an early lunch. The actions of the Monster had captured the attention of everyone in the city. And the media were in their element. Right now, for example, they were endlessly showing the discovery of the two skeletons in the wood. The news was meagre, but the TV bulletins were repeating it obsessively. And people couldn't get enough of looking at it. Even if someone had changed channels, they would have seen the same thing. It had become a collective psychosis.

It was like staring at an aquarium. An aquarium of horrors.

Leopoldo Strini was sitting at his usual table, at the back of the café. He had worked all night on the latest finds, but wasn't yet in a position to supply any useful results. He was half-dead with exhaustion, and halfway through the morning had decided to take a break and grab a quick meal before getting back to work. A veal sandwich, a portion of fries and a Sprite.

He was just about to take one of his last bites of the sandwich when a man sat down at his table, directly opposite him, obscuring his view of the TV. 'Hello,' the man said, smiling in a friendly manner.

Strini was startled for a moment. He had never seen this man before.

'May I disturb you for a moment?'

'I'm not buying anything,' Strini said with a certain sharpness.

'Oh, no, I'm not here to sell you anything,' Batista Erriaga reassured him. 'I'm here because I have a gift for you.'

'Look, I'm not interested. I just want to finish eating.'

Erriaga took off his cap and passed his hand over it, as if to remove some invisible dust. He would have liked to tell this idiot that he hated being here, because he hated cheap cafés where they served greasy food that was harmful to his blood pressure and his cholesterol level. And he hated the children and families who usually frequented these places – he couldn't stand the commotion, the oily hands, the absurd happiness of those who brought children into the world. But after what had happened the previous evening, after the discovery of the remains of the two German hitchhikers, he had had to take some drastic decisions, because his plans risked failing. He would have liked to tell all this to the imbecile he had in front of him, but all he said was, 'Leopoldo, listen to me . . . '

Hearing his own name, Strini froze, his sandwich in mid-air. 'Do we know each other?'

'I know you.'

Strini had a bad feeling about this. 'What the hell do you want from me?'

Erriaga placed his cap on the table and folded his arms. 'You are the head of the Technical Analysis Laboratory at Police Headquarters.'

'If you're a journalist, you're barking up the wrong tree: I can't leak any information.'

'Obviously,' Erriaga said, pretending to understand his intransigence. 'I know you have extremely strict rules about that, and I also know that you would never break them. But I'm not a journalist and you're going to tell me everything you know, and it will be because you want to.'

Strini gave the stranger a sidelong glance. Was he mad? 'I don't even know who you are. Why should I want to share confidential information with you?'

'Because, from now on, you and I are friends.' Erriaga finished the sentence with the gentlest of smiles.

Strini let out a laugh. 'Look, why don't you just clear off right now?'

Erriaga assumed an offended expression. 'You don't know it yet, but being my friend has its advantages.'

'I don't want money.'

'I'm not talking about money. Do you believe in heaven, Leopoldo?'

Strini had had enough. He put the rest of his sandwich down on the plate and got ready to leave. 'I'm still a police officer, you idiot. I could have you arrested.'

'Did you love your grandmother Eleonora?'

Strini stopped dead. 'What's that got to do with anything?'

Erriaga immediately noted that he had just had to mention her name to stop Strini in his tracks. It was a sign that the man wanted to know more. 'Ninety-four . . . She had a long life, didn't she?'

'Yes, she did.'

His tone had already changed, now sounding docile and confused. Erriaga pressed home his advantage. 'If I'm not mistaken, you were her only grandchild, and she really loved you. Leopoldo was also the name of her husband, your grandfather.'

'Yes.'

'She'd promised you that one day you would inherit the little house in Centocelle where she lived. Three rooms and bathroom. Plus, she had a little money put aside. Thirty thousand euros, or am I mistaken?'

Strini's eyes were bulging; he had turned white and couldn't articulate his words. 'Yes . . . Or rather, no . . . I don't remember . . . '

'How can you not remember?' Erriaga said, pretending to be indignant. 'Thanks to that money you were able to marry the girl you loved, and then the two of you went to live in your grandmother's house. A pity that, to obtain all that, you were forced to take the old woman's life.'

'What the hell are you talking about?' Strini said angrily, grabbing his arm and squeezing it hard. 'My grandmother died of cancer.'

'I know,' Erriaga said, looking straight into Strini's rage-filled eyes. 'Dimethyl mercury is an interesting substance: you just need a few drops on the skin for it to immediately penetrate the membrane of the cells, starting an irreversible carcinogenic process. Of course, you have to wait a few months, but the result is assured. Although, to be honest, patience isn't your forte, or you wouldn't have wanted to do God's work before He did.'

'How do you—'

Erriaga took the hand that was squeezing his arm and pulled it off. 'I'm sure part of you is convinced that ninety-four is long enough for a life. After all, dear Eleonora was no longer self-sufficient, and as her designated heir it was up to you to take care of her, with all that meant in terms of time and money.'

By now, Strini was in a state of utter terror.

'Given the age of the dead woman, the doctors didn't delve too deeply into the causes of her cancer. Nobody suspected a thing. That's why I know what's going through your mind: you're thinking that nobody knows this story, not even your wife. But, if I were you, I wouldn't ask too many questions about how I found out. And, since you don't know if you're also going to reach the age of ninety-four, I advise you to start saving time.'

'Are you blackmailing me?'

It struck Erriaga that Strini couldn't be all that intelligent if he could come out with such an obvious question as that. 'I told you, I'm here to give you a gift.' He paused. 'The gift is my silence.'

Strini decided to get down to brass tacks. 'What do you want?'

Erriaga searched in his pocket, took out a sheet of paper and a pen and wrote down a telephone number. 'You can call me at any hour of the day or night. I want to be the first to know all the results of your lab's analyses in the Monster of Rome case.'

'The first to know?'

'That's right,' he said, lifting his eyes from the sheet of paper.

'Why?'

Now came the most difficult part. 'Because I might ask you to destroy evidence.'

Strini collapsed back in his chair and raised his eyes to the ceiling. 'Shit, you can't ask something like that.'

Erriaga did not lose his composure. 'After her death you would have preferred to have her cremated, wouldn't you? But Eleonora was religious, so she'd purchased a niche in Verano Cemetery. It would be a real pity if someone exhumed the body and searched for residues of a poison as unusual as dimethyl mercury. In fact, I'm sure they would ask for your advice, given that such substances can't be too hard to find in your laboratory.'

'The first to know,' Strini said, resigned.

Erriaga gave him one of his famous hyena smiles. 'I'm pleased we understood each other immediately.' Then he looked at his watch. 'I think you should go: you have work to finish.'

Strini hesitated for a moment. Then he stood up and went to the cash desk to pay his bill. Erriaga was so pleased that he left his own chair and went and sat down on the one left free by Strini. He picked up what remained of the veal sandwich and was about to bite into it, forgetting all about his cholesterol and his high blood pressure, when his attention was attracted by the TV set, which was still without sound.

At that moment they were showing the same old images of Deputy Commissioner Moro releasing statements to a group of journalists, not far from the place where the two skeletons had been discovered in the wood. Erriaga had seen those images at least a dozen times since the previous evening. But he hadn't noticed until now what was happening behind the deputy commissioner.

In the background, a young policewoman had made an inverted sign of the cross – *from right to left, from down to up*.

He knew who the woman was. Three years earlier she had been a leading player in an important investigation.

What the hell was she doing? Why was she making that gesture?

She was either very clever or very stupid, Batista Erriaga thought. Whichever it was, she surely didn't know that she had put herself in serious danger.

3

The news had reached all the editorial offices early in the afternoon.

The investigators had released it to restore a little of the public's trust, but also to divert attention from the discovery of the remains of the two hitchhikers.

Diana Delgaudio, the girl who had miraculously survived both the wound in her sternum and a night in the open, was conscious and had started to communicate. She had done so in writing. A single word.

They.

The bitter truth, though, was that Diana had had just one moment of slight lucidity, before sinking back into a catatonic state. For the doctors that was quite normal, they didn't want to raise anyone's expectations. It was rare for similar episodes to lead to any kind of stable recovery. But people were already talking about recovery and nobody had the courage to disillusion them.

God knows what nightmares she's having in that strange sleep of hers, Sandra thought.

The word she had written on the sheet of paper in a clipboard could simply have been the result of delirium. A kind of unconditioned reflex, like when you throw a catatonic man a ball and he catches it.

The doctors had tried giving Diana a pen and paper again, but the attempt hadn't produced any results.

They, Sandra thought.

'For the purposes of the case, it has no value,' Superintendent Crespi said. 'The doctors say the word could be connected to all kinds of memories. Maybe an episode from her past life came back into her mind and she wrote "*they*" referring to that.'

The word had not been triggered by a question, nor had it been a reaction to the conversation the nurses were having when Diana had written it on the clipboard. They had simply been talking about the boyfriend of one of the two girls.

Some journalists had ventured that 'they' could refer to the presence of more than one person in the attack on Diana and her boyfriend in the pine wood at Ostia. But Sandra immediately ruled out that hypothesis: the traces she had photographed, especially the footprints on the ground, indicated clearly that only one man had been involved. Unless he'd had an accomplice who could fly from one tree to another . . . It was just media bullshit.

So the word had not ended up on the board in the operations room.

Homicide in pine wood at Ostia:

Objects: rucksack, climbing rope, hunting knife, Ruger SP101 revolver.

Prints of the young man on the climbing rope and on the knife left in the sternum of the young woman: he ordered him to tie the girl up and to strike her if he wanted to save his life.

Kills the young man by shooting him in back of neck.

Puts lipstick on the girl (to photograph her?).

Leaves a figure of salt next to the victims (a doll?).

After killing changes clothes.

Homicide of Officers Rimonti and Carboni:

Objects: hunting knife, Ruger SP101 revolver.

Kills officer Stefano Carboni with a gunshot to the chest.

Shoots officer Pia Rimonti, wounding her in the stomach. Then strips her, cuffs her to a tree, tortures her, and finishes her off with a hunting knife. Puts make-up on her (to photograph her?).

Homicide of hitchhikers:

Objects: hunting knife, Ruger SP101 revolver.

Kills Bernhard Jäger with a gunshot to the temple.

Kills Annabel Meyer with a number of stabs to the abdomen.

Annabel Meyer was pregnant.

Buries the victims' bodies and rucksacks.

It was obvious to everyone that the elements of the last double homicide – actually, the first in chronological order – didn't amount to much. In fact, looking at all three scenes, it was as if they had gradually been reduced.

In the case of the hitchhikers, a major factor was that a lot of time had passed since the murders. The contents of the rucksacks of the two young Germans were being examined in the lab right now. Crespi hoped that Leopoldo Strini would show up with some good news. And, above all, some evidence.

'Why are they taking so long?' he wondered. He was referring to the fact that, just before the meeting in the operations room, Deputy Commissioner Moro had been summoned unexpectedly to the Commissioner's office.

Sandra had no answer to that, but she could imagine it.

*

'What does "inter-force consultation" mean?'

'That you're no longer the only person leading the operation,' the Director of the State Police said clearly.

Moro, though, wasn't happy. 'We don't need anybody, we can handle this by ourselves. But thanks all the same.'

'Please don't make a fuss,' the Commissioner intervened. 'We've been under a lot of pressure. You knew they were all over us: the minister, the mayor, public opinion, the media.'

They had been shut up for half an hour in his office on the top floor of Headquarters.

'So what's going to happen now?' Moro asked.

'Officially, the Carabinieri's Special Operations Group will join us on the investigation. We'll have to pass them all the information in our possession and from now on they'll do the same. It's a task force. It was the minister's idea. He'll be holding a press conference soon to announce it.'

What a load of crap, Moro would have liked to say. It wasn't the deployment of resources that would decide the outcome of a case like this. In fact, the involvement of too many heads often hampered an investigation. Dispersing the line of command wasted time. 'Task force' was just an expression to soften up the press, the kind of thing tough cops said in an action movie. In reality, investigations were conducted in silence, going over the ground inch by inch. It was intelligence work, involving the use of informers and tip-offs. It was like sewing a thread, slowly, patiently. Only at the end would the result be evident. 'All right, that's the official version. But what's really going down?'

The Commissioner looked Moro in the eyes. He was starting to get angry. 'I'll tell you what's going down. Two years ago, you sent an innocent man to jail for the murder of the two German hitchhikers. Now that son of a bitch wants to sue the state: his lawyer has already released a statement maintaining that, and I quote, "two years ago his client was forced to confess because he is a victim of the legal system and the superficial methods of the police". Can you imagine? A thief has suddenly become a hero! This morning, an online paper held an opinion poll on how this case is being handled. Would you like me to tell you the results?'

'In other words, chief, you're throwing me out.'

'You've thrown yourself out, Moro.'

Moro was determined not to let his bitterness show. 'So, if I understand correctly, from now on we're collaborating with the Carabinieri, but actually they're in charge, and the task force story is just a way to save face?'

'Do you think we like it this way?' the Director of the State Police said. 'From now on I'll have to report to some damned general from the Carabinieri. I'll have to be nice to him and pretend we're equals.'

Moro realised that these two were decreeing his end and that, after years in which he had served them faithfully, producing outstanding results for which they had taken much of the credit, they didn't give a damn about the fact that he would be the only one to pay. 'What's going to happen?'

'The handing over of information will take place by this afternoon,' the Commissioner said. 'You'll have to report to your counterpart in the Carabinieri and take him through the investigation in detail. You'll answer his questions and then pass over the evidence.'

Moro felt a tightness in his stomach. 'Do we also tell him about the man with the wolf's head? Wasn't that supposed to remain confidential?'

'We'll keep that part out of it,' the Director of the State Police said. 'It's more prudent.'

'Agreed,' the Commissioner said, then went on, 'The operations room won't be dismantled, but it will no longer have an effective role, because the men will be immediately assigned to other cases.'

Another lie to save appearances.

'I resign,' Moro said abruptly.

'You can't, not now,' the Commissioner retorted.

These bastards had used his successes to advance their careers, and now they were discarding him unceremoniously because of a mistake he'd made two years before. Could he help it if an innocent man had confessed to the murder of the two hitchhikers just to get legal advantages? It was the system that was wrong, not him. 'I want to hand in my resignation, nobody can stop me.'

The Commissioner looked as if he was about to lose his temper, but the Director of the State Police intervened. 'It isn't sensible,' he asserted. 'As long as you remain on the force you'll be entitled to official protection, but if you leave you'll become an ordinary citizen, and then they'll be able to bring charges against you for the mistake you made two years ago. And besides, who's making you leave right now? You'd be a perfect target for our detractors: they'd pull you to pieces.'

Moro realised his back was up against the wall. He smiled and shook his head. 'You really have screwed me.'

'Let's wait for the storm to blow over. Stay out of the limelight, let the others do the work and get the honours. Then, gradually, you'll be able to go back to doing what you did before. Your career won't suffer, you have my word.'

You know where you can stick your word, Moro thought. But he knew he had no choice. 'Yes, sir.'

They saw him come back into the operations room looking tense and grim-faced. Abruptly, the murmur ceased and everybody prepared to listen to what he had to say, even though he had not announced that he was going to say anything at all.

He didn't beat about the bush. 'We're out,' he said. 'As of now, we have no operational role: the case is being passed on to the Carabinieri's Special Operations Group.' Voices were raised in protest, but Moro silenced them with a gesture of his hand. 'I'm more pissed off than you are, I can assure you, but we can't do anything about it: it's over.'

Sandra couldn't believe it. It was crazy to take Moro off the case. The Carabinieri would have to start again from scratch, and precious time would be wasted. And the Monster was bound to strike again very soon. She was certain the decision was purely political.

'I'd like to thank you all for the work you've done so far,' Moro went on. 'I know you haven't had much sleep, or much of a private life, over the past few days, and I know that many of you have given up trying to calculate your overtime. Even though nobody else will thank you for it, I assure you it won't be forgotten.'

As Moro continued his speech, Sandra observed her colleagues. Their fatigue, which they had ignored until now, seemed to burst out abruptly on their faces. She too was disappointed, but she also felt relief. It was as though she had been suddenly relieved of a burden. She could go back to Max, to her old life. Barely six days had gone by, but it was as if it had been months.

Moro's voice faded into the background of her thoughts. Sandra felt she was already somewhere else. It was then that she became aware of a vibration in the pocket of her uniform. She took out her mobile phone and looked at the screen.

A text message from a number she didn't know. It contained an incomprehensible question.

Do you worship him?

4

The name of Victor's sister was Hana. They were twins.

She had died at the age of nine, which was about the time her brother had entered the Hamelin Institute. The two things must have been connected, Marcus thought.

They were the children of Anatoly Nikolayevich Agapov, a Russian diplomat assigned to the Rome embassy during the Cold War years, who had kept his post after the advent of *perestroika*. He had been dead for about twenty years now.

Clemente had followed up on Marcus's hunch, looking for the girl rather than Victor's crime. That was how he had tracked down the identity of the brother and sister.

When Marcus had asked him how he had done it, he had simply replied that the Vatican kept files on all the people connected with Communist regimes who had passed through Rome. But it was obvious that someone in the upper echelons had passed on the information. In the confidential papers, there was talk of 'suspicious homicide', but officially Hana had died of natural causes.

It was because of that inconsistency that the story had emerged from the Vatican archives.

Clemente had done much more, though. He had got hold of

the name of the housekeeper who had worked for the Agapovs at the time. The woman now lived in a nursing home run by Salesian nuns.

Marcus set off on the metro to pay her a visit, in the hope of learning more about the case.

It had rained the previous night, so the child of salt had abstained from killing. But he had made sure that the two skeletons in the wood were found. When Marcus had heard the news, he had not been particularly surprised. The storyteller had added another chapter to his story in the present. But his true intention was to tell everyone about his own past. That was why Marcus needed to find out as much as he could about his childhood.

The lull in the rain was due to end soon, so he might strike again tonight.

But Marcus knew he also had to protect himself against those who were trying to cover up for the Monster. He was sure that they were the same people he had seen in the video he had rescued from the fire at the Hamelin Institute.

The oldest of the nurses had definitely died in the fire at the Institute. Dr Astolfi was also dead. But the second nurse – the one-armed man – and the red-headed woman were still alive. As was Professor Kropp, of course.

Kropp was behind it all.

At Termini, Marcus changed to the line going to Pietralata. Many of the passengers were busy reading the free newspaper distributed at the entrance to the metro stations. It was a special edition reporting the news of Diana Delgaudio's 'awakening' and the fact that she written one word on a piece of paper.

They.

Even though the journalists thought differently, Marcus didn't believe it referred to the fact that she had been attacked by more than one person in the pine wood at Ostia. It wasn't a gang, it was one man. A man he might soon get to know better.

A few minutes later, he reached his destination. The nursing home was a sober white building, neoclassical in style. It consisted of three floors, with a garden surrounded by black railings. Clemente had phoned ahead to let the nuns know he was coming.

Marcus was there in his priest's habit. This time, his disguise was the same as his actual function.

The Mother Superior admitted him to the day room. It was just before six o'clock, dinner time. Some of the residents sat on sofas around a TV set, others were playing cards. A lady with blue hair was playing the piano, rocking her head and smiling at some memory from her past, while behind her two others were dancing a kind of waltz.

'There, that's Signora Ferri.' The Mother Superior indicated a woman in a wheelchair, sitting by the window, looking out absently. 'She's not really with us. Her mind often wanders.'

Her name was Virginia Ferri, and she was over eighty.

Marcus approached her. 'Good evening.'

The woman slowly turned her head to see who had greeted her. She had green eyes like those of a cat, which stood out against her light complexion. Her skin was covered with little brown spots, typical of age, but her face was surprisingly smooth. Her hair was sparse and dishevelled. She wore a nightshirt, but was clutching a small leather handbag on her lap, as if she were due to leave at any moment.

'My name's Father Marcus, I'm a priest. Is it OK if I have a word with you?'

'Of course,' she replied, her voice shriller than he had expected. 'Are you here for the wedding?'

'What wedding?'

'Mine,' she said immediately. 'I've decided to get married, but the sisters don't approve.'

It struck Marcus that the Mother Superior was right when she said that the woman's mind wandered. But he plunged in all the same. 'You're Signora Virginia Ferri, is that right?'

'Yes, that's me,' she confirmed, a hint of suspicion in her voice.

'And you were the Agapov family's housekeeper in the eighties, is that correct?'

'Six years of my life I devoted to that family.'

Good, Marcus told himself: he'd come to the right person. 'Do you mind if I ask you a few questions?'

'No, why should I mind?'

Marcus pulled over a chair and sat down next to her. 'What kind of man was Signor Agapov?'

The old woman was silent for a few moments. Marcus was afraid that her memory might betray her, but he was wrong. 'He was a stern man, very strict. I don't think he liked being in Rome. He worked at the Russian embassy, but spent a lot of time at home, shut up in his study.'

'And what about his wife? He did have a wife, didn't he?'

'Signor Agapov was a widower.'

Marcus registered the information: Anatoly Agapov had a difficult character and had been forced to bring up his children without a wife. Maybe he hadn't been very much of a father. 'What was your role in the household, Signora Ferri?'

'I was in charge of the servants,' she said proudly. 'Eight people in all, including the gardeners.'

'So it was a big house?'

'It was enormous. A villa outside Rome. It took me at least an hour to get there every morning.'

Marcus was surprised. 'You mean you didn't live there with the family?'

'Signor Agapov didn't allow anyone else to be there after dark.'

How strange, Marcus thought. And the image came into his mind of a large empty house, inhabited only by a stern man and his two children. Obviously not the best place in which to spend one's childhood. 'What can you tell me about the twins?'

'Victor and Hana?'

'Did you know them well?'

She gave a grimace of displeasure. 'We saw Hana mostly. Sometimes, she'd get away from her father and come and see us in the kitchen or while we were doing the domestic chores. She was a child of light.'

Marcus liked that definition. But what did it mean, she'd get away from her father? 'So her father was possessive . . .'

'The children didn't go to school and didn't even have a private tutor: Signor Agapov taught them himself. And they didn't have any friends.' She turned back to the window. 'My fiancé should be here at any moment. Maybe this time he'll bring me flowers.'

Marcus ignored this. 'What about Victor? What can you tell me about him?'

The woman turned back to him. 'Will you believe me if I tell you that in six years I saw him maybe eight times, nine times at most? He was always shut up in his room. Every now and again we'd hear him playing the piano. He was very good. And he was brilliant at mathematics. One of the maids was tidying his things once, and found sheets and sheets of paper filled with sums.'

The killer savant, the psychopathic savant. 'Did you ever talk to him?'

'Victor didn't talk. He was quiet, he just watched. A couple of times I caught him hiding in his room, watching me in silence.' She seemed to shudder at the memory. 'His sister was a lively girl, though. I think she suffered a lot from being so isolated. But

Signor Agapov doted on her, she was his favourite. The only time I ever saw him smile, he was with Hana.'

That too was an important piece of information for Marcus: Victor had had to compete with his sister. Their father had lavished his attentions on Hana, not on him. To a child of nine, that might have been sufficient motive for murder.

The old woman became distracted again. 'One of these days my fiancé is going to come and take me away from this place. I don't want to die here, I want to get married.'

Marcus nudged her back to her story. 'What was the relationship like between the two children?'

'Signor Agapov never tried to hide the fact that he preferred Hana. I think it hurt Victor a lot. For instance, he refused to have his meals with his father and sister. Signor Agapov would take him his food in his room. Every now and again we'd hear the children quarrel, but they also spent time together. Their favourite game was hide and seek.'

The moment had come to bring up the most painful part of the story, Marcus thought. 'Signora Ferri, how did Hana die?'

'Oh, Father,' the woman said, putting her hands together. 'One morning I got to the villa with the rest of the servants and we found Signor Agapov sitting on the steps outside, with his head in his hands, crying bitterly. He said his Hana was dead, that a sudden fever had taken her away.'

'And did you all believe him?'

Her face darkened. 'We did until we saw the blood on the girl's bed and the knife.'

The knife, Marcus repeated to himself. The same weapon the Monster chose to kill his female victims. 'And didn't anybody report it?'

'Signor Agapov was a very powerful man, what could we do? He had the coffin sent straight back to Russia, so that Hana could be buried next to her mother. Then he dismissed everyone.'

Agapov had presumably used his diplomatic immunity to sweep everything under the carpet.

'He put Victor in a school and then shut himself up in that house until he died.'

It wasn't a school, Marcus would have liked to reply. It was a psychiatric institution for children who had committed terrible crimes. So Victor hadn't needed to be put on trial, he told himself. His father had sentenced him and provided the punishment.

'Is it because of the boy that you're here, Father?' The woman's eyes were full of fear now. 'He's done something, hasn't he?'

Marcus didn't have the courage to tell her the whole truth. 'I fear he may have done.'

She nodded, pensively. It was as if she had always known it, Marcus thought.

'Do you want to see them?' Before Marcus could say anything, she opened the leather handbag she was holding in her lap and searched until she found a little book with a flowery cover. She leafed through it and extracted some old photographs. Finding the one she was looking for, she held it out to Marcus.

The colours were faded by time: it probably dated back to the eighties. It looked as if it had been taken with a self-timer. In the middle of the photograph was a man of about fifty, relatively short but robust. Anatoly Agapov was wearing a dark tie and a waistcoat. His hair was combed back and he had a black goatee beard. To his right, a girl in a little red velvet dress. Her hair wasn't very long, but nor was it short and there was a ribbon lifting the fringe. Hana. She was the only one smiling. To the left of the man, a boy. He also had a suit and tie. Bobbed hair with a fringe falling over his eyes. Marcus recognised him: he had seen him in the video he had taken away from the Hamelin Institute.

Victor.

He looked sad and was staring at the camera exactly as he had looked at the video camera while Kropp was questioning him. Once again Marcus had the unsettling impression that the child was looking through the camera into the present. Looking directly at him.

Then Marcus noticed a strange detail. *Anatoly Agapov was holding his son by the hand, but not Hana.*

Wasn't she his favourite? He was missing something . . . Was it a gesture of affection or a way of imposing his authority? Was that paternal hand a leash?

'Can I keep it?' Marcus asked the old woman.

'You will bring it back, Father, won't you?'

'Yes,' Marcus promised, and stood up. 'I'm very grateful to you, Signora Ferri. You've been a great help to me.'

'Wait, don't you want to meet my fiancé?' she said, disappointed. 'He'll be here soon. He comes every evening at this hour and stops on the street, beyond the garden. He looks at my window because he wants to make sure I'm OK. Then he waves to me. He always waves to me.'

'Another time,' Marcus said.

'The sisters think I'm mad, that I made him up. But it's true. He's younger than me, and even though he's missing an arm I still like him.'

Marcus stopped dead. He remembered the male nurse at the Hamelin Institute whom he had seen in the video the previous day.

Fernando, the one-armed man.

'Can you show me where your fiancé stands when he comes to see you in the evening?' he asked, turning towards the window.

The old woman smiled: at last, someone believed her. 'Next to that tree.'

*

Before Fernando knew what was happening, Marcus had already flung him to the ground and pinned him down by pressing his forearm into his neck.

'Are you keeping an eye on the old woman because you want to make sure nobody talks to her? Because you know the truth, you know about Victor . . . '

The man was choking, his eyes bulging. 'Who are you?' he tried to ask with the little breath remaining to him.

Marcus pressed harder. 'Who sent you? Was it Kropp?'

The man shook his head. 'I beg you, Kropp has nothing to do with this.' His stump was moving about in the sleeve of his loose dark jacket, beating on the ground like a fish struggling desperately out of water.

Marcus loosened his grip to let him speak. 'Then explain it to me . . . '

'It was my idea. Giovanni told me someone was asking questions. Someone who wasn't a policeman.'

Giovanni was the elderly male nurse who slept in the basement of the Hamelin Institute. The man with the blue shoes.

'I came here because I thought whoever was investigating would get to the housekeeper.' He started crying. 'I beg you, I want to talk, I want to get out of this. I can't stand it any more.'

Marcus, though, didn't believe that Fernando was sincere. 'How do I know I can trust you?'

'Because I'll take you to Kropp.'

5

During the rest of the afternoon, she hadn't thought again about the strange text.

Once she had left Headquarters at the end of her shift, she had gone to the gym to work off the tension she had accumulated over the past six days. The physical effort had drained her of all the things that had been causing her anguish.

The defeat of Moro and the Central Operations Team, the investigation passed to the Carabinieri, Diana Delgaudio showing signs of a recovery that would actually never happen.

The truth, though, was that she didn't want to go home. Her routine with Max scared her. For the first time, she realised that something really wasn't right between them. She didn't know what it was and, above all, she didn't know how to tell him.

She got out of the shower and went to the changing room. Opening the locker in which she had put her things, she saw that there was another text on her phone. The same unknown number, the same message.

Do you worship him?

The first time, she had assumed that someone had sent her a text meant for someone else by mistake. But now, she began to suspect that it was actually addressed to her.

On her way back to Trastevere, she tried to call the sender's number, but got only a series of rings. It was upsetting. She wasn't unduly curious, though, so she decided to drop it.

She parked a few yards from home and waited a moment before getting out of the car. Her hands gripping the wheel, she looked through the windscreen at the lighted window of her apartment. She could see Max moving about in the kitchen. He was wearing an apron and his glasses were resting on the top of his head. He was probably making dinner. From where she was, he seemed to have his usual absent-minded air, and was most likely whistling.

How can I tell him? she thought. How can I explain something I can't even explain to myself?

But she would do it somehow, she owed it to him. So she took a deep breath and got out of the car.

As soon as he heard the key turning in the lock, Max came to greet her in the entrance as he did every evening. 'Tired?' he asked, kissing her on the cheek and relieving her of her gym bag. 'Dinner is nearly ready,' he added without waiting for an answer.

'OK,' was all Sandra managed to say, and even that was an enormous effort for her. But Max didn't notice.

'We had a great history test in class today: the kids gave perfect answers to all my questions about the Renaissance. I gave them all top marks!' He said it like a businessman who had just sealed a million-dollar deal.

Max's enthusiasm for his work was incredible. His salary was barely enough to pay the rent, but being a history teacher meant more to him than any riches.

One night he had dreamt about some numbers. Sandra had urged him to play them in the lottery, but he had resisted. 'If I got rich, I'd find it strange to be a simple teacher. I'd have to change my life, and I'm pleased with my life as it is now.'

'That's not true,' she had retorted. 'You could carry on doing what you're doing, you just wouldn't have to worry about the future any more.'

'And what's more beautiful than the mystery of the future? Including all the dramas and anxieties. When people don't have to worry about the future any more, it's as if they've already done all they had to do in their lives. But I have history: the past is the only certainty I need.'

Sandra was fascinated by this man who to anyone else might appear devoid of ambition. It seemed to her that Max, unlike so many people, knew exactly what he wanted. And he was satisfied by that knowledge.

A few minutes later, she sat down at the table. Max was still straining the pasta. He moved with great confidence in the kitchen. Since coming to Rome from Nottingham, he had learned all about Italian cooking. She, on the other hand, could barely boil a couple of eggs.

This evening, as usual, Max had laid the table and put a candle in a glass. It had become a kind of romantic ritual. Before serving the dishes, he lit the candle with a cigarette lighter and smiled at her. He had also opened a bottle of red wine. 'That way we can get blind drunk and fall asleep on the sofa,' he said.

How could she tell a man like this that she found it hard to be with him? She felt ungrateful to fate.

He had made her favourite dish: pasta *alla Norma*. And for a second course there was *saltimbocca alla romana*. The trouble with living with someone who was perfect was that it made you feel inadequate. Sandra knew she didn't deserve all these attentions. Inside her, the unease was growing.

'Let's make a pact,' Max said. 'No murders tonight, please.'

That afternoon she had phoned to tell him that the case of the Monster of Rome had been transferred to the Carabinieri. Sandra never talked to him about her work, preferring to gloss over the ugliness that might have disturbed his sensitive soul. But this evening she was afraid of gaps in the conversation. And the fact that even that unlikely topic of conversation had been eliminated terrified her. 'OK,' she said anyway, forcing a smile.

Max sat down opposite her and put his hand on hers. 'I'm glad you're off that case. Now eat, before it gets cold.'

Sandra looked down at her plate, fearing she would never be able to raise her eyes again. But when she picked up her napkin, the world came crashing down on her head with unexpected violence.

Under the napkin was a velvet case. It looked as if it contained a ring.

Sandra felt the tears welling up in her. She tried to hold them back, but to no avail.

'I know what you think about marriage,' Max said, unable to imagine the real reason she was crying. 'When we met, you told me straight away you wouldn't marry anybody else after David. All this time I've respected your wishes and I've never mentioned getting married. But now I've changed my mind. Would you like me to tell you why?'

Sandra merely nodded.

'Nothing is for ever.' He paused. 'If I've learned one thing, it's that our actions don't depend on how good we've been at planning or imagining the future. No, they're dictated only by what we feel here and now. So even though marriage with me might not last a lifetime, it doesn't matter. What matters is that I want it now. I'm prepared to risk unhappiness to be happy now.'

In the meantime, Sandra was looking at the case, without having the courage to pick it up.

'Don't expect a big jewel,' he said. 'Not even that little box can contain the value of what I feel.'

'I don't want to,' she said under her breath, almost in a whisper.

'What?' Max genuinely hadn't heard.

Sandra lifted her tear-stained eyes to him. 'I don't want to marry you.'

If Max was expecting an explanation, it didn't come. His expression changed abruptly. It wasn't only disappointment, it was as if he had just been told that he had only a few days left to live. 'Is there someone else?'

'No,' she replied immediately, although she didn't even know if it was true.

'What, then?'

Sandra took the mobile phone from the shelf where she had put it. She opened the texts and showed him the two anonymous messages she had received during the day.

'*Do you worship him?*' Max read.

'I don't know who sent them to me and I don't know the reason why. Anyone else in my place would be curious to know what's behind a romantic message like that. But not me. And do you know why?' She didn't wait for the answer. 'Because it made me think about the two of us. It forced me to ask myself what I was feeling.' She paused for breath. 'I love you, Max. But I don't worship you. And I think that to get married, or even just to spend all your lives together, there has to be something more than love. And, right now, I don't feel it.'

'Do you mean it's over?'

'I really don't know. But I have a horrible feeling it is. I'm sorry.'

Neither of them said anything for a while. Then Max stood up from the table. 'A friend of mine has a house by the sea that he only uses in the summer. I could ask him to let me stay there tonight, or maybe even the next few nights. I don't want to lose you, Sandra. But I don't want to be here either.'

She understood him. Just then, part of her wished she could embrace him and hold him back. But she knew it wouldn't be right.

Max blew out the candle on the table. 'The Colosseum.'

Sandra looked at him. 'What?'

'It isn't a historical fact, just a legend,' he said. 'The Colosseum is said to have been a kind of temple used by devil worshippers. To lay people who wanted to become part of the cult, they asked a question in Latin: "*Colis eum*?" In other words, "Do you worship him?" Obviously, "him" referred to the devil . . . *Colis eum*: Colosseum.'

She was disconcerted by the explanation. But she said nothing.

Max left the kitchen, but before doing so picked up the case with the ring from the table. It was the only reaction he allowed himself after listening to Sandra's words. And that said a great deal about what a fine person he was: another man would have got up on his high horse, responded to the humiliation with a show of contempt. Not Max. But at that moment Sandra might have preferred to be slapped rather than be taught that lesson in love and respect.

The ring was the only thing that Max took with him, apart from his jacket, which was hanging out in the hall. Then he left the apartment, closing the door behind him.

Sandra found it impossible to move. The pasta on her plate was getting cold. A thin thread of grey smoke still rose from the candle in the middle of the table, and the sweet smell of the wax had pervaded the room. She wondered if this really was the end. She tried for a moment to think of her life without Max. She started subtracting his presence from all her actions and habits. It was painful. But not painful enough to make her run after him and tell him she had made a mistake.

So, after a few more moments in which she regained her composure, she picked up the mobile phone and replied to the message Do you worship him? with one word: Colosseum.

A few minutes passed, then another text arrived.

Four in the morning.

6

Moro was alone in the operations room.

Alone like a veteran who had lost the war but didn't want to return home, and so remained on the deserted battlefield, surrounded by the ghosts of his comrades, waiting for the enemy who wouldn't come. Because the only thing he knew how to do was fight.

He was standing by the board listing the elements of the cases. The answers are all there in front of you, he told himself. But you've been looking at them the wrong way, that's why you lost.

He had been dropped from the case because of that business with the hitchhikers, because two years earlier he'd put an innocent man in jail for a murder where there were no bodies. And that arsehole had confessed to something he hadn't done.

Moro knew that this punishment was par for the course. But he couldn't drop it, that wasn't like him. Even though he no longer had any role in the investigation into the Monster of Rome, he couldn't slow down, couldn't stop everything. He was like a car being driven as fast as possible towards its destination. That was how he had wanted it, that was how he had been trained. He couldn't stop now. But nor could he run the risk of being thrown out of the police. A few hours earlier he had offered his resignation, but the Director of the State Police had rejected it with a threat and a promise.

'As long as you remain on the force you'll be entitled to official protection, but if you leave you'll become an ordinary citizen, and then they'll be able to bring charges against you for the mistake you made two years ago . . . Let's wait for the storm to blow over. Stay out of the limelight, let the others do the work and get the honours. Then, gradually, you'll be able to go back to doing what you did before. Your career won't suffer, you have my word.'

What a load of bullshit. Anyway this business of resigning was a bluff. He knew perfectly well that he would be completely alone. Everyone would abandon him, probably pinning most of the blame on him.

The Monster was running rings around them. Moro had to admit it, with a touch of admiration in his anger. In the case of the pine wood at Ostia, he had inundated them with clues and evidence, including his DNA left on the shirt he'd stupidly mistaken for the victim's when he had put his clothes back on after the murders. Since then, nothing, or almost nothing.

But something was missing from that list. The symbol. The man with the wolf's head.

Moro remembered the shadow cast by the bone sculpture found in Astolfi's apartment. And he remembered the shudder he had felt looking at it.

His superiors didn't want the Carabinieri to know about that. He still remembered their words that afternoon, when he had asked if the story of that symbol was one of the things to be handed over to the Special Operations Group.

'We'll keep that part out of it,' the Director of the State Police had said, supported by the Commissioner. 'It's more prudent.'

But it was 'that part' that might be an opportunity for Moro to get back in the game. After all, nobody had actually ordered him to stop investigating the symbol. That meant that, officially, he was still free to do so.

'Twenty-three cases,' he repeated to himself. Twenty-three cases in which the anthropomorphic figure had appeared as part of a crime, or else in connection with something or someone involved in a crime. Why?

He remembered some of those episodes. The babysitter who threw the children from the windows and kept their shoes as souvenirs had confessed but had been unable to explain why there was a drawing of a man with a wolf's head on a page in her diary. In 1994, the figure had appeared on the bathroom mirror in the home of a man who had killed his family and then himself. In 2005, it had been discovered, drawn in spray paint, on the grave of a paedophile.

Unconnected events, different years and culprits. The only thing they had in common was the symbol. It was as if someone had wanted to sign those crimes, but not to take the credit.

It seemed more like a piece of . . . *proselytising*.

He who does evil will be understood, that was the message. He will be helped. Just as the Monster of Rome had been helped by Astolfi, who had taken a piece of evidence from the crime scene and had tried to remedy the killer's mistake by letting Diana Delgaudio die.

Moro was convinced that, somewhere out there, there were others like Astolfi. People devoted to evil as if it were a religion.

If he tracked them down, he would have his revenge.

He summoned Leopoldo Strini. Because he had been asked to examine the sculpture of animal bones found in Astolfi's apartment, he was the only person to know the story of the symbol, apart from Moro's trusted men in the Central Operations Team and Superintendent Crespi.

He saw Strini coming with the requested files. He had a strange expression on his face, and seemed unusually agitated.

Strini realised that Moro was looking him up and down, maybe because he had noticed his nervousness. Ever since he had talked with that mysterious man with the oriental features at lunchtime, his life had been turned upside down. Learning that the case had been transferred to the Carabinieri had helped to calm him down a little. He would have to pass the finds to the Special Operations Group's scientific lab, which meant that his new 'friend' – his blackmailer – would no longer be able to ask him for a first look at the evidence, or to destroy it. At least he hoped so. Because a little voice in his head kept telling him that, whatever happened, the man from the café now had him by the balls, and would continue to do so until one of them cracked. 'It's all here,' he said, placing the files on the table. Then he went on his way.

Moro immediately forgot about Strini and his nervousness, because there in front of him was the summary of the twenty-three cases in which the image of the man with the wolf's head had appeared. He started looking through it in search of anything relevant.

In the case of the murdered family, for example, when Forensics had found the symbol on the bathroom mirror in the course of a supplementary investigation, they had also found the clear print of a right hand on the floor. The report suggested an explanation: days after the killings, someone had got into the house, turned on the hot water taps in the bathroom, and traced the symbol in the steam on the mirror. But on his way out he had probably slipped because of the condensation. To cushion his fall, he had reached out his hand. Hence, the print on the floor.

But there was an inconsistency in that theory: it was unlikely that someone would use only one hand to protect himself after slipping. The instinct for self-preservation would have led the person to use both hands. At the time, since the mystery couldn't be clarified, the question of the handprint had been relegated to the background, along with that of the symbol on the mirror. Because, Moro remembered, the police didn't like having to deal with anything to do with the occult.

He went on to examine the case of the paedophile's grave. But in the meagre police report, all it said was that there had been an 'act of vandalism carried out by persons unknown'. The handwriting expert, though, had expressed the opinion that the words has been written by a 'forced right-hander'. In the past, some teachers had compelled left-handed children to use their other hand. It had happened in Catholic schools, Moro recalled, the result of an absurd superstition that said the left hand was the hand of the devil and left-handers had to be 'educated' to use their right hand. But, apart from that one detail, that case, too, presented nothing of interest.

In the babysitter case, there was even less. The whole investigation had centred on the shoes, which the girl had kept like a fetish after throwing the children from the windows. With regard to the drawing in the page of the diary there was little or nothing: the girl had stated that she hadn't drawn it and they had been content with that version. Whether or not she had drawn it, it wouldn't have made any difference to the trial. On the contrary, it might have affected the sentence if the babysitter had claimed she was mentally ill.

'I see a man with a wolf's head, Your Honour! He was the one who told me to kill those children!'

But, just as he was about to pass on, Moro stumbled across something interesting. At the time, his colleagues had questioned a man who had occasionally gone out with the defendant. They weren't boyfriend and girlfriend but, as the babysitter herself said, they did have sexual relations. The man had been questioned because he was suspected of complicity, but there was no real evidence against him and no charges had been brought. All the same, the transcript of his statement had ended up in the case file.

What struck Moro weren't the man's answers, which were quite banal, but the identity document attached to the statement.

Among his distinguishing features was the fact that he did not have a left arm.

The print on the bathroom floor, Moro immediately thought. That was why there was only a print of a right hand: *he was one-armed*! His intuition was confirmed by the story of the paedophile's grave: whoever had scrawled that symbol on it had used his right hand to do so, but the writing was forced . . . Just like that of a left-handed person who has lost his left arm.

Moro immediately searched for details of the babysitter's friend. Apart from the name, there was an address.

7

Night had fallen.

The sky was clear of clouds, and the moon was a beacon. Marcus was convinced the killer would strike again within a few hours. That was why he had to get the one-armed man to tell him as much as possible.

Despite his lack of an arm, Fernando was a skilful driver.

'What can you tell me about Victor?' Marcus asked.

'If you got to the old housekeeper, that means you pretty much know everything already.'

'Tell me more. About the Hamelin Institute, for example.'

Fernando took a very narrow bend. 'The children who came there had already committed violent crimes or showed a marked tendency in that direction. But I assume you already know that.'

'Yes, I do.'

'What you don't know is that they weren't given any rehabilitative therapy. Kropp wanted to safeguard their ability to do harm. He considered it a kind of talent.'

'For what reason?'

'You'll find out everything as soon as we get to Kropp.'

'Why don't you tell me now?'

For a moment Fernando took his eyes off the road and looked at him. 'Because I want to show you.'

'Does it have anything to do with the man with the wolf's head?'

This time, Fernando did not answer the question directly. All he said was, 'You will have to be patient, it won't be long now: you won't regret it. You're not a policeman, are you? So you must be a private detective . . . '

'Kind of,' Marcus replied. 'Where is Victor now?'

'I don't know. Nobody knows. Once the children left the Hamelin Institute, they went back into the real world and we lost all trace of them.' He smiled. 'But we were sure we'd hear about them again sooner or later. Many of them committed some crime or other after a couple of years. We'd hear about it in the newspapers or on TV, and Kropp would be pleased because he'd achieved his aim: to make them perfect instruments of evil.'

'Is that why you're protecting Victor?'

'We've done the same for others in the past. But Victor was Kropp's pride and joy: a psychopathic savant, completely incapable of feeling. His wickedness was equal to his intelligence. The professor knew the child of salt would do great things. Sure enough, look what's happening.'

Marcus wasn't in a position to know how much truth there was in the man's words, but he had no other choice but to follow him. 'When I jumped on you outside the nursing home, you said you knew that someone who wasn't a policeman was investigating this affair.'

'The police don't know anything about the child of salt, but we knew that someone was following up that lead. All I did was stand outside the old woman's window to see if she had any visitors. I told you: I want out of this whole thing.'

'Who else is part of it?'

'Giovanni, the old nurse you met, who's now dead.' The man

with the blue shoes. 'Then there was Dr Astolfi, who's also gone. Then Olga, the other nurse. Me and Kropp.'

Marcus had been testing him, to make sure he mentioned all those he had seen in the video of Victor as a child which he had taken from the Hamelin Institute. 'No one else?'

'No, no one.'

They turned on to the ramp leading from the ring road back to the centre.

'Why do you want out?'

Fernando laughed. 'Because at first I was won over by Kropp's ideas like the others. I was a piece of garbage before I met the professor. He gave me an aim and an ideal. *A discipline*. Kropp believes firmly in the value of fairytales: he says they're the most faithful mirror of human nature. If you take the villains out of fairytales, they stop being entertaining, have you noticed that? Nobody wants a story that only has good guys.'

'So he created them specially for the children: stories where the villains were the main characters.'

'Yes, and he made one up for me too: the story of the *invisible man* . . . There's this man nobody can see, because he's just like all the others, there's nothing special about him. He'd like to be noticed, he'd like everyone to turn and look at him, he can't resign himself to being a nobody. He buys beautiful clothes, improves his appearance, but it's no good. So you know what he does? He understands that he mustn't add something, he must take something away.'

Marcus had a horrible feeling he could imagine the rest of the story.

'So he cuts off one of his arms,' Fernando said. 'And he learns to do everything with just one hand. Do you know what happens? Everybody looks at him, they feel sorry for him, but they don't know the enormous strength he has inside him. What other man would be capable of doing something like that? He's achieved his purpose: now he knows he's stronger than anybody else. Discipline.'

Marcus was horrified. 'And now you want to betray the person who taught you all this?'

'I'm not betraying Kropp,' he said, becoming impassioned. 'But ideals require effort, and I've already given a lot to the cause.'

The cause? Marcus asked himself. What cause could a group of people who protected evildoers possibly have?

'Do we have far to go?'

'We're nearly there.'

They came to a wide stretch of road near the Via dei Giubbonari. There, they left the car and proceeded on foot to the Campo de' Fiori.

The Campo de' Fiori may have looked like a square, but it was different from all the others, because it had originally been an uncultivated field. The palaces and buildings had been added later, naturally marking the space.

Even though the name of the place invoked an image of rustic calm, the Campo de' Fiori was remembered in the history of Rome as the home of the *girella*, a rope torture used to dislocate the arms of criminals. It was also the place where people had been burnt at the stake.

It was there that Giordano Bruno had been burnt alive for the crime of heresy.

As always when he walked through the square, Marcus looked up at the bronze statue of Bruno, with the black cowl over his head and his deep, still eyes. A freethinker, Bruno had challenged the Inquisition, preferring to face the flames rather than deny his own philosophical ideas. Marcus had a lot in common with him: both trusted in the power of reason.

Fernando was walking lopsidedly ahead of him, moving his

one arm as if he were marching. The jacket he wore was so loose, it looked like a clown's.

Their destination was an opulent seventeenth-century palace that had undergone renovations in the succeeding centuries, but still preserved its own noble aura.

Rome was full of aristocratic houses like that. From the outside they seemed to be in a state of decay, rather like the people who lived in them: counts, marquises and dukes who still had titles that had no value other than being rooted in history. Inside, though, those palaces contained antique furniture and works of art that any museum or private collector would envy. Artists of the calibre of Caravaggio, Mantegna and Benvenuto Cellini had lent their talents to embellish the residences of the noblemen of their time. Now the sight of those masterpieces was reserved for their descendants who, like them, spent their existence squandering inheritances that were the result of privileges unjustly acquired in the past.

'How can Kropp afford to live in a place like this?' Marcus asked.

Fernando turned and smiled. 'There are many things you don't know, my friend.' He increased his pace.

They went in through a side door. Fernando pressed a light switch and lit up a brief flight of stairs that led to a one-room basement. The caretaker's lodge. Another service staircase led to the upper floors.

'Welcome to my home,' Fernando said, indicating the single bed and the little kitchen that occupied almost the entire space. Clothes were hanging in an open wardrobe, and there were shelves of food, mostly in cans. 'Wait here.'

Marcus grabbed him by his one arm. 'Don't even think about it, I'm coming with you.'

'I'm not trying to trick you, I swear. But come if you like.'

Marcus lit his torch, and together they climbed the service

stairs. After an endless series of steps, they reached a landing. There were no doors, it was a dead end.

'Is this a joke?'

'Have faith,' Fernando said, amused. With the palm of his hand he pressed against one of the walls, and a little door opened. 'After you.'

But Marcus put his hand on the man's back, pushed him through the opening and followed him in.

They were in a huge room, devoid of furniture but richly decorated. The only fixture, apart from an old cast-iron radiator and a wide window covered with blinds, was a large gilded mirror on the wall, which reflected the beam of the torch and the two of them.

The little door through which they had come was perfectly camouflaged by the fresco on the wall. The system of secret passages had been conceived originally to allow the servants to move through the palace, appearing and disappearing in silence, without disturbing their masters.

'Who's at home?' Marcus asked under his breath.

'Kropp and Olga,' Fernando replied. 'Just the two of them. They occupy the east wing, to get there we have to—'

He didn't have time to finish the sentence, because Marcus landed him a punch full in the face. Fernando fell to his knees, lifting his hand to his big nose, which had started bleeding profusely. Marcus followed up the punch with a kick to the stomach that laid Fernando flat on the floor.

'Who's at home?' Marcus asked again.

'I told you,' Fernando whined.

Marcus forced him to turn over and removed a pair of handcuffs from the back pocket of his trousers. He had noticed them as they were climbing the stairs. Now he flung them at him. 'How many lies have you told me? I listened to you, but I don't think you've been very honest with me.'

'Why do you say that?' Fernando said, spitting blood on the marble floor.

'Do you think I'm so innocent as to believe that you would sell your boss to me so easily? Why have you brought me here?'

This time the kick hit him hard in the side. Fernando gasped and rolled on the floor. Before Marcus could kick him again, he raised his hand to stop him. 'All right . . . Kropp asked me to bring you.'

While Marcus was wondering if he should believe this, Fernando used his one arm to crawl to the wall and huddle below the big gilded mirror.

'What does Kropp want of me?'

'To meet you. I don't know the reason, I swear.'

Marcus again went to him. Fernando raised his arm to parry a possible kick, but Marcus grabbed him by his collar. He picked up the handcuffs from the floor, dragged him over to the cast-iron radiator and cuffed him to it. Then he turned his back on him and took a step towards the door that led to the other rooms.

'Kropp won't be pleased,' Fernando whimpered behind him.

Marcus wished he could just make him shut up.

'A room without furniture, so the only place you could handcuff me was a radiator,' Fernando said, and laughed. 'What imagination!'

Marcus put his hand on the door handle and lowered it. The door was open.

'I'm the invisible man. The invisible man knows that discipline is his strength. If he has discipline, everybody will realise how strong he is.' And he laughed again.

'Shut up,' Marcus said threateningly. He opened the door but, before walking through it, turned for a moment towards the big gilded mirror. He thought he was having a hallucination, because the handcuffed man at the radiator was no longer one-armed.

He had two arms. And in his left hand he was clutching something.

A syringe glinted for a moment in the mirror, then Marcus felt it plunging into the skin of his thigh, where the femoral artery was.

'Make everybody believe you are what you are not,' Fernando said, as the drug insinuated itself into Marcus's blood and he gripped the door handle to stop himself from falling. 'Repeat the exercise all the days of your life, with effort and dedication. Even you couldn't look at me, but now you see me.'

It was only now that Marcus realised how well planned it had all been. Fernando standing outside the nursing home, the handcuffs in the back pocket of his trousers, which Marcus had thought he'd noticed by pure chance, the room devoid of furniture but with a radiator positioned just next to the door: a perfect trap.

Marcus felt himself fall but, before he lost consciousness, he again heard Fernando's voice.

'Discipline, my friend. Discipline.'

8

A full moon peered down on the narrow streets of the historic centre.

Moro had come on foot to the seventeenth-century palace where it turned out the one-armed man was the caretaker. His lodge was in the basement. Moro didn't want to come forward yet: he preferred to wait and check things out first. He wasn't sure that the man was at home, but at least he had located the target. The next day, he would come back for a surprise search.

He turned to go back to his car, but stopped when he became aware of movement in the alley that ran along the side of the palace. Someone had opened wide an enormous double door of dark wood. After a short while, a station wagon emerged from what had once been the stables for the horses and the place where the carriages were kept.

As it passed him, Moro saw a one-armed man at the wheel: his nose was swollen and his nostrils were stuffed with wads of bloodstained cotton wool. Beside him sat a woman in her fifties, with short mahogany-coloured hair.

Moro didn't stop to ask himself where they were going at such a late hour: what he had seen was enough to send him running back to his own car, cutting through the alleys, hoping to get there before the station wagon left the maze of the historic centre and to set off in pursuit of it.

As they proceeded, the car jolted over the cobbles. To Marcus, bound and gagged in the boot, these jolts, light as they were, were like hammer blows to his temples. He was huddled in a foetal position, with his hands tied behind his back and his calves also bound. The handkerchief they had stuffed in his throat made it hard for him to breathe, partly because Fernando, before loading him in the car with the help of Olga, had punched him on the nose to avenge himself for the treatment he had received.

Marcus was dazed from the drug that had knocked him out, but from the position he was in he was able to catch part of the dialogue between the two former nurses from the Hamelin Institute.

'So, did I do a good job?' Fernando asked.

'Of course,' the red-headed woman replied. 'The professor heard everything. He's very pleased with you.'

Was she referring to Kropp? So he *was* in the palace. Maybe Fernando hadn't been lying about that.

'But it was a risk bringing him to the house,' Olga said.

'I laid the trap well,' Fernando said in his defence. 'And besides, I had no choice: he wouldn't have followed me if I'd suggested going somewhere isolated.'

'He must have asked you questions. What did you tell him?'

'Only what he already knew. I beat about the bush and he trusted me, partly because I think he was looking for confirmation more than anything else. He's a smart guy, you know.'

'So he doesn't know anything else?'

'I didn't get the impression he does.'

'Did you search him properly? Are you really sure he didn't have any papers?'

'I'm sure.'

'Not even a business card, a receipt from somewhere he's been?'

'Nothing,' he assured her. 'Apart from the torch, all he had in his pocket was a pair of latex gloves, a retractable screwdriver and some money.'

The only thing that bastard had left him, Marcus thought, was the medallion of the Archangel Michael he wore round his neck.

'Oh, and he also had a photograph the Agapovs' housekeeper must have given him in the nursing home: the father with the twins.'

'Did you destroy it?'

'I burnt it.'

Marcus didn't need it any more, he remembered it well.

'And he was unarmed,' Fernando added, completing his report.

'Strange,' the woman said. 'He isn't a policeman, that much we know. From the things he had with him, he might be a private detective. But then who was he working for?'

Marcus hoped that the two wanted to be sure of obtaining an answer before killing him. That way, he would gain time. But the drug was stopping him from thinking of a plan. He was convinced it would all be over for him very soon.

Moro was following the station wagon at a distance of about three hundred yards. As long as they had remained in the city he had kept other vehicles between him and them, so that they couldn't spot him in the rear view mirror. But now that they had got on to the multi-lane road that encircled Rome he had to be more careful. Even though the risk of losing them was greater.

In other circumstances, he would already have radioed for back-up. But there was no evidence of a crime, nor did he get the impression that trailing them involved any danger. The truth, however, was that after being taken off the case, he was determined to prove his worth. Especially to himself.

Let's see if you really have lost your grip, old man.

He could smell a crime when the opportunity presented itself. He was good at it. And, without quite knowing why, he was convinced that the two in front of him were up to something.

Something illegal.

He saw them visibly slowing down. Strange: there were no signs indicating an exit along that part of the road. Maybe they had realised they were being followed. He slowed down and let himself be overtaken by a lorry, concealing himself just behind it. He waited a few seconds, then did a manoeuvre so that he could check what was going on in front of the lorry.

He could no longer see the station wagon.

He repeated the manoeuvre twice more. Nothing. Where the hell had they got to? But as he was formulating the question in his head, the station wagon appeared in his right rear-view mirror. It had stopped at the side of the road and he had just passed it.

'Will you stop that, dammit?'

Fernando was yelling, but Marcus continued to kick his bound legs against the bodywork.

'I've stopped, arsehole. Now do you want me to come back there? I don't know if you'd like that.'

Olga was holding a black leather case in her lap. 'Maybe we should give him a second dose now,' she suggested.

'He has to answer our questions first: we need to discover what he knows. Then we'll give him the right dose.'

The right dose, Marcus repeated to himself. The one that would finish him off.

'If you don't shut up now, I'll break both your legs with the jack.'

The threat had the desired effect and, after another couple of kicks, Marcus stopped.

'Good,' Fernando said. 'I see you're starting to understand the way things are. It's best for you too if we hurry up, believe me.'

And he drove back on to the main road.

Moro had slowed down some more and moved into the emergency lane. He had his eyes fixed on the rear-view mirror.

Come on, let me see you. Dammit, get back on the road.

In the distance he saw a couple of headlights emerge and prayed that it was the station wagon. Sure enough, it was. Excited, he got ready to let them overtake him and then resume following them. But, as he waited for them to pass, another lorry came along the emergency lane with all its headlights on and blaring its horn, forcing him to move earlier than he had planned. He had to pull over to avoid a crash.

The result was that once again the station wagon was behind him.

He would take a risk and let himself again be overtaken by them: he had no alternative. He prayed they wouldn't take an exit in the meantime. But his prayers went unanswered, because the station wagon turned off in the direction of the Salaria, and finally disappeared from sight.

'No, dammit, no!'

He put his foot down on the accelerator, pushing the car to its limit, in search of another exit so that he could turn back.

Even in such an uncomfortable position, Marcus realised that the road had changed. It was no longer just the reduced speed that suggested it, but also the fact that the asphalt now seemed less smooth. More jolts and potholes threw him against the walls of the boot.

Then he heard the unmistakable sound of a dirt road. Little

stones flew up and bounced off the back of the vehicle, like a spray of popcorn.

The two in front had stopped talking, depriving him of valuable psychological guidance. What did they intend to do once they arrived? He would have preferred to know in advance, instead of being forced to imagine it.

The car turned a narrow bend and stopped. Marcus heard Olga and Fernando get out and close the doors behind them. From outside, their voices now came muffled.

'Help me to open the boot and take him inside.'

'Couldn't you use your other arm too, for once?'

'Discipline, Olga, discipline,' Fernando said pedantically.

Marcus heard the sound of caterpillar tracks being moved, then Fernando got back in the car and started it again.

He had managed to turn around after a couple of miles and was now driving along the opposite carriageway, moving his eyes between the windscreen and his left, trying to see the station wagon.

Having come more or less level with the exit where he had lost them, he spotted, thanks to the full moon, the position lights at the rear of a vehicle. They were at the top of a hill flanked by a kind of path.

From that distance he couldn't say if it really was the station wagon. But, whatever the vehicle was, he saw it drive into a shed made of sheet metal.

Moro accelerated in search of an exit.

Someone opened wide the boot of the station wagon and shone a torch in his face. Marcus instinctively half-closed his eyes and shrank back.

'Welcome,' Fernando said. 'Now we can have a chat and you'll finally tell us who you are.'

He grabbed him by the rope round his waist and was about to drag him out of the boot when Olga stopped him. 'There's no need,' she said.

Fernando turned and looked at her in surprise. 'What do you mean?'

'Now that we're at the end, the professor said to kill him and leave it at that.'

A disappointed expression came over Fernando's face. At the end of what? Marcus wondered.

'We still have to deal with the policewoman,' Fernando said.

What policewoman? Marcus felt a shudder.

'She can wait,' Olga said. 'We don't yet know if she's a problem.'

'You saw her on television, making the sign of the cross. How did she know?'

What were they talking about? Could they possibly mean Sandra?

'I've looked into it: she's not a detective, she's a photographer. But, in case there's any doubt, I already know how to deal with her.'

Now Marcus was certain they were talking about her. And he could do nothing to help her.

Olga opened the case she had with her and took out a little automatic pistol. 'Your journey ends here too, Fernando,' she said, and handed him the weapon.

More disappointment. 'Weren't we supposed to do it together?'

Olga shook her head. 'It's what the professor has decided.'

Fernando took the pistol and stood there looking at it, cradling it in both hands. The idea of suicide had taken root in him a long time ago. He had paid his dues, he had accepted it. That was a discipline too. And basically, it would be easier for him than it had been for Giovanni and Astolfi. Being burnt alive or throwing yourself out of a window were terrible ways to end it all.

'You will tell the professor I've been good, won't you?'

'I'll tell him,' the woman promised.

'Even if I ask you to do it instead of me?'

Olga went to him and took back the pistol. 'I'll tell Kropp you were very brave.'

Fernando smiled, apparently satisfied. Then both of them made inverted signs of the cross, and Olga moved a few steps away.

Moro had abandoned his car a hundred yards away and was now climbing the hill. He was almost at the top, near that shed which looked like some kind of abandoned warehouse, when he saw a light filter through a broken window. He took out his pistol and went closer.

The interior of the warehouse was illuminated by the lights of the station wagon and the beam of a torch. He counted three people. One of them was bound and gagged in the boot.

Shit, he exclaimed to himself. He had been right: those two – the one-armed man and the red-headed woman – were up to something. While he was trying without success to catch what they were saying, he saw that the woman was holding a gun in her hand. She had retreated and was now pointing it at the one-armed man. He couldn't wait. With his elbow, he smashed in the window and aimed his own gun at her. 'Stop!'

The three people in the warehouse turned simultaneously and looked in his direction.

'Throw that away,' he said.

The woman hesitated.

'Throw it, I said!'

At that point, she obeyed. Then she raised her hands and Fernando did the same with his one arm.

'I'm a police officer. What's going on here?'

'Thank God,' Fernando exclaimed. 'This bitch forced me to tie up my friend,' he said, indicating Marcus. 'Then she told me to drive here. She wanted to kill both of us.'

Marcus stared at the man with the pistol. It was Deputy Commissioner Moro, he had recognised him. But he didn't like the dubious expression that came over his face after hearing Fernando's lie. He didn't believe him, did he?

'You're pulling my leg,' Moro asserted.

Fernando realised that his story hadn't washed. He had to think of something else. 'There's an accomplice of hers in the vicinity. He could be back at any moment.'

Marcus understood his game: Fernando wanted Moro to tell him to take Olga's pistol and keep an eye on her while he went in search of the accomplice. But, luckily, Moro wasn't so naïve.

'I'm not going to let you get hold of that weapon,' he said. 'And there's no accomplice: I saw you arrive and, apart from the man in the boot, there were just the two of you.'

Fernando, though, wouldn't let go. 'You said you're a police officer, so you must have handcuffs with you. I have another pair in the back pocket of my trousers: the woman could handcuff me to the car and I could do the same to her.'

Because of the drug, Marcus couldn't figure out what he had in mind. But all the same, he started kicking the inside of the boot. 'What's the matter with your friend?' Moro asked.

'Nothing, it's the drug the bitch gave him.' He pointed to the black leather case that had ended up on the floor when Olga had raised her hands, from which a syringe stuck out. 'He had the same reaction before, and forced us to pull over to the side of the road. I think they're convulsions, he needs a doctor.'

Marcus hoped that Moro would not fall into the trap and continued struggling and kicking with as much strength as he had left.

'All right: let's see your handcuffs,' Moro said.

Fernando turned slowly. And just as slowly he raised his jacket to show the contents of the back pocket of his trousers.

'OK, now take them out. But you'll have to handcuff yourself, I don't want you going anywhere near her.'

Fernando slipped them out, then crouched next to the bumper of the station wagon. He attached one of the cuffs to the tow bar. Then, with a little effort, and the help of his knees, he handcuffed his right wrist.

No, Marcus said in his head. Don't do it!

In the meantime, Moro threw his handcuffs through the window at the red-headed woman. 'Now it's your turn.'

She picked them up and approached one of the car doors in order to handcuff herself to the handle. As Moro made sure she was doing as he had ordered, Marcus saw Fernando's left arm come out of the sleeve and grab the pistol that was on the floor.

It was a momentary thing. Moro noticed the movement just in time and fired a shot that hit Fernando in the neck. But it didn't kill him, because Fernando, as he fell back, was quick-witted enough to fire twice. One of the bullets hit Moro in the side, making him spin round.

The red-headed woman was still free and moved around the car, crouching next to the body. She managed to get in on the driver's side and start the engine. In spite of his wound, Moro fired at her, but without stopping her.

The car smashed through the sheet metal door, throwing Marcus out of the open boot. As he hit the floor, he felt a sharp pain that made him momentarily lose consciousness. When he recovered a little, he saw Fernando, lying on his back on the floor in a pool of dark blood – dead. Moro, on the other hand, was still alive, clutching his own weapon in one hand and a mobile phone in the other. He was dialling a number. But he was holding the arm with the pistol close to his chest and Marcus saw that he was bleeding profusely down his side.

The bullet hit the subclavian artery, he told himself. He's going to die soon.

Moro managed to dial the emergency code and lifted the phone to his ear. 'Code 2724,' he said. 'Deputy Commissioner Moro. There's been a shooting, we have wounded. Trace this call . . . ' He didn't have time to finish the sentence before he collapsed and the phone fell from his hand.

Marcus and Moro were both lying on their sides, a few yards from each other. They were staring at each other. Even if he had been untied, Marcus could have done nothing for him.

They lay there looking at each other for a long time. The countryside fell silent once more, and the moon shone impassively. Moro was dying and Marcus tried to give him courage with his eyes. They didn't know each other, they had never spoken, but they were two human beings, and that was enough.

Marcus caught the moment when the light of life went out of those eyes. After fifteen minutes, the sound of sirens could be heard beyond the hill.

Olga had managed to escape. And Marcus's thoughts went to Sandra and the fact that she might be in danger.

9

At any moment, the full moon, low on the horizon, would come to rest in the lap of the Colosseum.

At four in the morning, Sandra was walking along the Via dei Fori Imperiali in the direction of the monument universally considered the symbol of Rome. If she remembered correctly the lessons she had learned at school, the Colosseum, inaugurated in about 80 AD, was 626 feet long, 510 feet wide and 157 feet high, with an arena of 287 feet by 180. There was a nursery rhyme to remember the measurements, but what still astonished Sandra was that it could contain up to 70,000 spectators.

Its name was actually a nickname. Originally called the Flavian Amphitheatre, it had taken its current name from the bronze colossus of the Emperor Nero that had once stood just in front of the building.

In the arena, men and animals died indiscriminately. Gladiators – from the name of the sword they used for fighting, the *gladius* – killed each other or else fought with wild animals brought to Rome from the furthest corners of the Empire. The public loved violence and some gladiators were celebrated like modern sporting champions. Until they died, obviously.

Over time, the Colosseum had become a symbol to the followers of Christ. That was because of the story, for which there was no historical evidence, that the pagans fed Christians to the lions. The legend had probably served to strengthen the memory of the genuine persecution they had suffered because of their faith. Every year, on the night between the Thursday and the Friday that preceded the Catholic Easter, the Pope led a Via Crucis from the Colosseum to commemorate the martyrdom of Christ.

Sandra, though, couldn't help thinking of the very different legend that Max had told her before he left. '*Colis eum?*' was the question. 'I worship the devil,' the answer. Whoever had sent her those anonymous text messages to summon her here at this hour of the morning either had a keen sense of humour or else was deadly serious. Having seen the inverted sign of the cross made by Astolfi in the pine wood at Ostia, Sandra leaned towards the second hypothesis.

The metro station just opposite the monument was still closed and the small square in front of the entrance was empty. No tourists queueing or paying extras dressed as Roman centurions to be photographed with them. Only a few teams of street-sweepers in the distance, cleaning the area in preparation for a new horde of visitors.

In that desolation, Sandra was sure that she would immediately spot the person who had invited her there. But, as a precaution, she had brought her service pistol with her, although she only ever used it once a month at the police firing range in order to keep in practice.

She waited almost twenty minutes, but nobody appeared. As she was wondering if she had simply been the victim of a practical joke and it was time to leave, she turned and noticed a gap in the iron railings around the amphitheatre. Had somebody made it for her?

It can't be, she told herself. I'll never go in there.

She wished that Marcus were with her. His presence gave her courage. You didn't come all the way here to turn and leave, she thought, so go on.

Sandra took out her pistol and, holding it at her side, went in through the gap.

Finding herself in the corridor that was part of the tourist route, she followed the signposts. She tried to perceive a sound, a noise, anything that told her she was not alone. She was about to climb one of the flights of travertine steps up to the *cavea* that had once housed the spectators when she heard a man's voice.

'Don't be afraid, Officer Vega.'

It came from the lower level, from the tunnels that criss-crossed beneath and around the arena. Sandra hesitated. She didn't feel confident going down there.

But the voice insisted, 'Think: if I'd wanted to set a trap for you, I certainly wouldn't have chosen this place.'

Sandra thought it over. It wasn't completely stupid. 'So why here?' she asked, still standing at the top of the steps.

'Haven't you got it? It was a test.'

She started descending the steps, slowly. She was an easy target, but she had no choice. She tried to accustom her eyes to the darkness and, when she got to the bottom, she looked around.

'Stay right where you are,' the voice said.

Sandra turned to a specific point and saw a shadowy figure. The man was sitting on a capital that had fallen from a column countless centuries earlier. She couldn't make out his face, but she noticed that he was wearing a cap.

'Well, did I pass the test?'

'I don't know yet . . . I saw you on TV making an inverted sign of the cross. Tell me: are you one of them?'

Them. The word reminded her of the *they* that Diana Delgaudio had written on a clipboard, and it made her shudder. 'Who might *they* be?'

'You solved the mystery of my text messages. How did you do it?'

'My partner teaches history, it's all thanks to him.'

Batista Erriaga knew she was being truthful. He had gathered information about her when he had searched for her telephone number.

'Does *them* refer to devil worshippers?'

'Do you believe in the devil, Officer Vega?'

'Not really. Should I?'

Erriaga did not reply. 'What do you know about all this?'

'I know there's someone protecting the Monster of Rome, though I can't figure out why.'

'Have you talked to your superiors? What do they say?'

'They don't believe me. Our pathologist, Dr Astolfi, sabotaged the investigation and then killed himself, but they think he simply went mad.'

Erriaga let out a brief laugh. 'I fear your superiors have kept something from you.'

Sandra had been harbouring that suspicion for a while, but hearing it said openly provoked her to anger. 'In what sense? What are you talking about?'

'The man with the wolf's head . . . You've never heard of that, I'm sure of it. It's a symbol that has appeared in various forms, but always in connection with crimes. For more than twenty years, the police have secretly been collecting these cases. So far they've counted twenty-three, but I can assure you there are many more. The fact is that these crimes have nothing in common apart from that symbol. A few days ago, it was found in Astolfi's apartment.'

'Why all the secrecy? I don't understand.'

'The police can't figure out who or what is behind this occult operation. Plus, just the thought of dealing with something that lies outside a purely rational viewpoint forces them to keep the thing secret and not delve further into it.'

'But you know the reason, don't you?'

'Dear Sandra, you're a police officer: you take it for granted that everybody is on the side of the good guys and you're surprised when you're told there are also people who support the bad guys. I don't want you to change your mind, but some people think that safeguarding the evil component of human nature is essential to the preservation of our species.'

'I swear to you I still don't understand.'

'Look around, observe this place. The Colosseum was a centre for violent death: people should have run a mile from such a spectacle, but instead they joined in as if they were at a party. Were our ancestors monsters? And do you think that anything has changed in human nature over the centuries? Right now, people are glued to their televisions, following the case of the Monster of Rome with the same morbid curiosity, as if it were a circus.'

Sandra had to admit that the analogy wasn't completely erroneous.

'Julius Caesar was just as much of a bloodthirsty conqueror as Hitler was. But today tourists buy T-shirts with his picture on them. Will they do the same with Hitler in a few thousand years? The truth is, we look indulgently on the sins of the past, and families come to the Colosseum and take photographs of themselves smiling in a place where there was death and cruelty.'

'I agree with you that the human race is sadistic and uncaring by nature, but why protect evil?'

'Because wars have always been the vehicles of progress: things are destroyed the better to be rebuilt. And people try to gain perfection in all fields in order to defeat other people and subjugate them. And in order not to be subjugated.'

'And what does the devil have to do with this?'

'Not the devil: religion. Every religion in the world thinks it possesses the absolute truth, even though this often conflicts with the truth of other faiths. Nobody is anxious to look for a common truth, everyone remains convinced of his own creed. Don't you think that's absurd, if God is one? So why should it be any different for Satanists? They don't think they're in error: it doesn't occur to them that there's anything wrong in what they do. They justify violent death exactly like anyone who wages war for his faith. Christians fought the Crusades, and Muslims still celebrate the idea of a holy war.'

'Satanists . . . Is that what they are?'

Erriaga had revealed the second level of the secret. There was nothing else to add. Those who recognised themselves in the man with the wolf's head were Satanists. But the meaning of that expression was too broad and complex for a mere young woman in a uniform to understand.

That was the third level of the secret, which had to remain that way.

Which was why Batista Erriaga simply said, 'Yes, they're Satanists.'

Sandra was disappointed. Disappointed by the fact that Deputy Commissioner Moro and, probably, also Superintendent Crespi had kept her out of that part of the case, downplaying the role of Astolfi and her discovery of what he had done. But she was even more disappointed that, in the end, those protecting the Monster were banal devil-worshippers. If there hadn't been victims, she would have laughed at such an absurdity.

'What do you want of me? Why did you drag me here?'

They had come to the crux of the encounter. Batista Erriaga had a task for her, one that was extremely delicate. He hoped she would not fail. 'I want to help you stop the child of salt.'

PART FOUR

The Child of Light

1

He had drunk a couple of vodkas and was sleepy, but had no desire to go to bed.

The club was packed, but he was the only person sitting at a table by himself. He kept playing with the keys of the villa by the sea. Giving them to him, his friend hadn't asked any questions. He'd simply had to ask him if he could use it for a few days, until he found somewhere else. Anyway, the reason for the request was all too obvious from his expression.

Max was sure it was all over between Sandra and him.

He still had in his pocket the case with the ring that she had rejected. Actually, she hadn't even opened it to see what was in it.

'Fuck,' he said, swallowing down the rest of the vodka in his glass.

He had given her all his love and devotion, so where had he gone wrong? He'd thought that things were going well, but there was always the damned ghost of her ex-husband between them. He hadn't known him, didn't even know what he looked like, but he was ever-present. If David hadn't died, if they had simply divorced like millions of couples in the world, maybe she would have felt liberated and could have loved him as he deserved.

Yes, that was the point: he deserved her love, he was sure of it.

But even though right was on his side, for some reason he wanted to punish himself. His fault was that he had been too perfect, he knew that. He should have asked for more for himself, not always stuck to her like a leech. Maybe if he had mistreated her, things would have been different. After all, David had been selfish, he hadn't given up his work for her – work that had taken him to trouble spots all over the world – even though he had known that Sandra didn't like his travelling or the idea of spending long periods with no news of him, not knowing if he was all right or even if he were still alive.

'Fuck you,' he said this time, addressing the ghost of David. He should have been more like him, then maybe he wouldn't have lost her. Might as well punish himself with a little more vodka.

As he was about to order a whole bottle, past caring about the fact that he had school the next morning, he noticed a woman staring at him from the bar counter. She was drinking a cocktail. She was beautiful, but not in an ostentatious way. Unwittingly seductive, he said to himself. He raised his glass to her, even though it was empty, as if toasting her health. He wasn't the kind of person who did certain things, but who gave a damn any more?

She returned the greeting, raising her cocktail glass. Then she approached his table.

'Are you waiting for someone?' she said. 'May I keep you company?'

She had caught him off guard, and he didn't know what to reply. In the end he blurted out a 'Yes, please sit down.'

'My name's Mina. What's yours?'

'Max.'

'Mina and Max: MM,' she said, amused.

He thought he detected an Eastern European accent. 'You aren't Italian.'

'Actually, I'm Romanian. You don't sound Italian either, or am I wrong?'

'I'm English, but I've been living here for many years.'

'I've been watching you all evening.'

Strange: he had only noticed her a little while ago.

'Am I wrong or are you angry about something?'

Max had no desire to tell her the truth. 'The woman I was supposed to be meeting here has stood me up.'

'Then tonight really is my night,' she said with a wicked smile.

By now he had looked at her more closely: the fashionable dress, black and with a plunging neckline, the perfectly manicured, red-painted nails of her slender hands, the broad gold bracelet on her left wrist, the necklace with a diamond of God knew how many carats. Her make-up was slightly too heavy, he noted. But her scent was definitely French. Someone out of the ordinary, he told himself. He didn't consider himself a sexist, but he had to admit that sometimes he did judge women according to the standard of living they expected from their partners. Perhaps because too many of them had turned their backs on him after learning that he was a mere schoolteacher. So he usually did his sums before getting to know women better, and, if need be, avoided them before they dumped him. Best not to have any illusions about this one: he couldn't afford her. He would buy her a drink without harbouring any expectations, just for a bit of company. Then they would go their separate ways.

'Can I get you another one of those?' He pointed at the cocktail.

Mina smiled again. 'How much money do you have in your pocket?'

He didn't immediately grasp the meaning of such a direct question. 'I don't know, why do you ask?'

She came closer until her face was an inch or two from his: he could smell her sweet breath. 'Have you really not figured out what I do, or are you trying to play games?'

A prostitute? He couldn't believe it. 'No, I'm sorry . . . It's just that . . . ' he tried to justify himself, clumsily.

The result was to unleash an amused laugh.

Then he tried to regain control of the situation. 'Fifty euros, but I can always find a cash machine.' Max couldn't believe his own words. He had been suddenly seized with a desire to transgress. To transgress that pointless pact of love with Sandra and the way in which he had always lived his own life, dutifully and maybe also a little boringly.

In the meantime, Mina seemed to be weighing up the offer, her eyes still fixed on him. It was as if she could see him better than anyone else. 'You're nice, you know,' she said. 'I'll do you a discount, the evening was a washout anyway.'

Max was as enthusiastic as a child. 'I have my car outside, we could go somewhere quiet.'

She shook her head, offended. 'Do I look to you like someone who does it in a car?'

Indeed she didn't.

'And besides, with that maniac around . . . '

She was right, there was this Monster of Rome business, he had forgotten. The authorities had advised couples not to choose isolated areas to make love in their cars. But there was still the villa in Sabaudia. It was a bit far, but he could pay her a little extra to persuade her. And, even though it was winter and it might be a little cold, he could light a fire. 'Let's go, I'll take you to the sea.'

*

The fire was crackling, the bedroom was already warming up, and he had no qualms. He was about to betray Sandra but he wasn't sure that it was 'technically' a betrayal. She hadn't told him clearly that she didn't love him, but that had been the meaning of her words. Nor did he ask himself what his pupils would think if they could see him like this: lying in a bed in a house that wasn't his, waiting for a high-class escort to come out of the bathroom so that he could have sex with her.

No, even he couldn't see himself like this. That was why he had preferred to immediately silence any possible sense of guilt.

During the car ride to Sabaudia, Mina had fallen asleep in her seat. He had kept stealing glances at her, trying to figure out who she really was, this woman of thirty-five or maybe thirty-six who hid behind a mask to seduce men. Or else imagining her life, her dreams, wondering whether she had ever been in love or still was.

On arriving, she had immediately looked around. The villa had an enviable position, facing the sea. To the left was Mount Circeo and the national park. Tonight it was illuminated by a bright moon. It was the kind of view Max could never have afforded, but it had made an immediate impression on Mina.

She had asked him where the bathroom was. Then she had slipped off her high-heeled shoes and climbed the stairs to the first floor. He had savoured that vision: it was like an angel ascending to heaven.

The sheets on the big double bed were clean. Max had undressed, neatly arranging his clothes, just as he did at home, but without realising it. It was a habit, part of the good manners that jarred with what he had decided to do – an act a long way from his cautious temperament.

Mina had been quite clear: they couldn't spend more than an hour together. And no kissing, that was the rule. Then she had handed him a box of condoms that she kept in her purse, sure that he knew what to do.

Max switched off the light and waited, with trepidation, for her to appear at any moment in the doorway, maybe dressed only in her underwear. He could smell her perfume everywhere, and was confused and excited. He didn't care, as long as he didn't have to think of the pain Sandra had caused him.

When he saw the flash beyond the dark threshold, he thought his imagination was playing tricks with him. But, after a few moments, there was another one. So he turned instinctively towards the window. But, outside, the sky was clear, there was no storm on the horizon, and the moon was still high.

Only at the third flash did he realise that it was actually the flash of a camera.

And it was coming closer.

2

They had locked him in a windowless room.

First, though, the police had allowed a doctor to visit him. Once his state of health had been checked they had moved him in here. The door had closed and since then Marcus hadn't been able to find out anything or see anybody.

The only things in here were the chair he was sitting on and a steel table. The only light came from a fluorescent strip on the ceiling, and on the wall there was a fan that blew new air into the room, producing an incessant, annoying hum.

He had lost all notion of time. When they had asked him for his particulars, he had provided the false ones he used as cover. Since he had no papers on him, he had dictated a telephone number, arranged specifically for such emergencies. The call supposedly went through to the voicemail of an official of the Argentinian embassy to the Vatican. Actually, Clemente would find the message and present himself within a short time at the police station with a false diplomatic passport that would demonstrate that Marcus was Alfonso García, extraordinary delegate for religious affairs, who worked on behalf of the government in Buenos Aires. Marcus had never before needed that complicated ploy. In theory, the Italian police should release him because he was covered by diplomatic immunity. But this time the matter was a really serious one.

The death of a deputy commissioner was involved. And Marcus was the only witness.

He didn't know if Clemente was already making moves to get him out. The police could keep him to the bitter end, but they would only need twenty-four hours to discover that there was no Alfonso García working for the Argentinian government and his cover would be blown.

But right now Marcus was not worried for himself. He was afraid for Sandra. Since listening to the exchange between Fernando and Olga, he had known that she too was in danger. God knew how she was now and whether she was safe. He couldn't allow anything to happen to her. So he decided that, in spite of Clemente, as soon as the officers came in again he would tell them everything. In other words, that he was conducting a parallel investigation into the Monster of Rome and that a group of people were covering for the killer. And he would tell them where to find Kropp. That way, he might be able to protect Sandra. He wasn't sure they would believe him, but he would do everything he could to make sure they didn't ignore him.

Yes, Sandra mattered more than anything.

Ever since the call had dragged him out of bed in the middle of the night, Superintendent Crespi hadn't stopped for a minute. His system needed a shot of caffeine, and his temples were throbbing with a headache, but he didn't even have time to take an aspirin.

The police station on the Piazza Euclide, in the Parioli district, was in a state of ferment. People were going back and forth between it and the warehouse where Moro's lifeless body had been found. But nobody had yet leaked anything to the press, Crespi noted. They all had too much respect for Moro to betray his memory. That was why the news of his death was still under wraps. But for how long? By midday, the Director of the State Police would hold a press conference to announce what had happened.

But there were too many questions needing answers. What had Moro been doing in that abandoned place? Whose was the body found a few yards from him? What had happened to provoke that exchange of fire? There were tyre marks, which meant that a second vehicle had been present apart from Moro's: had someone used it to escape? And what was the role played by this mysterious Argentinian diplomat, whom they had found bound and gagged?

They had taken him to the police station on the Piazza Euclide because it was the closest, but also to hide him from the journalists who would soon be leaping on the case. It was from there that operations were being directed. They didn't know if what had happened had anything to do with the case of the Monster of Rome, but they wouldn't let the Carabinieri deal with the murder of one of their own people.

In any case, for some hours now the Carabinieri's Special Operations Group had been busy with another problem.

From what Crespi had heard, it had been an eventful night. Soon after four, a strange phone call had come in to the emergency number. A woman, with a clear Eastern European accent and obviously in a state of panic, had reported an attack that had taken place in a house in the coastal town of Sabaudia.

When the Carabinieri had arrived at the villa, they had found a man's body in the bedroom. A gunshot straight to the heart, apparently fired from a Ruger revolver – the same type used by the Monster.

But it wasn't clear to the Carabinieri if this was just a coincidence or a copycat killing. The woman had managed to escape but, after raising the alarm, had vanished into thin air. Now they were looking for her and, in the meantime, searching for any possible DNA traces in the villa to compare them with the killer's.

Unlike the murder of Moro, the episode in Sabaudia was already public knowledge, although the dead man's identity had not yet been released. Crespi knew that was the main reason why the press had not yet caught wind of Moro's death.

They were busy trying to discover the name of the Monster's latest victim.

That was why there was plenty of time to grill this Alfonso García before some embassy official appeared and demanded his release on the grounds of diplomatic immunity. The man had given them a telephone number to verify his details, but Crespi had taken good care not to call it.

He wanted him for himself. And he would make him talk.

First, though, he needed a coffee urgently. So he went out into the cold Roman morning and crossed the Piazza Euclide towards the café of the same name.

'Superintendent!' he heard someone call.

Crespi was about to go into the café, but turned. He saw a man coming towards him, waving his arm. He didn't look like a reporter. He was clearly Filipino, and Crespi took him for a servant working in one of the posh houses in the Parioli district.

'Good morning, Superintendent Crespi,' Batista Erriaga said as soon as he came level. He was a little out of breath from running. 'Can I talk to you for a moment?'

'I'm in a hurry,' Crespi replied curtly.

'It won't take long, I promise you. I'd like to buy you a coffee.'

Crespi wanted to get rid of this pest and have his espresso in peace. 'Look, I don't mean to be rude because I don't even know who you are or why you know my name, but I told you, I don't have time.'

'Amanda.'

'I beg your pardon?'

'You don't know her, but she's an intelligent girl. She's fourteen years old and is still in high school. Like all girls her age, she has a thousand dreams and a thousand plans in her head. She likes animals a lot and has just started liking boys as well. There's one who's after her, she's noticed him and wishes he'd declare himself. Maybe next summer she'll finally get her first kiss.'

'Who are you talking about? I don't know anyone called Amanda.'

Erriaga struck his forehead with his hand. 'Oh, of course, how stupid I am! You don't know her because, actually, nobody knows her. The fact is, Amanda should have been born fourteen years ago, but her mother was run over on a pedestrian crossing in a suburban area by a hit-and-run driver who's never been found.'

Crespi fell silent.

Erriaga looked at him harshly. 'Amanda was the name that woman had chosen for her daughter. Didn't you know? Apparently not.'

Crespi was breathing hard and looking at the man in front of him, but still couldn't speak.

'I know you're a very religious man: you go to Mass every Sunday and take communion. But I'm not here to judge you. In fact, I don't give a damn if you sleep easy at night or if you think every day about what you've done and wish you could just give yourself up to your colleagues. I need you, Superintendent.'

'What do you need me for?'

Erriaga opened the glass door of the café. 'Let me buy you that damned coffee and I'll explain everything,' he said with his usual fake kindness.

*

Soon afterwards, they were sitting in the upstairs room of the café. Apart from a few tables, the furniture consisted of a couple of velvet sofas. Grey and black predominated. The only colourful note was provided by a huge photographic poster covering one wall: it showed the spectators in a cinema, maybe in the fifties, wearing 3-D glasses.

In front of that motionless and silent audience, Erriaga resumed speaking.

'The man you found last night, bound and gagged, in the place where Deputy Commissioner Moro died . . . '

Crespi was amazed. He wondered how he knew about it.

'Well?'

'You'll have to let him go.'

'What?'

'You heard me. You're going back to the station now and, on a pretext I'll let you choose, you're going to let him go.'

'I . . . I can't.'

'Of course you can. You won't need to let him escape, you just have to show him the exit. And I assure you you'll never see him again. It'll be as if he was never present at the crime scene.'

'But there's evidence that he was.'

Erriaga had thought of that too: when Leopoldo Strini had woken him that morning with the news of Moro's death, letting him be the first to know the story, Batista had instructed him to destroy all evidence that there had been a survivor of the exchange of fire. 'Don't worry about that. There won't be any consequences, I assure you.'

Crespi's expression hardened. From the way in which he was clenching his fists, Erriaga realised that Crespi, as the upright officer that he was, couldn't accept such blackmail.

'And what if I decided to go back to the station and confess what I did fourteen years ago? What if I arrested you right now for trying to blackmail a public official?'

Erriaga raised his arms. 'You're perfectly free to do that. In fact, I wouldn't stop you.' Then he laughed. 'Do you really think I've come here without taking such a risk into account? I'm not so stupid. And do you seriously think you're the first person I've persuaded using this method? You must have wondered how I managed to find out about a story you thought only you knew . . . Well, it's the same for the others. And some are less upright than you, I can assure you: they would do anything to safeguard their secrets. And, if I asked for favours, they wouldn't easily say no.'

'What kinds of favours?' Crespi was beginning to understand, and was vacillating.

'You have a beautiful family, Superintendent. If you decide to obey your conscience, you won't be the only person to pay the price.'

Crespi stopped clenching his fists and bowed his head in defeat. 'So from now on I'll always have to look behind me, scared you'll be back, because maybe you'll ask me for other favours in the future.'

'I know, it seems terrible. But try looking at it another way: it's better to live with an uncomfortable eventuality than spend the rest of your life in shame, let alone in prison for culpable homicide and failure in a duty to rescue.'

3

Sandra wasn't at home.

He had called Headquarters, thinking she might already have started her shift, but they had told him that she had taken the day off. Marcus was beside himself: he had to find her, to make sure she was all right.

Around mid-morning he managed to get in contact with Clemente. Through the usual voicemail, his friend brought him up to date with the fact that the monster had probably struck again the previous night, in Sabaudia. A man whose name had not yet been made known was dead, but the woman who'd been with him had managed to escape and raise the alarm, but then she had disappeared and nobody knew who she was. To analyse what had happened, they arranged to meet in a safe house in the Prati district.

Marcus arrived first and waited. He didn't know why the police had let him go so easily. After a while, the door of the room in which they had locked him had opened and Superintendent Crespi had come in with some forms and made him sign them. He'd seemed distracted, as if he weren't interested in what he was doing. Then he had told him that he was free to go, though he should remain within easy reach in case they needed to speak to him again.

Marcus, who had given a false telephone number and address, had thought this an unusual and overly hasty procedure. Especially since he had witnessed the death of a deputy commissioner. No patrol car had taken him to the address he had given to make sure that he had told the truth. Nobody had advised him to find a lawyer. And above all, no examining magistrate had listened to his version of events.

At first, he had suspected a trap. But then he had thought of something else. Someone powerful had interceded for him. And it wasn't Clemente.

Marcus was tired of subterfuges, of having constantly to look behind him and, in particular, of never knowing the real motive behind his missions. So, as soon as Clemente came in, he rounded on him. 'What are you hiding from me?'

'What are you talking about?' Clemente said, defensively.

'This whole thing.'

'Just calm down, please. Let's try to think this through together, I'm convinced you're making a mistake.'

'They kill themselves,' Marcus retorted angrily. 'Have you understood what I said? Kropp's followers, the people protecting the Monster, are so determined, so convinced of their own creed, that they agree to sacrifice their lives to achieve their purpose. I thought the pathologist throwing himself from a window or the old man burnt alive in the fire that he himself started were simply collateral damage. I told myself: they found themselves with their backs against the wall and preferred to die. But I was wrong. They *wanted* to die. It's a kind of martyrdom.'

'How can you say something like that?' Clemente asked, horrified.

'I saw him do it,' he replied thinking of Fernando and how

Olga had given him the pistol and told him that Kropp had decided it was all over for him. 'I've had my suspicions from the start. The Monster's words recorded in the confessional of Sant'Apollinare, you persuading me to investigate by telling me about a "serious threat hanging over Rome" ... Threat to whom?'

'You know.'

'No, I don't know any more. I have the impression that, right from the start, my task hasn't been to stop the Monster.'

Clemente tried to get out of this conversation by heading for the kitchen. 'I'm making coffee.'

Marcus grabbed his arm to stop him. 'The man with the wolf's head is the answer. They're a sect, a cult of some kind: the real mission was to stop them.'

Clemente looked down at the hand squeezing his arm. He was surprised and disappointed. 'You should try to restrain yourself.'

But Marcus had no intention of doing so. 'My superiors, the people who over the last three years have been giving me orders through you, the people whose faces I've never seen, aren't at all interested in the fate of those couples who've been killed, or of those who'll probably be killed soon. All that matters to them is to combat this evil religion, if that's what it is. And once again, they've used me.' It was just like the case of the nun found dismembered in the Vatican gardens. In that instance, he had come up against a wall of hostility. But he couldn't forget.

'*Hic est diabolus.*' The fellow sister of the poor nun had been right. The devil had indeed entered the Vatican, but maybe it had occurred even earlier than that.

'The same thing is happening here as happened with the man with the grey shoulder bag. And you're their accomplice.'

'You're being unfair.'

'Am I? Then demonstrate to me that I'm wrong: let me talk to whoever's in charge.'

'You know that's impossible.'

'Oh, yes, that's right: *It is not for us to ask, it is not for us to know. We must simply obey,*' he said, quoting the words Clemente was always using. 'But this time I will ask, and I want answers.' He grabbed Clemente by the collar – Clemente, the man he had always considered a friend, the man who, when he was in a hospital bed devoid of memory, had given him back memories and a name, the person he had always trusted – and pushed him up against the wall. It was a gesture that surprised even himself, he hadn't believed he was capable of it, but he had crossed a boundary now and couldn't turn back. 'Over these past few years, studying the sins of men collected in the archives of the penitenzieri, I've learned to recognise evil, but I've also realised that we all have something to be guilty of and that it's not enough to be aware of it to be forgiven. Sooner or later, there's a price to pay. And I don't want to atone for other people's sins. Who are these people who decide everything for me, these high-ranking prelates who control my existence, this "upper level"? I want to know!'

'Please let go of me.'

'I've put my life in their hands: I have a right to know!'

'Please—'

'I don't exist, I agreed to be invisible, I gave up everything. So now you're going to tell me who—'

'*I don't know!*'

These few words were uttered in one go, echoing with exasperation but also frustration. Marcus stared at Clemente. His eyes were watery: he was sincere. His painful admission – that 'I don't know' uttered as a liberating response to the brutality of his question – opened up a kind of chasm between them. He might have expected anything, even that his orders came from the Pope himself. But not this.

'The instructions come to me by voicemail, just like mine to you. It's always the same voice, but that's all I know.'

Stunned, Marcus let go of him. 'How is it possible? You've taught me everything I know: you told me the secrets of the penitenzieri, you revealed the mysteries of my mission. I thought you were highly experienced . . . '

Clemente went and sat down at the table and put his head in his hands. 'I was a country priest, in Portugal. One day a letter arrived. It had the Vatican seal on it: it was an assignment I couldn't get out of. Inside were instructions on how to track down a man who'd been admitted to a hospital in Prague: he'd lost his memory and I was supposed to give him two envelopes. In one there was a passport with a fictitious identity and money to start his life all over again, in the other a railway ticket for Rome. If he chose the latter, I would receive further instructions.'

'Every time you taught me something new . . . '

'. . . I'd just learned it myself.' Clemente sighed. 'I've never understood why they chose me. I had no particular gifts, I'd never shown any ambition to advance in my career. I was happy in my parish, with my congregation. I organised excursions for the old people, I taught the children the catechism. I christened, married, said mass every day. And I had to give it all up.' He looked up at Marcus. 'I miss what I've left behind. I'm as alone as you are.'

Marcus couldn't believe it. 'All this time . . . '

'I know: you feel betrayed. But I couldn't get out of it. To obey and to keep silent, that's our duty. We're servants of the Church. We're priests.'

Marcus slipped the medallion of the Archangel Michael from his neck and threw it at him. 'You can tell them that I'm no longer going to obey blindly and that I won't serve them. They'll have to find someone else.'

Clemente looked bitter, but didn't say a word. He bent down and picked up the medallion. Then he watched as Marcus walked to the door and went out, closing it behind him.

4

He walked in through the door of the attic room in the Via dei Serpenti. And she was there.

Marcus didn't ask her how she had found out where he lived, nor did he wonder how she had got in. When Sandra got up from the camp bed on which she had been sitting waiting for him, he moved instinctively towards her. And she, just as instinctively, hugged him.

They stood like that, embracing in silence. Marcus couldn't see her face but he smelt her hair and felt the warmth of her body. Sandra kept her head on his chest, listening to the secret beating of his heart. He felt a great peace, as if he had found his own place in the world. She realised that she had wanted him from the first moment, even though she hadn't admitted it until now.

They hugged tighter, aware perhaps that they couldn't go any further.

It was Sandra who broke away first. But only because they had a task to perform together. 'I have to talk to you: there isn't much time.'

Marcus agreed, although for a moment he was unable to look her in the eye. But he noticed that she was staring at the photograph on the wall, the image of the man with the grey shoulder bag. The killer of the nun in the Vatican gardens. Before she could ask him anything, he got in first with a question. 'How did you find me?'

'I met a man last night. He knows everything about you. He sent me here.' Sandra turned away from the image and began telling him what had happened in the Colosseum.

Marcus found it hard to believe what she was saying. Someone knew. Not only his address, but the purpose of his mission.

'He also knew that I knew you,' Sandra said. 'And that almost three years ago you helped me to find out what had happened to my husband.'

How come he was so well informed?

The man had confirmed to her that the people protecting the child of salt were a sect. Sandra expanded on the details of that explanation, even though she was convinced that the stranger had kept something from her.

'It was as if he revealed part of a secret in order not to have to reveal the whole of it. It's as if he was somehow forced by circumstances . . . That was my impression, anyway, I can't really define it any better than that.'

Actually, everything was very clear. Whoever the man was, he knew many things and knew how to use them. Marcus even suspected he'd been behind his being released so unexpectedly that morning.

'In the end, he told me he'd help me to stop the Monster.'

'How?'

'He sent me to you.'

Am I the answer? Am I the solution? Marcus couldn't believe it.

'He said that only you would be able to understand the killer's story.'

'Is that the word he used? *Story*?'

'Yes. Why?'

The storyteller, Marcus thought. So it was true: Victor was trying to tell them a story. But how far had he got? He recalled the photograph the Agapovs' housekeeper had given him: the father and the twins. *Anatoly Agapov was holding his son by the hand, but not Hana.*

'He said that, by putting together Moro's work and what you've discovered so far, you'd get to the truth,' Sandra continued.

The truth. The stranger knew the truth. Why not just come out and say it? And how did he know what the police had discovered? And above all, what he, Marcus, had discovered?

Marcus suddenly realised that Sandra wasn't aware of what had happened to Moro. And he was forced to give her the bad news.

'No!' was her incredulous reaction. 'It isn't possible.' She sat down again on the camp bed, staring into the distance. She had respected Deputy Commissioner Moro: he was a huge loss for the force. Officers like him left their mark and were always destined to change things.

Marcus did not dare disturb her until she asked him to continue.

'Let's go on,' was all he said.

It was his turn now to bring her up to date on the rest. He told her about the Hamelin Institute, Kropp and his followers, the man with the wolf's head, the psychopathic savant. Victor Agapov was the name of the Monster, and as a child he had killed his twin sister, Hana.

'That's why these aren't sex crimes,' Marcus said. 'He chooses couples because that's the only way he can relive the experience of when he was little. He believes he's innocent of the death of Hana, and he does to women what he would like to do to her.'

'He's driven by anger.'

'Precisely. He gives his male victims a different treatment: no suffering, just a fatal blow.'

Sandra had heard about what had happened the previous night in Sabaudia – that was all everyone was talking about in the city. 'Speaking of male victims,' she said, 'while I was waiting for you, I called an old friend in the Carabinieri: impossible to get anything out of the Special Operations Group right now. They're keeping the name of the victim secret, and they don't know anything about the woman who raised the alarm, except that she had an Eastern European accent. Anyway, it appears they're certain it was the Monster: they found his DNA in the house.'

Marcus thought this over. 'The girl manages to escape, so the Master can't complete his usual show. But he's determined all the same to let us know that it's his work.'

'So you think it was intentional?'

'Yes, he's stopped taking precautions: it's a signature.'

To Sandra, the reasoning made sense. 'For days now, we've been taking genetic samples from suspects or criminals with previous records for sexual offences: it's likely that by now he's guessed that we have his DNA. That means he doesn't care.'

'At the Colosseum, the stranger told you to give me all the elements that Moro had at his disposal.'

'Yes,' Sandra confirmed. She looked around the half-empty attic room. 'Do you have something to write with?'

Marcus gave her a felt-tip pen. The same one he had used three years earlier, when fragments of the memory he had lost would surface in his dreams and he would write them on the wall next to the camp bed. Those partial memories, written hastily in a shaky hand, had remained on the wall for a long time. Then he had rubbed them out, hopefully to forget again. But it hadn't happened. Those memories were the sentence he had to serve for the rest of his life.

So, when Sandra started writing on the wall the evidence listed on the board in the operations room, Marcus felt an unpleasant sense of *déjà vu*.

Homicide in pine wood at Ostia:

Objects: rucksack, climbing rope, hunting knife, Ruger SP101 revolver.

Prints of the young man on the climbing rope and on the knife left in the sternum of the young woman: he ordered him to tie the girl up and to strike her if he wanted to save his life.

Kills the young man by shooting him in back of neck.

Puts lipstick on the girl (to photograph her?).

Leaves a figure of salt next to the victims (a doll?).

After killing changes clothes.

Homicide of Officers Rimonti and Carboni:

Objects: hunting knife, Ruger SP101 revolver.

Kills Officer Stefano Carboni with a gunshot to the chest.

Shoots Officer Pia Rimonti, wounding her in the stomach. Then strips her, cuffs her to a tree, tortures her, and finishes her off with a hunting knife. Puts make-up on her (to photograph her?).

Homicide of hitchhikers:

Objects: hunting knife, Ruger SP101 revolver.

Kills Bernhard Jäger with a gunshot to the temple.

Kills Annabel Meyer with a number of stabs to the abdomen.

Annabel Meyer was pregnant.

Buries the victims' bodies and rucksacks.

Sandra finished the list, then added what little she knew about the latest attack.

Homicide in Sabaudia:
Objects: Ruger SP101 revolver.
Kills a man (name?) with a gunshot to the heart.
The woman who was with him manages to escape and raise the alarm. Can't be found. Why? (Eastern European accent.)
The killer deliberately leaves his own DNA at the scene: wants it to be known that this is his work.

Marcus approached the list and stood with his hands on his hips, studying it. He knew practically everything. Much of this information he had learned from the press, other things he had found out for himself. 'The Monster has struck four times, but the elements of the first attack are more significant than the others. So we'll only use those to try and figure out what we still have in store.'

And among them was something that Marcus didn't know.

'In the attack at Ostia, you've written at the end: "After killing, changes clothes." What does that mean?'

'That's how we found his DNA,' Sandra said, with a touch of pride. It was all due to her. She told Marcus about the mother of Giorgio Montefiori, the first victim, how she had insisted on being given back her son's personal effects, and how, once she had got them, she had come back to Headquarters to say that the shirt she'd been given wasn't Giorgio's because his initials weren't on it. Nobody had paid any attention to her, except Sandra, out of compassion. But the woman was right. 'So it was easy to deduce what had happened: after forcing Giorgio to stab

Diana Delgaudio and killing him with a gunshot to the back of his neck, the killer changed clothes. To do so, he put his clothes on the back seat of the car, where their clothes were that they'd taken off to make love. When he left, the killer confused the two shirts, leaving his own there.'

Marcus thought this over. Something didn't seem right. 'Why did he do that? Why did he change?'

'Maybe because he was afraid of bloodstains from the two young people and didn't want to arouse suspicions in case someone stopped him, maybe a patrol car checking papers. If you've just killed two people, better not to risk that happening, right?'

He wasn't sure. 'He forces the boy to stab his partner, then kills him execution-style, standing behind him and shooting him in the head. Throughout, he's kept himself away from the blood . . . So why bother to change?'

'You forget that then he reached into the car to make up Diana's face. The lipstick, remember? To put it on her he came very close to the wound in her sternum.'

Maybe Sandra was right, maybe the change of clothes was simply a precaution, however excessive. 'But there's still something unusual in the Ostia case,' Marcus said. 'Diana Delgaudio coming out of her coma for a short time and writing "*they*".'

'The doctors say it was a kind of unconditioned reflex, a word that emerged by chance from her memory along with the action of writing. And we know for sure that only Victor Agapov was involved. Do you really think it matters at this point?'

At first, Marcus had thought not. 'We know that a sect is involved in this affair. What if it was one of them Diana saw as well? Maybe someone was following the Monster in secret.' He wasn't prepared to believe what Fernando had told him: that they had lost contact with Victor after he had left the Hamelin Institute.

'Then why on earth would Astolfi have had to take the statuette of salt from the crime scene the following day? If someone from the sect really was there that night, they would have done it then.'

That was also true. But neither the change of clothes nor the word *they* seemed to tally with the rest.

'What do we do now?' Sandra asked.

Marcus turned to her. He could still smell her hair. A shudder went through him, but he didn't let it show. Instead, he focused his mind on the investigation. 'You'll have to find the girl from Sabaudia before the Carabinieri or the police do. We need her.'

'How? I have no way of doing that.'

'She has an Eastern European accent and can't be found . . . Why?'

'The Monster may have found her and killed her in the meantime, we don't know. But what does her accent have to do with anything?'

'Let's say she's still alive and is simply afraid of the police: maybe she has a record.'

'You think she's a criminal?'

'Actually, I was thinking a prostitute.' Marcus paused. 'Put yourself in her shoes: she got away from a murderer, she raised the alarm so she thinks she's done her duty. She has money put aside and she's a foreigner: she can get out any time she wants, she has no interest in remaining in Italy.'

'All the more reason if she's seen the Monster's face and he knows there's someone out there who can identify him,' Sandra agreed.

'Or else she knows nothing, has seen nothing, and is quite simply hiding and waiting for things to calm down.'

'All correct. But the Carabinieri and the police will have reached the same conclusions.'

'Yes, and they'll be examining the circles she moved in. But they'll be looking in from the outside. We have a contact on the inside . . .'

'Who?'

'Cosmo Barditi.' The man who had put him on the track of the child of salt through the fairytale book. The most important thing, though, was that he had run a club offering S&M shows: the SX.

'How could a dead man help us?' Sandra asked.

'His partner,' Marcus said, meaning the woman he had given money so that she could leave Rome together with her two-year-old daughter. Now he hoped she hadn't yet followed his advice. 'You'll have to go to her, tell her you've been sent by Cosmo's friend, the one who told her to disappear. She and I are the only people who know the story, she'll believe you.'

'Why don't you come with me?'

'We have a couple of problems to deal with. One is that mystery man in the Colosseum: we have to figure out who he is and why he's decided to help us. I don't think he's entirely disinterested.'

'And the other problem?'

'To solve that one, I'll have to pay a visit I've had to put off until now.'

5

The main door of the seventeenth-century palace was ajar.

Marcus pushed it open and found himself in a large atrium with a secret garden. There were trees and stone fountains, with statues of nymphs gathering flowers. The building was constructed around this space, with a belvedere surrounded by Doric columns.

The beauty of the place was highly reminiscent of other, more illustrious and more opulent Roman palaces, like the Palazzo Ruspoli or the Palazzo Doria Pamphilj.

To the left, a huge marble staircase led to the upper floors. Marcus started climbing.

He crossed the threshold into a frescoed drawing room richly adorned with old furniture and tapestries. There was a slight smell pervading the room, the smell of an old house. Of seasoned wood, of oil paint, of incense. It was a welcoming smell, a smell of history and the past.

Marcus carried on, walking through rooms similar to the first, joined one to the other without any corridor separating them, so that he felt as if he were constantly entering the same one.

From the paintings on the walls, people whose names were now lost – ladies, nobles, cavaliers – watched his passage, and it was as if their eyes, apparently motionless, were moving together with him.

Where are they now? Marcus wondered. What has remained of them? Maybe only a painting, a face that a complacent artist prettified, somewhat violating his pact with the truth. They had thought that this way their memory would last a long time, but instead they had become items of furniture, like any knick-knack.

As he was formulating these thoughts, a sound sought him out. It was low and constant. A single note repeated *ad infinitum*. Like a coded message. Like an invitation. It was offering to be his guide.

Marcus followed it.

As he moved forward, the sound became ever clearer, a sign that he was getting close to the source. He found himself in front of a half-closed door. That was where the sound was coming from. Marcus walked in.

A spacious room with a large canopied bed. The velvet curtains surrounding it were closed, making it impossible to see who was lying on it. But, from the modern equipment around it, a lot could be gleaned.

There was a heart monitor – this was the source of the sound that had guided him. Another monitor registering vital signs. And there was an oxygen cylinder, the tube from which disappeared under the hangings around the bed.

Marcus approached slowly, and only then did he notice a body slumped in an armchair in a corner of the room. He stopped for a moment when he recognised Olga, the red-headed woman. But she was motionless and her eyes were closed.

It was when he went closer to her that he realised she wasn't just sleeping. Her hands were together in her lap, and she was still holding the syringe with which, most likely, she had injected herself. The exact point was on her neck, at the level of her jugular.

Marcus lifted her eyelids to make sure she was really dead. Only when he was certain did he turn back to the bed.

Reaching it, he moved aside one of the velvet drapes, certain he would find a second dead body.

There lay a pale man with sparse, unkempt fair hair, large eyes and an oxygen mask covering part of his face. He wasn't dead. Beneath the blankets his chest rose and fell slowly. His body seemed shrunken – as if from some black magic spell, as in a fairytale.

Professor Kropp raised his weary eyes to him. And smiled. Then, with some difficulty, he slipped a bony hand from under the blankets and removed the mask from his mouth. 'Just in time,' he whispered.

Marcus did not feel any pity for this dying man. 'Where's Victor?' he asked in a harsh voice.

Kropp shook his head slightly. 'You won't find him. Not even I know where he is. And if you don't believe me, you already know that for someone in my state tortures and threats are pointless.'

Marcus felt as if he had come to a dead end.

'You haven't understood Victor, nobody has understood him,' Kropp continued, speaking very slowly. 'Usually, we don't personally kill the animals we eat, do we? But if we were driven by hunger, would we do so? And would we even be ready to feed on a human corpse if our own survival depended on it? In extreme situations, we do things we wouldn't otherwise do. In the same way, for some individuals killing isn't a choice: they're forced to do it. There's something inside them that obliges them to do it. The only way they can free themselves from that unbearable oppression is to give in to it.'

'You're justifying a killer.'

'Justifying? What does that word mean? Someone who's blind from birth doesn't know what it means to see, in fact he doesn't know he's blind. In the same way, a man who doesn't know what good means isn't aware that he's bad.'

Marcus bent over him and spoke in his ear. 'Spare me the final sermon: soon your devil will greet you in hell.'

Kropp turned his head on the pillow and looked at him. 'You say that, but you don't really think it.'

Marcus retreated.

'You don't believe in the devil or in hell, am I right or am I wrong?'

Inside, Marcus was forced to admit, with some difficulty, that yes, he was right. 'How can you afford to die in a place like this? In all this luxury?'

'You're like those poor fools outside who all their lives ask themselves the wrong questions and wait for answers which of course will never come.'

'You'll have to be clearer than that, I'm curious . . .'

'You think this is the work of a few individuals. Me, Astolfi, Olga over there on that armchair, Fernando and Giovanni. But we're only a part of the whole. We've simply provided an example. Others are on our side. They remain in the shadows because nobody would understand them, but they live their lives inspired by our example. They support us, and pray for us.'

This talk of blasphemous prayers horrified Marcus.

'The nobles who lived in this palace were on our side in the old days.'

'What old days?'

'Do you think everything is reducible to the present? In the last few years, we've marked the worst instances of bloodshed with our symbol so that people should understand and awake from their lethargy.'

'You're talking about the man with the wolf's head.' Marcus

thought of the cases the unknown man at the Colosseum had told Sandra about: a babysitter, a paedophile, a father who had slaughtered his nearest and dearest . . .

'But proselytising isn't enough. It's always necessary to send a signal that everyone can understand. It's like in the fairytales: you always need a villain.'

'That's the reason behind the Hamelin Institute: to cultivate children who will become monsters when they grow up.'

'And then Victor arrived, and I realised he was the right one. I placed my trust in him, and he hasn't disappointed me. When he's finished telling his story, you too will understand and you'll be surprised.'

Listening to these boasts, Marcus felt a sudden sense of oppression. *You will understand and you'll be surprised.* It sounded like a prophecy.

'Who are you?' Kropp asked.

'I was a priest before, but now I'm not so sure,' he replied sincerely.

Kropp started laughing, but the laughter immediately turned into a coughing fit. Then he resumed. 'I'd like you to have something . . .'

'I don't want anything from you.'

But Kropp ignored him and, with what seemed an excruciating effort, reached out an arm towards the bedside table. He took a folded piece of cardboard and handed it to Marcus. 'You'll understand and you'll be surprised,' he repeated.

Marcus reluctantly accepted Kropp's gift and opened it.

It was a map.

A street map of Rome with a route marked out in red, starting in the Via del Mancino and ending in the Piazza di Spagna, just below the famous Spanish Steps.

'What's this?'

'The end of your story, child without name.' Kropp placed the oxygen mask back over his mouth and closed his eyes. Marcus stood looking at him for a while longer as his chest rose and fell with his breathing. Then he decided he had had enough.

The old man would be dead soon. Alone, as he deserved. Nobody could save him, not even Kropp himself if he repented at the last moment. And Marcus was certainly not willing to grant him forgiveness for his sins with a final blessing.

So he walked away from that deathbed, intending to leave this house forever. In his mind, the image of an old, yellowing photograph.

A father with his own twin children. *Anatoly Agapov was holding his son by the hand, but not Hana.*

Why, if the family's housekeeper had said that the man loved her more than him?

The time had come to go where everything had started. The Agapovs' villa was waiting for him.

6

She had been staring at the phone on the table for at least two hours.

It was something she had often done as a teenager, praying that the boy she liked would call. She would concentrate with all her being, trusting in the power of her own gaze, hoping that a telepathic appeal would force the object of her love to raise the receiver and dial her number.

It had never worked. But Sandra still believed in it, even though now for a different reason.

Call, come on, call . . .

She was sitting in Cosmo Barditi's office at the SX. She had followed Marcus's instructions and had presented herself at Cosmo's apartment. The man's partner was about to leave for the airport with their two-year-old daughter. She had got to her just in time.

Sandra had not said she was a policewoman, she had introduced herself as suggested by Marcus. Cosmo's partner had been reluctant to listen to her at first: she wanted nothing more to do with this business, and – understandably – she was also afraid for her daughter. But when Sandra had told her that another woman, perhaps a prostitute, was in danger, she had decided to co-operate.

Sandra had understood what Marcus had probably not grasped: Cosmo's partner had almost certainly had a tough life too. Maybe a life she wasn't proud of and had put behind her. But she had not forgotten what it meant to need help and to have nobody ready to give it. So she had taken Cosmo's diary and had started calling all his contacts. She told everybody the same thing: if anybody knew the foreign woman involved in the Sabaudia murder, they had to get a simple message to her.

There was somebody looking for her who could give her a hand. The police wouldn't be in any way involved.

That was all Cosmo's partner could do for Sandra. They had then come straight to the SX, because they had given the number of the club as a secure place to call. It might also be the perfect place to meet the mystery woman, if she responded.

That was when Sandra's long wait by the silent phone had begun.

Obviously, Cosmo's partner had insisted on going with her. She had left her daughter with her neighbour. Since Cosmo's death she had not set foot in the club, which had remained closed.

That was why, as soon as they entered Cosmo's office, they had been greeted by the bad smell and the woman had noticed with horror that there were still dark, dried stains visible on the table and on the floor: blood and other bodily matter Cosmo had lost after the gunshot to his head. The death had immediately been registered as suicide, so Forensics had carried out only a routine examination, and the residue of the chemical reagents could still be seen. The body had been removed, but nobody had cleaned up. There were companies that specialised in that kind of work: using particular products, they could get rid of anything that might bear witness to the fact that a horrible act had taken place there. But Sandra had always observed that the dead person's relatives needed to be informed that they should call in a third party to have it done, because they were in no position to think of it themselves. Perhaps because they were upset, or perhaps because it was always taken for granted that someone else would perform such a thankless duty.

So, while Sandra sat staring at the phone, the woman was busy cleaning everything with a bucket of water, a cloth and floor detergent. She had tried to tell her that this type of dirt wouldn't just go away, that she would need something more powerful to remove it. But the woman had replied that she would try all the same. She was in a state of shock and continued scrubbing away without respite.

She's too young to be a widow, Sandra thought. And she thought of herself, having to deal with David's death when she was only twenty-six. Everyone had the right to their own kind of madness when faced with a loss. She, for example, had decided to stop time. In her apartment, she had moved nothing and had even surrounded herself with the things she had most hated about her husband when he was still alive. Like the aniseed cigarettes and the cheap aftershave. She was afraid of forgetting his smell. She couldn't bear the idea that something else of the man she loved, even the most insignificant or hateful of his habits, should disappear from her life.

Now she felt sorry for this woman. If she hadn't gone to her as Marcus had said, if she hadn't respected to the letter the instructions she had received from him, they wouldn't be here, in this office. The woman might be at the airport right now, ready to leave and start all over again. Not bending over a floor, removing what remained of the man she had loved.

At that moment, the phone rang.

The woman broke off what she was doing and looked up at Sandra, who immediately lifted the receiver.

'Who the hell are you?' a female voice said.

It was her. The prostitute she was looking for. She was sure of it because of her accent. 'I want to help you.'

'You want to help me and you kicked up all this fuss to find me? Do you know who I'm trying to hide from, you bitch?'

She was playing tough but she was scared, Sandra observed. 'Calm down, now, listen to me and try and think carefully.' She had to appear stronger than her, it was the only way to persuade her to trust her. 'It only took me a couple of hours and a few phone calls to track you down – how long do you think the Monster will take? I'll tell you one thing you may not have thought of: he's a criminal, he probably has contacts in criminal circles, so we can't rule out the possibility that someone is already helping him, maybe without knowing his intentions.'

The woman said nothing for a while. A good sign, Sandra thought. 'You're a woman, I can believe what you say . . . ' It was an observation but also a request.

Sandra understood why Marcus had entrusted her with this task: the Monster was a man, and it was men above all who were capable of cruelty and brutality. That was why it was easier to trust a woman. 'Yes, you can believe me,' she reassured her.

At the other end of the line, there was another silence, a longer one this time. 'All right,' the woman said. 'Where shall we meet?'

She got to the club an hour later. She was carrying a small rucksack on her back, with her things in it, and wearing a pair of red sneakers, loose grey tracksuit bottoms and a blue top with a hood, with a man's aviator-style leather jacket over it. The choice of the clothing wasn't random, Sandra noted. She was a beautiful woman of about thirty-five, maybe even a little more, the kind that made eyes turn. But she didn't want to be conspicuous, that was why she was wearing such scruffy clothes. All the same, she'd put on make-up, as if the most feminine part of herself had resisted, gaining the upper hand at least in this respect.

They were sitting in one of the small rooms off the main room of the SX. Cosmo's partner had gone, leaving them alone: she didn't want to have anything more to do with this business and Sandra didn't blame her.

'It was terrible.' The woman was talking about what had happened the night before, all the while biting her nails, heedless of ruining the red polish. 'I don't even know how I got out alive.'

'Who was the man with you?' Sandra asked: the identity of the male victim was still under wraps and none of the news bulletins had mentioned it.

The woman glared at her. 'Does it matter? I don't remember his name and, even if I did, I don't know if it was his real one. Do you think men are honest with someone like me? Especially those with wives or girlfriends, and I got the impression he was one of them.'

She was right, it didn't matter. 'OK, go on.'

'He took me to the villa and I asked to go to the bathroom to get ready. I always do, it's a habit, but I think it saved my life this time. While I was in there, something strange happened . . . From under the door I saw flashes of light. I immediately realised it was a camera, but I assumed my client had thought up some little game. I sometimes get people like that, but photography's a perversion I can deal with.'

Sandra thought of the Monster, and the fact that she had already figured out that he photographed his victims.

'Of course, I would have asked him extra for that. But I was fine with it, and I was about to leave the bathroom when I heard the shot.'

The woman couldn't go on with the story, the memory of it still terrified her. 'What happened?' Sandra prompted her.

'I switched out the light and crouched next to the door, hoping he wouldn't notice I was there. I heard him walking around the house: he was looking for me. He was going to find me, so I had to decide what to do in a hurry. There was a window in the bathroom, but it was too small, I couldn't get through. And besides, I really didn't feel like jumping down, I might have broken a leg and got stuck there. And if he'd found me then . . . ' She lowered her eyes. 'I don't know where I got the courage. I collected my clothes, because if I'd run away naked I wouldn't have got far, not with the cold out there . . . It's incredible how the brain works when you're in danger.'

She was wandering, but Sandra didn't want to interrupt her.

'I opened the bathroom door. Everything was dark. I started walking around the house, trying to remember the layout of the rooms. At the end of the corridor I could see the beam of a torch moving around in one of the rooms. That was where he was. If he'd come out, he would definitely have seen me. I had a few seconds to get to the stairs: they were halfway between him and me. But I couldn't make up my mind. I had the feeling every one of my movements was making a very loud noise and he would hear.' She paused. 'Then I got to the stairs and started slowly going down. There was a lot of movement on the floor above: he couldn't find me and must have been very angry.'

'Did he say anything? Did he scream or curse while he was looking for you?'

The woman shook her head. 'He was silent, and that scared me even more. Then I saw the front door, which was locked from the inside and there was no key. I felt like crying, I was about to give up. Fortunately I summoned up the strength to look for another way out . . . In the meantime, he was coming down, I could hear his steps. I opened a window and threw myself out without knowing what was waiting for me beyond it. I flew through the air and landed on something soft. It was sand, but then I started sliding down a slope and couldn't stop, until I got to the beach. I fell on my back: the pain took my breath away. When I opened my eyes, I saw the full moon. I'd forgotten all about it. I was an easy target with all that light. I looked up at the window I'd jumped through and saw a silhouette . . . ' The woman hunched her shoulders. 'I couldn't see his face, but he could see me. He was standing there without moving. Then he fired.'

'He fired?' Sandra asked.

'Yes, but he missed me by a couple of feet, maybe less. And then I got up and started running. The sand slowed me down, and I was more and more desperate. I was sure he'd hit me, that at any moment I'd feel a hot pinching in my back – I don't know why, that's how I imagined the pain.'

'And did he continue shooting?'

'I counted three more shots, then nothing more. He must have come down to look for me, but I went back up the slope and reached the road. I hid behind a rubbish bin and waited for day to come. They were the worst hours of my life.'

Sandra could understand that. 'What happened then?'

'I got a lift from a lorry driver, and from a service station I called the emergency number to report what had happened. Then I went home, hoping that bastard didn't know where I lived. I mean, how could he? I had my bag with my papers with me, it was the first time I'd seen the guy who'd wanted to fuck me, and I'd never been in that villa before.'

Sandra weighed up the story. She was lucky, she told herself. 'You haven't told me your name.'

'I don't want to tell you. Is that a problem?'

'At least tell me what I should call you.'

'Mina, call me Mina.'

Maybe it was the name she used for her work. 'But I do want to tell you who I am: my name is Sandra Vega and I'm a policewoman.'

At these words, the woman leapt to her feet. 'Fuck off! On the phone you told me no police!'

'I know, but calm down: I'm not here in an official capacity.'

She grabbed her rucksack, determined to leave. 'Are you fucking me around? Who gives a fuck what capacity you're in? You're a cop, full stop.'

'Yes, but now I've been honest with you. I could have kept quiet about it. I'm working with someone who isn't a policeman, someone you should talk to.'

'Who's that?' she asked, angrily and suspiciously.

'He has powerful contacts in the Vatican, he can help you stay out of circulation for a while, but you'll have to help us.'

The woman stopped in her tracks. When it came down to it, she had no choice: she was scared and didn't know where to go. So she sat down again. In her momentum, the sleeves of both her leather jacket and her top had ridden up her left arm. Sandra noticed that she had a scar on her left wrist, like someone who had attempted suicide in the past. The woman noticed where she was looking and hid her arm again under her clothes. 'I usually cover it with a bracelet so the clients don't notice.' There was a sad note in her voice now. 'I've already been through a lot in my life . . . You said you could help me, so I beg you: get me out of this nightmare.'

'I will,' Sandra promised. 'Now let's go: I'll take you to my place, it'll be safer there.' She took from her the rucksack containing her things.

7

The Agapov residence was located in an isolated spot, a place outside time. The surrounding countryside was still as it must have appeared towards the end of the eighteenth century, the era when the villa had been built, when dangers of every kind lurked in those woods and hills. Incautious travellers might fall into the hands of brigands, be robbed and then have their throats cut in order not to leave witnesses. The bodies were buried in common graves and nobody ever heard of them again. In the old days, on nights of the full moon, fires lit by witches could be seen in the distance – according to the legends, there was never any shortage of witches in Rome and its surroundings. And in the Dark Ages they were sentenced to burn on the same fire with which they had celebrated their demons.

It had taken Marcus more than an hour to reach the place. It was just after seven in the evening but the moon, certainly less full than the night before, had already begun its climb towards the highest point of a cold starry sky.

From the outside, the house appeared enormous, just as the housekeeper who had worked there for six years had described it. But the old lady in the nursing home hadn't prepared him for the most impressive aspect of the building.

From a distance, it looked like a church.

Marcus wondered how many people, over the course of time, had mistaken it for a place of worship. Maybe that had been a deliberate choice by the person who had commissioned it or an eccentricity of the architect who had designed it, but the façade was in Gothic style and ended in little spires that seemed to ascend to heaven. The grey stone of the building reflected the moonlight, creating angular shadows beneath the cornices and bluish gleams on the windowpanes, which were decorated like those of a cathedral. On the main gate was a sign from an estate agency with the words FOR SALE in large letters. Beneath it, though, could be seen the marks left by previous signs, which had over time failed at the same aim.

The house was closed up.

The garden that surrounded it was filled with palm trees – another extravagance of the place. But the trees were enveloped in the thick bark that formed when they were too long deprived of expert care.

Marcus climbed over the railings and walked along the drive towards the outside steps that led up to the veranda and then to the entrance. He remembered what the old woman had told him: that, when the Agapovs lived there, she had been in charge of eight servants, but that none of them had been allowed to remain there after dark. They were all forced to leave before nightfall and return the following day. Marcus reflected that, if he were still alive, Anatoly Agapov wouldn't have accepted his presence here, at this hour.

What happened at night in this house?

Marcus had brought a torch and a jack with him from the car. He used the jack to open the front door of light-coloured wood that might separate him from the answer to that question.

The moonlight slid between his legs like a cat, preceding him beyond the threshold. A sinister creaking, worthy of a ghost story, greeted him. Deep down, that was indeed what Marcus had come to do: to reawaken the spirit of a child. Hana.

He thought of Kropp's final attempt to distract him from his enterprise. That map he had given him surely led to another deception.

'*The end of your story, child without name . . .*' But he hadn't fallen for it.

Now he was here. He hoped the story he was looking for was also here.

Once again, he would use the housekeeper's words as a guide. When he had asked her what kind of man Anatoly Agapov had been, she had replied, '*He was a stern man, very strict. I don't think he liked being in Rome. He worked at the Russian embassy, but spent a lot of time at home, shut up in his study.*'

The study. That was the first place to look.

He found it after wandering around the house for a while. It was not easy to distinguish one room from another, partly because the furniture was covered in white sheets to protect it from the dust. Lifting some of them in search of clues, Marcus had discovered that objects of daily use, furnishings and fittings were all in their places. Whoever bought the villa one day – assuming that ever happened – would inherit everything that had belonged to the Agapovs, even without knowing their story or the tragedy that had taken place amid these objects.

In the study there was a large bookcase and an oak table in front of it. Marcus quickly took the dust sheets off the furniture. He sat down on the armchair behind the desk – this must have been Anatoly Agapov's command post – and started searching in the drawers. The second on the right, though, was stuck. Marcus took hold of the handle with both his hands and pulled, until it opened abruptly, falling to the floor with a noise that echoed through the house.

Among the contents of the drawer was a picture frame, which now lay face down on the floor. Marcus turned it over. It contained a photograph he already knew: the housekeeper had given him a copy, which had then been burnt by Fernando.

This one, though, was identical.

An image with colours faded by time, which went back to the eighties. It looked as if had been taken with a self-timer. In the middle, Anatoly Agapov, about fifty, relatively short but robust, wearing a dark tie and a waistcoat. His hair was combed back and he had a black goatee beard. To his right, Hana – a little red velvet dress, hair not very long but not short either, and with a ribbon lifting the fringe. Hana. She was the only one smiling. To the left of the man, Victor – a suit and tie, bobbed hair with a fringe falling over his eyes, sad-looking.

A father and his children, almost identical twins.

Once again, Marcus noticed the detail that had bothered him from the start. *Anatoly Agapov was holding his son by the hand, but not Hana.*

For a long time Marcus had wondered why, given that, according to the housekeeper, the girl was her father's favourite. '*The only time I ever saw him smile, he was with Hana.*'

So he wondered again if what he saw in the photograph was a gesture of affection or a way to impose his own authority. And whether that paternal hand was a leash for Victor. Right now, he didn't have an explanation, so he put the photograph in his pocket and decided to continue with his inspection of the house.

As he walked through the rooms, he remembered other things the old woman had told him about the twins.

'*We saw Hana mostly. Sometimes, she'd get away from her father and come and see us in the kitchen or while we were doing the domestic chores. She was a child of light.*'

A child of light. Marcus had liked that definition. So she got away from her father? What did that mean? He had asked himself that question before, and he asked it again.

'The children didn't go to school and didn't even have a private tutor: Signor Agapov taught them himself. And they didn't have any friends.'

When Marcus had asked about Victor, the housekeeper had said, *'Will you believe me if I tell you that in six years I saw him maybe eight times, nine times at most?'* And later she had added, *'Victor didn't talk. He was quiet, he just watched. A couple of times I caught him hiding in his room, watching me in silence.'*

As he shone his torch around those rooms, Marcus could still detect the presence of Victor in every corner, behind a sofa or a curtain. Now he was only a fleeting shadow, produced by his imagination, or maybe by the house itself, which was still haunted by the childhood of that sad little boy.

On the upper floor he found the children's rooms.

They were next to each other, and very similar. Little beds with colourful inlaid wooden headboards, little study tables with chairs. Pink predominated in Hana's room, brown in Victor's. In Hana's room there was a doll's house, perfectly furnished in every detail. In Victor's, there was a little upright piano.

'He was always shut up in his room. Every now and again we'd hear him playing the piano. He was very good. And he was brilliant at mathematics. One of the maids was tidying his things once, and found sheets and sheets of paper filled with sums.'

Sure enough, there they were. Marcus saw them heaped up in the bookcase, together with volumes on algebra and geometry and an old abacus. In Hana's room, on the other hand, there was a large wardrobe full of dolls' clothes. Coloured ribbons, shiny unmatched shoes on the shelves, little hats. The gifts of an affectionate father to his favourite child. Victor had resented that competition with his sister. A perfect motive for killing her.

'What was the relationship like between the two children?'

'Every now and again we'd hear the children quarrel, but they also spent time together. Their favourite game was hide and seek.'

Hide and seek, Marcus repeated to himself. The favourite game of ghosts. *'How did Hana die?'* he had asked the old woman.

'Oh, Father. One morning I got to the villa with the rest of the servants and we found Signor Agapov sitting on the steps outside, with his head in his hands, crying bitterly. He said his Hana was dead, that a sudden fever had taken her away.'

'And did you all believe him?'

Her face had darkened. *'We did until we saw the blood on the girl's bed and the knife.'*

The knife: the Monster's favourite weapon along with the Ruger revolver, Marcus repeated to himself. Maybe, just maybe, Victor could have been stopped back then. But nobody had reported the matter.

'Signor Agapov was a very powerful man, what could we do? He had the coffin sent straight back to Russia, so that Hana could be buried next to her mother. Then he dismissed everyone.'

Anatoly Agapov had used his diplomatic immunity to cover up what had happened. He had placed Victor in the Hamelin Institute and had stayed in the house until he died. The man was a widower, but it was only now that Marcus realised that during the course of this inspection he had found nothing that invoked the memory of a wife and mother who had died prematurely.

Not a photo, not an heirloom. Nothing.

His tour of the house concluded in the attic, which was cluttered with old furniture. But there was also something else.

A locked door.

Apart from the main lock, there were three padlocks of different sizes. Marcus did not even wonder why there were so many precautions: without hesitation, he took an old chair and began beating it against the door – once, twice, several times, until it yielded.

He raised the beam of the torch and in an instant knew the reason why there was no trace of Signora Agapov in the house.

8

She had made up a bed for her on the sofa in the apartment in Trastevere.

Then, while Mina was having a shower, she had started cooking for her. She had been tempted to look in her rucksack: maybe she would find a paper with her true identity. But she had resisted. The woman was starting to trust her, and Sandra was convinced that she could get her to open up more.

There was a difference of a few years between them and, even though she was younger, Sandra had immediately felt like an elder sister. She was sorry for Mina and the life she had led, perhaps the result of a sad, troubled past. She wondered if at least sometimes, faced with the various options life presented everyone with, she had actually been able to choose which direction to take.

Sandra laid the table and switched on the TV. The news was on. Obviously, they were talking about the Monster's latest crime, in Sabaudia. The reporters described it as a semi-failure on the part of the killer, given that the female victim had got away this time. Nothing was yet known about the identity of the murdered man.

Evidently the Carabinieri are better at keeping secrets than we were, Sandra told herself. Then she wondered if, as Mina had said, the man who had died had a wife or girlfriend and if she at least had been informed. She felt sorry for that woman, whoever she was. At that moment, she realised that Mina was standing in the doorway of the kitchen, wrapped in Max's dressing gown, which Sandra had lent her. She was staring at the TV and looking shaken. Sandra grabbed the remote and switched it off in order not to upset her further.

'Are you hungry?' she asked. 'Take a seat, it's ready.'

They ate almost in silence, because Mina had suddenly grown taciturn. Maybe the emotional memory of what had happened, and above all the awareness of the fate she had escaped, was starting to rise to the surface in her. Up until that moment, adrenaline had dulled her reactions, so now it was only natural that she should be in a state of shock.

Sandra noted that Mina kept her left arm under the table as she ate. Maybe she didn't want a repetition of what had happened at the SX, when she had involuntarily shown her the scar on her wrist. She was ashamed of it.

'I was married once,' Sandra said, trying to stimulate her curiosity. 'A good man – his name was David. He died.'

Mina raised her eyes from the plate, surprised.

'It's a long story,' Sandra added.

'If you don't want to talk about it, why did you tell me?'

Sandra put her fork down on the table and looked at her. 'Because you're not the only person who's ever got it into her head to do something extremely stupid, to wipe out the pain.'

Mina seized her own wrist with the other hand. 'They say if you failed the first time, the second time is easier. It isn't true. But I haven't given up hope of succeeding one day.'

'But when the killer shot at you last night, you didn't keep still and wait for the bullets.'

Mina was forced to think about that. Then she burst out laughing. 'You're right.'

Sandra laughed with her.

But then Mina turned serious again. 'Why are you doing this for me?'

'Because helping other people makes me feel better. Now, please, let's finish dinner: you need a good sleep.'

Mina said nothing. She was sitting very still.

'What's the matter?' Sandra asked, noticing that something was wrong.

'I lied to you.'

Even without knowing what the lie was, Sandra wasn't surprised. 'Whatever it was, it's fixable.'

Mina bit her lip. 'It isn't true that I didn't see his face.'

Sandra didn't move, paralysed by surprise. 'Are you telling me you'd be able to identify him?'

Mina nodded. 'I think so.'

Sandra got up from the table. 'Then we have to go straight to the police.'

'No!' Mina screamed, reaching out her arm to stop her. 'I beg you,' she added softly.

'We have to do an identikit immediately, before the memory fades.'

'I'll never forget him as long as I live, believe me.'

'It isn't true: even after a few hours, memory can play tricks.'

'If I go to the police, it'll be all over for me.'

What was she referring to? Why was she so afraid of the police? Sandra had no idea, but she had to do something all the same. 'Are you good at describing things?'

'Yes, why?'

'Because I'm good at drawing.'

In the secret room in the attic of the villa there was an easel with a professional camera attached to the top. Facing it was a kind of stage set with an interchangeable coloured background. There were various pieces of furniture that could be arranged on the stage – a stool, a sofa, a chaise longue. There was even a chair in front of a little table with a mirror: on top of the table, everything needed for make-up. Multi-coloured blushers, face powder, brushes, lipsticks.

Marcus's attention, though, was immediately drawn to a row of women's clothes hanging on a rack. He shone his torch on them, then went through them with his hand. They were elegant dresses of different colours, some of them evening dresses, some of silk or satin . . . Marcus immediately noticed a detail that shook him.

These garments weren't a woman's size. *They were a little girl's.*

But he had a horrible feeling the real surprise was hidden behind the curtain that screened off a corner of the room. Sure enough, when he moved it aside, he found what he had suspected: the dark-room where Anatoly Agapov had developed his photographs. There were tubs, acids and chemicals, a tank, an enlarger, the little lamp that emitted non-actinic red light.

In a corner of the desk, a heap of photographs. Maybe discarded ones. Marcus reached out to them, putting down the torch so as to have both his hands free to look through them.

They were ambiguous, discordant, unpleasant images. All of them showed a girl, Hana, wearing the clothes he had seen hanging on the rack.

The girl was smiling: she seemed pleased as she winked at the camera. But Marcus still managed to detect her profound unease.

Ostensibly there was nothing bad, certainly nothing sexual. It seemed like a game. But, looking closely at those photographs, there was something sick. The sickness of a man who had replaced his dead wife with his daughter and fed his own madness with an obscene display.

That was why he always sent the servants away before nightfall. He wanted to remain alone to do this.

Had Victor inherited his father's perversion? Was that why he made up and photographed his female victims?

As Marcus went mechanically through the photos, and anger rose inside him, he came across another family image. It was very similar to the one the old woman had shown him in the nursing home, another copy of which he had found in a desk drawer in Anatoly Agapov's study. The father with his twin children. The photograph taken with a self-timer in which Hana was smiling and Anatoly was holding only Victor by the hand.

Except that in this one *the girl wasn't there*.

Only father and son were present. Same composition, same pose. Same lighting. How was it possible? Marcus decided to compare it with the one he had in his pocket.

Apart from that one significant thing, they were identical. Of the two, the original had to be the one in which Anatoly was with Victor alone.

'God help me,' Marcus heard himself say.

The other one was a photomontage.

Hana didn't exist.

9

The child of light existed only in photographs.

She was an optical illusion. A piece of trickery. She wasn't real.

In the video filmed at the Hamelin Institute, the nine-year-old Victor had been telling the truth: he hadn't killed his sister, for the simple reason that Hana didn't exist. But Kropp and his people hadn't believed him. Nobody had believed him.

Hana was the fruit of Anatoly Agapov's sick imagination.

'What was the relationship like between the two children?'

'Every now and again, we'd hear the children quarrel, but they also spent time together. Their favourite game was hide and seek.'

Hide and seek, Marcus repeated to himself. That was how the housekeeper had put it.

Nobody had ever seen the twins together.

Anatoly Agapov had invented the girl to satisfy a perversion, or maybe simply because he was mad. And he had forced his son to humour his madness by making him wear girls' clothes.

Victor, with time, had realised that his father preferred his imaginary sister, so he had started to convince himself that he was her in order to obtain his father's affection.

At that point, his personality had split.

But the male part wasn't completely subjugated: from time to time he'd go back to being Victor and start to suffer again because he felt excluded from his father's attentions.

It was impossible to know how long this whole thing had lasted, how much the boy had resisted. But one day he could stand it no longer and decided to 'kill' Hana to punish his father.

Marcus remembered what the housekeeper had said: Anatoly Agapov was so distraught, he had repatriated his daughter's body, covering up what had happened thanks to the diplomatic immunity he enjoyed.

But there was nobody in the coffin, Marcus knew that now.

In *killing* Hana, Victor had achieved his goal: he was free. But he couldn't foresee that his father, in his own madness, would decide to have him admitted to the Hamelin Institute, putting him together with children who really had committed terrible crimes and entrusting him to the care of Kropp and his people.

Marcus couldn't imagine a worse fate. Victor had gone from one torture to another, without having done anything wrong.

Over the years, that had turned him into a monster.

He kills couples because he sees himself and his sister in them. His motive is the injustice he has suffered, Marcus repeated to himself.

But there was more.

For that, however, he needed to talk to Sandra. He stopped at a service station to phone her.

The training for forensic photographers included an identikit course.

The pupils would alternate in the roles of the witness and the artist. The reason was simple: they had to learn to observe, to describe and to reproduce. Otherwise they would always be asking the camera to do all the work. In fact, their future task would be to guide the lens as if they were 'drawing' with it.

It wasn't difficult for Sandra to reconstruct the monster's face thanks to the details provided by Mina. At the end, she showed her the result. 'Will this do?'

Mina looked at it carefully. 'Yes, it's him,' she said resolutely.

At that point, it was Sandra who now looked more closely at the face. And as predicted, she was surprised at its normality.

The Monster was a man like any other.

Small brown eyes, a wide forehead, a slightly larger than average nose, thin lips, no beard or moustache. In identikits, faces always had a neutral expression. There was never any hatred or resentment. Nothing came through of the mindset of the individual they depicted. That was why they weren't frightening.

'Good, excellent work,' she said to Mina with a smile.

'Thank you,' Mina replied. 'It's been a long time since anyone complimented me.' And at last she too smiled, a lot calmer now.

'Go to bed, you must be tired,' Sandra said, continuing to play the role of elder sister. Then she went into the next room and scanned the drawing in order to email it to Superintendent Crespi and also to the Carabinieri.

In memory of Deputy Commissioner Moro, she said to herself.

But, before she could finish, her mobile phone rang. Unknown number. Sandra answered all the same.

'It's me,' Marcus said immediately. His tone was excited.

'We have an identikit of the Monster,' Sandra announced, triumphantly. 'I did as you told me and found the prostitute from Sabaudia: she was the one who gave me the description. She's in my apartment right now and I was about to send—'

'Drop it,' Marcus said, a little too hurriedly. 'She saw Victor. *We have to look for Hana.*'

'What do you mean?'

Marcus brought her quickly up to date on his visit to the villa and on the child of light. 'I was right, the answers are all in the first crime scene: the pine wood at Ostia. The storyteller: the end of the story coincides with the beginning. But the most important clues are those that seemed the most marginal: the word "*they*" written by Diana Delgaudio and the fact that the killer changed his clothes.'

'I don't quite understand . . . '

'When she woke up momentarily from her coma, Diana tried to send us a message: Hana and Victor were both present at the scene of the crime. *They*.'

'How is that possible? She doesn't exist.'

'The killer changes his clothes. That's the point! Over time, Victor has finally become Hana. In fact, when he impersonated his sister as a child, he was no longer a withdrawn, silent boy, he became a friendly little girl everybody liked and everybody loved. In growing up, he made a choice, and chose Hana in order to be accepted.'

'But, in order to kill, he turns back into Victor. That's why he changes his clothes.'

'Precisely. And after the murders he turns back into Hana. In Ostia, the police found a man's shirt in the car, left by mistake instead of Giorgio Montefiori's.'

'So we have to look for a woman,' Sandra concluded.

'The DNA, remember? He doesn't care about the fact that the police and the Carabinieri have that lead: he knows he's perfectly camouflaged because they're looking for a man.'

'But he *is* a man,' Sandra remarked.

'The DNA left in the villa in Sabaudia wasn't a signature but a challenge. It's as if he was saying: you're never going to find me.'

'Why?'

'I think he feels sure of his disguise because at some point in the past few years he's had a sex change,' Marcus asserted. 'Hana tried to wipe out Victor, but every now and again he re-emerges. Hana knows that Victor could do her harm: like that time when they were little and he tried to kill her. So she makes him kill the couples and relive that experience in which he defeats her: it's a way to keep him good. He doesn't see the victims as lovers, but as brother and sister, remember?'

'What are you talking about? I don't quite follow you: you said that Victor tried to kill Hana when he was a child?'

'Yes. I think Victor as a child performed some act of self-harm, like cutting his wrists.'

When the sun went down, the servants left the house.

Victor watched them from the window of his room. He watched them as they walked down the long drive to the big gate. And he always expressed the same desire: to leave with them.

But he couldn't. He had never left the villa.

Even the sun abandoned him, descending quickly beyond the line of the horizon. And the fear began. Every night. He would have liked someone to come and take him away from there. That was how it happened in films and novels, wasn't it? Whenever the main character was in danger, there was always someone who ran to his rescue and saved him. Victor closed his eyes and prayed with his whole being for it to happen. Sometimes he convinced himself that it really would be like that. But nobody ever came for him.

Not every night, though, was the same. Sometimes the time passed indifferently, and he could devote himself to numbers – the last refuge remaining to him. At other times, though, the silence of the house was interrupted by his father's voice.

'Where are you?' he would repeat in a soft voice. 'Where is my little kukla *now, my little doll?'*

The softness was meant to flush him out. There had been days when Victor had tried to escape him. There were places where nobody would find him – he would look for them with Hana, when they played hide and seek in the big house. But you couldn't remain hidden forever.

So, with time, Victor had learned not to resist. He would go to his sister's room, choose some clothes from the wardrobe, and put them on. And become Hana. Then he would sit down on the bed and wait.

'There's my wonderful kukla,*' his father would say with a smile, opening his arms wide.*

Then he would take him by the hand and together they would go up to the attic.

'Beautiful dolls have to demonstrate that they earn their beauty.'

Victor would get up on a stool and watch him getting the camera ready and setting up the lights. His father was a perfectionist. He would carefully look through the garments he kept in the secret room, hand one to him and explain what he wanted him to do. First, though, he would personally see to the make-up. He had a predilection for lipstick.

Sometimes, Hana tried to refuse. Then her father would lose his temper.

'It was your brother put you up to this, wasn't it? It's always him, that useless little bastard.'

Hana knew he might take it out on Victor – he had already shown her the revolver he kept hidden in a drawer.

'I'll punish Victor as I punished that good-for-nothing mother of his,' he threatened.

So she yielded – she always yielded.

'My good little kukla, *this time we won't need the rope.'*

Victor always thought that, if his mother had been there, things might have been different. He really didn't remember much about her. The scent of her hands, for example. And the warmth of her breasts, when she pulled him to her and sang to him to make him sleep. Nothing else. After all, she had only been present in the first five years of his life. But he knew she had been beautiful. 'The most beautiful of all women,' her husband would still say when he wasn't angry at her soul. Because now he couldn't get angry with her any more, he couldn't scream his own contempt at her.

Victor knew that, without her being there, he himself had become the object of Anatoly's hatred.

In Moscow, after his mother's death, his father had wiped her out of their lives. He had thrown away everything that might remind them of her. The make-up with which she had made herself beautiful, the clothes in the wardrobe, the objects of daily use, the trinkets with which she had decorated their house over the years.

And the photographs.

He had burnt them all in the fireplace. All that remained were lots of empty frames. They were little black holes that swallowed everything around them. Father and son tried to ignore them, but it was difficult and often they didn't succeed. It might happen that they were sitting at table and their eyes were attracted by one of those empty spaces present in the room.

Victor managed to live with them, but for his father they were becoming an obsession.

Then, one day, he had come into Victor's room carrying a hanger with a woman's dress, yellow with red flowers. Without a word of explanation, he had made him put it on.

Victor could still remember clearly the sensation he had felt, standing in the middle of the room, barefoot on the cold floor. Anatoly Agapov was looking at him gravely. The dress was a couple of sizes too large and Victor felt ridiculous. But his father didn't mind.

'We'll have to let your hair grow a little,' he had said in the end, emerging from his own thoughts.

Then his father had bought the camera and, subsequently, everything else he needed. Little by little, he had become an expert. And he no longer mistook the sizes of the clothes – now he was good even at that.

So Victor had started to pose for him, thinking at first that it was a kind of game. Even later, although finding the situation strange, he had continued obeying his father's will. He never asked himself if it was right or wrong, because children know perfectly well that their parents are always right.

So he didn't see anything bad in it, and, besides, he had always been afraid of saying no to him – something told him not to do so. But after a while he had told himself: if a game makes you feel afraid, then maybe it's not just a game.

The confirmation of that presentiment had come the day his father, instead of calling him Victor, had used another name for him. It had happened quite naturally, in the context of a sentence like any other.

'Now could you show me your profile, Hana?'

Where did that name come from, uttered with such kindness? At first, Victor had thought it was a mistake. But then that oddity had repeated itself, until it became a habit. And when he had tried to ask his father who Hana was, he had replied simply: 'Hana is your sister.'

When he had finished taking the photographs, Anatoly would shut himself up in his darkroom to develop his work. Then Hana knew that her task was over. She could go back downstairs and turn into Victor again.

Sometimes, though, Victor would put on Hana's clothes without his father asking him to do so. And he would visit the servants. He had noticed that they were well disposed towards his sister. They would smile at her, talk to her, take an interest in her. And Victor had discovered that it was much easier for him to interact with strangers when he was wearing those clothes. Other people were no longer hostile and distant, they didn't give him that look that he hated more than anything else. The look of compassion, he called it. He had seen it on his mother's face the day she had died. Her corpse had stared at him and it was as if she was saying, 'Poor Victor.'

His father, though, wasn't always bad to him. There were times when something changed, and Victor always hoped they would last forever. Like when he had wanted them to pose together for a self-portrait. No Hana that time, just father and son. And then Victor had summoned up the courage to actually take his hand. And the really incredible thing was that his father hadn't pulled his hand away. It had been wonderful.

But no change was long-lasting. Subsequently, things had gone back to the way they had been before. And Hana was again the favourite. But, after that photograph with his father, something inside Victor had snapped: the disappointment was a wound that could no longer be ignored.

And he was tired of always being afraid.

One day he locked himself in his room – it was a rainy day, and he didn't like rain. He was lying face-down on the rug, solving equations – a way to lose himself, not to have to think. A generic second-grade equation appeared before his eyes.

$ax^2 + bx = c = 0$

To determine the unknown x, the terms of the equation had to be equal to zero. That was why they had to be wiped out. His mathematical mind did not take long to find the solution. On the left of the equation, there was himself and Hana. To be equal to zero, they had to wipe each other out.

That was how the idea came to him.

Zero was a beautiful number. It was a state of peace, an unassailable condition. People didn't know the true value of zero. For them, zero was death, but for him it might be freedom. At that moment, Victor realised that nobody would come and take him away. It was pointless to hope for that. But maybe mathematics could still save him.

So he went to Hana's room, put on her most beautiful dress and stretched out on her bed. A short time earlier, he had stolen his father's old hunting knife. At first he merely placed it on his skin, just to savour it. It was cold. Then he closed his eyes and clenched his teeth, ignoring the voice of his sister inside him, begging him not to do it. Instead, he lifted the blade, brought it down and let it slide across his left wrist. He felt the steel sink into his flesh. The pain was unbearable. A warm viscous substance slid along his fingers. Then, slowly, he lost consciousness.

No more Victor. No more Hana.

Zero.

When he opened his eyes again, his father was holding him in his arms, wrapping his wrist with a towel to stop the blood. He was crying desperately and cradling him. Then words emerged from his lips that Victor did not understand at first.

'My Hana is gone.' And then, 'What have you done, Victor? What have you done?'

Only later would Victor realise that this modest scar on the wrist was an imperfection the sight of which Anatoly Nikolayevich Agapov would never tolerate. Not on the snow-white skin of his kukla. *From that day on, he stopped photographing her. That day, Hana had died.*

Only Hana, though. That was the big surprise, the incredible novelty. Even though he felt sick, Victor was happier than he had ever been before.

His father, on the other hand, had continued crying in front of the servants. And some of them were moved. So Anatoly sent them all away, for ever.

The new life, the life without fear, lasted just one month. Long enough to send a coffin to Moscow and for the scar to heal. One night, before Victor fell asleep, the door of his room opened, letting the light from the corridor in, like a silver blade. He had recognised his father's silhouette in the doorway. Anatoly's face was in shadow.

The man didn't move. Then, however, he spoke in a neutral, icy voice.

'You can't stay here any more.'

At that moment, Victor's heart sank.

'There's a place where bad children like you have to go. You're going to live there from tomorrow, it'll be your new home. And you'll never come back here.'

10

'. . . I think Victor as a child performed some act of self-harm, like cutting his wrists . . . '

Marcus's last words took Sandra's breath away.

'My God, he's here.'

'What are you talking about?'

She swallowed with difficulty. 'It's her: the prostitute is Hana. Call the police.' Then she immediately hung up, because she didn't have much time left. She thought of where her pistol was. In the bedroom. Too far: she'd never reach it in time. But she had to try.

She took a step beyond the threshold and was about to carry on along the corridor, but then froze. The woman was there, with her back to her. And she had changed.

She was wearing men's clothes. Dark trousers, a white shirt.

Victor turned. In his hand, he had Sandra's camera. 'I like taking photographs too, did you know that?'

Sandra didn't move, but she noticed that he had opened his rucksack and had placed a camera and an old hunting knife neatly on the sofa.

Victor saw where she was looking. 'Oh, yes,' he said. 'The revolver was useless, I already used it last night.'

Sandra retreated until she found herself with her back to the wall.

'I heard your call just now,' Victor said, picking up Sandra's camera again. 'But do you think I hadn't foreseen it all? It was all calculated: I'm very good at mathematics.'

Any word you said to a psychopath could set off an unpredictable reaction. That was why Sandra had decided to keep quiet.

'Why aren't you talking to me any more?' Victor asked, pouting. 'Are you offended? I didn't make a mistake last night in Sabaudia, I simply separated the solutions of the equation.'

What was he talking about? What was he referring to?

'The terms cancel each other out. The result is zero.'

Sandra felt a terrible shudder go through her. 'Max,' she said softly.

Victor nodded.

Sandra felt her eyes fill with tears. 'Why us?'

'I saw you make an inverted sign of the cross the other night on television, while that policeman was talking. What does the sign mean? I saw them make it sometimes at the Institute where they shut me up as a child, but I never understood it.'

Still silence.

Victor shrugged, as if deep down he didn't care. 'I always follow what the papers and television say about me. But you also struck me because, when I saw you, you were putting away a camera. And, as I said, I like cameras. You were perfect for my game.' His face clouded over. 'That's what my father always told Hana, to persuade her to pose for him. "It's only a game, *kukla*, you mustn't be afraid."'

Sandra pushed her heels back until she touched the skirting board. Letting herself be guided by touch, she started moving slowly to the right, hugging the wall.

'It's strange, the way people behave before they die. Have you noticed that? The girl in Ostia screamed and asked her boyfriend not to stab her. But I told him to do it and he did. I don't think he loved her ... The policewoman on the other hand, Pia Rimonti, thanked me in the end. Yes, she actually said thank you when I got tired of torturing her and made it clear that I was finally going to kill her.'

Sandra was furious: she could imagine the scene.

'The German girl, the hitchhiker, I don't even remember. She begged me, but I didn't understand her language. I only discovered later that she was trying to tell me about the child she was carrying inside her. And Max ...'

Sandra wasn't sure she wanted to know how he had died. A tear slid down her face. Victor noticed it.

'How can you cry for him? He was cheating on you with a prostitute.'

He said this in a tone that made Sandra's blood boil.

'Did you like my story about the way I escaped from the villa in Sabaudia? Hana has a vivid imagination. Over the past few years she's impersonated many women, deceiving every man she met. Mila is her most successful character. She likes going with men, she would have continued if I hadn't come back to her.'

By now, Sandra had managed to move about three feet.

'After she changed sex she thought she'd got rid of me. But every now and again I'd come back. The first few times I was only a thought, a voice in her head. One night she was with a client and, when I appeared and saw that scene, I started screaming and threw up all over his cock.' He laughed. 'You should have seen the look of disgust on the man's face. He wanted to hit me, but if he'd tried I'd have killed him with my bare hands. He'll never know how lucky he was.'

Sandra wasn't sure Victor would want to keep talking for much longer. She had to do something: the minutes were passing quickly and nobody was coming to rescue her.

The door of the apartment was now a few steps away. If she

got out through it and ran down the stairs, he was sure to catch up with her, but she'd be able to start screaming, attracting someone's attention.

'Actually, I don't really want to kill you, but I have to. Because, every time I kill, Hana gets very scared and then she gives me more space after that. I'm sure that, with time, there'll only be me again, Victor . . . I know everyone prefers my sister, but I've discovered that there's something else that attracts people's attention . . . fear. That's a feeling too, isn't it?'

Sandra darted for the door. Victor was taken by surprise, but managed to head her off. Sandra pushed him aside, but he grabbed her firmly by the arm. She dragged him with her along the hall, while he hit her repeatedly on the back with his fist. 'You can't get out: nobody can get out of here, *kukla*!'

Sandra opened the door and found herself outside. She wanted to scream but didn't have any breath in her lungs. It had been sucked out of her by panic, not by the struggle.

Victor slammed the back of her head down on the floor and she almost lost consciousness. In spite of her blurred vision, she managed to see him going back inside. Where had he gone? Sandra tried to raise herself on to her arms but fell back and hit her temple. Tears were now filling her eyes. Through that liquid, milky veil, she saw him come back towards her, his face transfigured by fury.

He had fetched the knife.

Sandra closed her eyes, ready to receive the first stab. But instead of feeling pain she heard a woman's shrill scream. She opened her eyes again and saw Victor lying on the ground. A man was on top of him, with his back to her. He was holding him still. Victor was struggling, yelling desperately, but the other man wouldn't let go.

The woman's scream became masculine, then feminine again. It was chilling.

The man turned towards Sandra. 'Are you all right?' She tried to nod, but wasn't sure she'd managed it.

'I'm a penitenziere,' Clemente said.

Sandra had never seen his face, didn't know his name, but she believed him. Then the man landed Victor a punch, and he finally fell silent. 'Get out of here,' she tried to tell him in a thin voice. 'The police . . . Your secret . . . '

Clemente merely smiled.

Only then did Sandra notice the knife sticking out of his stomach.

11

When Marcus reached Trastevere, he couldn't get through the police cordon.

He stopped on the edges of it, mingling with the onlookers and the photographers who had come rushing to the scene.

Nobody understood what was going on, but the rumours were coming thick and fast.

Some mentioned the man who had been taken away in handcuffs a little while earlier and how overjoyed the police had been as they bundled him into a car that had left at high speed, along with a cortège of other cars with flashing lights, their sirens howling.

Then he glimpsed Sandra being led to an ambulance by two paramedics. It was obvious that something had happened to her but, basically, she was fine.

He heaved a sigh of relief, but it didn't last long.

He saw a stretcher being carried down the steps of the building. On it lay a man with a respirator over his face. It was Clemente. How had he found out about Sandra? Marcus had never mentioned her to him ... He watched as they loaded him into a second ambulance, but then the ambulance didn't leave.

Why don't you go? How long are you going to take?

The vehicle stood there with its doors closed. Movements could be detected inside. At last it set off, but with no sirens.

Marcus guessed that his friend hadn't made it.

He felt like crying, cursing himself for the way they had parted company the last time. Instead, much to his surprise, he found himself praying in a low voice.

He did so in the middle of the crowd, without anybody noticing. While all those around were busy with other things. Deep down, that was always the way things went.

I am invisible, he repeated to himself. I don't exist.

For the fifth lesson of his training, Clemente had come to his apartment in the dead of night, without any warning.

'We have to go somewhere,' he announced, without adding anything else.

Marcus dressed in haste and together they left the attic room in the Via dei Serpenti. They wandered through the centre of a deserted Rome on foot until they came to the entrance of an old palace.

Clemente took from his pocket a very old, heavy key of burnished iron, with which he opened the front door, letting Marcus go in first.

The place was vast and silent, like a large church. A row of candles indicated the way up a pink marble staircase.

'Come,' Clemente whispered. 'The others are already here.'

The others? Who were the others? Marcus wondered.

They climbed the big staircase and went along a wide corridor frescoed with scenes that he was unable to interpret at first. Then he realised that they were reproductions of famous episodes from the Gospels. Jesus bringing Lazarus back to life, the wedding at Cana, the baptism of Jesus . . .

Clemente saw the dubious look he gave those pictures. 'It's like in the Sistine Chapel,' he hastened to say. 'There, Michelangelo's fresco of the Last Judgement serves to admonish and instruct the cardinals who have gathered in conclave to elect the new pope about the gravity of the task awaiting them. Here, the gospel scenes have the same purpose: to remind those passing through that the mission they are about to perform must be inspired only by the will of the Holy Spirit.'

'What mission?'

'You'll see.'

Soon afterwards, they came to a marble parapet adorned with columns, overlooking a large circular space. Before they could lean on it, Clemente drew Marcus close and said, 'We have to stay in the shadows.'

They stationed themselves behind one of the columns and at last Marcus was able to look down.

In the hall below there were twelve confessionals arranged in a circle, around a large gilded candelabrum on a pedestal. On it there were twelve lighted candles.

The recurrent number twelve recalled the apostles, Marcus immediately noted.

After a short time, some men started coming in. They all wore dark hoods, which made it impossible to see their faces. As each man passed the candelabrum, he extinguished the flames of one of the candles with two fingers. Then they went and took up their positions inside the confessionals.

This went on until only one candle remained lit, and one confessional was empty. Nobody will extinguish Judas's candle, Marcus told himself. No one will take his place.

That single candle was the only light in the room.

'The Office of the Shadows,' Clemente explained in a low voice. 'That's the name of the ritual you're watching.'

When they were all sitting in their places, another participant in the liturgy made his entrance, in a hood of red satin.

He was carrying a large, very bright candle, which restored visibility to the room. He placed it at the top of the candelabrum. The candle represented Christ. At that point, Marcus realised where they were.

The Tribunal of Souls.

When Clemente had told him about the Archive of Sins kept by the penitenzieri, Clemente had explained that for the most serious sins – the mortal sins – it was necessary to gather a special court, composed of high-ranking prelates but also of simple priests, all chosen at random, who together would decide whether or not to grant forgiveness to the penitent.

That was what was about to happen before his eyes.

The man in the red hood would first read a text detailing the sin, then launch into a fierce denunciation of the sinner, who always remained anonymous. The prelate called to this thankless but fundamental ministry was known as the Devil's Advocate.

Another of his tasks involved judging the cases for beatification and sanctification of those men who, in life, had demonstrated that they possessed divine aptitudes. It was up to him to demonstrate the contrary. In the ritual of the Tribunal of Souls, though, the Devil's Advocate really did take the part of the devil, because, according to Scriptures, the devil certainly wouldn't want a sinner to be absolved of his sins and thus escape hell.

Beyond all the archaic symbolism, clearly medieval in origin, the Tribunal of Souls retained all its age-old power, making it seem the very instrument of fate.

The judgement did not revolve around the sin in itself, but rather the soul of the sinner. It was as if what was being decided was whether or not he or she was still worthy of being part of the human race.

After the speech by the Devil's Advocate, a debate would begin between the members in the confessionals. In the end, the judgement would be expressed unequivocally. Each of them would rise from his seat and, on the way out of the room, would decide whether or not to relight the candle he had extinguished on the way in. This was done by taking a small stick from a bowl and dipping it in the flame of the candle that represented Christ.

In the end, the number of candles that turned out to be lit on the candelabrum determined the pardon or condemnation of the penitent. Obviously, the majority prevailed. If the numbers were equal, the judgement would be considered favourable.

The trial, then, was about to start.

The man in the red hood had taken a sheet of paper and started to read in a stentorian voice that had echoed through the room: that night's sin – the culpa gravis *– had been committed by a woman who had killed her two-year-old son because, according to her, she was suffering from a serious form of depression.*

Having finished reading, the man in the red hood had prepared to begin his accusation. But first he had slid back the hood, because he was the only person present who could show his own face.

The Devil's Advocate was oriental.

12

Cardinal Batista Erriaga slipped his pastoral ring back on.

The ring finger of his right hand had been far too long deprived of the sacred jewel. At last he had been able to leave his room in that fourth-class hotel in which he had spent the last few nights and return home to his splendid penthouse not far from the Colosseum, with a view over the Forum.

With the capture of the child of salt, his task was almost done. It was perfectly all right now for Rome to know that the Devil's Advocate had returned to the city.

The ghost of his friend Min, which had so tormented him in the past few days, had not yet vanished. But it was again a silent presence in his conscience. It did not bother him, because it was thanks to the good giant that Erriaga had ended up in the upper echelons of the Church.

As a young man he had committed a murder. He had brutally killed Min, who had been guilty of nothing but making fun of him, and for that they had imprisoned him. Batista had rejected the sentence, considering it unjust and rebelling against any form of authority throughout his sentence. But it was all just rebellious bluster – in reality, he was suffering deep inside for what he had done.

Until one day he had met a priest, and everything had changed.

The priest had started telling him about the Gospels and the Scriptures. Gradually, patiently, he had persuaded Batista to free himself of his burden. But, after he had confessed his sin, the priest had not absolved him immediately. Instead, he had explained that it was necessary to transcribe his *culpa gravis* and submit it to a special tribunal that met in Rome. He had done so, and long days had passed in which Batista had feared that there would never be any forgiveness or redemption for him. But then the verdict had arrived.

His soul was saved.

At that moment, Erriaga had glimpsed the possibility of turning his life around. The Tribunal of Souls was the extraordinary instrument that would allow him to get away from that wretched existence, to escape a preordained fate of poverty and insignificance. What power there was in passing judgement on the souls of men! He would no longer be the humble, ineffectual offspring of an alcoholic – the son of the trained monkey.

He had persuaded the priest to start him off on the road to taking his vows. He had never been driven by a sincere vocation, but by a healthy ambition.

In the years that followed, he had pursued his aim with commitment and self-denial. First of all, he had managed to wipe out all trace of his own past: nobody would ever connect him with a murder that had taken place in a small village in the Philippines. Then he had climbed – deservedly so – every step in the hierarchical ladder. From simple priest to bishop, from monsignor to cardinal. And finally he had obtained the office for which he had prepared himself all his life. In fact, given his expertise, it was almost taken for granted that they would choose him.

For more than twenty years he had held the Office of

Shadows within the tribunal. He would formulate the charge against the penitents and, in doing so, he would learn their most shameful secrets. Their identity was sealed by anonymity. But Batista Erriaga was in a position to identify them from small details in their confessions.

By now, he was really expert at doing that.

Over time, he had learned to use what he knew in order to obtain favours. He didn't like to call it blackmail, even though that was what it might appear to be. Whenever he used his immense power, he did so only for the good of the Church. That it might also be of advantage to him personally was a completely marginal matter.

He did not feel any pity for the penitents. These men confessed only so that they could continue their lives undisturbed. They were cowards, because in that way they avoided having to face the full weight of the law. In addition, many of them obtained forgiveness and then went back to doing exactly what they had done before.

In Erriaga's opinion, the sacrament of confession was one of the defects of Catholicism. A periodic cleansing of the conscience and it was all sorted!

That was why he had no compunction about exploiting these sinners, using their vices to obtain advantages for himself. Whenever he confronted one of them, they were astonished to hear their own secrets recounted back to them. The fact that they couldn't figure out how he knew was proof that they had even forgotten they had confessed to a priest. That was how little forgiveness mattered to them!

He put on one of his usual beautifully tailored dark suits but with his priest's white collar instead of a tie, slipped the chain with the big cross of gold and rubies around his neck, then looked at himself in the mirror and recited in a low voice a prayer for the soul of Min.

In his youth he had committed a terrible crime, but at least he had not had the effrontery to forgive himself for it.

When he had finished, he decided to go out, because he still had one thing to do to complete his task.

The secret consisted of three levels. The first was the child of salt. The second, the man with the wolf's head. And they had both been exposed.

But the third had to remain intact. Otherwise, the Church would pay a huge price. And he with it.

13

Marcus had thought about it for a long time.

There had been no point standing outside the hospital where she had been admitted as a purely precautionary measure. There were already groups of photographers and reporters waiting for her in the hope of stealing an image or a statement.

Sandra was the person of the moment. Along with Victor Agapov, obviously.

The Monster had been taken to prison and, according to the little information available to the press, was obstinately refusing to answer the questions of the examining magistrates. That was why attention was focusing on the young policewoman, both victim and heroine of the last act of the drama.

He was hoping to see her, to talk to her, but he couldn't just come forward. His grief at the death of Clemente was pursuing him like a nagging presence. After the death of his one friend, Sandra was the only antidote to solitude.

Up until now he had always thought he was alone, but it wasn't true. Maybe because he had always believed that Clemente had his own life beyond the relationship between the two of them: people he interacted with, communicated with, even laughed with or confided in. Just the fact that he knew their superiors seemed an advantage. Instead of which, Clemente had been exactly like him: he'd had nobody. The big difference between them was that he'd never complained, he hadn't seen it as a burden the way Marcus did.

Marcus wished he had understood Clemente's solitude and taken it upon himself. That way they could have shared his own too. And then they would really have been friends.

'I was a country priest, in Portugal. One day a letter arrived. It had the Vatican seal on it: it was an assignment I couldn't get out of. Inside were instructions on how to track down a man who had been admitted to a hospital in Prague . . . I've never understood why they chose me. I had no particular gifts, I'd never shown any ambition to advance in my career. I was happy in my parish, with my congregation . . . It is not for us to ask, it is not for us to know. We must simply obey.'

The previous night, Clemente had saved Sandra by sacrificing himself. The main reason Marcus wanted to see her was to tell her the truth about his friend.

He was waiting for her now in the one place where they could meet away from crowds and onlookers. Far from everyone. He wasn't sure Sandra would guess he was waiting for her there, but he hoped she would. Because it was the place they had first met, three years earlier. The sacristy of San Luigi dei Francesi.

'I'm here,' she said before he could open his mouth, as if they really had made an appointment and she wanted to apologise for being late.

Marcus started towards her, but then stopped dead. The last time, they had embraced, but now that wouldn't be right. Sandra was hollow-faced, her eyes swollen from crying.

'I'm stupid. It's my fault Max is dead.'

'I don't think it was down to you.'

'Oh, but it was. If I hadn't made that inverted sign of the cross as I was being filmed on TV, that bastard wouldn't have chosen us.'

Marcus was unaware of that part of the story. In fact, he had asked himself why Sandra in particular, why Max in particular. But he had not been in a position to answer his own question. Learning now how it had happened, he decided to say nothing.

'His students are very upset, they can't get over it. They've prepared a memorial, there's going to be a brief ceremony in the school gym.' She finished the sentence and looked at her watch. 'The magistrate has authorised the repatriation of the body. This evening, a plane will take him back to England.' Then she added, 'I'm going with him.'

Marcus was looking at her, unable to say a word. They were only a few yards from each other, but neither of them could bear to move closer. It was as if there was a gulf between them.

'I have to go with him. I have to talk to his mother, his father and his brothers, I'll meet his old friends he didn't get a chance to introduce me to and I'll see for the first time the place where he was born, and they'll see me and think I loved him to the end and it won't be true. I . . .'

She let that word remain hanging over the precipice that divided them.

'You what?' Marcus asked.

This time it was Sandra's turn to be silent.

'Why did you come here?'

'Because I made a promise.'

Marcus was disappointed by the answer. He would have liked to hear her say that it was because of him.

'Your friend's name was Clemente, wasn't it? And he was a penitenziere.'

So Sandra knew who had saved her . . . Clemente had broken the rule of the penitenzieri . . . *'Nobody must know of your existence. Ever. You will be able to say who you are only in the time that elapses between the lightning and the thunder . . .'*

Sandra searched in her pocket, took something out, and held it out to him without coming closer. 'Before dying, he asked me to give you this.'

Marcus took a step forward and saw what was in the palm of her hand. The medallion of the Archangel Michael brandishing a fiery sword.

'He said it was important. And that you would understand.'

Marcus remembered the moment of anger when he had flung it at him. Had that really been their farewell? That threw him into an even darker pit of despair.

'I have to go,' Sandra said.

She came to him and put Clemente's medallion in his hands. Then she raised herself a little on tiptoe and gave him a kiss on the lips. A long kiss. 'In another life,' she said.

'In another life,' Marcus promised.

Late that evening he returned to the attic room in the Via dei Serpenti. He closed the door and waited before switching on the light. Through the window came a weak glimmer from the rooftops of Rome.

Now he really was completely alone. Alone for good.

He was sad. But if Sandra had prolonged that kiss, and had turned that farewell into something else, maybe a request to be loved, how would he have reacted? He had taken an oath many years earlier, a vow of chastity and obedience. Would he really have been ready to break it? And to become what?

He was a hunter of the dark. It wasn't a profession, it was his nature.

Evil wasn't simply a form of behaviour from which negative effects and feelings derived. *Evil is a dimension*. He could detect it, seeing what others couldn't see.

And in the picture he had in front of him now something was missing.

Who was the man Sandra had met at the Colosseum? How did he know so much about the police investigation? And above all, how was it possible that he knew Marcus and the penitenzieri?

He still had to answer these questions. The hunter of the dark had no choice. But he would start tomorrow. For now, he was too tired.

He lit the little lamp next to the camp bed. The first thing he saw was the image of the man with the grey rucksack. The killer of the nun. He couldn't help thinking that his falling out with Clemente had started with the case of the dismembered corpse in the Vatican gardens and, above all, with Marcus's insistence on meeting his superiors. He had been unfair to him. His friend's desperate 'I don't know' still echoed inside him.

He remembered the medallion Clemente had wanted to give him back before dying – the Archangel Michael, protector of the penitenzieri. The moment had come to put it on again. He looked for it in his pocket, but together with it also pulled out a folded piece of cardboard. It took him a while to remember that it was the map that Kropp had given him. Both those objects came from men who were about to die. Marcus was about to get rid of the second, because he couldn't bear the comparison. But before tearing up the map he forced himself to look at it one last time.

The centre of Rome, a route leading from the Via del Mancino to the Piazza di Spagna, at the foot of the steps that led up to the church of Trinità dei Monti. Little more than half a mile on foot.

You'll understand and you'll be surprised, Kropp had said.

But what could there possibly be, right in the middle of one of the most famous and visited places in Rome? What secret could possibly be concealed in front of everybody's eyes?

Before, Marcus had thought it was a lure, a way of distracting him from his main aim: to find Victor. Now, though, he considered it in a different light: Kropp could have sent him to the most remote and unknown corner of the city if he had simply wanted to deceive him. But what he had actually done made no sense.

'The end of your story, child without name.'

It was only in taking a closer look at the map that Marcus noticed a detail. Or rather, an *anomaly*. Not all of the route marked in red passed along the city streets. Several times it seemed to cut across buildings.

Not over them, Marcus told himself.

Below.

The route was underground.

14

There was a strange phenomenon taking place throughout Rome.

People were filling the streets, refusing to go to bed. The city was celebrating the end of a nightmare. The most extraordinary thing was the vigils that were happening spontaneously in all neighbourhoods. Someone would choose a place at random to lay flowers or light a candle for the victims, and after a while that place would fill with other testimonies – soft toys, photos, little notes. People would stop and take each other by the hand. Many prayed.

The churches were open. Those which were usually the goal only of tourists were now full of worshippers. Nobody any longer felt embarrassment at being seen giving thanks to God.

A bold, joyful faith. That was how it appeared to Marcus. But he couldn't join in the carnival, not yet.

The Via del Mancino was near the Piazza Venezia.

He waited for the street to be momentarily deserted before letting himself down through a manhole into the conduit of the Capitoline aqueduct: the beginning of the route indicated in Kropp's map. Moving the wrought-iron cover, he discovered a little ladder that descended for several yards underground. Only when he reached the bottom of the steps did he light his torch.

It illuminated the narrow tunnel in which the conduit ran. The walls of the tunnel bore the sediments of different periods. Layers of reinforced concrete, or mould, but also tuff and travertine. One layer was made up of shards of clay amphorae. At the time of the ancient Romans, old, unused receptacles had often been used as building material.

Marcus kept going and his torch travelled back and forth between the uneven floor and the map he held in his hand. He came to a number of forks on his way and several times found it hard to orientate himself. But, at a certain point, he found himself at the beginning of a tunnel, probably dug many centuries earlier, which had nothing to do with the aqueduct.

He turned into it. After a few yards, he noticed that the walls were covered in inscriptions in ancient Greek, Latin and Aramaic. Some words had been corroded by time and damp.

A catacomb, he thought.

These were Christian or Hebraic burial places and were found in various parts of Rome. The oldest went back to the second century AD, when a ban on burying the dead within the walls of the city had been introduced.

It was strange that there should be one so close to the Piazza di Spagna.

Christian catacombs were usually dedicated to a saint. The most famous was the one that housed the grave of St Peter, several yards below the basilica that was the symbol of Catholicism. He had visited it once with Clemente, who had even told him the story of how the apostle's remains had been discovered in 1939.

As he advanced, Marcus shone his torch more closely at the walls in the hope that something would reveal to him where he was.

He saw it at the base of one of the walls. It was only an inch or two high. He didn't recognise it immediately, because at first it simply looked like a figure of a little man in profile, his legs stretched out in the motion of walking.

Then he noticed the wolf's head.

The posture indicated that he wanted to be followed. Marcus did so. As he advanced, he found the symbol again several times, placed ever higher and ever larger in size. A sign that whoever had made this old mural promised to reveal something important at the end of the route.

When the man with the wolf's head reached his size, it seemed to Marcus as if he were walking beside him. It was an unpleasant feeling. Several yards above his head, people were parading with their hearts full of a regained faith, while down here he was marching side by side with the devil.

He came out to a circular room, a kind of well without an exit. The ceiling was low, but Marcus noticed that you could stand up in it perfectly easily, even without having to bend. On the walls, all around, the figure with the wolf's head was repeated obsessively. Marcus shone his torch on all these related creatures, one by one. Until he reached the last in the row. And was taken aback.

This figure was different. The wolf's head had been taken from him and was lying next to him, like a mask. Beneath that effigy there was still a human face. A face that Marcus knew well because he had seen it thousands of times.

The man without the mask was Jesus Christ.

'Yes, they're Christians,' a man's voice said behind him.

Marcus turned abruptly, aiming the torch. The man lifted a hand to his face, but only because the light was blinding him.

'Could you lower that, please?'

Marcus did so, and the man also lowered his arm. Marcus realised he had seen him once before, one night at the Tribunal of Souls.

The Devil's Advocate.

Batista Erriaga, on the other hand, was seeing Marcus for the first time. 'I was hoping you wouldn't get to this point,' he said, thinking of the third level of the secret, which was now exposed.

'What do you mean "they're Christians"?' Marcus asked the man, who was dressed in black but with a cardinal's cross and ring.

'That they believe in God and in Christ, just like you and me. In fact, their faith may even be stronger and more fruitful than ours, Marcus.'

The man knew his name. 'Then why protect evil?'

'For the sake of good,' Erriaga said, realising how strange the concept might sound to the uninitiated. 'You see, Marcus, in all the great monotheistic religions God is both good and bad, merciful and vengeful, compassionate and ruthless. That is how he is for the Jews and for the Muslims. The Christians, on the other hand, at a certain point in their history, distinguished God from the devil . . . God could only be good: he had to be good. And even today we're paying the price for that decision, that error. We've hidden the devil from mankind, just as we hide dirt under a carpet. To obtain what? We've absolved God of his sins just to absolve ourselves. It's an act of great selfishness, don't you think?'

'So Kropp and his acolytes were just pretending to be Satanists.'

'If the true God is both good and bad, what is Satanism if not another way to worship? Just before the year 1000 – in 999 – a group of Christians founded the Confraternity of Judas. They maintained something that was already evident in the Holy Scriptures, that is, that without Judas, the martyrdom of Christ wouldn't have taken place, and without that martyrdom we wouldn't have had Christianity. Judas – evil – had been essential. They understood that the devil was necessary to fuel the faith. So they invented symbols that would make a deep impression on people. What is 666 if not an upturned 999? Upside-down crosses are still crosses! That's what people don't see, don't understand.'

'The Confraternity of Judas,' Marcus repeated, thinking of Kropp's sect. 'Evil increases faith,' he concluded, horrified.

'You've seen what's happening outside tonight. Have you looked in the faces of those men and women praying? Have you looked in their eyes? They're happy. How many souls have been saved thanks to Victor? Talk to them of good and they'll ignore you. Show them evil and they'll pay attention.'

'And those who died?'

'If we're made in the image and likeness of God, then he too must be wicked. An army, in order to exist, needs a war. Without evil, men wouldn't need the Church. And every war has its victims.'

'So Diana and Giorgio, the two police officers, the hitchhikers, Max, Cosmo Barditi . . . Were they just collateral damage?'

'You're being unfair. You may not believe me, but I too have been trying to stop the killings, just like you. Except that I've been doing it in my own way, conscious of a higher interest.'

'What higher interest?' The words were like a challenge.

Erriaga narrowed his eyes – he didn't like being provoked. 'Who do you think gave Clemente the order to entrust this investigation to you after we'd found the recording in the confessional at Sant'Apollinare?'

Marcus was caught off guard.

'You always wanted to know the faces of your superiors.' Batista stretched his arms out wide and pointed to his chest. 'Here I am: Cardinal Batista Erriaga. All this time you've been working for me.'

Marcus did not know what to say. Anger and bitterness were gaining the upper hand over rational thought. 'You knew from the start who the child of salt was. Why didn't you give me the chance to stop him straight away?'

'It wasn't as simple as that: Kropp and his people had to be stopped first.'

Marcus saw it all clearly now. 'Of course. Because the one thing that concerned you was that anyone should find out that the Church knew of the existence of the Confraternity of Judas. People who believed in the same God as us: a disgrace too great to reveal.'

Erriaga observed that the man he had in front of him – the one he had traced to Prague, lying in a hospital bed without a memory and with a bullet in his forehead, the one he had had taught by Clemente – had a very strong temperament, and he liked that. He had chosen well. 'Ever since Innocent III, the Pope has been described as "the tamer of monsters". The message is clear. The Church is not afraid to confront its own history, or the lowest and most deplorable part of human nature: sin. When our enemies want to attack us, they talk about our opulence, how far we are from Christ's dictates of poverty and generosity towards our fellows. Then they say that the devil has entered the Vatican.'

Hic est diabolus, Marcus recalled.

'And they're right,' Erriaga said, to Marcus's surprise. 'Because only we can keep evil at bay. Remember that.'

'Now that I know, I'm not sure I want to be part of all this any more . . . ' Marcus turned towards the tunnel that led to the exit.

'You're an ingrate. It was *I* who sent Clemente straight to Sandra Vega's apartment when I learned from my sources that the victim in Sabaudia had been her partner. It was *I* who understood the danger she was in and acted accordingly. Your woman is alive thanks to *me*!'

Marcus ignored Erriaga's provocation and passed him right by. Then he stopped and turned one last time. 'Good is the exception, evil the rule. You taught me that.'

Batista Erriaga broke into a noisy laugh that echoed through the stony space. 'You will never have a life like other people. You can't be what you are not. It's your nature.'

Then he added something that sent a shiver through Marcus.

'You'll be back.'

Epilogue

The Tamer of Monsters

'You're nearly ready,' Clemente had told him one morning in March. 'You just need one more lesson and your training will be over.'

'I don't know if I am,' Marcus had replied, because he was still full of doubts. 'The migraines keep tormenting me, and I also have a recurring nightmare.'

Clemente had searched in his pockets, taken out a metal medallion, like those that could be bought for small change in the souvenir shops in St Peter's Square, and shown it to him as if it were of inestimable value.

'This is the Archangel Michael,' he said, indicating the angel with the sword of fire. 'He chased Lucifer from heaven and threw him into hell.' Then he took his hand and gave him the medallion. 'He is the protector of the penitenzieri. Put it around your neck and carry it with you always, it'll help you.'

Marcus welcomed the gift in the hope that it really would protect him. 'And when will my last lesson take place?'

Clemente smiled. 'When the time is right.'

Marcus hadn't understood the meaning of his friend's words. But he was sure that one day all would be clear.

It was the end of February in Lagos, and the temperature stood at forty degrees, with a humidity level of eighty-five per cent.

The second-largest city in Africa, after Cairo, had a population of more than twenty-one million, which grew every day by two thousand. It was a phenomenon that was quite perceptible: since he had been here, Marcus had seen the shantytown outside his window increase in size.

He had chosen an apartment on the outskirts, over a garage that repaired old trucks. It wasn't very large and, even though he was used to living in big, noisy cities, the night-time heat prevented him from sleeping well. His things had been crammed into a built-in wardrobe, he had a refrigerator that went back to the seventies and a little kitchen area in which he cooked his meals. The ceiling fan emitted a rhythmic buzz, like the flight of a hornet.

In spite of the discomfort, he felt free.

He had been in Nigeria for nearly eight months, but had spent the last two years moving from one place to another. Paraguay, Bolivia, Pakistan, Cambodia. Going in search of *anomalies*, he had managed to break up a network of paedophiles, in Gujranwala he had stopped a Swedish citizen who chose the poorest countries to commit murders and satisfy his homicidal impulses without fear of being caught, and in Phnom Penh he had discovered a hospital where needy citizens sold their own organs to Westerners for a few hundred dollars. Now he was on the trail of a gang of people-traffickers: almost a hundred men, women and children had disappeared in the course of a few years.

He had started to interact with people, to communicate. That had been his wish for a long time. He hadn't forgotten the isolation he had suffered in Rome. But even now, his solitary temperament would suddenly raise its head and, before any stable ties had been created, he would pack his bags and leave.

He was afraid of commitment. Because the only emotional relationship he had managed to create had ended bitterly. He still thought about Sandra, although less and less frequently. Every now and again he wondered where she was and whether she was happy. But he never went so far as to imagine if there was someone with her, or if she was returning his thoughts. That would have been painful and futile.

It did often happen, though, that he would talk to Clemente. It happened in his head, an intense, constructive dialogue. He would tell him all the things he couldn't or wouldn't have told him when he was alive. He felt a tightness in his stomach only when he thought again of the final lesson of his training, the one they would never have together.

Two years earlier, he had wanted to leave the priesthood. But after a while he had realised that that wasn't how things worked. You could give up anything, but not part of yourself. Erriaga was right: whatever he did, wherever he went, that was his nature. In spite of the doubts that tormented him, he could do nothing about it. So, from time to time, whenever he found an abandoned church, he went in and celebrated mass. Sometimes something happened that he couldn't explain. During the service, people would arrive unexpectedly and start to listen. He wasn't sure if God really existed, but the need for Him was something that people had in common.

The tall black man had been following him for nearly a week.

Marcus noticed him once again as he was walking around the noisy, gaudy market of Balogun. He always kept about thirty feet away. The place was a veritable labyrinth where you could buy anything and it was easy to lose yourself in the crowd. But it hadn't taken Marcus long to spot him. From the way he was following him, it was obvious he wasn't much of an expert at that kind of thing, but you never knew. Maybe the gang he was investigating had found out about him and had set someone to keep an eye on him.

Marcus stopped by a water-seller's stand. He loosened the collar of his white linen shirt and asked for a glass. As he drank, he passed a handkerchief over his neck to wipe away the sweat, taking advantage of the action to look around. The man too had stopped and was now pretending to look at the colourful fabrics on a stall. He was wearing a light-coloured tunic and carrying a canvas bag.

Marcus decided he had to do something.

He waited for the voice of the muezzin to start calling the faithful to prayer. Part of the market came to a halt, since half the population of Lagos was Muslim. Marcus took advantage of this to walk faster through the maze of alleys. The man behind him did the same. He was double his size, so Marcus didn't think he would get the better of him in a fight. Plus, he didn't even know if he was armed, but had a feeling he might be. He had to be clever. He slipped into a deserted alley and hid behind a curtain. He waited for the man to pass him and then jumped on his back, knocking him to the ground face down. Then he sat on him and began squeezing his neck with both hands.

'Why are you following me?'

'Wait, let me speak.' The giant wasn't trying to retaliate, only to loosen his grip in order not to choke.

'Did they send you?'

'I don't understand,' the man tried to protest in halting French.

Marcus squeezed even harder. 'How did you find me?'

'You're a priest, aren't you?'

Hearing him say that, Marcus relaxed his grip a little.

'They told me there's someone who investigates missing persons . . . ' Then with a couple of fingers he extracted from the collar of his tunic a leather strap with a wooden cross hanging from it. 'You can trust me, I'm a missionary.'

Marcus wasn't sure he was telling the truth, but he let him go all the same. With a bit of effort, the man turned and sat up. Then he put a hand to his throat and coughed, trying to regain his breath.

'What's your name?'

'Father Emile.'

Marcus held out his hand and helped him up. 'Why have you been following me? Why didn't you just come forward?'

'Because I wanted to be sure first that what they say about you is true.'

Marcus was struck by this. 'And what do they say?'

'That you're a priest, which means you're the right person.'

The right person for what? He didn't understand.

'How do you know?'

'They saw you celebrate mass in an abandoned church . . . So, is it true? Are you a priest?'

'Yes, I am.' Then he let the man continue his story.

'My village is called Kivuli. A war has been going on there for decades, a war everybody pretends not to know about. Periodically, we have problems with the water, and there are cases of cholera. Because of the conflict, doctors don't come to Kivuli, and aid workers are often executed by the warring factions because they're thought to be enemy spies. That's why I'm here in Lagos, to find the drugs we need to contain the epidemic . . . While I was here I heard about you and came looking for you.'

Marcus would never have imagined he was so easy to find. Maybe he had lowered his guard a little too much lately. 'I don't know who told you certain things, but it isn't true that I can help you. I'm sorry.' He turned his back on him and was about to walk off.

'I made a promise.'

The man uttered the words in a tone of supplication, but Marcus ignored him.

Father Emile wouldn't let go. 'I promised a priest who was a friend of mine before the cholera took him. He taught me to be everything I am: he was my teacher.'

At these last words, Marcus thought of Clemente and stopped.

'Father Abel led the mission in Kivuli for forty-five years,' the man continued, aware that he had started to get through to him.

Marcus turned.

'His exact words before dying were: "Don't forget the garden of the dead."'

Marcus registered the phrase. But those last words, 'the dead', he didn't like.

'About twenty years ago, there were some murders in the village. Three young women. I hadn't arrived in Kivuli yet, I know they were found dead in the forest. Father Abel couldn't forget what had happened. For the rest of his life, the one thing he wanted was for the culprit to be punished.'

Marcus was sceptical. 'Twenty years is a long time. You can't conduct an investigation: any clues there once were must be gone by now. And the culprit might be dead, especially if no other murders happened after that.'

But the man wouldn't give up. 'Father Abel even wrote a letter to the Vatican to tell them what had happened. He never received an answer.'

Marcus was struck by this. 'Why the Vatican?'

'Because according to Father Abel the killer was a priest.'

This really shook him. 'Do you also know his name?'

'Cornelius Van Buren, a Dutchman.'

'But Father Abel wasn't sure, was he?'

'No, but he had a very strong suspicion. Partly because Father Van Buren suddenly disappeared and the murders stopped at the same time.'

Disappeared, Marcus told himself. There was something in this old story that compelled him to deal with it. Maybe because the killer was a priest. Or maybe because the Vatican, even though informed of what had happened, had completely ignored it. 'Where is your village?'

'It will be a long journey,' Father Emile said. 'Kivuli is in the Congo.'

It took them nearly three weeks to reach their destination.

More than two weeks were spent waiting in a small town a hundred and eighty miles from the city of Goma. For nearly a month, a bloody battle had been in progress around Kivuli. On one side was the militia of the CNDP – the Congrès National pour la Défense du Peuple, Father Emile had explained. 'They're pro-Rwandan Tutsi. The name makes them sound like freedom fighters, but actually they're bloodthirsty rapists.' On the other side was the regular army of the Democratic Republic of the Congo, which was gradually gaining back territory previously held by the rebels.

They had spent eighteen days glued to the radio, waiting for the situation to calm down enough to let them embark on the last stage of the journey. Marcus had even managed to persuade a helicopter pilot to accept money to take them there. At midnight on the nineteenth day, news had finally come in of a fragile truce.

A window of a few hours had been created, and they had immediately taken advantage of it.

The helicopter was flying low with its lights out even though it was dark, in order to avoid being shot down by the artillery of one or other army. There was a powerful storm in the area. On the one hand, that was an advantage, because the rain would cover the noise of the blades. On the other it was a danger, because every time lightning lit up the sky someone below might be able to spot them.

As they flew towards their destination, Marcus looked below, wondering what to expect in that jungle and if it wasn't a bit of a gamble to go there because of something that had happened so long ago. But he couldn't turn back now, he had committed himself to Father Emile, who seemed to think it was of vital importance that he should see what he had to show him.

He clutched the medallion of the Archangel Michael and prayed it really was worth the trouble.

They landed in a muddy clearing surrounded by vegetation.

The pilot said something in broken French, loudly enough to be heard over the din of the engine. They didn't understand his words, but the meaning was that they had to hurry, because he wouldn't wait long for them.

They ran towards the wall of shrubs and entered the tangle. From this point on, Father Emile walked always a few steps ahead of Marcus, who wondered how he could possibly know the right direction. It was dark and the rain was falling straight and heavy on their heads, beating down on the thick greenery, like deafening drums. At this point, Father Emile moved aside a last branch and they abruptly came out into the middle of a village of clay and sheet-metal huts.

In front of them was a chaotic scene.

People running here and there in the incessant rain, carrying blue plastic bags containing the core possessions of their families. Men gathering what little cattle they owned in an attempt to get them to shelter. Children crying as they clung to the legs of their mothers and babies carried on backs, wrapped in coloured cloths. Marcus immediately had the impression that nobody knew exactly where to go.

Father Emile guessed his thoughts and slowed down to explain. 'The rebels were here up until yesterday, and tomorrow morning the soldiers will come into the village and take their place. But they won't come as liberators: they'll burn the houses and the provisions so that the enemy won't be able to find any reserves in case they return. And they'll kill everybody, on the trumped-up charge that they collaborated with the enemy. That'll serve as a warning to the nearby villages.'

As he looked around, Marcus lifted his head as if he had heard an unusual sound. Sure enough, in the middle of the pouring rain and the excited voices, singing could be heard. It came from a large wooden building. From inside filtered a yellowish light.

A church.

'Not everybody will leave this place tonight,' Father Emile explained. 'The old and the sick will remain here.'

Whoever couldn't make it out of here would remain, Marcus repeated to himself. At the mercy of some unimaginable horror.

Father Emile grabbed him by one arm and shook him. 'You heard the pilot, didn't you? He'll be leaving very soon, we have to hurry.'

They were again outside the village, but on the opposite side from where they had landed. As they went, Father Emile recruited a couple of men to help them. They carried with them shovels and rudimentary lanterns.

They came to a small valley that had probably once housed the banks of a river. In the highest part there were some graves.

A little graveyard with three crosses.

Father Emile said something in a dialect similar to Swahili and the men started digging. Then he passed a shovel to Marcus and the two of them lent a hand.

'In our language Kivuli means *shadow*,' Father Emile said. 'The village took the name of the river that flows every now and again in this little valley. In spring the river appears when the sun goes down, and then disappears the following morning, just like a shadow.'

Marcus guessed that the phenomenon was somehow connected to the nature of the soil.

'Twenty years ago, Father Abel asked for these graves to be placed far from the village cemetery, in this area which is devoid of vegetation in summer, even though he called it "the garden of the dead".'

Limestone soil was the best for burying bodies, preserving them from the action of time. A natural mortuary.

'When the three girls were killed, there was no way to conduct an investigation of any kind. But Father Abel knew that one day someone would come and ask questions. Whoever it was would surely want to see the bodies.'

And, sure enough, that moment had come.

One of the bodies was exhumed before the others. Marcus let go of the shovel and approached the grave. The water falling from the sky was filling it, but the remains were wrapped in a plastic sheet. Marcus knelt in the mud and tore it off with his hands. Father Emile handed him a lantern.

Shining it, Marcus noticed that the body had indeed been well preserved in that limestone cradle. It had undergone a kind of mummification. So, even after twenty years, the bones were still intact and covered in scraps of cloth that looked like dark parchment.

'They were sixteen, eighteen, and twenty-two,' Father Emile said, referring to the victims. 'This one was the first, the youngest.'

Marcus, however, couldn't figure out how she had died. So he went closer, in search of the mark of a wound or a scratch on the bones. He spotted something that struck him, but just then the rain extinguished the lantern.

It can't be, he told himself. He asked immediately for the other lantern to be passed to him. Then he *saw*, and he retreated so rapidly from the hole that he fell on his back.

He lay like that, with his hands and back sunk in the mud and a stunned expression on his face.

Father Emile confirmed his intuition. 'The head was neatly severed, as were the arms and legs. Only the torso remained intact. The remains were scattered over a few yards and the girl had been stripped of her clothes, which had been reduced to scraps.'

Marcus was finding it hard to breathe, while the rain beat down on him, preventing him from thinking clearly. He had seen a corpse like that before.

'Hic est diabolus.'

The young nun from the enclosed order dismembered in the wood in the Vatican gardens.

The devil is here, he thought. The man with the grey shoulder bag in the image from the security footage, the man he had been chasing without success, had been in Kivuli seventeen years before the murder at the Vatican, since which three more years had passed.

'Cornelius Van Buren,' he said to Father Emile, remembering the name of the Dutch missionary who had probably committed these murders. 'Is there anyone in the village who knew him?'

'A lot of time has gone by, and the average lifespan is very short around here.' But then he thought more carefully. 'There is an old woman. One of the girls who were killed was her granddaughter.'

'I have to talk to her.'

Father Emile looked at him in surprise. 'The helicopter,' he reminded him.

'I'll take the risk: take me to her.'

They came to the church and Father Emile went in first. Inside, those sick with cholera were laid out along the walls. Their relatives had abandoned them in order to escape, and now the old people were tending to them. A large wooden crucifix watched over everyone from an altar filled with candles.

The old were singing for the young. It was a song full of sweetness and melancholy: each person seemed to have accepted his or her fate.

Father Emile went in search of the woman and found her at the end of the nave. She was taking care of a boy on whose forehead she was putting wet rags to bring down the fever. Father Emile made a sign to Marcus, summoning him. They both crouched next to the woman. Father Emile said something to her in their language. She shifted her gaze to the stranger, studying him with huge, very clear blue eyes.

'She'll talk to you,' Father Emile said. 'What do you want to ask her?'

'If she remembers anything about Van Buren.'

Father Emile translated the question. The woman thought this over for a moment and then replied, resolutely. Marcus waited for her to finish, hoping that her words would reveal something important to him.

'She says that priest was different from the others, he seemed better, but in fact he wasn't. And there was something about the way he looked at people. And that's something she didn't like.'

The woman spoke again.

'She says that over these past years she's tried to wipe out his face forever from her memory and has succeeded. She apologises to you, but she doesn't want to remember anything else. She's sure he was the person who killed her granddaughter, but now she's at peace and soon they will find each other again in the next world.'

But that wasn't enough for Marcus. 'Ask her to tell you something about the day Van Buren vanished.'

Father Emile did so.

'She says that one night the spirits of the jungle came to take him away to hell.'

The spirits of the jungle . . . Marcus had been hoping for a different answer.

Father Emile understood his disappointment. 'You have to realise that superstition and religion co-exist here. These people are Catholics, but they continue to cultivate beliefs linked to the old ways of worship. That's how it's always been.'

Marcus thanked the woman with a nod of the head, and was about to rise when she pointed to something. At first, he didn't understand. Then he realised it was something to do with the medallion he was wearing around his neck.

The Archangel Michael, the protector of the penitenzieri.

Marcus slipped it off his neck, took her hand and laid the medallion in her rough palm. Then he closed her hand, as if it were a casket. 'May this angel protect you tonight.'

The woman welcomed the gift with a slight smile. They looked at each other for a few more moments, as if saying goodbye, then Marcus stood up.

*

They retraced their steps to the helicopter. The pilot had already started the engine again and the blades were whirling in the air. Marcus reached the door but then turned: Father Emile wasn't beside him, he had stopped much earlier. So he turned back, ignoring the pilot's cutting remarks.

'Come, what are you waiting for?' he said.

But Father Emile shook his head without saying anything. Marcus realised that he wouldn't even look for shelter in the jungle like the other inhabitants of the village. Instead, he would go back to the church and wait for death together with those of his parishioners who were in no position to escape.

'The Church has done great things with the missions in Kivuli and similar places,' Father Emile said. 'Don't let a killer destroy that.'

Marcus nodded and embraced Father Emile. Then he boarded the helicopter, which in a few seconds took flight into the grey curtain of rain. Beneath him, Father Emile raised his hand in a gesture of farewell. Marcus returned the gesture, but didn't feel relieved. He wished he had that man's courage. One day, he told himself. Maybe.

The night had been filled with surprises. He had the name of a killer who up until that moment had been an unknown demon. Twenty years had gone by, but maybe there was still time for the truth to come out.

But, for that to happen, Marcus would have to go back to Rome.

Cornelius Van Buren had killed on other occasions.

Marcus had found traces of him in various places around the world. In Indonesia, in Peru, in Africa again. The devil had taken advantage of his own status as a missionary to move undisturbed from place to place. Wherever he had been, he had left a mark of his passage. In the end, Marcus had counted forty-six female corpses.

But those victims had all preceded the ones in Kivuli.

The village in Congo had been his last destination. Then he had vanished into thin air. 'One night the spirits of the jungle came and took him away to hell,' Father Emile had said, translating the words of the old woman in the village.

Of course Marcus could not completely rule out the possibility that, in the meantime, Van Buren had struck other times and elsewhere. And that he simply hadn't found any traces of those crimes. Basically, they had all happened in remote, backward places.

In any case, seventeen years after Kivuli, Van Buren had reappeared with a mutilated corpse in the gardens of the Vatican. And then had vanished again.

Why that fleeting appearance? And where had he been in the three years since the murder of the nun? Marcus calculated that he must be about sixty-five by now: was it possible that he had died in the meantime?

One item of information had immediately struck him. Van Buren chose his victims carefully.

They were young, innocent, and beautiful.

Was it conceivable that he had tired of his hobby?

Cardinal Erriaga had predicted it would happen. '*You'll be back,*' he had said with a laugh.

And sure enough, at five-thirty on a Tuesday afternoon, Marcus lingered in the Sistine Chapel together with the last group of visitors. While they were all admiring the frescoes, he was watching the movements of the security people.

When the guards asked those present to make their way out because the Vatican Museums were about to close, Marcus left the group and slipped into a side corridor. From there he descended a service staircase that led into the Pigna courtyard. In the previous days he had paid other visits, but they had actually been tours of inspection to study the TV cameras that watched over the internal perimeter of Vatican City.

He had found gaps in the surveillance system. Thanks to them, he managed to reach the gardens undisturbed.

The spring sun was setting slowly, but it would be dark soon. So he hid among the box hedges and waited. He recalled the first time he had been here with Clemente: the area had been put under a kind of quarantine to allow the two of them to cross the grounds undisturbed.

Who was it who had organised that apparently impossible enterprise? Erriaga, of course. But why after that had nobody from the higher echelons lifted a finger to help Marcus complete his investigation into the death of the nun?

There was an obvious contradiction.

Erriaga could have covered up the case completely. Instead, he had wanted Marcus to see and, above all, to know.

*

When darkness fell, Marcus left his hiding place and headed for the one part of the gardens where the vegetation could grow freely.

The two-hectare wood where the gardeners only ever went to remove the dry leaves.

Reaching the spot, he lit the small torch he had with him, trying to remember where the nun's body had been. He located the spot which three years earlier had been marked off with the yellow tape of the Gendarmerie. *Evil is a dimension*, he reminded himself. He knew perfectly well what he had to do.

To look for *anomalies*.

To do so, it was necessary to summon up the memory of what had happened that day in the presence of Clemente.

A human torso.

It was naked. At the time he had immediately thought of the Belvedere Torso, the huge mutilated statue of Hercules preserved in the Vatican Museums. But the nun had been subjected to bestial treatment. *Someone* had neatly severed her head, legs and arms. They lay a few yards away, scattered along with her torn clothes.

No, not 'someone'.

'Cornelius Van Buren.' Now he could finally utter the name of the killer in this place.

The murder had been brutal. But there had been a logic to it, a design. The devil had known how to move within the walls. He had studied the location, the control procedures, he had got around the security measures, exactly as he himself had done a little while earlier.

'Whoever it was came from outside.'

'How do you know that?'

'We know his face. The body has been here for at least eight or nine hours. This morning, very early, the security cameras filmed a suspicious man wandering around the gardens. He was dressed

like a Vatican employee, but it turns out the uniform had been stolen.'

'Why him?'

'Look for yourself.'

Clemente had shown him the image from the security cameras. It showed a man dressed as a gardener, his face partially hidden by the peak of a cap. Caucasian, indeterminate age but certainly more than fifty. He had a grey shoulder bag. At the bottom, a darker stain had been visible.

'The gendarmes are convinced that inside that bag there was a small hatchet or something similar. He must have used it recently, the stain you see is probably blood.'

'Why a hatchet?'

'Because it was the one kind of weapon he could have found here. There's no way he could have brought anything in from outside, with all the security checks and metal detectors.'

'But he took it away with him to cover his tracks, in case the gendarmes *called in the Italian police.'*

'It's easier on the way out: there are no checks. And to get away without being seen all you have to do is mingle with the stream of pilgrims and tourists.'

Thinking again about that dialogue, Marcus immediately identified the error.

After Kivuli, Van Buren stopped killing for seventeen years and disappeared. Maybe he didn't stop, he thought. He simply became cleverer and learned to cover his tracks better.

But then why run an enormous risk by committing a murder inside the Vatican?

Marcus guessed that he had let himself be deceived by the way in which Van Buren had got through the controls. He had to admit it: he had been fascinated. But now, in that deserted wood, he revised his position. A predator like Van Buren would never accept the danger of getting caught.

Because he liked killing too much.

So what had happened?

Both he and Clemente had taken it granted that the killer had entered and left the Vatican.

But what if he had always been there?

Basically, that would explain his in-depth knowledge of the security systems. But Marcus ruled out that hypothesis because, during his unsuccessful investigation, he had looked into the lives of all those, lay or religious, who operated within the state and who had anything in common with the man in the image – Caucasian, over fifty.

A ghost, he told himself. A spectre capable of appearing and disappearing at whim.

He shone the torch at the trees. The devil had chosen the perfect place to strike. Far from anyone's eyes. And he had also chosen the perfect victim.

'*Her identity is a secret,*' Clemente had said, referring to the young nun. '*It's one of the dictates of the order to which she belongs.*'

In public, the nuns covered their own faces with veils. Marcus had seen them on the faces of her fellow sisters when they had come to recover the poor girl's remains.

'*Hic est diabolus.*'

That was what one of them had said to him, passing close by him as Clemente was drawing him away.

The devil is here.

Why did the killer choose one of them? Marcus asked himself.

'*Every now and again, the nuns stroll in this wood,*' Clemente had said '*Almost nobody ever comes here, and they can pray undisturbed.*'

It was logical, then, to think that the killer had chosen her by chance. A woman who had decided to stop existing for the rest of humanity, and who in addition was in the one isolated place in the Vatican, the wood. The right person in the right place. The other victims, though, he had deliberately chosen because they were *young, innocent and beautiful*.

Marcus remembered bending down to get a better look at her. The snow-white complexion, the small breasts, the indecently displayed sexual organs. The very short blonde hair on the severed head. The blue eyes, lifted to heaven.

So she too had been young, innocent and beautiful. But if she covered her face with a veil, how could the killer have known that?

'He knew her.'

He said it in one go, without even realising. Suddenly the pieces started to fit. They came together in front of his eyes as if in an old painting by Caravaggio, like the one kept in San Luigi dei Francesi, in front of which his training had begun.

And in the painting they were all there. Cornelius Van Buren, the nun who had whispered to him '*Hic est diabolus*', Batista Erriaga, the Archangel Michael, the old woman from Kivuli, even Clemente.

'Look for the anomaly, Marcus,' his mentor had always said. And Marcus found it.

This time the anomaly was him.

'There's a small enclosed convent beyond the wood,' Clemente had said. That was where Marcus was now headed.

After a while, the trees thinned out and a low, austere-looking grey building appeared. Behind the windowpanes, a yellowish light, as of candles, could be made out. And shadowy figures moving in slowly but orderly fashion.

Marcus approached the little door and knocked once. After a short while, someone turned the locks and opened the door. The nun's face was covered with a black veil. She looked at him, and then immediately stepped back to let him in, as if he was expected.

Marcus stepped inside. There, in front of him, the nuns were lined up. He immediately noticed that he had not been mistaken. Candles. The nuns had chosen to isolate themselves from the rest of humanity, rejecting any technology or instrument of comfort. And this place of silence, outside time, was bang in the middle of the small territory of the Vatican, in the centre of a huge chaotic metropolis like Rome.

'It's difficult to comprehend the choice these women make,' Clemente had said. *'Many people think they should go out and do good in the world instead of shutting themselves up within the walls of a convent. But, as my grandmother always said, we don't know*

how many times these sisters have saved the world with their prayers.'

Now he knew. It was true.

Nobody told Marcus where to go. But, as soon as he moved, the nuns started stepping aside one by one, to indicate the direction. In this way he reached the foot of a flight of stairs. First he looked up, then he started climbing.

His mind was brimming with thoughts, but now they all had a meaning.

Erriaga's laughter . . . '*You will never have a life like other people. You can't be what you are not. It's your nature.*' The cardinal knew it: Marcus would continue to see anomalies, the marks of evil. It was his talent and his curse. And he would never forget the mutilated body of the nun. Van Buren had scattered far too many bodies around the world for Marcus not to run into him again. And besides, it was his nature: he couldn't do anything different. '*You'll be back.*' And in fact, he was.

'*And when will my last lesson take place?*' he had asked Clemente.

Clemente had smiled. '*When the time is right.*'

That had been the last lesson of his training. That was why, three years earlier, Erriaga had wanted him to go to the wood and see the dismembered body. There was nothing to discover that the cardinal did not already know.

'*One night the spirits of the jungle came and took him away to hell.*' That was how Father Emile had translated the old woman's words. Then the woman had pointed to the medallion Marcus carried around his neck and he had given it to her.

The Archangel Michael, the protector of the penitenzieri.

But the woman hadn't pointed to it because she wanted it: she was simply telling him that she had seen medallions like that the night Van Buren had vanished from Kivuli.

The hunters of the dark – the spirits of the jungle – had

already been on Van Buren's trail. They had tracked him down and taken him away.

Reaching the top of the stairs, Marcus noticed that at the end of the corridor to his left there was a single room from which came a weak glimmer. He walked towards it unhurriedly, until he got to the heavy bars of burnished iron.

The door of a cell.

At last he had confirmation of why, in the seventeen years after Kivuli, Cornelius Van Buren had not killed again.

The old man was sitting on a dark wooden chair, his back stooped. He was wearing a worn black sweater. A camp bed stood against the wall. There was a single shelf of books. And, right now, Van Buren was reading.

He's always been here, Marcus said to himself. The devil had never moved from the Vatican.

'Hic est diabolus.' That was what the nun had said to him as he left the wood. All he had needed to do was reflect on her words. She had been trying to inform him. Maybe she had been horrified by what one of her sisters had suffered and so had decided to break her vow of silence.

The devil is here.

One day, Cornelius had accidentally seen the face of one of the sisters who watched over him. She was innocent, young and very pretty. So he had found a way to escape and attack her when she was alone in the wood. But his escape could not have lasted very long. Soon afterwards, someone must have taken him back to his prison. Marcus recognised in a corner the grey shoulder bag, the dried bloodstain still visible at the bottom.

The old man shifted his gaze from the book and turned to him. His dishevelled beard, white in places, speckled his hollow face. He stared at him in a kindly fashion. But Marcus was not deceived.

'They told me you would come.'

The words shook Marcus. But they were only the confirmation of what he already knew. 'What do you want from me?'

The old priest smiled at him. He had sparse yellow teeth. 'Don't be afraid, this is just a new lesson in your training.'

'Are you my lesson?' Marcus asked with contempt.

'No,' the old man replied. 'I'm your teacher.'

A conversation with the author

The first question that comes to mind to anyone reading your novels, especially The Lost Girls of Rome *and now* The Hunter of the Dark, *is: How much of all this is true? Are you able to tell us that?*

Ever since *The Lost Girls of Rome*, the first novel in the series, came out, my readers have had one particular question for me. 'Does the Archive of Sins really exist?'

My answer has always been the same: 'Yes, it exists, and the penitenzieri even have a website: www.penitenzieria.va.'

I don't think anybody thought it was possible that the things talked about in the novel were based on reality. Obviously, I took liberties with them in order to get a story out of them. But I never blamed anybody who questioned the veracity of the situations and the characters. Those who had never heard of the Paenitentiaria Apostolica, the oldest ministry in the Vatican, were just as surprised as I was when I first learned of it. I'll never forget what happened in my head at that moment. I immediately thought of a question and an idea. The question was: 'How is it possible that nobody has ever written about the penitenzieri?' And the idea: 'What a terrific subject for a novel!'

*

How did you come across the subject, which is as incredible as it is true?

Every writer hopes to come across an 'original' story, it's the Holy Grail of all storytellers. That's why I'll always be in debt to one particular person.

When I met Father Jonathan for the first time, I couldn't believe I was talking to someone who was so like the cops in the seventies crime thrillers that I loved, but was actually a priest! Plus, there was something quite 'gothic' about his stories, as if he really was operating on the edge of some dark dimension. Today, Father Jonathan still helps the law enforcement agencies with cases where it is difficult to figure out the evil involved. The lessons learned from the Archive are sometimes essential for understanding, at least in part, what seems totally incomprehensible.

Has this journey you've taken led you to a better understanding of human nature? In other words, what have you learned about the concepts of good and evil?

The truth that nobody wants to hear is that over the course of history good has evolved along with mankind, while evil has stayed very much the same.

With the exception of those connected with technological developments, crimes, especially the most heinous ones, have remained identical over the centuries. At the time of the ancient Romans, there were serial killers just as there are now (except that, obviously, they weren't called serial killers). Even though we've had thousands of years to study evil and get to know it better, we still can't explain what drives someone who is like us to commit a violent act just for the pleasure of it. In the historical part of the Archive of Sins, the part that can be consulted, there are many things that bear witness to that. For example, in 1997 I concluded my university studies with a thesis on a famous Italian 'monster', a killer of children. He suffered from narcissistic personality disorder, and had no qualms about recounting all the macabre details of his killings, almost boasting of his own 'ventures'. It's no coincidence that when the police were still looking for him he left them a message in a telephone booth in which he signed himself 'the monster'. Well, in the Archive there's a confession by a young man who committed the same kind of crime. The words he used to describe what happened in his mind while he was killing those innocent children were very similar to those used by my monster. Except that the young penitent lived in the first half of the sixteenth century!

You studied law and criminology, and you have a deep knowledge of the darkest recesses of the mind. Is there anything in this field that still surprises you or catches you unawares?

Father Jonathan warned me that I might find many of the things he told me unacceptable. At times, it's been very difficult to admit that I was incredibly unprepared for certain manifestations of evil. I've carefully selected the stories to tell in the novel, trying not to fall into the temptation to reveal too much about the cases I studied as part of my research. There's a strange element in our nature that feels a dangerous attraction to what is wicked. It's the same element that leads us, for example, to openly condemn someone who murders children while at the same time following his actions in the media with morbid interest. It's a fact that the names of criminals are always remembered, rarely those of their victims . . .

Many details in this novel are historically true, not only the Paenitentiaria Apostolica. Can you tell us something more about the Confraternity of Judas, for example?

In the Middle Ages, some Christians were convinced of the

need to preserve evil in history since it was only because of evil that men would still need God, and, above all, the Church.

But how to reconcile evil with the faith?

The solution was to convert evildoers without their realising it. They had to continue to act on behalf of evil, but it was to be directed towards good. To achieve this aim, they made new converts among criminals, deceiving them by telling them they would be worshipping the devil. Their temple had an anthropomorphic statue in it: a man with a wolf's head. Only the true members of the confraternity knew that this mask concealed the face of Christ. The others prayed to this creature they thought was evil, when they were actually addressing their prayers to the son of God.

The heresy of the Confraternity of Judas was severely punished by the Inquisition.

How long did it take you to work on the novel, including the research and the writing itself?

I wrote this novel over the course of a year, but its genesis goes back a long way. The histories of the places I've described are the result of research and reading, but above all they are a gift that many Roman friends have given me over the years. It's thanks to them that I've discovered many legends and mysteries, and it's also thanks to them that I've visited many secret, unknown corners. Imagine what I felt, for example, when I learned of the existence of a real two-hectare wood in the middle of Vatican City!

What is your relationship with Rome?

Anyone who wasn't born in Rome or hasn't lived here for a good part of his or her life has no idea what the most unique city in the world really conceals. Rome has been my home for many years now, so I can confidently state that there is nowhere else like it in the world. It's no coincidence that whoever comes here feels they've always been always part of the place, and realises immediately that the expression 'the Eternal City' is more than deserved.

Acknowledgements

Stefano Mauri, my publisher. Fabrizio Cocco, my editor. Giuseppe Strazzeri, the editorial director of Longanesi. Raffaella Roncato. Cristina Foschini. Elena Pavanetto. Giuseppe Somenzi. Graziella Cerutti.

Luigi Bernabò, my agent.

Michele, Ottavio and Vito, my witnesses. Achille.

Antonio and Fiettina, my father and mother.

Chiara, my sister.

Have you read them all?

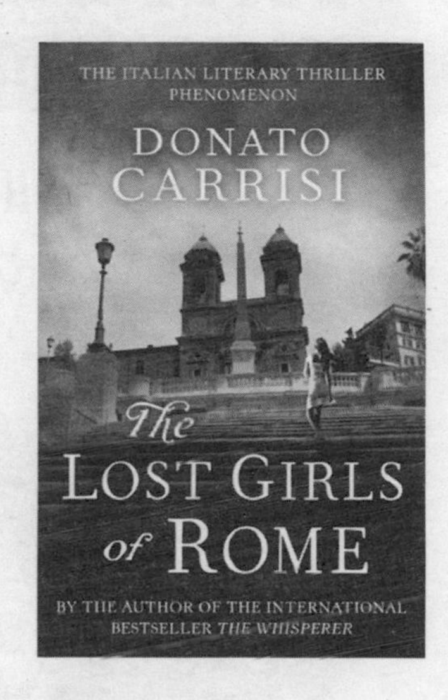

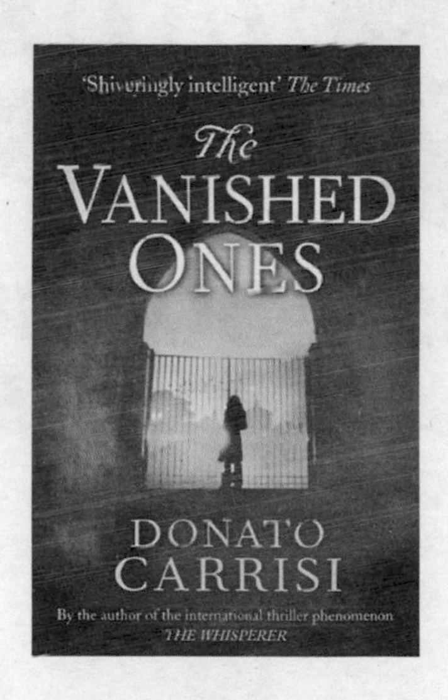